GRAY WIDOW'S WAR

GRAY WIDOW'S WAR

BOOK THREE OF THE GRAY WIDOW SERIES

DAN JOLLEY

Charlotte, NC

FALSTAFF
BOOKS
WWW.FALSTAFFBOOKS.COM

For Tracy — Always

I

THE CALM

1

C hief Resident Carla Gates had no more than closed her eyes when the burner phone in her pocket buzzed. Her stomach clenched, and a wave of nausea rolled through her as she clawed it out and jabbed the green button. She didn't have to look at the display, which showed her the words "UNKNOWN CALLER." Only one person contacted her on this phone. Her voice trembled as she swung her legs over the side of the couch and sat up, staring into the dimly-lit confines of her office.

"Hello?"

"Did you look into the cases I sent you?"

Carla's stomach clenched again. The voice on the other end of the line purred—but it was the purr of a big cat. Husky and low and feminine and deadly.

"I...I did, but...but those were anomalies. Spontaneous recovery, it, it happens sometimes, it doesn't prove—"

A tinge of impatience threaded its way into the Gray Widow's words. "Did you find the evidence worth exploring, Doctor? More important, does your current patient have anything to lose?"

Carla Gates propped an elbow on one knee and let her face drop into her hand. "Maybe not, but *I* could lose my license. Or get arrested."

"If I'm wrong, Doctor, will the patient be in any way worse off?"

Carla went over the cases in her mind: the three instances over the past three weeks in which terminal patients—patients who had zero chance of recovery—had miraculously regained their full health, literally overnight. Two of them were stage four cancer patients. The third was a child who'd been struck by six stray bullets during a shootout between police officers and a man barricaded inside his trailer with a cache of ille-gally-modified, fully-automatic assault rifles. All three of them had been sent home and provided with hospice care.

And now all three of them had returned to their normal lives as if nothing had happened. The adults, a man and a woman, were even healthier now than before their initial diagnoses. The only trace left of the world-shattering trauma the little girl had endured was a series of thin scars on her torso.

Carla had fibbed, just now. There were no instances of spontaneous recovery from multiple gunshot wounds. She took a deep breath. "How do I know this was you? That you did this?"

"What would I gain by lying about it?"

Carla made a fist. Thumped it against her leg. "All right. All right. Room 2617." She checked her watch. "2:03 a.m."

"I'm trusting you, Doctor. Trusting you not to disappoint me. Or betray me."

The hairs on the back of her neck and her forearms abruptly standing straight up, Carla said, "Making threats is counterproductive."

The Gray Widow chuckled. A sound devoid of humor. "That's the spirit, Doc. See you in an hour. And, listen—once you're there? Open the curtains."

Carla spent the next forty minutes talking to nurses and filling out forms. At 1:46 a.m., she huddled close with the nurse manager of the ICU, a stout middle-aged woman named Milly Rae. Milly Rae's forehead had become a topographical map of combined worry and skepticism. "I just don't see the point," she said for the second time. "A private room? Carla, we're taking him off the ventilator in the morning. The family's already signed for the organs. Unless we have somebody else who needs the bed, why go to the effort?"

"Dignity." Carla tried to sound convincing. "Not every family member has said their goodbyes yet. It's the kind of thing best done in a little bit of privacy."

4

Milly Rae cocked her head to one side, her forehead wrinkles not letting up. "Has somebody called? They let you know they're coming?"

Slowly Carla nodded. "Yeah. Yes. A grandparent. I get the impression it's the kind of grandparent Cullen wants to, y'know…impress."

Milly Rae's eyes slid half closed. Carla recognized the nurse's "unimpressed" face. "Oh. So it's a donor thing. Slide the grandson into a private room, show Grandpa Moneybags how special he is. And then the hospital gets a big fat check."

Carla shrugged. "I can't say for sure, but…yeah, maybe."

Milly Rae snorted as she turned to walk away. "2617 is open."

Under her breath, Carla said, "I know."

At 1:52 a.m., Carla Gates, a nurse, and an orderly transferred Michael Eugene Hayslip from the ICU to private room 2617. After the orderly left, Carla watched as the nurse checked the function of the ventilator, changed out Hayslip's catheter bag, and registered her activities on the tablet computer built into the monitor stand. When she'd finished, the nurse came and stood beside Carla. The two of them watched Michael Hayslip for a moment, the soft repeating hiss of the ventilator the only sound in the room.

"Need anything else, Doc?"

"No. No, you can go. I'm going to stay here with him for a few minutes."

The nurse nodded and left, and Carla pushed the door shut and leaned against it. She raised her wrist and watched as the time ticked from 2:02 to 2:03. Forcing herself to take long, deep breaths, Carla crossed to the window and pushed the curtains aside, revealing the face of the hospital's south wing and the night sky above it.

From behind her, the Gray Widow's voice reached out of the shadows of the bathroom: "Good to see you again, Doctor."

Carla spun, and her breath hitched and got stuck. She recognized the tall, lean, graceful woman who stepped out of the shadows, the long curves of the Gray Widow's frame hugged by a suit of segmented body armor. She could feel the eyes behind the black mesh eye-spots of the helmet tracking her, marking every movement, every twitch of every muscle. But the Widow wasn't alone, and Carla Gates almost cried out as the second figure emerged from the darkness, tall and quick and whip-thin.

It was a man. The shoulders were too broad, the hips too narrow, and when she saw him move, the gait was too masculine not to be. Beyond that, Carla had no clue as to his identity. He wore combat boots, snug dark jeans, and a fitted, cream-colored long-sleeved shirt that ended in supple leather gloves...and, like the Widow, his entire head was covered, but not with a helmet. Instead he wore a white ski mask over what appeared to be a white nylon stocking. Carla couldn't tell his age, his ethnicity, nothing.

The Gray Widow moved closer to Carla, and the doctor couldn't help wincing, just a little. The Widow's helmet had six other black spots, painted to mimic a spider's eight eyes, and when she turned her head, the effect made the chill bumps on Carla's arms pucker up even harder. "This is the one? He has the kind of injury we discussed?"

Carla frowned. She wouldn't have called the limited communication they'd had a *discussion*. "Michael Hayslip. Twenty-six. Traumatic head injury resulting from a motorcycle crash." The man in the white mask moved past Carla and went to stand next to the bed. He gazed down at Hayslip. Carla thought she caught a faint trace of something in the man's wake—something dark. Spicy. Cologne? "What's your friend doing?"

Instead of answering her, the Widow said, "And his brain function. Compromised?"

Carla's eyes tightened. "Gone. Here, I'll show you." She beckoned, and the Widow followed her to the opposite side of the bed from the man in the white mask. Carla gestured toward Hayslip's hairline, which was obscured by gauze and heavy bandages. "The...um. In layman's terms, the left side of his skull was caved in. This young man no longer has any brain function. His family has signed the release forms. We'll be taking him off the ventilator at the beginning of the morning shift. Unless..."

And here it was. The promise of what the Gray Widow had told her. No, not promise, but *possibility*. If such a thing could exist...if the three other cases the Widow had pointed her to actually were the result of... what? Was it something this new person did? The man in the mask hadn't made a sound since he and the Widow had arrived.

Carla put her thoughts into words the best she could. "Can you really do this? Can you really...*heal* him?"

The Widow's bizarre, unsettling head lifted. Looked across Michael Hayslip's all-but-corpse at the man in the white mask—who nodded.

Once. The Widow turned to Carla and gently took her arm in one gloved hand. The lights of the ventilator's readout danced across some kind of metal bracket folded across the back of the Widow's gauntlet. "Let's give him some space, Doc."

Carla let the Widow guide her to one corner of the room, so that she could only see the man in the white mask from behind. His shoulders moved, and Carla realized he had taken off the leather gloves, but she couldn't see his hands—couldn't watch as he reached forward and touched Michael Hayslip's face.

Instantly something happened. Carla couldn't tell what she was seeing, only that the man in the mask finally made a sound, grunted in effort, in *pain*, and she started toward him, but the Widow's fingers tightened on her arm like four steel hooks. "No no, Doc," the Widow whispered. "Let it happen."

Carla's eyes hadn't left the man's back, and as she watched, as she stared with raw eyes, she saw the air above him warp and tremble as waves of heat rolled across the room. Carla's voice came from some tiny, distant place, and sounded strange to her own ears. "Is that—is this normal? Is it supposed to work like this?"

"Just relax," the Widow breathed, and the man in the mask gave out a long, shuddering sigh and straightened up. Carla saw him tugging the leather gloves back on as he turned, and the Widow crossed the floor to him in a heartbeat. "Are you okay?" the Widow asked, and "You good?"

In that instant, as he nodded, it became crystal-clear to Carla Gates how the Gray Widow felt about the man in the white mask.

The Widow and the thin man moved back toward the bathroom. Carla said, "So—what happens now? Is there, I mean, how long does it—"

She would have said more, but Michael Eugene Hayslip surged upright in bed, his eyes open and staring wildly around him, and before Carla could even get to his bedside he wrenched the ventilator tube up and out of his throat, and when she arrived at his side he grabbed her by her coat and bellowed, "Where am I? How'd I get here? Where's Kim? Where's my wife?"

Carla threw a frenzied glance over one shoulder, but the Gray Widow and the man in the white mask had vanished.

"Are you a doctor? Am I in a hospital? Shit, I'm in a hospital! What happened?" Hayslip prodded at his head. "Are these bandages?"

Carla started to say, "Mr. Hayslip, if you'll just calm down," but her words broke off in a yelp when Hayslip yanked the bandages off his head in one grunting motion, revealing the smooth, perfectly-formed, unblemished cranium beneath.

Janey Sinclair stood on the roof of Gavring Medical's south wing, gazing down into Room 2716. Tears welled in the winter-sky-blue eyes behind the black mesh of her helmet's face plate, but Janey regulated her breathing and willed them away. It wasn't easy. Especially when she saw the plump, dark-haired young woman burst into the room, rocket past Carla Gates, and throw herself into Michael Hayslip's arms. Janey's eyesight was good, but not quite good enough to see the tears flowing freely down Kim Hayslip's face, not without a pair of binoculars. She didn't need to see the tears. The way Kim's shoulders shook, the way Michael held her and smoothed her hair with one hand, the way he kept his lips close to her ear, she knew the kind of soothing reassurances her miraculously-recovered husband must have been murmuring to her.

Things like *I'm fine,* and *It's okay,* and *You don't need to cry.*

Janey turned and sat down next to Tim Kapoor, putting her back against the short brick wall that ran around the building's edge. On one of the bricks, while waiting for Carla Gates to make the necessary arrangements earlier in the evening, Janey had chiseled a symbol that mirrored the pattern of eye-spots on her helmet.

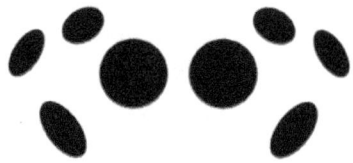

She didn't think there would be very many crimes committed on the roof of a major hospital, but the "Eyes of the Widow" had begun to serve as at least something of a deterrent around Atlanta. She figured it couldn't hurt.

Tim had his stocking-and-ski-mask combo pulled up far enough to free his nose and mouth, and was almost done eating a protein bar.

"Will that be enough? Should we get you a cheeseburger or something?"

Tim shook his head. "I haven't been needing as much. The, ah, the healing doesn't seem to be taking as much out of me. I'm getting more efficient, I guess?" He popped the last bite of the protein bar into his mouth, folded the wrapper and slipped it into a pocket, and talked with his mouth full. "Everything look good over there?"

Janey nodded. "Wife just arrived. It's all happy reunion."

Tim didn't look at her. "Need to get ready for yours, then." When Janey didn't respond, he chewed a couple of times and spoke again. "This was it, right? The final test. Make sure I can pull it off."

Janey opened her mouth to speak, but words refused to form on her tongue. She squeezed her eyes shut, deftly loosened the buckles at the base of her helmet, and slid it off. There wasn't enough light for Tim to see her face clearly—the thatch of tight chestnut curls on top of her head, the golden-brown complexion, the long-ish nose, the ample lips—but she didn't want him to see how puffy her ice-blue eyes were getting, so maybe that worked out all right.

Janey saw Tim perfectly, light or not. She willed her night vision up to full power, taking in the lines of his jaw, the flash of his straight white teeth, the tendons in his neck that bunched and flexed beneath his dark-copper as he chewed. She had long ago memorized every square millimeter of his face.

But what could she say? What words were there, in a moment like this one?

I'm sorry?

Thank you?

...I love you?

Janey reached out a gloved hand, aiming to touch Tim's knee, and Tim swallowed and said, "Please don't."

She recoiled as if stung. Tim seemed to pretend not to notice. Eventually, after starting and stopping a few more times, Janey thought she might have control of her voice. "So...what're you going to do? I mean —afterward?"

Tim tilted his head back to rest it against the wall. Absently, he pulled his mask back down so that it covered his whole head again. His voice came out a tiny bit muffled. "Today's Wednesday, so if we go up there Friday, you'll have the weekend." He shrugged. "I guess more of this. Healing people. I'll still help out with the office, Mom and Dad and all, but... it's not like I can stop, y'know? I figure, even if I'm kind of leisurely about it, I can do a thing like this once a week without alerting anybody. Maybe more often if I get better at it. Of course, it'll be harder without someone to pop me in and out of places, but I'm sure I can figure something out."

I'm sorry.

Thank you.

...I—

"Tim—"

For the first time since they flickered from Michael Hayslip's room to the roof, Tim turned his head and looked at her. She couldn't see his face, his beautiful, noble face, his warm, compassionate, dark-as-the-night-sky eyes, and she wanted to pull his mask off and take him in her arms the way Nicole Hayslip had done with her husband.

"It is what it is," Tim said as he got to his feet. "C'mon, we should get out of here."

Numbly, mutely, Janey rose and put a hand on Tim's shoulder. He didn't object. Janey focused on their destination, and in a burst of savage heat that scorched the nearby bricks, she and Tim flickered and vanished into the dark.

2

I n her apartment on the eleventh floor of the LaCroix Building, Sha'dae Wilkerson sat on her couch, staring at the frenzied action of a video game on her television. Beside her, Nathan Pittman held the controller, fingers and thumbs jabbing and twitching as he navigated a huge, armored simian character through a frantic battle against a large group of antagonists. Nathan wore a blindfold. Sha'dae's eyes shimmered violet now and then as Nathan watched the screen through them.

"I think I need to get my eyes checked," Nathan said as he dispatched an opponent. "You've got, like, better than 20/20 vision, don't you? This looks like some kind of ultra-ultra HD."

"I guess. I've never been to an eye doctor."

Nathan wore jeans and a black tank-top, and in her peripheral vision, she noticed the long lines of ridged muscle in Nathan's forearm as he leaned forward, waggling the controller at the screen. His body had changed in the last month, since the night up on the roof when she and Nathan and Tim Kapoor had been Augmented. He'd told her he'd been working out, but changes like this didn't come from just lifting weights for a few weeks. His Augmentation was...augmenting itself.

Sha'dae didn't figure she should be surprised. She and Janey had been practicing as well, refining what Sha'dae could do with her telepathy. But that produced no visible signs. Unlike what had happened—what was happening—to Nathan.

Sha'dae kept her vision locked straight forward, and clamped down hard on anything flowing to Nathan's mind other than what her eyes saw. No thoughts. No communication of any kind. Not for the first time, she debated the wisdom of letting him hang out at her apartment as much as he did now.

At the same time, though, Sha'dae felt grateful for the company. Janey and Tim were off doing what they were doing—just the thought of which threatened to open a whole mental can of worms that made her squirm in pained sympathy—and Garrison Vessler and Scott Charles had disappeared again. Zach Feygen knew what they were all going through, but he wasn't an Augment, and now that the Sender had fallen from the sky and died, she didn't guess he ever would be.

No one will be. We're the last ones.

Sha'dae didn't even consider reaching out to Special Agent Grassley or Ashley Strandjev. Those two had made it very clear that when they had something to say, they'd be the ones doing the reaching out.

So that left the one available person Sha'dae could be honest with sitting next to her on the sofa. Just barely eighteen years old, skin pale as milk, his short hair now dyed a brilliant royal blue. He'd had to give up his piercings, since his skin had forced them out as it healed, and it would take something like a jackhammer now to put them back in. She didn't figure he could get tattooed anymore, either. Of course, the horrible scars on his chest had also smoothed out and vanished, and she knew he considered that a more than fair trade-off for not being able to wear piercings.

Dad would kill me.

Sha'dae had been timing Nathan's visits around her step-father's frequent "check-ups." She'd tried to tell him that that made him sound like a doctor, that what he meant to say was that he was "checking in" on her, not giving her a check-up, but he either didn't grasp that particular idiomatic difference or didn't care. Mashal Sulemankhel had agreed that Sha'dae could keep the name Wilkerson when he married Sha'dae's mother fifteen years ago, and he had reluctantly agreed that Sha'dae could get her own apartment when she started college, but those were the only two concessions to "Westernism" he had allowed. Everything else stayed set in stone: the reading and following of the Quran, the five-times-a-day prayer schedule, the hijab, the strict pork prohibition, etc. If he knew his step-daughter was entertaining a male guest by herself, a male guest only recently turned eighteen, no less, Sha'dae feared he'd have an aneurysm.

She also feared he'd have a good point. Sha'dae was halfway through her twenty-fourth year. The differences between an eighteen-year-old and a twenty-four-year-old were…she groped for the right word. Staggering? Insurmountable?

Nathan finished the match and quit out of the game. "Okay. I think that's enough for now." His voice had gotten slowly, steadily deeper since his Augmentation, and while he still sounded nothing like Detective Feygen or Mr. Vessler, he no longer sounded like a boy, either. That didn't help. Nathan scooted forward to the edge of the couch and pulled the blindfold off, and stretched as he stood and put the controller back on the entertainment center. Sha'dae severed the telepathic connection between them, and tried not to watch the muscles in his shoulders flex and roll. She felt vaguely ashamed of herself, and wondered if she should feel ashamed for feeling ashamed.

Nathan moved over to the picture window near the front door and pushed aside the blackout curtain. Sha'dae had selected the heavy curtain around the same time she'd had the security system installed, which was right after returning from the Brittain ranch in Texas. Images of red sparks dancing in front of a topaz-yellow background flashed across her mind, and she shuddered at the memory.

"What're you looking at?" Sha'dae got up and went to the galley kitchen, but glanced over her shoulder at Nathan. He stood there, peering up at the night sky. "Or…are you looking *for* something?"

Nathan let the curtain fall back into place and came over to the breakfast bar. He leaned against it, his thick forearms flat on its surface. "Distractions are…well. Y'know. Distracting. But my guts haven't unclenched yet. I'm starting to think I'll never know what it's like not to be on edge."

Sha'dae opened the refrigerator and took out two bottles of soda. She handed one to Nathan, and leaned back against the edge of the counter. The Plowman's words echoed around in her head: *I am sorry. It is too late for your world.*

Nathan said, "Janey would've told us if she'd heard anything, right? I mean, if Agent Grassley or Mr. Vessler or somebody knew anything, they'd let us know, wouldn't they?"

Sha'dae tapped the side of her head. "Instantly, I'm pretty sure." As part of their practice, Janey had teleported all the way to the west coast, and though the connection felt strained, Sha'dae had still heard her when she'd called out telepathically.

Nathan used his thumbnail to pop the metal cap off the soda bottle. It flipped into the air, tumbling over and over, and he caught it between his thumb and forefinger. Using only those two fingers, he bent the metal cap in half, then again, then again, crimping and folding it until it was little more than an irregularly-shaped ball bearing. "This would make one hell of an Instagram feed, y'know." His eyes met hers. "If we could tell anybody about it."

Sha'dae toyed with the edge of the emerald-green hijab that covered her hair and framed her face. *If.* If only.

Dad, I'd like you to meet my boyfriend, Nathan. Why yes, he is a lot younger than I am. And white. And not a Muslim. And his hair is blue. At the moment. Why don't we all sit down and have a nice dinner?

"You ever read any comics?" Nathan asked.

Sha'dae blinked. "You mean, like comic books?" When Nathan nodded, she said, "I've read a few, here and there. I've always liked Storm from the X-Men."

He grinned for a second. "Storm's one of my favorites. But yeah, I'm glad, 'cause I was going to bring up the X-Men. Like, I know everybody's seen the movies now, and a lot more people know about them from the movies than've ever read the comics, right? But I used to read the comics a lot. Like, a *lot*. Years and years worth. And one day something occurred to me." He took a swig of his soda. "In the real world, you get somebody that goes through something traumatic, and it might take them, like, a whole decade to get over. Y'know? They've gotta go to therapy, maybe some kind of support group or something. Right? And that's like if somebody gets mugged and beaten up. Or if they see somebody get killed. Or they get, like, raped or something."

"Right...?"

"But in the X-Men comics, stuff like that happens in *every issue*. Somebody gets hurt so bad they almost die, or they see their friend get disintegrated right in front of them, or, like, what about when Professor X got turned into an alien, and they had to take his brain out and clone him a new human body?"

Sha'dae couldn't repress a tiny chuckle. "That really happened?"

"Back in the eighties. But think about it for a second. One thing like that happens, and a real, ordinary regular person might not get over it. Like, might not *ever* get over it. Except stuff like that is happening. Now. To us."

She moved closer to him, and set her bottle down on the bar. "Well, Janey told you what happened to her, right? When she and her father got shot? She had to be institutionalized for a while." After a pause: "Are you afraid of something like that happening to you?"

He flashed another grin, but turned his face away, and she saw color rise into his cheeks. "Me? Nah. I mean, I survived getting shot, too, and all it did for me was let me drop out of school. No, I mean, I'm more worried about…um. I don't want *you* getting hurt."

Sha'dae sucked in a quick breath and hoped it wasn't loud enough for Nathan to notice. She couldn't tell how long the silence stretched out between them.

Say something. Say something!

"I guess I'd better get going," Nathan said, as Sha'dae's stomach clenched. "There's a chance my parents might wonder where I am. Not a huge chance, but, y'know, they might notice I'm not there."

She tried for a casual smile. "You couldn't send them a text?"

"They'd have to turn their phones on to get texts. Thanks for letting me hang out tonight."

"Anytime."

He came around the breakfast bar and gave her a quick hug. That was a first. She wondered how soft and flimsy her body must feel to him, as the rock-like muscles in his back flexed under her fingers.

Nathan let her go and waved as he walked out the door. Sha'dae locked it behind him, engaged the security system, and not for the first time wished she drank alcohol.

Chattanooga's Incline Railway opened in 1895. At one mile in length, it was one of the steepest passenger railways in the world, starting down at the mountain's base in the St. Elmo neighborhood and extending all the way to Point Park at the top. The houses up on the crest, typical of most mountain-top communities, represented many of the city's wealthiest families—grand brick or mountain stone abodes worth many hundreds of thousands of dollars, some even topping a million, especially along East Brow Road, looking far, far down into the valley. Out over the working class. Safe in their lofty vantage points.

One such house, a short walk from the Incline's upper station, was listed as belonging to a Dr. Hubert Mills. Dr. Mills had cultivated a reputation for eccentricity as he'd gotten older. He'd taken to purchasing automobiles exclusively painted in a metallic purple, which he insisted on parking along the street, and often mowed his lawn dressed only in boxer shorts and a pair of red high-top sneakers. The good doctor suffered a stroke at the age of sixty-eight, several years after his retirement, at which point his public eccentricity shifted into extreme social withdrawal. His neighbors breathed quiet sighs of relief when the purple cars vanished from in front of the house, and slightly louder sighs of relief when a regular lawn service showed up to take care of the lengthening grass.

These days, Dr. Mills rarely showed his face. He had his groceries delivered once a week, paid in cash, and aside from a monthly visit from his investment man, received no callers. Neither did he bother anyone. His shutters remained drawn, day in and day out, and no one ever heard excessively loud music or the blaring of a television. As far as the rest of the community was concerned, the Mills house was a well-maintained empty shell.

Thursday morning, seven hours after Tim healed Michael Hayslip, a teenage boy rang the doorbell at the Mills house, struggling to keep his grip on the two overflowing bags of groceries in his arms. After a few seconds, the massive oak double doors opened, revealing Dr. Mills. He stood there, staring dully at the boy, a rheumy-eyed, frail old man dressed in layers of rumpled cardigans and sagging khaki pants. His small, weak feet poked out from under the pant hems, clad in striped socks, and his voice sounded more like a wheeze than spoken words.

"How much?"

"Um..." The boy shifted around, proffering a long, narrow slip of paper. "It's there. On the receipt."

Mills took the receipt, slowly balanced a pair of reading glasses on the tip of his nose, and peered at the faint blue print. "Very good. You can just set those down…there, yes. That's fine. Here. Keep the change." Mills handed the boy a sheaf of twenties.

"Thanks, Doc! You, uh, you have a good day, all right? And call us if you need anything else."

Mills nodded and closed the door.

With his back to the oak, he slid down to a sitting position on the foyer's marble floor, and the Mills façade melted away. The old man's skin lost its age spots and its wrinkles, evening and smoothing, and his coarse gray hair turned to a lustrous sheet of fine, straight blonde. In seconds, Hubert Mills had disappeared, replaced by a slim young woman who called herself Aphrodite Lupo. Aphrodite's dark blue eyes flashed with pain and effort.

She felt the floor vibrating before Julian Roth materialized in front of her. His image blurred, a shimmering cloud of sheerest black, expanding and contracting, scraping the air with its painful susurration. Roth's body, when Aphrodite could see it, was emaciated to the point of non-viability, his head so like a skull that the presence of eyeballs within the socket seemed wrong. Obscene.

Roth crouched in front of her. "Did he suspect anything?"

She shook her head. "I'm still just a feeble old man."

He reached out. Helped her to her feet. Tried to make his words sound soothing and reasonable. "You should let me go. You need help. We both do."

In less than a heartbeat, Aphrodite's eyes shifted from dark-blue-on-white to the red-sparks-on-yellow, and Roth winced and tried to draw away from her. But Aphrodite opened the channel, her mind to his, forced wide the crack in Roth's psyche and hammered the point home one more time.

"No one. Is going. Anywhere. Not until I—until we—" She grunted. The foyer flooded with the sound of thousands of whispered voices. "Until *I* regain my strength."

Roth's shoulders slumped. His jaw went slack. "Yes. Yes, Aphrodite. Of course."

"You understand me?"

"Yes. Yes. I understand."

"Good. Now. I'm ready for another meal. Go and find us someone."
The whispers grew louder. "Go. Now. Hurry."

Peering out from behind the ventilation grate, the eyeball watched the girl. The eye was small. Careful. The thread of shiny pink tissue that trailed from the back of the eye barely thicker than a hair. So easy to miss. Especially tucked into a corner, the way Parker Schutz kept it. The thread of tissue ran along the length of the air duct, down into Parker's room and along the floor and up to where it connected to his foot. Sometimes it connected to his finger. Once he had sent the eye out, questing, watching, from the tip of his penis, but that made him feel odd and uncomfortable and he didn't like it so he didn't do that anymore.

The eyeball watching the girl could hear her, too. Fine hairs grew out of the eyeball's surface in the shape of a ring, and her voice made them tremble, and Parker understood her. He knew her name was Anastasia. Anastasia Coletti. He liked that name better than "Parker Schutz." Parker lay on his bunk in the room down the hall from Anastasia and watched her with the eyeball.

Mostly she was boring. But she was pretty, and watching her made him happy. Not like watching the others. The other four. Five of them, total, in the Special Wing. Parker and Joey and Beverly, and old Mr. Burl, and...and Trina. Parker clenched his jaw when he thought about Trina. But she was quiet now, they kept her quiet now, so that was okay.

Mr. Stamford and all the people in white coats thought the Special Wing was so safe from everyone and everything else, but Parker could see them because his eye and his ear could sneak out and nobody else knew he could do that.

They called him Number 2. He didn't like that. The other kids had said number 2 meant poop, he remembered that, like if you pooped your pants, you went number 2. Number 1 was pee. That made Parker laugh a little, especially when he thought about who Number 1 was. Trina's number 1! Trina's number 1! He remembered those other kids. Saw their faces, clear as day. But that was a long time ago. How long? Years? It felt like years. Parker had grown a lot since then.

He knew his name was Parker. Parker Schutz. Even if nobody here called him that.

There were a bunch of other kids, over in the other hallway, over where they kept Anastasia. He didn't know much about them. He'd stopped exploring when he found Anastasia, because she was so pretty and she made him happy.

The eye in the ventilation shaft twitched when Anastasia's door opened. A man in a white coat came in and said, "Were you having an event, Anastasia? We saw your vitals spike. Did you see something?"

But Anastasia shook her head. "No, I just had a nightmare. It was nothing."

The man in the white coat said okay, and went back out, but when Anastasia lay back down on her bed, Parker's little eye heard her whisper. It was barely any sound at all, but he heard it, because the hairs on the little eye were very sensitive, and when Anastasia whispered, "I understand, Scott," Parker heard that just fine.

One of his other little eyes was watching the hallway, and saw the same man in the white coat as he pushed buttons next to the door to the Special Wing and let a light shine in his eye and put his hand on a screen. The door to the Special Wing opened up, and Parker disconnected from his little eyes. They shrank up into the ventilation shafts and stayed there, quiet. Waiting. Waiting for him to reconnect. He knew he had a few hours to do that, before the little eyes shriveled up and went dead and he'd have to grow some new ones.

The door to his room opened, and the man in the white coat said, "How're we doing, Number 2?" and Parker wanted to laugh at that. *Poop! It means poop!* That was funny. But he never said anything to the people here. Or to Mr. Stamford. The man in the white coat looked at a panel set into the wall beside the door, and Parker thought he seemed satisfied with the numbers on the panel, and he went back out and the door shut.

Parker Schutz never said anything. But he remembered.

He remembered everything they'd ever done to him.

And everything they'd ever done to the other five in the Special Wing. Because he'd seen it all. Parker remembered.

He'd never forget what Trina did. What she always did. Before they made her get quiet. One time Trina had paid attention to him for a whole week before they made her stop. Parker's jaw clenched again.

A thin thread of tissue sprouted from the heel of Parker's right foot and felt its way down. Down to the level below this one, where another thread waited, and he reconnected, so that he could see what his Other Self had been doing in the Space Underneath.

No one knew about the Space Underneath.

No one knew about his Other Self.

Parker Schutz's Other Self had been down there for a long time now. Since right after Parker got to this place. He'd been down there, making the Space Underneath bigger, so that he could grow.

Parker let his mind slide out along the shiny pink thread, slide into his Other Self's body. He had to be very careful not to let anyone know about this. Not until he was ready. Not until the time was right to bring his Other Self up into the place with the rooms and the halls and the needles and the drills and the saws. And Trina. He thought that day might be soon. He hoped so.

His Other Self was getting so hungry.

3

At 11:00 Friday morning, Janey and Tim pulled into the parking lot of the Leslie O'Brien Care Facility in two separate cars— Janey's little Civic and Tim's battered old Monte Carlo. Tim avoided Janey's eyes when he got out, and though that hurt, in a perverse way Janey was grateful.

It felt like walking through mud, making her way up to the front door. For weeks she'd been on a mental loop, whenever she allowed herself to think of what was about to happen, her mind banging around and around on a track lined with razor blades.

She couldn't even begin to imagine what Tim was feeling.

No. That's not true. Of course I can imagine.

How could she react to what Tim was doing? Of his own free will? She knew what he'd say about it if she asked him. The same thing he'd said to her before, after they'd returned to Atlanta from that God-awful day in Texas. "I have to do it. You know I do. I couldn't live with myself if I didn't. And if I didn't…you wouldn't want to be with me."

Janey pulled open the front door. As she strode across the lobby toward the front desk, she felt as if she were marching toward her own execution. *How much sense does that make?* How could she view this as going to her death?

Except it wasn't her death…it was the death of this part of her life. The grieving. The struggling to cope.

The hope she'd found in Tim.

But it was a rebirth as well, wasn't it? Of course it was. It *had* to be. She kept telling herself that.

"Ms. Sinclair!" Beth, the duty nurse, broke out into a wide grin when she spotted Janey. The grin faltered when she took in Janey's expression, and the large suitcase Janey carried, and dropped entirely when she looked over Janey's shoulder and saw Tim. Janey didn't dare turn around to see what Beth saw. "This isn't your usual visiting day," Beth said. "Is everything all right?"

In as few words as she could manage, since she didn't trust the steadiness of her voice, Janey explained that she had made alternate arrangements for Adam's care, and that she and her friend Tim had come to move Adam to his new home. Beth immediately summoned Dr. Humphreys, the staff physician assigned to Adam's case, as well as Mr. Pomeroy, the head account manager, both of whom expressed caution and polite skepticism about this sudden departure. Janey reminded them, as quickly and tactfully as she could, that she was legally responsible for Adam, and that the decision had been made and would not change. She numbly signed the necessary release papers, and assured them that she'd return for whatever belongings of Adam's she didn't take today.

Tim never spoke.

When she opened the door to Adam's room, she found him sitting cross-legged in the corner, playing with a set of brightly-colored Bristle Blocks. His curly, shoulder-length blond hair had been pulled back to the nape of his neck with a black hairband, and the light from the window created a deep shadow in the broad indentation on the left side of his skull. He had flecks of something pink around his mouth. Janey recognized them as remnants of the Frankenberry cereal he liked to have for breakfast.

It took Adam's clear, ocean-green eyes a couple of seconds to focus on her, but when they did, he said, "Janey!" and got to his feet. His movements were staccato, imprecise—his left leg hadn't worked very well since he'd been shot—and while she didn't think he was going to fall, Janey nonetheless darted forward and steadied him. He said, "Did you bring any candy?"

Janey guided him over to sit on the edge of the bed. "Not today. Today's going to be something special. All right? We're going to go on a little trip."

Adam saw Tim standing in the doorway. "Who's that?"

"You remember Tim. Tim Kapoor. He was here once before. I introduced you."

Adam favored Tim with wide, blank eyes. "He's your friend?"

Janey almost lost it. She couldn't look at Tim in that moment. Dared not. "Yes, Adam, he's my friend. He's your friend, too."

"We're going on a trip? Out to the yard? I saw a butterfly in the yard."

"A little farther than the yard, honey. But first we need to pack up your things."

Wordlessly, Tim laid the suitcase on its side and opened it, and began transferring Adam's clothes into it from the closet. Adam watched him, wide-eyed. "I get to take my toys, right? And my books. They read me my books. *One Fish Two Fish.*"

Janey's vision blurred and swam. "Of course, honey. Anything you want."

Janey and Tim had spent a long, agonizing conversation discussing the logistics of what they were about to attempt. It would've been easiest, from a purely pragmatic standpoint, to do it right there in Adam's room in the O'Brien House, but that would have prompted several thousand questions from the staff that neither of them wanted to answer. Best to take him someplace else. Janey could have simply teleported him back to her apartment, but depending on his awareness of his surroundings, that might have caused him to panic. Ultimately Janey had decided to rent a small cabin near the care facility. A neutral place to which they could transport him by car, and where they could have enough privacy.

Adam waved goodbye to Beth and Dr. Humphreys as Janey helped him into the Civic's passenger seat. She closed the door, circled around to the driver's side, and caught Tim's eye for half a second as he climbed into the Monte Carlo.

In one of her art classes, the professor had told the students about a painter's attempt to execute a portrait of the early American writer Bret Harte. According to the professor, Harte's eyes had contained so much pain, such enduring anguish, that the artist was finally forced to paint the portrait with Harte's eyes closed. In that moment, looking across the

Civic's roof at Tim, Janey knew she could never capture his pain on a canvas.

"Where are we going?" Adam asked as Janey pulled away from the O'Brien House. A glance in the rearview showed her Tim following behind.

"I'm taking you to a nice place."

Adam had held onto a couple of the Bristle Blocks, and he hummed as he pressed them together and pulled them apart, together and apart.

Ten minutes later, Janey parked in front of the small cabin and led Adam up the stairs. The morning chill had yet to leave. Janey's breath became a plume of white as she exhaled. She fitted the key she'd been given at the rental office into the lock, and the tumblers clicked as Tim climbed the stairs behind them. "Here we go, honey," she said to Adam, leading him with a hand on his elbow. He followed her inside without question. Tim closed the door.

It wasn't a big place. Just one room, really, with partitions creating the illusion of walls. Good enough for a romantic weekend getaway. Janey could see the waters of Lake Lanier past a section of woods, if she squinted hard enough through the kitchen window. The furniture was all cheap rustic. Lots of exposed wood and claw feet. Janey gestured toward the biggest chair in the small living room. "Adam, honey, why don't you sit there?"

Adam did as he was asked. His wide eyes hadn't stopped darting around since he'd crossed the threshold. "Is this my room now?"

Janey took a deep breath through her nose, exhaled through her mouth, and turned to Tim. "Maybe you could stand behind him?"

Tim locked eyes with her this time. It was like looking into the eye of a hurricane. Janey didn't know how long they stood there before Tim nodded and slid behind the chair. He closed his eyes and tilted his head from side to side, cracking his neck.

Janey knelt beside Adam and took his hand. "Now, I want you to relax, okay? Maybe think about going to sleep? Can you do that?"

Adam yawned. He said, "Kinda tired." He leaned back in the chair, letting his head sink into the soft headrest cushion, and Tim laid his palms on Adam's forehead and face. Janey let go of Adam's hand in a hurry and almost sprawled on the floor, the surge of power she felt was so strong. Heat spread out from Tim's body, and Janey knew from personal experience, from the many times he'd healed her own catastrophic wounds, that that warmth radiated through Adam now, starting at the top of his head and spreading all the way down to the soles of his feet.

Adam's fingers twitched. The tendons in his neck stood out, and as Janey watched, his back arched. He made a guttural sound deep in his throat.

Tim took his hands away, and Adam collapsed, and Janey had to fight not to make any noise. The horrible dent in Adam's head was gone. Just like with Michael Hayslip. Adam's forehead was perfectly symmetrical again, for the first time in three years. Whole. Undamaged. As if the bullet that had taken her husband away had never been fired.

Tim took an unsteady step out from behind the chair. Janey sprang off the floor to help him, but he waved her away. "I'm good. I'm good." He moved past her, and got a hand on the front doorknob. "I'll see you, Janey."

Tim opened the door, and from behind her, Adam said, "Janey?"

She spun. Somewhere in the far, faint back of her mind, she heard the sound of the door as it closed and latched, but she didn't pay it any attention, she *couldn't*, because her heart was trying its best to explode inside her ribcage. That was Adam's voice. Coming from Adam's lips. Not the stranger she'd first met in the recovery room at the hospital. Not the innocent, sleepy child she'd visited at the Leslie O'Brien home. It was *Adam*. The real one. The one she'd fallen in love with. The one she'd promised to spend the rest of her life with.

Her husband.

Slowly Adam got up from the chair, and Janey couldn't have stopped the flood of tears down her cheeks if someone had been holding a gun to her head. Intelligence had come rushing back into Adam's clear green eyes, along with recognition and...confusion. His eyebrows drew together as he stared around him. "Where are we?" His gaze shifted to her. "What happened to your *hair*? Are you—Janey, why're you crying?"

Years fell away. Years of impotent, helpless rage, of long, cold nights spent crying alone, of mourning the life and the love that had been taken from her with the pull of a trigger.

If the ground around them had cracked and broken and fallen away, if the cabin had turned to dust, if the sun had turned black in the sky and died, Janey wouldn't have noticed. Her world had narrowed, raggedly, involuntarily, to the resurrected figure standing in front of her.

Janey threw her arms around him and buried her face in his neck and didn't even try to talk through the tears. The scent of Adam's skin filled her nostrils, and he lifted her face and his lips found hers and his kiss felt like coming home.

S o…what do you remember? Anything?"

Janey and Adam sat on a broad, flat rock on the shore of Lake Lanier, watching the sun go down through the trees beyond the far shore. Adam had picked up a twig, and as he spoke, he broke small lengths of it off and tossed them in the water. "It's sort of…kind of like waking up from a really vivid dream. The kind where you open your eyes and you think, 'Did that really happen?' And, y'know, for a while, you're not sure what's real and what isn't. And there are parts that…they sort of fade in and out. Like looking at something in really dim light? The more I think about some things, the less I can get straight in my head." He shifted his eyes toward her. "Three years? It's been three *years*."

Janey rested her cheek on his shoulder. "I've got so much to tell you. You wouldn't believe…you *won't* believe a lot of it. Because it's fucking crazy. But it all happened."

"If I believe that your friend Tim has super healing powers, and repaired my brain after I went all *Regarding Henry*, I don't see you telling me much I'll just flat deny." He threw another bit of the twig into the water. "How…how did you pay for…for me? For everything? As I recall, we didn't even have insurance when, uh. When it happened. When I… damn. When I got shot in the head."

"You remember I told you my dad had left me some money?"

"Yeah. You didn't want to touch it. Not unless we really had to."

"Right. Money from that account paid for my own time at the O'Brien home. And I used what was left to get you started."

Adam frowned, and dropped the twig. "But that ran out?"

"Eventually. It's okay, though, I—uh, I'm doing okay. With my paintings."

"And you're still teaching at the dojo, too, I guess?"

"Um. No. I'm painting full-time now. For money, I mean."

He pulled away enough to look her in the face. "You're making a living as a painter?"

She nodded, and watched as Adam's eyebrows climbed up his forehead. "Enough to pay for medical care? At a place like that? How successful *are* you?"

Janey tried to decide whether or not to let pride show through in her smile. "Well…not too bad…"

"Janey."

"My last painting went for, um, twenty-eight thousand."

Adam tried to downplay how hard he choked on his own spit. She waited while he coughed and cleared his throat. He stood and took a couple of steps away, giving her an uplifted pointer finger: *just a minute.*

He's taller than Tim.

Janey winced inwardly at the comparison. It had flared up, unannounced, like the piercing jab of an earache. Adam said, "I don't mean to react…however it looks like I'm reacting. I'm just surprised, is all. I mean, *shit*, you're doing that well? That's like, like, winning the fucking lottery!"

Janey stood and threaded her fingers through his. "Let's go back to the cabin, okay? Like I said, a lot has happened. More than just that. And I need to tell you. All of it. And it's going to take a while, so we should go get comfortable."

Adam smiled. It looked as if he were trying to be brave. "You're right. I've got an awful lot to catch up on. Hey! If it's been three years—who's president now?"

Janey groaned. "You're not going to believe that, either."

Twenty minutes later, she and Adam settled into the cabin's living room, and Janey talked. From right after sundown, through a frozen-pizza dinner, all the way to just past midnight, Janey talked. She told him everything. When she got to the part about being able to teleport from one patch of darkness to another, Adam demanded proof, and Janey turned off the lights and obliged, flickering from the darkened kitchen to the bathroom. Adam reacted to that better than she'd hoped. She was expecting more shock. Instead he just leaned back on the plaid-upholstered loveseat and closed his eyes and rubbed his temples.

Janey turned the lights on and came to sit beside him. "Are you all right?"

He sighed. "I think...I think I already knew. Like when you remember something, but you're not sure if it was something that really happened, or just something you dreamed? I think...I think I remember some of what I saw. I think I saw you do the..." He gestured vaguely from the bathroom to the kitchen and back. "It feels like something I used to know." He sighed. "But you're probably going to have to tell me all this more than once. Because right now I'm not convinced that I'm not still lying in a hospital bed, having some kind of mind-fuck fever dream."

"I guess that's fair."

He straightened up and sat forward. "And you've been able to do this, this thing, for how long?"

"Since just before I turned eighteen."

"Were you ever going to tell me?"

Janey took her time answering him. She stood, and slowly paced back and forth, her long legs covering the length of the living room in only a few steps. "Number one, aside from what my father could do, I had no idea anyone else could do anything like this. I sure as hell didn't know about the extraterrestrial part of it." She grimaced. "I get where you're coming from, Adam. I do. Just talking about it out loud still makes me feel ridiculous. But to answer your question, no, I don't think I ever would've told you. I never planned to do anything with it. It was...it was like being born with a tail. Right? You get it removed when you're a baby, and nobody would ever have to know about it. It wouldn't affect your life. At all. Why would you tell anyone if you didn't want to? Or have to? Why would I have opened myself up to that kind of...whatever. Scrutiny? For what purpose?"

"All right. Okay. And there's more, right?"

Janey kept going. She told him about the Vylar suit she'd stolen, and her very public declaration that Atlanta was hers to protect, and that the only reason she'd done any of it was because of him. Because she didn't want to let anyone else suffer the way he had...the way *she* had. She told him about Brenda Jorden and Simon Grove, and Garrison Vessler and Scott Charles, and Detective Feygen, and Derek Stamford. With a hitch in her voice, she told him about Aphrodite Lupo and her two followers, Julian Roth and Trent Davis. And about Nathan Pittman and Sha'dae Wilkerson. And finally about Nicole Grassley and Ashley Strandjev, and the bizarre version of a job offer they'd made her.

Janey's voice had turned scratchy and strained by the time she'd finished. Adam stood and walked over to a window, staring out into the blackness of the forest night. Staring into nothing. He said, "None of that seems real to me. Not yet. Not even your...what you can do. You're telling me all this, all these things that affect the whole world, but I just woke up. Here. All I've seen so far is this cabin, and these trees and the lake. It's familiar. I mean, I'm pretty sure I believe it. All of it. But at the same time, it's all just a story."

Janey joined him at the window, facing him. She folded her arms under her breasts and leaned her shoulder against the wall. "So what're you saying?"

He turned toward her, and reached out and gently pulled her arms to him, tracing his fingertips along her wrists to take her hands in his. "I'm saying that what I know is true—right now, the only thing I know to be a hundred percent real—is that I'm here. With you. With my wife."

Janey felt the rush again—the collapsing of reality around her. The trembling, deep in her foundation. Trembling that, she realized in a heart-beat of combined horror and joy, could bring down all the walls she'd built inside herself, once and for all. The walls that had barricaded off her old life, when her goals and her happiness and her pain were all simple. When sliding into bed each night, wrapped up in Adam's arms, she felt truly, unquestionably safe.

Adam said, "I know it's been three years for you. I know you've had to deal with...things that I can't wrap my head around, not yet. But for me, this just feels like waking up. And I guess what I'm trying to say is, I love you. Janey, I love you, and I need you. I'll always need you."

Before she could decide how to respond to that, before any words even formed in her head, Adam slid forward and pulled her arms around his waist, and kissed the side of her neck in *that spot oh God he still knew the exact spot* and he kissed the lobe of her ear and grazed his teeth across it and Janey's stomach fluttered and clenched and a wave of heat rushed down into her groin and spread out along her thighs.

Adam pulled his head back and rested his forehead against hers as his fingers found their way under her shirt, sliding up her sides and along the contours of her back, and his nails scratched gentle spiral patterns on her skin in *exactly* the way she loved the most, and that almost-forgotten sensation combined with Adam's scent and shot a thrill of pleasure deep into the most primitive part of her brain. Her bra unhooked under his touch and his hand dropped to caress her lower back and *oh God oh God he remembers he remembers everything.* Memories crashed through Janey's mind, memories of the days in their first apartment, the days when their love still held the unquenchable glow of the new.

She didn't resist when Adam maneuvered her shirt up and over her head. She didn't resist when he slid the bra straps down her arms and uncovered her breasts. She didn't resist when he kissed her lips and that sweet, perfect spot on her neck that they had discovered together, and made his way down her chest, the furnace-heat of his breath engulfing one tightening nipple, then the other, and while his gentle lips and tongue took her, bathed and caressed her, she ran the fingers of both hands into his hair and pressed him harder against her.

Three years. It's been three years.

Adam straightened, leaving her nipples cool and hard and aching for more, and shrugged out of his shirt. The time in the Leslie O'Brien home had diminished the long, wiry muscles that once covered his frame, but it was still him, still her husband, still the man she'd vowed to love and honor and cherish for the rest of her life.

Janey melted against him and kissed him, her tongue desperate against his, her entire body a construct of need and loneliness, and as he pulled her toward the cabin's bedroom, all the walls in Janey's mind crumbled to dust.

4

Janey awoke to dark clouds, filling both the sky and her mind alike. She fumbled for her phone on the nightstand. Seven minutes after noon. Janey closed her eyes again, trying and failing to relax.

The night before, when she'd finally drifted off to sleep, it had seemed as if she'd managed to travel back in time. To a place before she ever thought about stealing a suit of body armor, to a place before she'd ever heard the names Simon Grove or Aphrodite Lupo, to a place where she had no idea what lay beyond the planet's mundane confines. This morning, as she stretched out one arm and felt the empty space where Adam had lain the night before, gently snoring, the reality of her world seemed sharp and raw and sore as a skinned knee.

Adam stepped out of the bathroom, tucking his shirt into his pants. "I notice we don't have anything to eat here."

Janey sat up and stretched, the sheet falling away from her, and Adam gave a long, low whistle. "Now *that* is a sight that'll never get old."

Janey wished she could return that feeling with a smile, but unease gripped her mind and her heart. She wanted to swat it away, as if it were a pestering insect. She swung her legs over the edge of the bed and felt around for her clothes. "You ready to head back to Atlanta?"

He leaned against the bathroom's doorframe. "Ready to try to figure out how to fit back into my life, you mean?"

Janey stood, tugging her pants up. "Maybe we just go back to my apartment, to start with. And you're right, there's nothing to eat here, so we'll stop somewhere on the way. Grab a breakfast sandwich or something."

Adam came over and picked her shirt up off the floor. As he handed it to her, he said, "That's the most solemn I've ever heard anyone sound while talking about breakfast sandwiches."

Janey fastened her bra and took the shirt from him. "Yeah, well...all the stuff I told you last night? There's one more bit we need to go over."

Adam's face darkened. "Is it about Tim?"

Janey froze. Paralyzed for a long heartbeat. "Why do you ask?"

He cocked his head to one side. "You know I said it's like a dream. Fades in and out. I...think I'm starting to remember some of my time there, in the home. I think I remember you coming there with Tim. More than once. Did you—were you...together?"

With every word Adam spoke, Janey's blood grew colder and colder, until it felt so thick her heart could barely beat. "Nothing ever happened. Between us."

His eyes narrowed, but not in an accusatory way. He was simply thinking. She had seen that look on his face...how many times?

I know every expression he's got. Just as well as he knows me.

Adam said, "You mean nothing happened, physically." Janey didn't say anything. The buttoning of her shirt became very important. "I'm asking if something *happened*."

"Adam..."

"You said I was severely brain-damaged. That my personality was gone. That there was no hope of getting me back. Why wouldn't you connect with someone else?"

"Adam, don't."

"Don't what?"

"Don't be so *damn understanding*." Janey's raised voice surprised her as much as it did him. "Tim and I—we went through—look, there's no road map for this, okay? You're right. You were gone. Your mind was gone. You didn't know who I was. But you were alive, and you were my husband, and now you're back and *we're still married*."

He slid his hands into his pockets. "Is that why you're here? Because you took a vow? Because you're obligated?"

She threw her hands up. "What was last night, then? You think I was faking that? You think I didn't want you back? The love of my fucking life? The man I promised myself to? You think I just—just *moved on?*"

"I spent three years not knowing what was real and what wasn't. I'm only trying to figure out where I stand."

She brushed past him and walked out of the bedroom. He followed her and watched as she slipped her shoes on. Janey said, "I don't want to talk about this right now."

He folded his arms across his chest. "Why not?"

"Because we've got other things to discuss. Because, like I tried to tell you, there's something else you need to know about. Something more important than—" Janey couldn't stop herself, she knew she should before the words left her mouth, knew the kind of damage they could cause, but after what she'd done, what she'd sacrificed, the words came barreling out like a train leaving a tunnel. "—your fragile male ego."

Adam went pale. "You think…you think me being concerned about my wife's emotional state comes from worrying about getting my ego bruised?" He took a step forward. His voice grew softer, but that just made it worse. "You think wanting to know whether or not my wife is in love with another man comes from my own insecurity?"

Janey faced him square-on. "I don't want to discuss it right now because you need to know that the *fucking world might be ending.* All right? After we beat Aphrodite—after Stamford ran away—the Plowman came back. I didn't tell you this last night because I wanted us to be close! I wanted to start off on the right track, and I don't figure there's a much better mood-killer than this. But the Plowman came back and told us, and I quote, 'It is too late for your planet.' He said a signal got sent, and his people are going to come and *annihilate* us. How's that for a paradigm-changer? How's that for not caring so much about *feelings?*"

Adam slumped down into a chair. It took him several moments to speak, and when he did, a lot of sputtering and false starts came first. "But…but then…what's being *done* about it?"

Janey leaned back against the front door. She shrugged. "No one's seen or heard from him since that day. We don't know if he's dead, or if he went home, or if he's in hiding, or what." She squeezed her eyes shut. "We also don't know if he's *right*. There's no way to confirm it."

"So…everyone's just…waiting?"

"Waiting. Watching. Trying to deal with the things we can. Agent Grassley hooked me up with a new suit, since my last one got shredded. We've been trying to figure out where Derek Stamford is, and what he's doing, but the son of a bitch *excels* at covering his tracks."

Adam stared blankly into space. "And you can't warn the rest of the world…?"

She sighed. "The only way to get anyone to believe us would be to expose ourselves. Come out publicly as Augments. But then what if the Plowman's wrong? We've just given ourselves over to the government for nothing. If I'm going to get imprisoned or, or fucking *vivisected*, I want it to be for a good reason."

"And there's been no indication of anything. No, uh, signs of invasion? I guess?"

"None that we've seen."

Janey blew out a long breath, and made a gesture with both hands as if to shoo all the badness away. She walked over and held out a hand to him. Adam took it, and rose to stand very close to her, and Janey touched the side of his face, ran her fingertips along his jaw. He closed his eyes and nuzzled into the palm of her hand. She said, "You've come back to me. We're together. Let's make the most of it."

He nodded, his eyes still closed. "Okay." And then, "Honestly, I don't think I can process any of that right now anyway."

Janey said, "It's…I think…it's kind of like being told you *might* have terminal cancer. But you won't know until the test results come back. What do you do in the meantime? Sit in a corner and tremble? Or try to live your life?"

"Again, a lot to process."

"Yeah. So let's go get some breakfast. I'm starving."

Adam followed her out to the car. Clouds scudded overhead, low and gray. Not the kind that bring rain—instead, they diffused the morning sunlight and created a glare that found its way into every crack and crevice.

You've come back to me. We're together. Let's make the most of it.

As Janey started the car, the unease tightened around her again, and she wondered how much she meant all the things she'd said.

J aney drove through Midtown, headed for the LaCroix Building. Adam stared out the window again as they went, but now his eyes darted around. Janey realized he was looking for familiar sights. As they turned a corner onto Ponce, she wondered whether she should say anything about the store coming up on their right.

Adam spotted it before she'd made up her mind. "Chandler's is...it's gone?"

"Closed about eighteen months after you got hurt."

They cruised past the pizza restaurant that now occupied Adam's old place of employment. He slumped in his seat. "So my driver's license is expired. And not only do I not have a job now, there's not even a job I might be able to go back to."

Words floated up and presented themselves to Janey. *You managed an art-supply store. You can find another management gig.* She looked the words over and decided against saying them out loud.

Adam went on. "Would anybody even hire me now? How's it going to look on a résumé—a three-year gap?"

"Well, you could tell them the truth. You got hurt, and it took a long time to recover."

He rubbed the bridge of his nose. "That's not the truth. The truth is I was a brain-damaged idiot for three years."

"You weren't an *idiot*. You were sweet."

"You said I had the mental capacity of, what, a three-year-old? Maybe four?"

Janey didn't answer. More words floated in front of her, waiting to be voiced. *It's not like you were dead.* And *Maybe you could try being happy, instead of feeling sorry for yourself?*

Inwardly she flinched. How could she even think something that cold? How would she feel in Adam's shoes?

They ran into a construction slow-down—Janey kicked herself for not checking her traffic app—and by the time they pulled into her space at the LaCroix, the sun had begun to set. She preferred the summer, when it didn't get dark until past nine o'clock. Not only because one of her favorite things to do was drive around at night with the windows down, blasting the stereo, but also because the summer daylight hours meant fewer crimes committed under cover of darkness.

Adam gazed up at the building as they climbed out of the rental car. "Went for a high-rise, huh?"

Janey remembered the apartment they had shared after they got married: a second-floor walk-up over a dry cleaners. The place had had zero curb appeal, but Janey always thought of it as a hidden gem, with its spacious bedrooms and twelve-foot ceilings. Adam was the one who'd found it, pulled in by the architectural details and the transoms above the bedroom doors. She thought about the featureless beige box she lived in now. It wasn't even apples to oranges. There was no comparison at all.

Adam slipped his arm around her waist in the elevator, and she leaned her head against his. For some reason she couldn't identify, her stomach clenched and trembled, as if she were about to face some dangerous combatant. Adam said, "You okay?"

"Yeah. I'm good. Why do you ask?"

"You tensed up for a second."

Janey let a smile curl her lips and gave him a quick kiss. "Just excited." The elevator thunked and chimed, and Janey led Adam down the hallway to her apartment door. Her fingers only fumbled with the keys for a second.

When Adam didn't say anything after walking into her living room, Janey leaned against the doorframe and folded her arms, waiting. He turned in a circle, his expression unreadable, and wandered into the kitchen. Janey still didn't speak. When he went from the kitchen into the bedroom, and she heard him open the door to the bathroom, Janey just stood, calmly, waiting. Imagining his reaction. Something like, "The place certainly has possibilities, doesn't it?" Or maybe, "Decorating didn't fit into the budget, huh?"

She knew the place was Spartan. Sha'dae had told her it looked as if she had either just moved in, or was just about to move out. Truthfully, Janey hadn't given personal decorations much thought in the last three years. She hadn't given her personal *life* much thought...

...except for Tim.

Janey winced, and fought down unbidden thoughts. Adam came back out into the living room, and Janey said, "Well? What do you think?"

Adam threw his arms wide. "Where's all my stuff?"

Janey faltered. "Your—huh?"

He made exaggerated gestures with both hands. "Where's the furniture we picked out together? Where's that TV I saved up for? Where's my guitar, and that Japanese screen I got in college? Where's all my *books?*"

"Adam...I..."

"Please tell me it's all in storage. You've got a storage unit somewhere. Right? You had that, that *basement* place you told me about. Surely to God you've got a storage unit."

Janey couldn't decide what to do with her hands. "Adam...honey. I got rid of all that."

His eyes bugged out of their sockets. "You got *rid* of it? What do you mean? You sold it? Gave it away?"

Janey's vision had gone a little blurry. She crossed to the couch and sat, and patted the cushion next to her. "Just come and sit down, okay?"

Adam lowered himself onto the couch, but stayed perched on the edge of it, facing her. "Do you remember who you sold it to? Could we buy it back?"

"Some of it I gave to the Salvation Army. I took all the books to a used book store. A lot of the other stuff...the Japanese screen, I...um. I took it to the dump."

She might as well have slapped him across the face. "*Why?* Why the *fuck* would you do that?"

"*Hey*. I do not appreciate being cursed at."

He stood and paced to the kitchen before turning around to face her. "Well I don't appreciate you getting rid of everything I owned, either."

Tears spilled down Janey's cheeks before she even realized she was crying. She leaned forward and hid her face in her hands—for about two seconds. Then she was up and on her feet and within striking distance of Adam's outraged face. "I didn't think I was ever going to get you back! How do you not see that? There was no way to get you back, Adam! I had no reason to hope! Not—"

His face darkened. He swallowed hard. "Not until Tim turned up with his healing thing. Right?"

She spun away from him. "Why are we doing this? Why are we fighting? You just got home!"

From over her shoulder, Adam said, "I didn't just get home. I just got to *your apartment*."

Janey's back stiffened. Without looking at him, she walked to the closet halfway down the hall. "There's food in the fridge. Make yourself as comfortable as you're able."

"Huh? Where're you going?"

"I need a few minutes."

"In a closet—? Oh. Oh, I get it. We actually start talking about something, and you're going to do your disappearing thing—"

Janey didn't hear the rest of what he said, because she closed the door and, bathed in welcome darkness, flickered away.

Adam's demands about a storage unit, in retrospect, almost made Janey laugh, since she teleported from the darkness of her closet to the darkness of a 10 x 20 storage unit she'd rented after her Basement got replaced by a massive burning crater.

She'd recreated the work bench and the pegboard, and was well on her way to stocking it with newer versions of all the blunt and edged weaponry that had decorated it before. There was no room, of course, for the bales of hay with the targets pinned to them, or the modest lawn furniture she'd occasionally relaxed in...or the now-destroyed poster of her father in full stage-magician regalia. That had been a one-of-a-kind item. She tried not to think about it.

She did shrug into the new Vylar suit Agent Grassley had provided. Janey still wasn't sure exactly what agency Grassley was part of, or if it was even accurate to call her "agent," but she hadn't looked a gift horse in the mouth. Grassley's people, whoever they were, had tailored the new suit to Janey's exact measurements, making it a damn sight more comfortable than the old one. No more putting Band-Aids over her nipples to prevent chafing. It was made of second-generation Vylar, too, or so they said. Even more bullet-proof than the last model. Janey seated the helmet and strapped it down, slung her "dark pouch" around her back, grabbed up a couple of telescoping aluminum batons, and flickered out into the city.

Janey still patrolled. She'd added a few more Eyes of the Widow symbols around town, and kept a regular watch over them, but in recent weeks hadn't seen very much crime in any of those spots. She didn't know if she just wasn't paying close enough attention, or kept missing the trouble, or if, perhaps, the patrol was actually working. Perhaps word had gotten out that you shouldn't cause any problems around those places, or the Widow would get you. She liked the idea that she'd become a cautionary tale.

Winter was just about to give way to Spring, but though the days had warmed up enough that she didn't need much more than a T-shirt and jeans, the nights and early mornings still held a chill. Janey left spots of heat around the city as she flickered from location to location. First a bus stop…then an alleyway behind a nightclub…then a gas station in an area tagged with gang-related graffiti.

Nothing.

She'd hoped the patrol would serve as a distraction from what was going on with Adam, and in a way it did. But at the same time, it let an all-too-familiar thought loop start playing in her head. How many other people on Earth knew what she knew? How many other people knew that extraterrestrials—beings whose proper name she still didn't know—weren't just watching us, hadn't just visited us, but were actively experimenting with human DNA, viewing it as raw material in an effort to create military assets for their own use off-world. It lent Janey a perspective she didn't welcome.

What was the point?

The question bounced around in her brain. Yes, she'd managed to prevent some small percentage of street-level crime in one city. But on a higher level, humans still warred and feuded and killed and maimed each other *everywhere else on the planet.* And on a level higher than that one, what did it matter? Why should she even concern herself with the petty bickering of individual humans, when now she knew that Earth was just one world of…how many? One world out of a multitude, probably a multitude of multitudes. Could humans survive in the face of a threat as advanced and ruthless as the one they faced?

Did they even deserve to?

The thought loop broke when Janey stepped out of the shadows of a church rooftop and heard an unmistakable sound: the combined boom and crunch of a car wreck. She sprinted to the far corner of the roof and saw an old, battered Camaro that had just driven full-speed directly into a telephone pole. A half-step backward into darkness and Janey reappeared in a doorway at ground level, thirty feet from the crash. She ran toward it.

Agent Grassley had at one point commented on the insulating properties of Vylar, and Janey hoped Grassley hadn't exaggerated, because she saw the driver of the car—a balding, paunchy, middle-aged black man—slumped against the wheel, blood pouring from a laceration in his scalp. The driver's-side window had shattered. Janey noted bits of glass all over the man as she called out: "Sir! Sir, can you hear me?" The driver didn't respond, and when Janey tugged on the door handle, the door didn't move, crimped into the frame from the impact.

She reached into the car, past the man, and turned off the ignition switch. The last thing she needed was an explosion. Another tug on the door still didn't budge it, so Janey grabbed the door with both hands, braced one foot against the body, and wrenched the door completely off its hinges. It hit the ground with a hollow thud as she released the man's seat belt, and as she went to maneuver him out of the car, the shifting of his body exposed a long piece of metal protruding from his right side, high up under the armpit.

Janey took hold of the man, not quite as firmly as she'd gripped the Camaro's door, and flickered with him to a dark spot she knew right outside the entrance of Gavring Medical's Midtown emergency room. She laid him down as gently as she could and ran for the entrance.

Half an hour later, Janey emerged from the shadows a block down from the emergency room entrance, now dressed in civilian clothes. The Vylar suit had gotten more than a little of the Camaro driver's blood on it, so it was back in the storage unit, soaking in a big plastic tub. Ordinarily she'd just take it straight to her apartment and clean it off in the shower, but she'd read enough about forensics not to want to get strangers' blood in her grout, plus...she wasn't ready to see Adam again quite yet.

She couldn't have said what she was doing here, though. She hadn't even caught the driver's name, and didn't want to attract any police attention by claiming she'd seen the accident. A half-formed notion that she might catch a glimpse of the man through a window flitted around her, but she batted it away.

Halfway between her and the ER entrance, on the other side of the street, was a MARTA stop. The kind that consisted entirely of a MARTA sign poking up out of the sidewalk. No bench. No enclosure. Just a place for people to stand and wait.

Janey squinted. She moved closer, and saw a young girl, no older than thirteen, with skin a little darker than Janey's and a glorious head of natural hair. The girl sat on the sidewalk with her back to the MARTA signpost, crying.

Is that the Camaro driver's daughter?

Janey realized how unlikely that was. Just a crazy thought, brought on by how vividly the man's injuries still stood out in her mind. Janey walked at a measured pace toward the girl, and when she got within easy earshot, she said, "Hello? Are you okay?"

The girl whipped her head around and stared, and Janey thought for a second she was about to get up and bolt away, but then the girl's shoulders sagged and she slumped back down against the signpost. She made an attempt at drying her eyes with the sleeve of her shirt, but Janey could see both shirt sleeves were already soaking wet.

Janey stopped ten feet away. "Do you need some help? Is there anything I can do?"

The girl sniffled, and when she spoke, her voice held so much bitterness that for an instant Janey thought she might have misjudged her age. "Can you fix my dad's legs?"

Janey came closer, and crouched down to put herself on eye level with the girl. "I wish I could. What, uh…what's wrong with your dad's legs?"

The girl's eyes narrowed. Grew dangerous. "They got broken." She closed her eyes the rest of the way. "Now he can't work. Now he can't do anything. So me and Mom and James are gonna have to find someplace else to live. Shit…" She dragged the word out. *Sheeeit.* "We're gonna be payin' off hospital bills the rest of our lives. Prob'ly my kids' lives, too."

Janey groped for something positive to say. "Insurance won't help?"

Soaked in bitterness: "Insurance is a *fucking* joke. Plus it don't pay none when…when Dad got hurt the way he did."

As carefully as she could, Janey said, "How'd he get hurt?"

The girl snapped out words like repeated strikes of a venomous snake. "The Gray Fucking Widow. The Gray Widow broke his goddamn legs. Only thing Dad was ever good at was tree work. Cuttin' 'em, trimmin' branches and shit. Now he can't do that. Doctors say his knees got fucked up so bad, he prob'ly won't ever *fucking walk again*."

Janey almost fell over backward. Her breath grew short in her chest, and she started sweating. "What—I'm sorry, I just—doesn't the Gray Widow—what was—"

The girl glared at her. "What was he doin'? That's what you want to ask me? 'The Gray Widow protects people, he must've been doin' somethin' awful.' Right? That's what you want to say?" Janey couldn't think of anything that wouldn't make the situation even worse. The girl didn't wait for her. "Yeah, he was dealin'. It was a stupid-ass thing for him to do, but you know what? 'Less you the boss, tree-trimmin' don't pay shit. Not enough to keep us all alive. So he did what he had to do, and the police say he was dealin' to kids, and 'cause of that, that goddamn bitch *cunt* ruined him." She hugged her knees, her cheeks wet. She didn't bother wiping them dry. "Ruined all of us."

Janey stood, and had to take several long, deep breaths to keep from vomiting. Finally, she said, "What's your name? I'm Janey."

The girl kept her eyes lowered. Staring holes in the sidewalk. "I don't need nothin' from you, Janey."

Before Janey could come up with anything else, a MARTA bus arrived, and the girl stood and climbed aboard. Janey watched her through the window as she took a seat and tilted her head forward, her face hidden in shadow.

With a hiss and a squeal, the bus pulled away.

5

Twenty minutes later, with the still-damp but non-bloody Vylar suit tucked under her arm in a small bundle and her boots in her other hand, Janey stepped out of the shadows on the roof of the LaCroix Building. She intended to take a couple of minutes and calm down, or maybe psych herself up—or possibly both—before heading back to the apartment and Adam.

The roof of the building lent itself to a complicated form of reflection for her these days. The first time she'd ever been up here was when Simon Grove had abducted Tim and tried to kill him. The next time, a dying alien weapons researcher had used Janey's body as a conduit to Augment —she suspected randomly—Tim and Nathan and Sha'dae. Now Janey liked to hang out there on quiet nights and stare up at the stars. Partly to admire their beauty.

Partly to see if any of them weren't moving right.

Tonight she materialized on the roof, heard the crunch of gravel under her feet, and froze. Tim stood not even ten feet away, leaned against the edge wall, smoking a cigarette. And looking at her.

Janey felt as if every word had been slapped out of her mouth and down her throat, where they bunched up and tried to choke her. After several long, painful seconds, she said, "Since when do you *smoke?*"

Tim blew out a long plume and looked up at the stars. "My uncle's smoked all his life. He always says it calms his nerves. I thought I'd give it a try." He took another drag. "It's not like I'm going to get lung cancer. Or emphysema. Or, y'know. Anything, ever." He looked at her from the corner of his eye. "Been out patrolling?"

Janey nodded.

"So where's Adam?"

"Oh, he's—he's—he's down in the apartment."

"How's that working? If I may ask. You two going to try to make a go of it?"

"Tim, I don't—"

He put up a hand and stopped her. "Forget it. Sorry. Sorry. None of my business. Of course you're making a go of it. You're married. You took vows." Tim dropped the cigarette on the roof and ground it out with his heel. He walked past her toward the stairs, his gaze sliding across the bundled-up suit. "I'm glad he's okay with you going on patrol. City still needs the Gray Widow, right?"

Janey stood there like a statue, kicking herself on the inside as hard as she could, until Tim was gone. She moved back into the shadows, flickered...

...and emerged from the closet in her apartment.

The first thing she noticed was the candlelight. The second was the smell of roast chicken.

"Janey? Is that you?"

Janey dropped the suit and the black boots on the floor and took the corner fast into the kitchen. Adam, a floral-patterned apron around his waist, opened Janey's oven—which she couldn't even remember the last time she'd used—and pulled out a baking pan with what looked like a professionally-prepared chicken in it. Two place settings adorned Janey's tiny breakfast table, complete with tall candles and wine glasses, and on the stove she spotted two other dishes: one filled with glazed carrots, the other with mashed potatoes.

Adam said, "Turns out I still know how to cook." He put the chicken down near the carrots and the potatoes, and came to her, pulling off oven mitts as he moved. Adam took Janey's hands in his. "Baby, I'm sorry. I'm really sorry. I've been acting like a giant dick. I don't know how to do what I'm doing, how to, y'know, *be* how I am, where I am. But there's got to be a better way to do it than what I did today." He gestured toward the food. "This is supposed to be a peace offering. A good, solid, healthy meal, like I used to cook for us."

Janey had all but forgotten how much Adam liked to cook.

"Unless, I mean, unless you already ate? Because all of this can keep."

Janey made her mouth smile. "No. No, I haven't eaten. I'm starving."

He grinned, his perfect teeth flashing in the candlelight. "Then sit! Sit, please. Let me serve you."

Janey sank into one of the uncomfortable, straight-backed chairs in her breakfast nook, and watched as her husband brought dinner to her.

The next morning, Janey and Adam rode in silence. Adam had insisted they go back to the O'Brien Home and pick up the remainder of his belongings, and Janey had agreed, on the condition that he stay in the car and not let any of the staff see him, so as not to provoke a billion questions. Now, with two plastic bins full of toiletries, knick-knacks, and toys in the back seat, they were headed back to Atlanta.

Adam stared out the window at the passing scenery, and when Janey said, "Hey, I'm going to stop up here and fill the tank," he only grunted in assent.

She pulled the Civic into a Sav-A-Ton gas station about a mile north of where Peachtree Industrial Boulevard started. The place sat on a relatively lonely stretch of tree-lined road, on the edge between rural and suburban, and sold live bait along with Slim Jims and ethanol-laced gasoline.

Adam stayed in the car while Janey pumped the gas, and when she got back in and shut the door, he said, "That pretty-boy over there's been staring at us this whole time."

"What guy?" Janey craned her neck around to see where Adam was pointing.

She didn't bother stifling a short, clipped scream.

Simon Grove leaned against the wall of the gas station, dressed in the same suit he'd been wearing in the barn on the Texas ranch, smoking a cigarette and smiling.

Smiling at Janey.

She cranked the car and jammed it into drive and made the tires squeal, getting them out of the parking lot and back onto the road. As the engine whined in protest, the speedometer needle climbing far too slowly for her taste, Adam shouted, "What the fuck? What's going on, what's wrong?"

Janey started to say, "That's Simon Grove, the guy I told you about," but as the next words in the sentence died in her mind—*That's the guy who almost killed Tim*—Janey glanced in the rearview and saw Simon Grove sprinting after them on foot.

And gaining.

Janey floored the gas pedal.

It was early enough in the morning, and few enough people were out on a Sunday, that they were the only car on this stretch of road. That would change soon enough, especially at this speed, since Janey had set them barreling toward downtown. But that shouldn't have mattered, because he was on foot, for God's sake, he was on foot and they were in a car and there was no way he could catch them—

Janey risked another look into the rearview mirror, and said, "No *fucking* way," and Adam twisted around to look out the back window, and this time he was the one who screamed.

As Simon Grove ran, his body changed. From one bounding stride to the next, he hunched forward, abruptly running on all fours, and he began to *grow*. The suit ripped and fell behind him in tatters, and his skin turned a noxious gray-green, and as his distended jaw opened to reveal rows of long, needle-like teeth, his eyes turned a hollow white.

He ran faster.

Janey stared through watering eyes as Simon's spine elongated, and his feet—all four of them—stretched and sprouted massive claws that ripped chunks out of the concrete as he sprinted after the Civic, and his skull flattened and lengthened and became something feline and horrible.

Janey realized he was going to catch them, and she looked around wildly for someplace dark, someplace she could take Adam and dive into, any place with any shadow to it, but there was nothing. The morning glare of the clouds eliminated every shadow, and she hadn't brought any weapons with her, and she didn't have time to process anything more because the fifteen-foot-long gray-green panther-beast that had been Simon Grove only moments before launched itself off the roadway and landed on the car.

Seven-inch talons exploded through the side windows as the beast clamped down on the car's roof, and Janey tried to shield Adam from the spray of shredding metal and glass as the beast ripped the roof free and tossed it to the side, where it clanged and deformed as it tumbled on the pavement. Janey struck at the beast's head, at its face, driving fists and elbows into it with all the strength she could muster, but if it felt the blows, it gave no indication beyond a steady, bone-deep, snarling growl. One talon snipped through Janey's seat belt, and the beast reared upright, hitching forward, and pain shot through Janey's shoulders as its rear talons curved around her arms and cinched tight below her armpits—

—and the creature's forelegs *became wings.*

The Civic skewed to the right as the beast plucked Janey out of the car, and to her horror she saw it rocket straight toward a tree, Adam's flailing arms trying to reach the steering wheel. The last glimpse she got of him was as the car rammed straight into the tree, the passenger-side airbag triggering in a burst of gas and fabric.

Janey squirmed, struggled, folded her body in half and kicked up toward the beast's face, and in response the beast shook her hard enough to make black spots float in her vision. In an utterly non-human voice, it grated out, *"Be still."*

Janey shrieked. "Let me go you son of a bitch I'll kill you *I'll kill you again fucker let me go!"*

The winged creature skimmed low over the tops of trees, the road and the crashed Civic rapidly fading behind them. Janey tried and tried again, but couldn't break the thing's grip around her shoulders, and finally she hung there, limp. Not daring to think of Adam, back there in the wrecked car, maybe bleeding, maybe dead.

Ahead of them, a small, bare hilltop rose out of the trees. The creature ground out more words. "I'm going to set you down. Don't run. I'll just catch you again." The massive wings kicked up twin plumes of dust as the beast and Janey dipped, slowed, and settled to the earth. The talons released her, and while Janey rubbed the pain away and the blood back into her muscles, the huge winged monstrosity shrank.

Its skin hissed and popped, its bones crunching and cracking as they slid across each other, and as Janey stared, her gorge rising, it became Simon Grove again. He stood there naked for a few seconds, before seeming to realize Janey's discomfort, at which point the suit he'd been wearing *emerged* from folds in his skin, and with a horrible, wet sound, his body shifted and settled back into it.

After several false starts, she said, "If you've hurt Adam—"

He grunted dismissively. "Your hubby's fine. I didn't smell any blood after the car hit the tree, and his breathing and heart rate were normal. Accelerated, to no one's surprise, I guess, but within standard parameters." Simon Grove folded his arms across his chest and popped his neck. Janey saw the scar where her father's sword had decapitated him, clear as day, and she saw him notice that she was looking at it.

"How? *How?* I killed you. I cut your fucking head off!"

Simon sat down on the ground, cross-legged, and gestured with his chin toward a patch of earth ten feet in front of him. "If you'll make yourself comfortable, I have words you need to hear."

6

Janey's hand flew to the outline of the phone in her pocket, but stopped. Adam didn't have a phone. She wasn't about to call 911 and have unsuspecting people show up and get torn to pieces. Agent Grassley and whatever backup she might be able to provide couldn't get there in time to do any good. Her eyes darted toward the woods surrounding them, gauging distances, seeking out the deepest shadows. Every second the sun rose higher in the sky, the more intense the glare got.

Simon sighed. "Look, if I wanted you dead, I would've ripped you in half already. I just want to talk. Try to stop shaking and maybe listen, all right?"

She *was* shaking. It felt as if adrenaline had replaced every drop of blood in her veins.

I killed you once, I can do it again.

He lifted his hands and waggled them, fingers spread wide. "I'm just sitting here. I want to talk to you. And I don't know how much time we have, so if we could get on with it, please? Pretty please? Cherries and such? Come on, sit your ass down."

"I'll stand, thanks." A sense of unreality settled over the scene. Janey wondered if this could be all some sort of illusion—some sort of Augmentation like Aphrodite Lupo's assault on her mind, making her believe things were happening that really weren't. "I saw you *die*. You were dead. Lying there in your own blood."

Simon massaged his neck with one hand. "Yeah. About that. Stamford collects Augments. You know that, right?"

Derek Stamford. The private defense contractor, once partnered with Garrison Vessler. Janey knew about the deal Stamford offered any Augment he encountered: work for him willingly, or get brainwashed. And if the brainwashing didn't take, Stamford had them killed. Stamford was the one who'd located the Plowman's base of operations, underneath the ranch in Texas, and tampered with the extraterrestrial systems enough to, according to the Plowman, ring an alarm bell. A bell heard by the Plowman's people, resulting in the potential conquest of Earth. That thought was too big, too full of dread, and too infuriating for Janey to entertain at the moment.

"Yeah. He 'collects' them. What of it?"

"Stamford had a healer in his stable. Her name was Caroline. He wanted to see what she could do with me, and left her alone with my corpse." Simon's matter-of-fact tone made Janey's skin crawl. "Caroline saw something in me. Once she started working on me. Saw, I guess, some potential. She put me back together, but..." His voice tightened. "But it killed her. The strain was too much."

Janey thought of the heavy toll healing had always taken on Tim's body. She could easily imagine him pushing himself too hard to be able to recover. *I wonder where he is now?* The thought sprang up, unbidden, a spike of sadness amid the quivering tension of this conversation.

"I opened my eyes and saw her, and she kissed my face. The way my mother used to. And she asked me to promise that I'd stop Stamford. Any way I could. Whatever way I had to. And she died before I could tell her I would."

Janey folded her arms and shook her head. "You were working with Stamford. You beat the shit out of me at the ranch. You told him about my —that I had to have darkness."

"That's the thing, Janey." Hearing her name on his lips made her gorge rise. "What Caroline did for me—it's still working on me. Still changing me. I was under the influence of Stamford's brainwashing when you saw me at the ranch. All the conditioning. All the drugs. But my brain was still healing. And when it healed enough to reject all of that, I left. I left, and I started looking for you."

Janey's eyes narrowed. "Why me?"

"Because you *did* kill me. Because the only way I could get you here now, make you listen to me, was by coming at you in broad daylight. Whatever shape I can take, do you think it would've made any difference after dark?"

She repressed a shudder, thinking of all the times she'd gone after Aphrodite Lupo. Dark or light hadn't made much difference. Only by working with the...she hesitated to use the words. The *combat squad* she was part of, along with Sha'dae and Nathan and...and Tim. Only working as a team had they been able to bring Aphrodite down.

"But why come to me at all? What do you want from me?"

Simon slowly stood and stretched. Hundreds of hard, sharp objects pushed up from underneath his skin for a second, but disappeared when he stopped flexing, and Janey threw up in her mouth a little. "Look, I was a scared kid when I ran away from home. I can't pretend that's not what it was. I wasn't a young man out seeking his fortune. I just ran away."

"You killed people. That's what you did. You took innocent young women and you drained their blood out of their bodies. Scared kid my brown ass."

Simon winced. "I know. I know. And after what Brenda Jorden did to me...it only got worse. It'd be easy if I could say she made me do it. I wish I could say that. I wish I could say she had me under some kind of mind control. But she didn't. She...she took away what little I had in the way of inhibitions, all right? I did horrible, horrible things, and I know ultimately I'll have to pay a price for that. But what Caroline did for me—Janey, the sacrifice she made. Because she saw a possibility in me. She made me understand. It's taken a long time, but I get it now, and...basically, I need your help."

"You've got to be fucking *kidding* me."

Simon's gaze fell to the ground at her feet. "I understood some things, while I was there in Stamford's, whatever you want to call it. His *flock*. Janey, he's not just brainwashing and enslaving adult Augments. He's doing things to children, too." A chill ran up Janey's spine at that, but Simon went on. "And more. I think I get what this thing is—what's been done to people like you, and Brenda, and Ned Fields, and Garrison

Vessler. I can see the patterns. You're all fighters. You're all different ways to win a war."

Military archetypes. That's what the Plowman had said the Augments were meant to be. Foot soldiers. Scouts. Interrogators, Infiltrators, etc. To be perfected, shipped off-planet, and replicated. Janey didn't know if she would have ever picked up on that if the Plowman hadn't told her, and couldn't help but be a tiny bit impressed that Simon had put it together.

"But then there's me. I'm a mistake. I know I am. I'm some kind of God-forsaken mashup. And so is Aphrodite Lupo."

Janey drummed the fingers of one hand against her biceps. "Can't argue with you. But I don't see your point."

Simon lifted his head and looked her in the eye. "My point is that Stamford's got a place. Hidden, heavily fortified, heavily defended. And he's got five more people like...like me. Like Aphrodite. Holding them there, locked up. Waiting for...something. I don't know what."

Janey heard herself groan, and covered her face with her hands. Five more like Aphrodite Lupo? Five more unstoppable, unkillable engines of destruction? Simon seemed to pick up on her despair, and said, "I know, right? It's the kind of thing you want to nuke from orbit. Which I would try to do, if the place wasn't like half a mile underground, and I knew anything about nukes or satellites."

Janey dropped her hands and glared at him. "Let's say I believe you. Which I have no reason to."

"Other than the fact that I didn't kill you just now."

She waved that away. "What do you expect me to do with this information? I don't know how much you saw on the Brittain ranch, but Aphrodite Lupo was basically impossible to kill, and with my luck, she probably still isn't dead. Despite Nathan punching her heart out of her chest. Now you want me to go up against five more of her?"

Simon's eyebrows lifted. "The kid punched her heart out? Wow. Wish I'd seen that." For a moment, to Janey's dismay and annoyance, Simon Grove seemed very much like Nathan Pittman—a simple kid, ready to be amazed by the world around him. She knew he couldn't be any older than twenty. Maybe even eighteen or nineteen. Janey brought her anger with Simon back to the forefront by remembering what Tim had looked like when she took him to the hospital. After Simon had beaten Tim to within an inch of his life and dropped him off the side of a twenty-story building.

Simon said, "I'm not asking you to believe me. Well, okay, yes I am, but I'm not just asking you to take my word for it. I can give you the location of this place. Go, take a look, check it out for yourself. Then you can decide what you want to do about it. And…whether or not you want me to help you."

Janey's eyes rolled. "I can tell you that right now, *Simon.*"

He put his hands up. "I know. I know. I get it. But like I said, there's a time limit involved. You know that creepy little kid that Brenda used to take care of? The one who could see people like us at a distance?"

Scott Charles. Janey didn't say Scott's name.

"Yeah, well, Stamford's got his own version of that kid. Little girl named Anastasia. She's just as good as Scott was, maybe better. She's the reason we showed up at the ranch in the first place." He craned his neck, looking up at the low white clouds. "She might be looking at us right now. And if she is, you can bet Stamford knows that *you* know what *I* know."

"Janey!"

Adam's voice drifted up out of the woods below the hilltop, accompanied by the sound of crashing underbrush and snapping twigs.

Simon Grove raised his head and sniffed. He looked faintly amused. "That's that blond fellow you were in the car with, I believe. See, I told you he was fine."

Janey ran toward Adam's voice. "Adam! Stay where you are, okay? Don't come up here!"

Adam burst out of the trees, caught sight of her and Simon, and though he slowed to a cautious walk, made his way up the hill nonetheless. Simon said, "Not great with following directions, is he?"

Janey snapped, "Shut the fuck up, Simon."

Panting hard, his skin criss-crossed with shallow scratches, Adam reached Janey's side, never taking his eyes off Simon. He held a three-foot section of tree branch in one hand like a cudgel. "Are you—are you okay?" Adam could barely get the words out. "What happened back there? Is this —this is the guy, right? He turned into—that thing?"

Simon got to his feet and took a step toward Adam. "Simon Grove. Pleased to meet you."

Janey bludgeoned Simon with her gaze. "If you even think about trying to shake his hand I'll break your arm *off.*"

Simon shrugged. "Whatever. We're going to need a way to communicate." He took a flip-phone out of an inside jacket pocket and tossed it to Janey. "It's a burner. The only number on it is mine."

Having regained a tiny bit of his breath and composure, Adam squinted at Simon and spoke to Janey. "Wait—is he on your side?"

Janey opened her mouth to answer, but Simon beat her to it. With a humorless grin, he said, "Right now I'm on *my* side." He gestured at the phone in Janey's hand. "It's the side where I'm less likely to die a horrible death. I'll be in touch. Once you've thought it over."

Simon turned and leaped from the hilltop into the branches of the nearest tall tree. He covered a distance of at least forty feet, and Janey heard Adam's breath lock in his throat. Seconds later, Simon Grove had disappeared into the woods, leaving Janey and Adam alone under the morning sun's cloud-filtered glare.

Adam sat down, pulled his knees up to his chest and wrapped his arms around them. Janey squatted next to him. "You all right?"

"I don't know." He made a few false starts. "I don't think I believed you. Even after you showed me your, the thing, the, uh...the flickering thing. Even then. I don't think I really *believed* you."

"And do you now?"

"I kind of want to crawl in a hole somewhere."

She extended a hand and helped him back to his feet. "I'd say that's a healthy reaction. Come on. We need to figure out what to tell the cops about my car's roof getting ripped off."

Adam nodded, and walked down the hill beside her. As they went, Janey dug her phone out of her pocket and called Zach Feygen. The detective's voice made the phone vibrate in her hand. "Damn, girl, what are you now, a mind-reader?"

"Huh?"

"I was just about to call you. Listen, we've got a situation—hang on. Why were you calling me?"

7

Janey couldn't think of any way Simon Grove could have known about her storage unit. She had rented it right after the chaos at the Brittain ranch had happened, which meant at the time, Simon had been working for Derek Stamford. Not spying on her. At least she hoped that was what it meant. After she ran out and picked up a phone at the nearest gas station, Janey and Adam flickered straight from her apartment to the storage unit.

Janey tugged the pull-chain, lighting the single bare bulb overhead. Adam said, "So I'm just supposed to sit here."

She unfolded a camp chair and set it up. "Until I come and get you, yes."

"Okay. Sit here and do what? Also, uh…what if I have to go to the bathroom?"

"They've got a bathroom in the rental office if you really have to go, but I'd prefer you didn't leave the unit. There's a bucket on one of the shelves."

"A bucket. Seriously."

"Look, this is for your own safety, all right?"

"If it's for my own safety, why are you leaving me here? Why aren't you staying with me?" He winced. "Sorry. I heard the 'whiny bitch' right after I'd said the words out loud."

Janey took his hands in hers. "I wish this wasn't necessary. But you saw what Grove can do. Maybe he's gotten better, maybe he hasn't, but I don't want him knowing where you are." She kissed the knuckles of his right hand. "Just hang tight, okay? I won't be gone too long. And if you need me, call or text, and I'll get here really damn fast."

He kissed her. She didn't stop him. "Okay."

Janey left the storage unit and called a cab from the rental office. While she waited, she reached out to Sha'dae. *Hey. You there?*

The cool, silver thought-stream splashed into Janey's mind. *What's up?*

I need you to grab Tim and meet me at Agent Grassley's office. Also...Tim should get his parents to leave town for a while. Not like out of the country or anything, they should just stay out of the building.

Janey. What's going on?

In a rush of words and images, Janey told her.

Half an hour later, Janey walked into a deliberately non-descript office in Buckhead. No signage anywhere indicated what kind of business occupied the space, and the bland, beige-and-brushed-nickel décor gave no clues either. Zach Feygen sat in one of the three chairs in what passed for a lobby, eating a bagel with cream cheese and lox and sipping coffee. Janey recognized the paper bag. "Bagel Palace?"

He swallowed a bite. "Is there anywhere else to get bagels?"

Feygen stood, and he and Janey hugged briefly. She could almost rest her chin on the top of his head. Janey squeezed his shoulders. "Still lifting, obviously."

Feygen waggled the bagel at her. "Got to, if I'm gonna keep eating what I want."

"Who's here?"

"So far just you and me. Have a seat."

Janey perched on the edge of a chair facing Feygen. "It's good to see you."

He nodded, chewed and swallowed, and after a moment said, "Fuckin' Simon Grove."

"Afraid so."

"Fuck."

"Yeah."

After a brief silence, which Janey did not want to turn awkward, she tried for a smile. "So, are you done with the police now? Or what?"

"Nah, I'm still on the job, but I'm also officially a 'security consultant' for Grassley. Makes me feel like I'm moonlighting for Blackwater or some shit."

"How's Heather?"

"Got a job as a flight attendant."

"No kidding? She enjoying it?"

"Seems to. Plus, we can pretty much fly for free now." He dropped his napkin into the brown paper bag and wadded it up. "How's, uh…how's your…situation?"

Janey sat back in the chair and drummed her fingertips on the armrests. "It worked. Tim healed Adam."

Feygen let out a low whistle. "He's back? Your husband? I mean, back to, I guess normal?"

"Yeah. I can't say it's like he never left, because oh my God, it is so *not* like he never left. But his mind is whole again."

"So, you and Tim…?"

Janey tilted her head back until she was staring at the ceiling. "It's… well, Adam's my husband. We never got divorced. And now he's back, and…" Janey stopped herself. *What am I trying to say here?* She sat up straighter in the chair and focused on Feygen. "What would you do, if Heather fell into a coma, and stayed there for three years? And the doctors told you she was never going to come out of it?"

Feygen took a sip of his coffee. "That's not something I want to think about. Hey, here's everybody else. What'd you guys do, carpool?"

Janey looked over her shoulder, to see Nicole Grassley and Ashley Strandjev coming through the front door, followed by Sha'dae and Nathan…and Tim, bringing up the rear. Janey stood, nodded at Grassley and Strandjev, and gave Sha'dae a quick hug when she came forward. Nathan flashed her his shy grin, which Janey returned, and then almost did a double-take when she noticed how much mass Nathan had gained.

Tim didn't look at her. Instead he pulled out his phone and stared at it.

Janey initiated telepathic contact, guiding her thoughts so that only

Sha'dae could hear her. *What's up with Nathan? When did he go from skinny kid to professional wrestler?*

He says it's just happening on its own. He's not even working out.

As Janey received that message, she saw a sparkle in Sha'dae's eyes, and had to work hard to keep her own eyes from widening. *Sha'dae!* Nathan? *Are you serious?*

I don't want to talk about it. Okay, that's not true, I really really want to talk about it. But not right now!

Nicole Grassley spoke, and Janey gave Sha'dae what she hoped was a subtle but very meaningful glance before she turned toward Grassley to listen. "Thanks, everyone, for coming in. This is definitely an all-hands-on-deck situation. Please follow me."

Grassley led the group down a hallway and opened the door to a conference room, and Janey had to hold in an exclamation when she saw Garrison Vessler and Scott Charles seated at the table. She all but ran to Scott, and wrapped him up in a hug. "Scott! You look amazing! How are you?"

He *did* look amazing. Even better than the last time she saw him. His formerly colorless hair had turned a healthy, normal blond, and he even had a bit of a tan. It took Janey a few seconds to realize how worried he was. Garrison Vessler stood and reached across the table, and Janey shook his hand. "Sir. If I'd known you were already here, I would've come in and said good morning."

Vessler said, "Not so sure it's good, especially after the news about Mr. Grove. Scott has something to tell everyone."

Grassley motioned for everyone to sit. One by one, they settled into chairs around the table. Tim waited until Janey sat down, and took a seat out of her line of sight.

Scott said, "Okay, it's—" and his voice broke. The urge to hug him and feed him pancakes and help him with his homework flooded through Janey, but she didn't move or make a sound. Scott cleared his throat, and when he continued speaking, Janey realized his voice had dropped an octave. *First Nathan grows up, now Scott?* She wasn't prepared. At that moment, Janey didn't feel prepared for *anything*. Scott said, "Okay, it's like this. You guys know I can see other Augments, out in the world, right? It's basically my whole, uh…*raison d'etre*."

Grassley's eyebrows rose. Vessler said, "I know. His vocabulary's better than mine."

Scott went on. "Well, a few nights ago, I kind of...sort of ran into somebody. Not like it normally is, 'cause, y'know, you guys all look like squiggly wave-forms in my head, right? Except this one didn't. This one I could see. What she was like."

Nathan leaned forward. "She? Dude, you met a girl?"

Pink spots appeared in Scott's cheeks. "Yeah. Sort of. Except in a really, profoundly fu—" He bit off the word and glanced at Vessler. "In a really screwed-up way. Guys, she's like me, but Stamford has her."

Janey sucked in a sharp breath.

Ashley Strandjev said, "Stamford? Derek Stamford?"

Scott nodded. "He's got this place. I'm figuring out where it is, or trying to, anyway, 'cause she doesn't know. He's got her there, along with some other kids, and, uh, he's got like this...I don't want to say 'zoo.' But people like Aphrodite Lupo? He's got more of them. In this place called the Special Wing."

Janey groaned. Grassley said, "Something to add, Janey?"

"Details. You already know Simon Grove contacted me. Well, what he told me lines up with what Scott was just saying."

Vessler stood and started pacing. "And you said he didn't attack you. Just talked."

Janey rested her palms on the table. "He tore the bloody hell out of my car, but he didn't hurt me. Or Adam. He...seems to be different. His mindset. His motivations."

Tim leaned forward and, for the first time that morning, looked Janey in the eye. "Different how, exactly? And how did he come back from— from what you did to him?"

As succinctly as she could, Janey told everyone what Simon had said about the healer called Caroline, and about his own realization that Derek Stamford was a monster, and that the information he gave her synched with what Scott had just told them. She pulled the burner phone out of her messenger bag. "He gave me this. Said he'd be in touch."

Ashley Strandjev made a hissing noise. "Shit. Janey, he could be tracing you with that."

Janey took the battery and the SIM card out of her bag and held them up. "I had that thought already."

Ashley visibly relaxed, until a muffled voice spoke from down the table. "Hey. Hello? Can you guys hear me?"

With a look of horror on his face, Tim took out his phone, holding it with two fingers, while Simon Grove's voice spoke from it. "Hellooo."

Tim said, "I didn't—it never even rang!"

Simon's voice crackled. "It doesn't have to, Beanpole. Not when you've got the right kinds of spyware on it. Getting your mom and dad out of the building was a nice touch, but you can relax. If I wanted to fuck them up, I could've done it while I was cloning your phone."

Scott Charles seemed to have shrunk. He recoiled from Simon's voice, turning paler by the second.

"Now. Who'm I talking to, Janey? Let me guess. You've got the old man and little Scottie, and of course your pal Tim—it is just 'pal' these days, right, Tim? And I recognized Nathan Pittman, or at least some jacked guy with Nathan Pittman's face. Been hitting the steroids, Nate?"

Grassley gestured with her chin toward Ashley, and then the door. Ashley silently rose from her seat and slipped out of the room. As she left, Nathan stood and leaned close to the phone. "Fuck you."

"Not sure about that fine young lady in the hijab, though, or the government spook. You'll have to introduce me. And what do you call yourselves? Collectively, I mean? The Fun Bunch? The Barrel o' Monkeys? The Once-Were-Humans?"

Janey said, "You just can't help being a dick, can you, Simon? Whether you're mind-controlled or not, you're still a creepy little bastard."

"I love it that we're on a first-name basis now, Janey." Static crackled from the phone. Janey thought it sounded as if Simon were moving as he spoke. "But hey, enough with the pleasantries. I've never had any talent for small talk. Oh—I will say this, though. Tim? You still there, buddy? Can you hear me?"

Tim glanced from Janey to Vessler and back. "Yeah, I can hear you."

"Just wanted to apologize for, y'know, almost killing you last year. I guess I should also apologize to you, Janey, since holy *shit* did I try my best to kill you, too. But Tim didn't have his gifts back then, did you, Tim? Never stood a chance. That wasn't a fair fight. I was wrong to go after you."

Tim's face darkened, and he seemed to chew over a few responses before he answered. "That's swell of you to say."

Janey heard Vessler mutter to Grassley, "Little shit tried to kill me, too, for what that's worth."

"Anyway. Like I was saying. You've had some independent, uh, what's the word—corroboration now, right? What Scott was saying to you, about his new girlfriend, and all of Stamford's shenanigans?"

Janey's fists clenched and unclenched. "Let's say that we have."

"Great! Then we can pool your knowledge and my knowledge, and go and kill just a *shit-ton* of bad guys. What do you think? Sound like a plan?"

Janey reached out and picked up the phone. Held it close to her lips. "All you've done is prove how big a threat you are. Do not approach us. We will not be alone. And we will kill you."

"So business-like! Nothing better than a confident woman. I'm not the bad guy here, Janey. Or, well, okay, I'm not the *worst* guy. Try not to put your emotions ahead of what's right, huh? Also, when you're ready to talk, just pop the battery and the SIM card back into that burner and give me a shout."

The line went dead. Tim dropped the phone onto the floor and stomped it into pieces.

Ashley Strandjev came back into the room as quietly as she'd left. "He's nowhere close." She glanced at Grassley. "Location's still burned, though."

Grassley waved the thought away. "We've got a dozen offices around the city. I'll give you all a new address before we leave. Memorize it. Do not write it down." The weight of her icy blue eyes fell squarely on Janey. "Right now, we have to decide on a course of action."

Several hundred miles above the meeting in the office building in Buckhead, a small black object entered the Earth's atmosphere. Not much bigger than a butane lighter, it was far too small to register on any radar system, and it moved too slowly to build up heat from atmospheric friction. The object drifted down, and as the air around it grew thick enough to navigate, tiny fins grew from its sides. The object had been programmed to strike the ground in a specific location. The fins maneuvered it deftly, guiding it as it sailed through the ocean of air, zeroing in on its target.

The object touched down at the edge of an elementary school playground. Class was in session, the playground stood empty, and no eyes witnessed the object as it penetrated the earth as swiftly and easily as a pebble breaking the surface of a pond.

It left no trace once it had vanished underground. It simply held its position. Waiting.

8

J aney called Adam and asked him to turn out the storage unit's light bulb and stand by the door. Ten seconds later, she materialized in the middle of the unit's floor and turned the light back on. Adam watched her with an unreadable expression on his face.

"Hey. How are you? Have you eaten?" She glanced at her phone. 11:58 a.m.

"No. I was waiting for you. Plus, there's no real food here."

Janey gestured for him to sit back down, and pulled another camp chair off a shelf. "I could go get us some lunch. What do you feel like? There's a new Thai place I know you'd love."

"I'm not that hungry, to tell you the truth. You could let me borrow your phone, maybe? I need to be looking at job listings."

Janey leaned forward and put her elbows on her knees. "Listen, if you don't want to get a job yet, you don't have to."

"Oh? Oh—that's right. You're a successful artist. I forgot." He didn't look at her as he spoke.

Janey cut off a sigh, fearing it would come out sounding exasperated. "That's not what I'm saying. Anyway, now that I'm not sending a fee to the O'Brien House every month, we've got some breathing room. I just—what I'm trying to say is, I don't want you to feel pressured."

Adam folded his arms. She recognized it as a defensive gesture, and she knew he caught that recognition, but he kept them folded none-theless. "Maybe I'll go back to school. Maybe I'll get my degree and land some steady job, with good insurance and a retirement plan. Maybe I don't want to be an artist anymore."

You weren't an artist to begin with. You were a manager at an art supply store.

The viciousness of the thought took Janey off-guard. Where the hell had that come from? She fought down a rising wave of shame. "If you want to go back to school, that's fine with me. We ought to be able to swing tuition, I mean, depending on where you wanted to go. Especially now that I'm getting some money from Agent Grassley's outfit, I can support both of us."

Adam stared at the spot where the far wall met the floor. "How much *are* you getting? You never said."

"It's a—officially it's a consulting fee. I've only gotten one payment so far, but it's," she coughed lightly, "ten thousand a month."

Adam's jaw dropped. "And you're still living in that shitty little one-bedroom?"

With her teeth not quite clenched, Janey said, "I've been living frugally. Because I was taking care. Of you."

"And mauling criminals. And fighting aliens." Adam stood and jammed his hands in his pockets. He didn't seem able to look at her. Not just meet her eyes, but look in her direction. He paced slowly around the unit's confined space.

"What's wrong?"

"*What's wrong.* What's wrong, you ask."

Janey stood, but didn't approach him. "Speaking of which. I've got a…a thing I've got to do. Tonight."

Adam stopped and finally faced her. "What kind of thing?"

"I guess you'd call it a…a work thing? Derek Stamford—Vessler's old business partner? Remember I told you about him? We found out where he is. So we need to go and try to figure out what he's doing. Stop him from doing it. Probably."

He frowned. "You and who else?"

She shrugged, and counted off on her fingers. "Me, Sha'dae, Nathan. Tim. Ashley Strandjev and maybe Zach Feygen. I'm hoping they stay out of it if things get tense, though. They're not, uh, not as resilient as the rest of us."

Adam sat down in the camp chair and leaned forward, fingertips against his forehead. "You're telling me that you're going on, on, on some kind of *raid?*"

"I guess so. Yeah."

"And you're going to do what? Kill the guy?"

She frowned. "Maybe. I don't want to kill him. I don't want to kill anybody. But he's dangerous on his own, and he might have more people like...like us. And maybe some regular humans with guns."

"Oh my *God*, Janey. Do you hear yourself? 'Regular humans?' Do you hear how you said that? You said it like *you're* not human!"

"I don't think I am. I don't think any of us Augments are. Not anymore."

"And what if one of these *humans with guns* shoots you? What if you end up facing somebody like, like Simon fucking Grove? I saw you! I saw you when he jerked you out of the car! You squirmed like a fish, but you couldn't do shit to him! How many more of these *things* are going to be at this place you're raiding?"

"We're not sure. Now that Scott has a place to focus on, we're hoping he'll be able to tell us."

Adam stared straight at her. Through her. "No. No, forget it."

"Excuse me?"

"You heard what I said. No. I don't want you going."

One of Janey's eyebrows quirked upward involuntarily. "You're forbidding me?"

"I'm saying think about it from my perspective! What if I told you I was about to—to—shit, I don't know enough about it to describe it intelligently. What if I told you I was about to put some friends together and go take down a crack house in the worst part of Atlanta? Would you be okay with that? Or would you try to talk me out of it?"

"You're not trying to talk me out of anything, Adam. You're flatly telling me I can't go."

"Answer the question. Please."

"The question's irrelevant, because you're drawing a false equivalency between me doing this and you doing something really stupid. You're not an Augment." Adam snorted. "Listen, okay? A few weeks ago, one of Aphrodite Lupo's henchmen told me that my power was all about running away. And in a way, I guess he's right. I can escape from *anywhere*. I'm meant to be a Scout, for God's sake. That's what I'm going to do tonight. I'm going to scout the place out. The point is, I know what I'm doing."

Yeah right. I have no idea what I'm doing.

Adam stood and came to her. He put his hands on her elbows and gently tugged her arms until she unfolded them and let him take her hands in his. "Okay. Then I'm not forbidding you. I'm not trying to persuade you. I'm all-out *begging* you. Please. Janey. Don't do this. I woke up, and everything is so different now, the whole world is fucking *crazy*, and you're the part of it I need the most. I love you, and I want to spend the rest of my life with you, and I don't want you hurt. That's number one. But I'm not even going to try to pretend that I don't need you for other reasons, too. You're the only thing keeping me from going bug-nuts insane. All of a sudden my wife has fucking super-powers and she's part of some kind of super-powered strike force and there's aliens and—" His voice caught. Hung as if on some kind of snag in his throat. Janey realized he was on the verge of tears. "Janey, I'm—I'm not sure any of this is *real*. I'm not sure I'm not hallucinating every bit of this. I think...I think I might still be in that bed in the O'Brien House."

A rush of pain flooded through Janey's chest. She pulled Adam to her and slid her arms around him. "You're not hallucinating. This is real. I know it's different from the world you knew, but it's real. I'm real. I'm here."

He pulled back just enough to touch his forehead to hers. "Then don't go. Don't put your life in danger. Stay here. Stay with me."

"If I don't go...if I, if *we* let Stamford do whatever it is he's doing... *that's* what's going to put my life in danger. Mine. Yours. Everyone's. I have no choice. It doesn't mean I'm not your wife anymore. It doesn't mean..." She broke off.

What does it mean?

Uncertainty yawned before her, a gulf as wide as outer space.

Adam pulled back from her. "Is this what our life is going to be from now on? You love me, you want to be with me, but things like this are going to come first?"

She pursed her lips. Considering. "Police officers do this. Firefighters do this. FBI agents, soldiers, rescue pilots. You don't have to think of it as anything more than that. I'm just…I'm on call."

Adam let out a long, groaning sigh.

Janey said, "Something I've been telling myself a lot lately: this is uncharted territory. Let's just take it as it comes. We'll figure it out."

He didn't look convinced. He looked like someone who's just been given months to live. Maybe weeks. But he said, "Okay."

D erek Stamford's silver-headed cane rang out hollow and crisp on the concrete floor, a sound which most of the Facility's staff had come to heed as a warning. Stamford made his way down a long corridor lit by near-blinding LED lights set into the walls and ceiling behind bullet-proof glass. He knew the Gray Widow was still out there. She haunted his dreams. Crawled up out of his nightmares.

Access to any place not bathed in bright light.

Part of that haunting came from the unbearably tantalizing possibilities that someone with her abilities presented—possibilities that hung just out of his reach as long as she remained free. Part of it came from the knowledge that, sooner or later, chances were excellent that he would find himself in the dark. And he wasn't sure what he could do to stop her from getting to him if and when that happened.

At first, when he'd acquired Kyle Gutierrez, Stamford had believed he had his answer. One teleport to cancel out another one. If only Gutierrez hadn't proven so unstable. The current facility was built like a fortress, but that had limited advantage when dealing with someone who could literally appear out of thin air.

He didn't regret his decision to de-centralize. The other children Anastasia's age were better off at the new place in Arizona. He would've sent Anastasia there herself if he hadn't needed her close by.

Stamford's left ear rang now. Constantly. Sometimes he succeeded in tuning it out. Other times it made him want to put a gun in his mouth. He both blamed the Gray Widow and feared her for it, because it was one of her ridiculous, amateur-hour crew that had detonated a helicopter back on the ranch in Texas and blown out his eardrum. The one result of the permanent tinnitus was that Stamford now stayed in a foul mood, from the moment he opened his eyes to the moment he drifted off to a chemically-aided sleep. His employees had learned to stay out of his way.

Stamford wasn't sure he approved of referring to the subjects in the Special Wing as "Abominations." It struck him as overly dramatic. Pulpy, even. But Stamford had read and heard plenty of Brenda Jorden's data on Simon Grove, and he'd seen a tiny bit of what Aphrodite Lupo had been capable of, and he knew they didn't fit the pattern that he and the Gray Widow and the rest of the Augments fit into. The denizens of the Special Wing had much more in common with Grove and Lupo than they did anyone else. Horrible mish-mashes of deviant mental patterns and grotesque physicalities, uncontrollable, non-viable. Too often displaying the need to be kept sedated.

Reg Fasolo opened one of the doors lining the corridor Stamford presently stumped his way down and fell in step beside his boss. Stamford said, "There's been a signal change in the array, hasn't there?"

"There has, sir. How did you know?"

I felt it.

Stamford didn't answer that. "Give me the latest on Grove."

Fasolo grimaced. "Still in the wind, I'm afraid, sir. He's apparently ejected all three tracking devices we implanted in him, and he's leaving no trace anywhere. Definitely no credit card or ATM usage, and no witness sightings, either."

"Doesn't really surprise me. Hell, it wouldn't surprise me if we found out he was living in the woods and eating fucking raccoons. Keep looking."

"I've got five different teams on it, sir."

Stamford reached the end of the corridor, which terminated in a massive door that would not have looked out of place on a bank vault. He punched a sixteen-digit code into a keypad beside it, and opened his right eye wide for a retinal scanner. As the door hissed and clunked and began to swing open, Stamford said, "Want to take a look at it?"

Fasolo blinked. "Seriously?"

Stamford made a beckoning gesture with his head. "Sure. I think you've earned it. Plus, I get the feeling something big is about to happen."

"I'd be honored, sir."

Fasolo followed Stamford through the door, which hissed shut and locked behind them, and Stamford took a measure of satisfaction in Faso-

lo's sharp intake of breath as they walked out onto the balcony over-
looking the Array.

Very few of the Facility's staff had gotten even a glimpse of the sweeping, unearthly mass of six-foot-tall, swaying columns in the chamber
below the Brittain ranch. Not before the Gray Widow had destroyed it
when she turned the barn above it into a massive fireball. Stamford wasn't
entirely sure the reproduction he'd managed was a faithful one, but it was
working. That was the important part.

The cavern Stamford and Fasolo looked out across had floor space
roughly equal to two football fields, the ceiling above festooned with
stalactites. All the stalagmites had been cleared away, though, the stone
surface leveled and polished, and now another array of swaying columns
spread out through the cavern, billions upon billions of tiny colored lights
swimming just below their surfaces.

"What's…" Fasolo didn't seem to be able to form words for a moment.
"What—sir, what am I looking at?"

"It's a communications array," Stamford said, and didn't bother trying
to hide the pride in his voice. "Whatever did this to us—whatever is
responsible for our Augmentations—comes from them. From off-world,
Reg. You're looking at an alien antenna."

Fasolo's eyes glistened with awe. "What are you—are you, sir, have you
been communicating with them? With…with extraterrestrial
intelligences?"

Stamford shook his head. "Not yet. I've gotten pretty far, learning
their language, but there's only so much I can do without some interac-
tion from their side. And I don't even know if they're aware of us. Though
today we might get an answer to that question." As he gazed out over the
swaying, shimmering display, the waving columns moving like the
tendrils of some fantastical undersea giant, Stamford's penis engorged,
pressing hard against the fly of his pants. He could feel his heartbeat in it,
mirrored in the rush of blood in his head, making the din in his left ear
pulsate.

Fasolo said, "What's happening today? Is it the signal change you
mentioned?"

"I think so. I think we're finally going to get something in return.
Something's coming, Reg. And I think it might be something big."

As Fasolo stared at the array, Stamford pulled a .38 revolver out of his pocket and shot Fasolo in the right temple. The bullet punched its way through and exited the other side of the skull, spraying Fasolo's brain onto the nearest wall, and Stamford's whole body shuddered with a thunderous orgasm.

After Fasolo's corpse had thumped to the floor at his feet, Stamford said, "That's for losing Simon Grove, you careless son of a bitch."

The Plowman crouched in a dimly-lit, brick-lined space, surrounded by the humming of machinery. None of the residents of the skyscraper knew he was there, down in the basement, existing in the space between walls. He hadn't left it for weeks, taking all of his nourishment from the building's electrical supply.

Electronic components sat stacked around him. It had taken these long weeks for him to modify them sufficiently for his purposes. The Plowman had begun imagining things in the frame of reference of Earth's dominant species, and occasionally practiced speaking, quietly. "This would be like building and launching a Space Shuttle using equipment from the Dark Ages," he murmured. Gone was the communication array that had accompanied him on the transit craft. The Plowman had taken what he needed from a Best Buy, and after days of non-stop labor, was finally ready.

He reached out and flicked a switch. He needed his voice for this, but the words he spoke were in no human language, and could not have been pronounced by any human tongue. "Evaluator reporting. Acknowledge."

The hum around him intensified. "We are not able to pinpoint your location, Evaluator."

"That is by design." The Plowman had arranged his communication beam in such a way that it registered as originating from 1,715 separate points on the Earth's surface, covering most of the Western Hemisphere.

"You do yourself great harm in this approach."

The Plowman considered his response. "What are your intentions, should I fail to surrender my location?"

"We are authorized to offer you a choice, Evaluator. The first option is the most preferable to us."

"State the option."

"Deactivate yourself. Use your current method to transfer your consciousness to its point of origin. There you will stand trial and face punishment."

A return to his physical body... The Plowman could hardly imagine it. "There are multiple reasons why I reject that option."

"Elaborate."

"First: your negligence cost my brother his life. Second: in the process of dying, my brother unlocked a genetic potential in this planet's dominant species equivalent to the most virulent of plagues."

"We are not concerned with the well-being of that planet's dominant species. Regulation has already been deployed, and will soon activate."

"You misunderstand me. This species poses a threat to *us.*"

Silence descended. Stretched out. Eventually the hum intensified again. "Your attempt to frighten us only weakens your position, Evaluator."

The Plowman sighed. He recognized it as a human expression. "I did not anticipate convincing you. I merely wish my warning to be recorded."

"So noted. Your defiance has led us to pursue the second of your two options."

"Which is what?"

The voice didn't answer. In the silence, the Plowman switched off the communications equipment, and wondered at the source of the chill making its way up his spine.

9

In the house on East Brow Road, in a room that once contained a pool table, Aphrodite Lupo sat in a corner and pulled her hair hard enough for big hanks of it to come loose from her scalp. They immediately grew back.

"I'm not ready. I told you. I'm not ready yet."

Aphrodite had her eyes squeezed tightly shut, her eyelids wrinkled, her brows touching as she grimaced. The rasping, whispering voice in her head spoke to her. Again. Still. The voice never stopped. Around the room, ice crystals began to accumulate as whispers echoed.

"I need to be at full strength. I'm not at full strength yet."

Aphrodite opened her eyes, just a crack, and saw the world splintering, sliding, re-forming, splintering again. The deep blue irises turned brilliant red-orange and splintered as well, knife-sharp crimson shards against a sudden, vivid yellow glow. The voice spoke. The voice never stopped.

Aphrodite ignored the splintering, rasping, shattered world around her. Willed her eyes to return to what she desperately wanted to believe was normal.

Aphrodite's current body could have been anywhere from seventeen to thirty years old, and fulfilled the dictionary's definition of "willowy."

Long, slender arms, long, long legs, a flat, narrow waist that curved only gently down to delicate hips. Only the merest hint of a bosom below finely sculpted collarbones, sweeping up into a graceful neck. Once before, Aphrodite had decided she needed to improve upon her appearance. Back when she still looked younger than her actual age. Back when she still could have shopped in the children's section. When she'd changed the first time, she added length of bone and additional thickness of muscle, but also softness where it mattered. A firm, round ass, along with high, heavy breasts and sensuous, full lips.

Aphrodite fell gracelessly over onto her side. The voice cared nothing for aesthetics. She had absorbed the necessary mass from the last three offerings Julian had brought her, and now the voice told her exactly how to make use of it. Aphrodite began to scream as her clothes tore, forced apart at the seams by the rapidly swelling muscles of her limbs and torso.

Aphrodite would not have cared even if she had known that Julian Roth stood just outside the pool table room's doorway, listening to her cry out in agony, watching her through the crack between the frame and the door. She took no notice at all as he backed away from the door, closed his eyes, and vanished.

<hr />

J aney held an encrypted phone in one hand, her thumb poised over the green TALK icon, and worked to regulate her breathing. Ashley had pulled a single number off the SIM card Simon had given her, and Janey already had it punched in.

Nathan said, "Is this a stupid idea? Are we going to regret this?"

Janey scowled down at the phone. "If Simon's telling the truth...if Stamford's got a bunch of Augments as powerful as Aphrodite Lupo, along with a girl who can do what Scott does? If we don't do *something*, he's going to come after us. Eventually. There won't be anywhere we can hide, and no security system that would make a difference."

The group had reassembled, minus Vessler and Scott, in an equally non-descript office in northern Marietta. Janey didn't blame Vessler for whisking Scott back off into hiding. Neither of them needed to be there for what they were planning.

Tim stood with his back to a wall, his lean arms folded. He looked at no one. He said, "Janey's right. I don't like it, but I don't think we have any choice."

Janey glanced around at the group. "Sha'dae? Thoughts?"

Sha'dae worried the edge of her hijab between a finger and thumb. "If Simon and Scott are both right about this, and we don't do anything, I don't think I'll ever sleep again."

Nicole Grassley nodded. "Pre-emptive strike it is."

Janey let out a long, ragged exhalation. Trusting Ashley that there was no way for Simon to trace this phone's location, she initiated the call, and seconds later Simon Grove's voice crackled out into the room. "Taking me up on my offer, then?"

Janey said, "I'm going to give you a location. We'll meet there, and you'll tell us the rest of what you know. If you try anything, I'll hack you to pieces and burn each part separately. Got it?"

"Ooh, so forceful! Sure thing, Janey. Just name the spot. But let's get on with it. Correct me if I'm wrong, but Scotty's wispy little girlfriend wasn't able to give you guys a location. Right? Well, I can. And time is not our friend."

"All right. Bellwood Quarry. 9:00 p.m."

Simon chuckled. "Nice, big open place. No lights around. Well after sunset. I can't complain."

"Come alone." Janey ended the call and sat back in her chair, rubbing her temples. "All right. We've got three hours to get ready for this—" She sat up, every muscle in her body tensing, as a staccato series of vibrations sounded out from her own phone, resting on the table. Janey grabbed it and tapped the screen, and her gold-brown skin turned a little gray as all the blood drained out of it.

Tim was at her side before she'd even realized he'd moved at all. "What's wrong?"

She looked up at him, icy blue eyes wide. "Motion sensor in my apartment just went off." Janey held the phone up, displaying a grainy image, and Tim made a choking sound.

"What is it?" Grassley demanded, knuckles on the tabletop.

Tim said, "Julian Roth. He just teleported into Janey's apartment." Then he and Grassley had to get out of the way as Janey bounded over to the conference room's light switch. She hit it, bathing the room in darkness, and vanished.

Forty-five seconds after Janey's exit from the conference room, during which she made a visit to her storage unit and scared Adam half to death, Janey stepped out of her apartment's coat closet with her rainbow-finish katana in one hand and a canister of mace in the other. She felt the buzzing in the air immediately, right before she heard a familiar floor joist creak in the living room, and her legs tensed, ready to spring.

Julian Roth called out, "Ms. Sinclair? Is that you? Please don't hurt me."

Janey pulled a small remote control out of her pocket and hit a button, shutting off electricity to the apartment and plunging the place into unbroken darkness.

She took two silent steps toward the living room and brought up her night vision. Roth stood there in the middle of the floor, his image crackling, expanding, shrinking, a living cloud of black static. When she caught a glimpse of his face, she almost gasped. How could a man in his condition even stand upright? He reminded Janey of photos she'd seen of the victims in World War II death camps.

"Please don't hurt me," Roth said. "I can't—I can't see in the dark like you can. You *can* see in the dark, right? …Are you here?"

Janey took a step closer. The tip of the katana's blade didn't waver. One good thrust through the eye socket should do it. But…Roth had saved her life. Janey would have been reduced to a thin red layer of tissue and pulverized bone if he hadn't plucked her out of the bright morning sky, high above the ranch in Texas.

"You told me you'd help me. You promised. Please. I don't want to die."

"Mr. Roth," Janey said from two feet in front of him, and Roth jumped. "I'm going to take your wrist. And we are going to leave."

His voice shook. "It'd be easier if you just told me where we were going. Staying… staying tangible… I can only do it for a few seconds at a time."

Janey clipped the mace to her belt. "This will only take a few seconds." She reached into the static cloud and grasped Roth's wrist—she could feel the bones of his arm, stark and brittle as the branches of a dead sapling— and flickered both of them to the roof. Roth cried out, and Janey said, "Keep it together," as she took them thirty yards up into the sky. One more flicker, and she and Julian Roth arrived on a wide expanse of concrete, next to a tall array of antennas.

Chill wind howled around them. The Vylar suit cut most of the cold, but Roth immediately hugged himself and hunched his shoulders. "Fuck, it's freezing! Where are we?"

"The roof the Georgia-Pacific Tower."

Roth's eyebrows shot up, despite his shivering. Janey knew that, from where she'd dropped them, it seemed as if they were surrounded by nothing but night sky. But Roth slowly walked toward the edge of the roof, Janey following ten paces behind him, and she heard him suck in a sharp breath as the vast display of downtown Atlanta opened up below.

Roth turned around, and took another startled breath at the sight of Janey's katana pointed at his face. "Let's get one thing straight," Janey said, and Roth flinched. "You are never, *ever* coming near my apartment again."

"Honestly, ma'am, I'd get rid of that place if I were you. Aphrodite knows where you live."

Janey's father, Alexander Sinclair, had now and again made reference to an experience he'd had on his own grandfather's farm as a teenager. In the story, Alexander hadn't been paying attention and wandered too near an unpleasant mule, at which point the mule had kicked him in the chest. A visit to the hospital and tape for his two broken ribs later, Alexander had been fine, but he'd always gone into great detail about the shattering impact.

Janey felt as if she'd been mule-kicked.

She took an uncertain step backward, the katana wavering. "Aphrodite's alive? You're sure?"

"I came straight from her to your place. She finally got distracted enough, she let the…the influence…the hold she has over me. She let it slip." His trembling grew more pronounced, and Janey realized he was terrified. "I saw this thing on *Animal Planet*. This lion in Africa, that caught a baby gazelle. And she didn't eat it, didn't hurt it. But she didn't let it leave, either, and she wouldn't let it get any food. She just kept it, like a plaything, until it starved to death." He made a sound a little like laughter and a little like glass breaking. "I'm nothing to her. I'm an instrument. A tool. She's going to let me die." He wiped tears out of the corners of his eyes, and his body's static-like distortion intensified. "Ms. Sinclair, I don't know if there's anything you can do for me. But please. Help me, and...and keep me away from Aphrodite, because if she's in the same room with me and paying attention, I'm pretty sure I'll just go right back under. But help me, and keep her away from me, and I'll tell you anything you want to know. I'll help you any way I can."

When she'd first laid eyes on Julian Roth, after he'd killed one of his high-school tormentors by teleporting chunks of the man's body away, Janey had felt a primal spike of fear. Julian had looked like some kind of specter. A demon. A creature of darkness and hunger. But now he was just...*pitiful*, more than anything else. "Can Aphrodite track you?"

He shook his head. "I don't think so. You know...you remember how she gets in your brain, like she's split open your skull and crawled inside it?"

Janey repressed a shudder. She remembered that sensation vividly. It had felt as if Aphrodite had forced a crack in the walls of her mind, and poured a swarm of poisonous biting insects through it. "Yeah, I know what you're talking about."

"Well, she's done that to me...uh...let's call it a lot. And I got to the point where I could sort of, I guess, narrow the opening? She'd have to come looking for me. I couldn't ever close it, not all the way, but I'm pretty sure she doesn't know where I am now unless I want her to."

"Fuck. You're 'pretty sure'? And you came to my fucking apartment?"

He took a step closer to her, but Janey didn't feel threatened. She half-expected him to fall to his knees and clasp his hands in front of his face. "I won't go back to it! I'm sorry, I didn't know any other way to get in touch with you! But please, Ms. Sinclair, I am literally starving to death! If there's any way you can help me, for God's sake, *please!*"

Janey wondered about the mysterious Research & Development division Grassley had access to. Whether they might have anything to prevent a mostly-intangible Augment from dying of malnutrition.

"All right. All right, I'll talk to some people, and maybe they can help you. But first things damn sure first: where is Aphrodite?"

Fifteen minutes later, Janey crouched beside a tree on someone's front lawn and peered at the house across East Brow Road. Beyond the house, Chattanooga stretched out, its lights twinkling in a much more restrained version of the panorama Julian Roth had seen from the top of the Georgia-Pacific Tower. Janey would have arrived here sooner, but had gotten a bit lost in the winding roads atop Lookout Mountain, and had finally descended to the valley floor and followed the straight-shot tracks of the Incline Railway up to the top.

She had also called Nicole Grassley to tell her what she was doing, and to get her up to speed on what might help Julian Roth. That conversation had involved a lot of sputtering on Grassley's part, followed by full-throated demands that Janey not face Aphrodite Lupo alone, so Janey had promised and promised and then promised again that she wouldn't. This was to be a reconnaissance mission only. Verify and return.

Except she didn't think there would be all that much to verify, since the massive front door of the house hung askew, held in place by only one hinge. If she'd had to guess, Janey would have surmised that someone or something inside the house had exited in either a great hurry or an intense fit of pique.

Someone or something.

Which one applied to Aphrodite Lupo now? Maybe both? Behind the helmet's face plate, Janey grimaced. If both terms applied to Aphrodite, did that mean they applied to Janey as well? To Nathan and Sha'dae? To Tim?

Maybe. Maybe so.

Janey flickered across the street and inside the house.

It was a place of money. That much was obvious. But it had also been demolished, and very recently, judging by the amount of water on the floor, spewing from the exposed pipes of the kitchen sink that had been torn completely away. Mahogany-paneled walls sported deep, wide slashes gouged almost certainly by oversized claws; marble floors bore cracks and craters; heavy, antique, leather-upholstered furniture lay in pieces, torn into chunks.

Janey didn't think this was evidence of a fight. She thought it looked more like the aftermath of a tantrum, and not one she wanted to see an encore of. Janey executed a search pattern, flickering through an ever-widening spiral away from the house, but Aphrodite seemed to have vanished. Janey flickered over to the roof of the Incline Railway's upper station and tapped out a quick text to Grassley: SHE'S NOT HERE. RETURNING NOW.

The trip back to Atlanta was much easier. I-24 led straight to I-75, which took her back to the Marietta office in three minutes flat, traveling twenty miles at a jump, high in the night sky. Janey walked back into the conference room, her helmet in her hand and the katana in a scabbard across the back, and Sha'dae almost took her off her feet with a forceful hug. "Are you okay? Tell me you're okay!"

Janey set the helmet down on the table. "Yeah, I'm fine. This is turning out to be the weirdest night I've had in a while, but I'm okay."

Quietly, Tim asked, "Is Adam all right?"

Janey cleared her throat before she answered him. "He's safe. He wasn't at the apartment. I've, uh, I've got him stashed."

Nicole Grassley had been on the phone when Janey walked in. Now she ended the call and dropped the phone into a pocket of her pantsuit. "So what you're asking me to do, Janey, is provide some sort of safe haven for an Augment who, until a month ago, was actively trying to kill you?"

Janey sighed. "I think he was under Aphrodite's control. She'd pulled a Brenda Jorden on Roth and Trent Davis both. Roth managed to get away, and he's asking for our help. For what it's worth, he's vulnerable to mace, so if you need to rig a failsafe, I'd go for some sort of chemical option. Tranquilizer gas or something." At Grassley's expression of incredulity, Janey said, "Look, he saved my life, all right? I would've died. And I promised him I'd try to help him. So if you don't want to, I'll see what I can do on my own."

Grassley sat down heavily in one of the chairs. "No. No, you don't have to do that. Our research guys are keen to get a look at him. Where is Roth now?"

"Roof of a skyscraper downtown, unless he chickened out and ran. Where do you want me to take him?"

Grassley pulled a small pad of paper out of another one of her pockets and started writing on it. Nathan came to Janey's side and said, "Are you still planning to talk to Simon Grove tonight? After all this?"

Janey slowly shrugged. "I don't see that we have any other choice. And I know, it's a lot. Feels like everything's coming at us at once." She glanced around. "Speaking of which. We just got confirmation that getting her heart punched out of her chest only slowed Aphrodite down for a while. She's alive, she knows where we live, and there's no reason to think she won't come for us. Nathan, Sha'dae, Tim...basically all of us. We need to stay somewhere else until we get her figured out. Uh, Tim—where are your parents...?"

Tim's face grew tight. He checked his watch. "They should be checking into a B&B in Savannah right about now. I told them they'd won a trip. Courtesy of a now-maxed-out credit card."

Grassley said, "We can reimburse you for that."

Tim shrugged. "Is Savannah far enough away?"

Janey chewed her lower lip. "I'd rather us all be somewhere completely off the grid. Or at least someplace no one can trace us to."

Ashley Strandjev spoke up. "Nobody knows anything about me. Not Simon Grove or Aphrodite Lupo, I mean. And my folks have a cabin up in Gatlinburg. Sleeps about sixteen. We can go there. Here, I'll give you directions."

A minute later, after everyone agreed that Janey would go and collect Julian Roth, Janey excused herself and walked down the hallway to get a drink out of a water fountain. She had just straightened up when she heard three sets of footsteps, and saw that Tim, Nathan, and Sha'dae had followed her.

Tim said, "So I'm about to have to explain to my parents that aliens are real, and they've been experimenting on humans, and I'm one of the experiments. And they have to go hide because their lives might be in danger. Any tips on how I should do that?"

"Do a better job than I did with Adam?"

Tim hesitated. "I guess Adam will be joining us in Gatlinburg too?"

Janey groaned. She didn't mean to, and wished she could take it back. But the sound hung there in the air between them, and rather than watch Tim as he tried to decide what it meant, Janey put her helmet on and latched it into place. "I guess so," she said, her voice slightly muffled by the face plate. She held up the yellow notepad sheet that bore the cabin's address. "Sha'dae? You ready to help me find this place, as soon as I get back from dealing with Julian?"

Tim put a hand up. "Listen...it's going to take the rest of the night if I have to drive to Savannah, convince my parents to go along with this, and drive them all the way up to Gatlinburg. Once you've got the cabin set up, think you could give me a lift?"

Janey nodded, expressionless under the helmet. "Of course. Just give me a few minutes." She stepped into the dark confines of a nearby janitorial closet.

Tim said, "That'll give me time to figure out what the hell I'm going to say to Mom and Dad."

Janey closed the closet door and vanished in a burst of heat.

10

By taking Sha'dae to the cabin first and leaving her there, Janey could then follow Sha'dae's telepathic "beacon" back to it as she went to retrieve everyone else. It had thrilled Janey when she and Sha'dae had first figured out how manage that, as it gave her an elegant workaround for having to spend eighteen boring hours meditating in a place before she could flicker to it from out of her line of sight.

The two young women materialized along the tree line beside the cabin's gravel driveway, and Sha'dae said, "What was Ashley's last name again? Rockefeller? Trump?"

"Lodge" was much more accurate a description than "cabin." Janey had seen places like this as a girl, but only from a distance, driving through the Smokies with her father. Perched above an almost-sheer drop of several hundred feet, the place was a three-story Bavarian-style house of the sort usually rented out by large groups. Janey flickered inside through a window, disarmed the security system with the code Ashley had given her, and unlocked the door.

She found the décor a bit over the top. The few surfaces not made of dark, rough-hewn wood were covered in dark brown or black leather with big, exposed brass studs—with the exception of the recently-updated kitchen, which seemed to belong in a different, much more modern house. The main floor had two master suites, as she discovered on a high-speed flickering sweep, but the second and third floors were crammed with bedrooms, each of which was in turn crammed with bunk beds. Janey tried to imagine staying there for a family reunion, or a corporate getaway, or a sorority ski trip to Ober Gatlinburg. The thought of that many people packed into one house made her clench her teeth until her jaw ached.

"I'll be right back," Janey told Sha'dae. In the next few minutes, Janey returned with Tim, Nathan, Ashley, and Nicole Grassley. To Tim, she said, "Ready to go get your parents?"

"Not quite yet." Tim waved his phone at her. "Just talked to Mom, she and Dad are okay, but I still haven't figured out how to approach this. Maybe go get Detective Feygen first?"

Janey nodded. "Oh. Yeah. I'd better do that. All right, let me call them —give them a chance to throw a few things in a bag or something."

As Janey spoke to Zach Feygen on the phone, Ashley offered a tour of the lodge to anyone interested. Only Nathan and Sha'dae took her up on it, and when Janey ended the call to Feygen, it left her, Tim, and Grassley standing in the living room.

A sudden, near-palpable awkwardness descended on the three of them like a sodden blanket. Janey started to speak twice and stopped herself both times. Finally, she turned to Grassley. "So. How's your R&D department doing? Other than, I guess, analyzing Julian Roth. Got any more gadgets cooked up? Like those black fog grenades? They really saved our asses at the ranch."

"Nothing quite like that. We've manufactured more of the grenades— you can pick them up before this Stamford venture kicks off—but what we did gain access to was quite a bit of experimental tech designed for Mars exploration."

Janey's forehead creased. "Mars exploration?"

"Design work for Elon Musk and a few others." When Janey's forehead failed to uncrease, Grassley said, "What? We're dealing with aliens, aren't we? Things involving outer space?"

Janey nodded slowly. "Yeah. Yeah, that makes sense. I suppose that's the kind of thing you have, but hope you don't need."

"Quite." Grassley shot a glance back and forth between Janey and Tim. She said, "I just need to make a call," and walked out onto the front porch. The door clicked and latched behind her. Long seconds passed, as the only voice in the house now—Ashley's—faded above them, floor joists creaking as she and her diminutive tour group moved down what Janey assumed was the second-floor hallway. Tim studiously examined a large stuffed deer head on the wall. Janey shifted her weight from foot to foot.

Tim said, "Time to grab the Feygens?"

"Actually, I need to go get Adam. He's been sitting in my storage unit all day, being really patient."

"Okay. I, uh…"

Tim was still staring at the deer head, but Janey felt pretty sure he wasn't seeing it. "Yes?"

Tim cleared his throat. "I was just going to say, assuming we're all going to be staying here until Aphrodite's taken care of, we're going to need a lot of clothes. And toiletries. And food."

Janey felt pretty certain that was not what Tim had been about to say, but she didn't press it. Instead she looked down at the Vylar suit. Not exactly what she would choose to hang out around a house in. "Yeah. I'll take care of that. I'd, uh, I'd better go."

"Right."

Janey went to the front door and stepped outside. She was about to flicker away when Nicole Grassley spoke from the shadows. "Janey. I'd like you to pick up Mr. Vessler and Scott, as well."

Janey answered as she buckled on her helmet. "Vessler won't like that. Putting all our eggs in one basket, so to speak. Just because we don't think anyone can find us here, doesn't mean no one can find us here. One good drone strike and our whole operation's gone."

Grassley tapped her phone. "He just agreed to it. I want to try something, is the thing. An experiment of sorts. They won't need to stay here for long."

"All right. I'll be back shortly." She walked off the steps into the darkness and flickered away.

———

Upstairs, Nathan Pittman trailed along the second-floor hallway, listening to Ashley Strandjev talk about how her parents had bought this place in the early nineties, and trying not to be distracted by the way Sha'dae's hips swayed as she walked. A lengthy series of what he hoped had been furtive, inconspicuous glances had convinced him that the long, loose-fitting clothes Sha'dae always wore hid a *slamming* body. Nathan ducked his head, his cheeks turning pink at the thought.

That's not nice. Don't think about her like that.

He'd been able to do little *but* think about her like that, though, ever since the night when he and Sha'dae and Janey and Tim had gathered in the motel room in Nebraska. After he'd found out that Aphrodite had only been using him to get to Janey. After he and Sha'dae and Tim had all become Augments, up on the roof of Janey's apartment building.

What is it with me and older women? Older women way the fuck out of my league?

Ashley finished the tour on the third floor, where a small, dimly-lit sitting area with floor-to-ceiling windows peered out over the valley below them, which at the moment looked like nothing more than a mass of darkness punctuated by the lights of other houses. Ashley said, "Well, there's a beer downstairs with my name on it. You guys want one? Wait. I'm asking a Muslim and a guy who's not old enough to drink. Never mind."

To his own intense surprise, a surprise profound enough that it didn't feel or sound as if the words were coming out of his own mouth, Nathan said, "Um, Sha'dae, I'd like to talk to you for a minute. If I could."

Sha'dae's gorgeous, ink-black eyes widened. "Sure. Of course." She glanced at Ashley, who gave them a casual little two-fingered salute and headed back toward the stairs. Once Ashley was out of earshot, Sha'dae said, "What's up?"

It was at that point that Nathan realized he had no idea what to say. "I just, uh…does this seem real to you?"

She didn't quite gasp. Nathan had zero clue as to how to interpret that. "Does what seem real?"

"Oh. Uh. All of this, I mean. Everything we're doing. Everything we're about to do."

"You mean…"

"Stamford! Stamford, going and, I guess, attacking him, and Simon Grove and all that shit? Oh—sorry." Nathan tried his best not to curse around her if he could help it.

"Right…right. Yeah. No, it doesn't seem real to me, either. If that's what you were trying to say."

"And, it's…I'm…since all this is…like, we're all gonna go, and do this thing. Right?"

Sha'dae's lips curled into a smile, but only on one side of her mouth. He loved it when she did that. "I guess we are. I've been trying to decide whether or not to call my parents. Would they try to talk me out of this? Would they even believe me? Is it better that they remain blissfully ignorant?"

Nathan rubbed the back of his neck. "Right. Like Tim's folks. Too bad they live in the same building as you guys, huh? They might've been able to stay out of it all."

She took a step closer to him. Close enough that he could smell…what was it? Perfume? Some kind of hair product? Just her skin? He had to fight to keep his thoughts in order. "Nathan, are you worried about your parents?"

The question shook him out of his scent-based daydream. "What? *God*, no. The less they know about me the better. Not just about all this…I can't believe I get to say these words and mean it. Not just about all this alien stuff. Those two have always seen me as an embarrassment, at *best*. Screw them."

"Okay." Her voice dropped. Did it get a little huskier? Was he imagining that? "Then what did you want to talk to me about?"

"I…uh…it's…" Nathan screamed at himself inside his head. "I just wanted to tell you—I…" The words dug their claws into the insides of his brain and refused to be dislodged. Nathan groaned and turned to face the window—and almost left the floor when Sha'dae's words entered his mind on the cool silver stream.

Would this make it any easier?

You smell really good! Wait! What I mean is, I think you're gorgeous! Oh God oh God I didn't mean to say that! I meant to say I really want to kiss you! OH MY GOD CAN WE STOP PLEASE JUST A SECOND I REALLY NEED A BREAK HERE

Sha'dae broke the connection. She'd taken a step backward, sliding into the thickest of the shadows in the room, and Nathan couldn't see her face well enough even to guess at what she might be feeling. He put his back to the wall next to the window and slid down to a sitting position, his hands covering his face. "That was really not how I wanted to say those things."

He felt Sha'dae settle onto the floor in front of him. "How did you want to say them?"

Okay. Okay, she's not laughing. And she's not screaming. And she's still here. Maybe I'll just be maimed with embarrassment instead of dead from it.

"I don't know. Better than that. Or maybe not at all. But definitely better than that."

Sha'dae reached out and gently pulled one of his hands away from his face. "Why would you not bring it up at all?"

He let the other hand drop, but thumped the back of his head against the wall. Not too hard, he knew, or he'd break the wood. "Why? Because you're amazing. You're an engineer. You're six years older than I am. You're *way* smarter than I am. Plus, y'know, I didn't know how interested you'd be in somebody who's never worn a hijab."

Sha'dae laughed. Nathan was reasonably sure it was because she thought what he'd said was funny, and not because she thought he was an idiot. "Only women wear hijab, Nathan."

"Seriously?" He groaned. "*See?* I'm nothing but a dumbass eighteen-year-old white boy. You're not just out of my league. I'm not even qualified to play."

"Come on. Get up. Come sit over here." She gestured toward a pair of chairs on the other side of the picture windows. Nathan slowly got up and gingerly sat down in one of them. The chair creaked, but supported his weight. Sha'dae settled into the other one and leaned forward, her elbows on her knees. "One of the smartest things I ever heard: anyone who clings to their limitations is entitled to keep them."

Nathan started to speak, but stopped himself. He could feel the words sinking in. "Wow, that's...kind of..." He was going to say, "awesome," but instead finished his statement with, "...profound."

"Thanks. Like I said, I didn't come up with it."

"Could we...uh...try the telepathy again?"

She smiled. *You're not afraid of blurting something else out?*

Oh, I'm pretty sure I'll blurt lots of stuff out. But I think I might not trip over my tongue as much. All right...I'm going all in, here. I've had a crush on you the size of the Hoover Dam since Nebraska.

She gave him that perfect crooked smile again. *I could sort of tell.*

Really? Wait...did you read my mind?

No. Your body language. And...here's the thing...it's not one-sided.

Nathan thought his heart might have stopped. *Seriously?*

Nathan, you're the sweetest boy I've ever met. And you're funny, and honest, and a lot smarter than you give yourself credit for. Also...and please understand, those other qualities take priority, but I can't kid myself...have you looked in the mirror lately?

His thoughts left his mind in a rush. *What? Why? Do I have something stuck in my teeth? It's my hair, isn't it? You hate the blue. I can go back to red!*

No! No, no, listen. I'm trying to tell you...

Sha'dae reached out and traced the sharp line that divided his right biceps and triceps, and Nathan immediately got so hard he thought he might split the zipper on his jeans. *This gets kind of...distracting.*

Holy shit holy shit this is real it's actually really happening she likes me too holy shit OH NO I'M BLURTING AGAIN SORRY SORRY SORRY

Sha'dae laughed.

Aloud, Nathan said, "But...I mean, it's sort of the, uh, what is it, the 400-pound gorilla in the room? Wait, that's not right. The religion, is what I'm trying to say. Could you...would you ever go for a guy who wasn't Muslim?"

She sighed. "I know this is a weird thing. There are more obstacles in the way than logical reasons to go for it. Probably a lot more. But it's like I heard Janey say—we're in uncharted waters. No one has ever been in our situation before. Ever. In the history of humanity."

He winced. "Yeah. Longshot. Longest of longshots."

"And I love my faith. It's part of me." She touched her hijab. "I choose this to help me define who I am. Not just as the daughter of a Muslim mother and father—well, step-father—but as myself. It's part of my identity. And, I'll just go ahead and tell you, Dad would *not* be thrilled if I brought you home. *But.* But..."

Sha'dae stood and, as Nathan's breath came to an abrupt halt, sat down in his lap and put her arms around him. Her scent filled him from the top of his head to the tips of his toes, an impossible blend of flowers and cinnamon. "We are not, strictly speaking, human anymore, are we?"

Nathan didn't know what to say. He didn't think he could have spoken even if he had known what to say.

She went on, "So maybe what we need to do is *add* to our lives. Add to the human experience. Define what's right for us." She dipped her head and kissed his lips, and she tasted even better than she smelled, and

Nathan thought if he died during the raid on Stamford's place, he could die happy.

He whispered, "Do you think we could continue this conversation somewhere slightly more private?"

Sha'dae bit her lower lip. "You mean like one of those bedrooms?"

Nathan stood and lifted her in his arms, and this time she did gasp out loud. "You just picked me up like I weigh *nothing!*"

He grinned. "That's not the only trick I know how to do." Sha'dae giggled as he carried her through the nearest doorway and kicked the door shut behind them.

Tim still stood and stared into the glass eyes of the taxidermied deer as footsteps descended the stairs. Ashley Strandjev walked past him toward the kitchen. "Want a beer?"

"No thanks." Tim moved to a large leather couch and flopped down onto it. "Where's Nathan and Sha'dae?"

Ashley pointed up. She came over and settled into a matching chair that faced the couch over a coffee table carved out of a massive tree stump. "Settling in, I'd say."

Tim shrugged with his eyebrows. "Did not see that coming."

Ashley took a long swig. "I've seen stranger. Depends on what her type is, I guess, too, right? Awfully limited pool to choose from if she's going for—" She seemed to roll the words around in her mouth before saying them. "—another Augment." Ashley propped her feet up on the coffee table and crossed her legs at the ankles. "So what's up with you and Teleportia?"

Tim surprised himself by laughing. "Teleportia? Is that what you call her?"

Ashley grinned. "Nah, I just came up with that, like, two seconds ago. But seriously, what's going on with you guys? It's not that I'm nosy. Or not that I'm *just* nosy. If there's a weird dynamic in the team, I want to know about it. Pretty sure Boss Lady does too."

Tim slid down in the seat and leaned his head back against the cushion. "It's pretty straightforward, I guess. Janey and I were together—well, not together in the fullest sense, but still. A couple. Except her husband was still alive. He'd been shot in a mugging, had massive brain damage, and didn't know who she was anymore. He was like a child, basically. But after I got…y'know. Zapped. Along with Nathan and Sha'dae. I realized I could heal him. So I did."

Ashley whistled. "And she just dropped you and went back to him?"

Tim stared at the ceiling. "What choice did she have? It's not like they got divorced. He didn't die. And he was the love of her life. It would've been…I mean, if she hadn't gone back to him?" He shook his head and pushed his fingers into his mop of wavy black hair. "I just keep thinking, 'What if that had been me?' Y'know? What if I'd been shot, but then I got better. I'd sure as *fuck* want my wife to come back to me. Would've been disappointed in her if she hadn't done it."

"But you're not happy about it."

Tim slid the rest of the way down, picked up a throw pillow, and pressed it over his face, muffling his voice. "No. I'm not." He tossed the pillow aside and pushed himself back upright. "Got any advice? What would you do in my position?"

"Jesus. Listen, Tim, I like you, and I like Janey, but *fuck* your position. You couldn't pay me enough to mess with all that shit."

Tim frowned. "Never had your heart broken, huh?"

"Nope. And never will."

"You sound awfully certain about that. I mean, you're really young."

"First of all, I'm only a few years younger than you are, so suck it. Second, I'm never going to get involved with all this 'dating' and 'romance' and 'other bullshit.' Never have, never will."

The light dawned. "Ah—you're ace?"

"Completely. No romance, no sex, none of this bullshit about urges and longing and whatever week-old garbage. All I see is it making people miserable. Fuck all of that. Sideways." She pointed at her groin. "Anything to do with this, I can take care of myself. Way, way, way easier than…" Ashley waved her beer bottle in a broad, sweeping gesture. "…all this shit." She took another swig. "No offense."

Tim sighed and stared at the ceiling again. "None taken."

More of the small black objects had been landing. Each one unnoticed, each one disappearing under the ground. No ripples. No debris thrown up out of the holes.

But enough had touched down now that they no longer had to wait. Each object dissolved into the hundreds upon hundreds of thousands of microscopic machines that composed it, each of which made its own tiny tunnel through the ground, parallel to the surface.

The machines expanded, linking, slowly but steadily forming a monofilament lattice a few inches below ground, and when each one had achieved its optimal state—a configuration spread out over several hundred square meters—they entered the next stage of their programming.

11

J aney materialized in the dark of the storage unit, pulled the light's chain, and in the weak glow unbuckled her helmet. Half an hour before, she'd deposited Tim's parents—and his brother Cary, at their near-manic insistence—at Ashley's lodge, and her ears still rang from all the outrage, indignation, confusion, and fear. Never had she felt so rotten for teleporting anyone to safety before. It hadn't helped her state of mind that she'd immediately had to go and effectively loot a department store, grabbing toothbrushes and toothpaste and shampoo and huge armfuls of clothes for everyone. She'd left a guilt-laced wad of cash tucked under a register, flickered back to the mountains, and dumped all the items in one of the lodge's third-floor bedrooms.

Now Adam crossed the floor of the storage unit in a heartbeat and clamped himself to her. She returned the embrace, but his happiness at seeing her competed in her heart with the dread of what was to come.

Pulling away, he said, "Well? What's going on?"

"We've got a safe place lined up. Or at least the safest place we can think of. I'm about to take you there."

He tried for what she took as a brave smile. "Will there be food? And, uh…maybe a shower? Indoor plumbing of some kind?"

"I know this has been a lot to ask. But please, just bear with me a little longer."

Sha'dae? Can you hear me?

Janey felt the telepathic connection slide into place—but there was an odd hesitation to it, and when Sha'dae answered, her words came through...not garbled, exactly. More like scattered. Janey hadn't seen Sha'dae when she'd dropped off the Kapoor family, and now that she thought about it, her thoughts had seemed a little erratic then, too.

Yes. Here. I'm here. Yes, I can hear you.

Sha'dae, are you all right?

Totally. Completely all right, yes. More than all right! I'd like to talk to you. When're you coming back?

I'm with Adam. We'll be back in a minute. What's going on with you?

See you soon! I'll leave the beacon running.

Adam had frowned as soon as Janey started speaking silently with Sha'dae, and his frown just grew deeper as the conversation continued. "You're doing it right now, aren't you? The telepathy thing?"

Janey nodded. "Just making sure we can find our way to where we need to go."

"That's...it's so weird. Seriously, I mean, it's like you're getting texts but there's no way I can see them."

In spite of herself, right in the middle of a genuine need to grab Adam and go, Jane said, "Why would you need to see texts if they were sent to me?"

"What? No, no, I just mean...I guess it's like I'm stuck somewhere surrounded by people who speak a different language. And you guys are all, y'know, chattering to each other, and I'm just wondering what's going on."

"Sha'dae's Augmentation doesn't work on non-Augments. Believe me, we've tried often enough." She slipped a gauntleted hand around his upper arm. "And what's going on is that we're on a time crunch and I'm— trying to keep you safe." She'd almost said, *I'm trying to keep you from getting killed*, but she didn't want to alarm him, and then she wondered why she was trying to protect his feelings.

I've had to deal with all this on my own. No one tried to protect my feelings.

...Except I haven't been in a coma for three years and I'm being ferociously unfair to my husband.

My husband. The words felt strange and unfamiliar to her.

"Where are we going?" Adam asked, sort of meekly, and to her shame Janey felt the annoyance build.

"At this point it's probably better if you don't know." Janey wasn't sure that was true, but she *was* sure she didn't want to explain things just then. "We're going farther this time. So brace yourself."

"More up-in-the-sky stuff?"

"It's faster that way," Janey said, and with a burst of heat that left scorch-marks on the metal shelving, she and Adam vanished.

Janey brought them back to earth in the lodge's driveway. Tim stood outside, leaning against one of the porch's support columns, smoking another cigarette. Before he realized Janey and Adam had arrived, he dropped the cigarette on the ground and crushed it under his heel. "Calm nerves, my ass," he muttered, and then jumped when Janey and Adam walked up out of the shadows.

Time to get this part over with.

Janey took off her helmet, sucked in a deep breath, and said, "Tim, this is Adam. Adam, this is Tim."

Adam stuck his hand out first. "Tim. I hear you're the reason I'm up and moving again. I don't know how to thank you."

Janey's heart cracked. Some part of her was surprised no one else seemed to hear it.

She hadn't known what to expect when Adam and Tim met, but—especially in light of Adam's clingy suspicion about Sha'dae's telepathy—Janey had not anticipated sincere, earnest gratitude.

Tim's eyes flicked from Adam to her and back, super-quick, before his perfect white teeth appeared in an easy smile. He shook Adam's hand. "Think nothing of it."

The crack widened, and in an explosion that felt like two tectonic plates rending, Janey's heart broke in half.

When she thought she had her voice under control, she inclined her head toward the front door. "I still have to pick up Mr. Vessler and Scott. Adam, let's go inside, I'll introduce you to everyone else."

As the three of them walked up the front steps, Tim said to Adam, "Want a beer?"

Adam said, "*God*, yes," and Janey wondered what the hell was going on with her life.

Everyone had gathered in the lodge's huge, taxidermy-infested living room, except for Nathan and Sha'dae, but before Janey could ask about them, they came down the stairs—*holding hands.* Janey's eyebrows twitched.

Sha'dae? Did you want to talk to me about Nathan? DID SOMETHING HAPPEN, Sha'dae?

Janey only got a silent, joyful giggle in response. Sha'dae dipped her head, her eyes sparkling.

Mr. Kapoor, a tall, thin Indian man with unruly gray hair, sat on a big leather couch next to his wife Rhonda, a sweet-faced white woman with red-going-gray hair cut in what Janey thought of as a "mom helmet," her features lined with worry and her cheeks streaked with barely-dried tears. Tim's brother Cary sat on the floor with his long legs splayed out, his rust-colored hair in shoulder-length dreadlocks, fear and confusion plastered across his intensely-freckled face. Mr. Kapoor stood, chin thrust out and eyes all but bugging from his sockets, but before he could say anything, Heather Feygen said, "Holy shit, that's her?"

Zach and Heather Feygen had been sitting on a leather love seat, but Heather surged to her feet, a dazzling smile lighting up her face. Janey had been in the same room with Heather before, but they'd never been formally introduced, and it took Janey completely off-guard when Heather all but ran over, threw her arms around her, and gave Janey a spirited hug. Heather stepped back and craned her neck to look Janey in the eye.

She's like some kind of doll.

Petite, fine-boned, and beyond gorgeous, Heather sported the sort of hair Janey used to have—a glorious mane of tight curls that bobbed and swayed as she moved. "Jesus God, I feel like Mini-Me standing next to you. How tall are you, anyway?"

Heather's grin was infectious, and Janey returned it. "Six feet on the dot."

"Girl, I just want to say. You kick *so much ass.* I can't even begin to tell you." Heather looked over her shoulder at her husband. "Why have you not properly introduced me to this goddess before?"

Feygen opened his mouth and spread his hands, but Nicole Grassley answered her. "It's not a good policy for Janey and the detective to be seen together."

Feygen said, "Right. See, baby? Not my fault."

Mr. Kapoor pushed forward, getting in between Heather and Janey. He spoke technically perfect English, but with a pronounced Marathi accent. "As if it were not bad enough that you *drug* us and bring us here, like—like—like B.A. Baracus on *The A-Team*..."

Janey heard Nathan say, "What's '*The A-Team*'?"

Mr. Kapoor went on, blustering himself into a higher and higher state of agitation. "Now you stand there in that get-up, telling us that you're this...this *vigilante*? And Tim, you've been associating with her? Knowing this?"

Heather had sat back down. "Oh, she's not just *a* vigilante, sir. She's *the* vigilante." Mr. Kapoor shot Heather a look that Janey figured was as polite as he could muster. The look said, *You are not helping, young lady.*

"She didn't drug you, Dad," Tim said, and Janey got the impression that he'd said those words more than once already. "She teleported you. Like I explained."

"Preposterous!" Mr. Kapoor put his fists on his hips. "Impossible! Obviously she gave us some sort of hallucinogen. And you're cooperating with all this!"

Tim sighed. "Everyone here deserves an explanation, we all know that. And when Janey goes and gets the last two..." He trailed off and cast a glance toward Janey and Agent Grassley. "We really need to decide on a name for ourselves. Just for convenience's sake if nothing else." He turned back to his father. "Two more people are coming. And then we'll explain everything. Right, Janey? ...Okay, Dad?"

Mr. Kapoor huffed and went to sit beside his wife again.

Janey beckoned to Nathan and Sha'dae, who'd been hovering near the kitchen. They both came over, and Janey said, "Can you two keep Adam company while I'm gone?"

Nathan clumsily cut his eyes toward Tim, but Sha'dae stayed focused on Adam. "Absolutely. Adam, it is such a pleasure to meet you. I'm Sha'dae Wilkerson, and this is Nathan Pittman. Can we get you anything while Janey's gone?"

Timidly, Adam said, "Well, Tim mentioned there was beer..."

Sha'dae guided Adam toward the kitchen while Janey buckled on her helmet. As she made her way toward the front door, she passed Tim, and murmured, "Thank you."

Just as quietly, Tim said, "For what?"

Janey's words jumbled up in her mouth. "Just..." She couldn't even finish the sentence. Instead she opened the door and fled into the dark.

I don't like this," Vessler said, as he and Janey and Scott materialized in the deep shadows outside the lodge. "I understand the necessity for it, but I don't like having only one exfil option."

Janey knew she was that option. "I'll get you both back to safety as soon as possible. This shouldn't take long, and if Agent Grassley's hunch is right, it could really help us."

Scott said, "I'm happy to do whatever I can, Janey." His voice didn't crack this time, and sounded about an octave deeper than when she'd first met him. Healthy living had accelerated Scott's previously-stunted development in a big way. Janey led the way up the front steps and into the living room, where she did another quick round of introductions.

"Okay, bro," Cary said to Tim, sounding less than half as cool as Janey thought he meant to. "This is everybody, right? Your whole Rotary Club. Now please. For the love of God. Tell us why we're here and what's going on."

Tim cleared his throat. "Okay, this is...it's going to take a little time to wrap your heads around it, all right? So just bear with me. I know it's going to be a lot to take in, but I'll explain everything, and I'll do my best to answer all your questions. Ready?"

Janey said, "Tim, I hate to interrupt you. But we're wasting darkness." She addressed the whole room. "Aliens are real. They've been experimenting on humans, trying to figure out how to turn us into military assets. A bunch of us here were supposed to become archetypes suitable for off-world transport, where they were going to clone us and use us to fight in some war we don't know anything about." She tapped her chest, then pointed around the room. "I'm Reconnaissance. Tim's Medical. Sha'dae is Communication, Nathan's Infantry, Scott's Surveillance. We refer to each other as Augments. A dangerous individual named Derek Stamford has been collecting other Augments, brainwashing them, and forcing them to work for him, and he's got someone like Scott. If we don't go get her, Stamford will be able to find any of us, any time. We're all in danger. Unfortunately, so are you."

Into the silence that descended after Janey stopped talking, Tim said, "You should consider writing blurbs."

Zach Feygen put his arm around Heather. Held her close to him. "Janey—tell them about Aphrodite."

Janey leaned against one of the couches. "There's someone else out there, too. The most dangerous Augment we've ever met. She calls herself Aphrodite Lupo, and we thought she was dead, but it turns out she's not. So, again, that puts all of you in danger, which is why you're here instead of at home. We're going to go after her. but we need to get this girl away from Derek Stamford first."

Tim's mother had leaned forward and rested her forehead on the heels of her hands. She said, "Wait. Hang on." Her head lifted. "If this young man over here—" She gestured at Scott, who blushed. "—is like the person you want to go after, why doesn't he tell you where this Aphrodite person is?"

Tim's eyebrows threatened to disappear into his hair. Cary lightly bumped his mother's knee with one fist, and said, "Look at Mom, playing right along!" He got to his feet. "Okay, Tim, Janey. Enough with the costumes and the tall tales. Maybe you are the Gray Widow, but come *on*. Aliens? What is this? Do you have the house rigged with hidden cameras? Is some B-list celebrity host about to pop out and tell us we've all been pranked?"

Nathan walked over to the fireplace and picked up a wrought-iron poker. He crossed the room and handed it to Cary. "Here. This is real, right?"

Frowning, Cary hefted the poker. Tapped it against his shoe, and the coffee table. "Yeah. I mean, it's a real poker. What's that got to do with anything?"

Nathan took the poker back. His newly-gained muscles popped out in stark relief as he twisted the poker around his wrist, turning it into a corkscrew. "Before our friends from outer space did this to us, I weighed a buck twenty-five soaking wet, and while yeah, I could run like the wind and throw a mean roundhouse kick, I could never bench more than about one-ten. Last time I checked, I tip the scales at four-thirty-five, and this doesn't even make me break a sweat."

Mr. and Mrs. Kapoor, in the kind of mirrored expression only truly found between long-married couples, had both let their jaws fall open.

Cary's eyes appeared to be trying to bug out of their sockets, and when Nathan handed him the poker, Cary's jaw dropped.

Heather made a sound not unlike a squeal. "Holy *fuck*, that was *fire!*" She leaned closer to Feygen's ear. "You think you could do that if you worked out more?"

Feygen watched the non-Augmented crowd's reactions with undisguised amusement. "Not even close, baby."

Scott spoke up. "Um. Sorry. To, uh, to answer your question? Ma'am? I can't find Aphrodite because her brain is…she's…there's something wrong with her. What I do, it just doesn't work where she's concerned."

Nathan took the corkscrew-shaped poker back from Cary and, with only a tiny bit more effort than it had taken the first time, straightened it back out. It didn't look perfect, and Janey thought she could see Nathan's fingerprints in the surface of the metal, but it seemed functional enough.

"Now," Nicole Grassley said, also addressing the whole group, "there's something we need to attend to. Mr. Vessler, Scott, Sha'dae? If you'll come with me, please?"

Sha'dae said, "I'd like Janey to be there, too."

Grassley nodded. As Janey followed the others out of the room, Tim said, "Okay. Janey gave you the Reader's Digest Condensed Version. Anybody got any follow-up questions?" All three Kapoors, Heather, and Adam flung hands in the air.

Agent Grassley led them into one of the master bedrooms. "All right. Now, Scott, correct me if I'm wrong, but your connection to this Anastasia has been spotty so far."

He nodded. "At best."

"Fine. Since Sha'dae is our Communications specialist, as Janey just stated, and since the two of you—" She pointed a long, bony finger at Janey and Sha'dae. "—combined your mental capacities when you briefly overpowered Aphrodite Lupo, my thought was to see if Sha'dae and Scott working together could give us a clearer indication of what we're going to be facing."

Vessler put a hand on Scott's shoulder. "Son? You up for this?"

"Yeah. Yes. We should at least see if there's anything to it, right?"

Sha'dae turned to Janey. "I'd like your eyes there with me. Could I loop you in?"

Janey said, "I was going to ask you to, if you hadn't volunteered it."

Grassley shut the bedroom door. "Very good. Then let's get on with it. Janey was right when she said we were wasting darkness." To Sha'dae: "How do we do this? Do you need to lie down?"

Sha'dae went to Scott's side. "No, we just need to hold hands. Might be better if we were sitting, though." She perched on the side of the bed, right in the middle, and patted both spots beside her. "Janey, why don't you come over here, and Scott, just have a seat right there."

Once she and Scott had taken their spots, Sha'dae gently took their hands in hers. "Let's take this slow. All right, Scott?"

He bobbed his head. "I'm ready."

Sha'dae's words entered Janey's mind on the thought-stream. *Here we go.*

Janey felt the connection when it opened with Scott Charles's mind—

—and suddenly the cool, comforting, smooth silver stream became more like the thundering wave of a tsunami. Janey and Sha'dae found themselves riding that wave, right on the crest, at such a breakneck speed that Janey thought her neck might snap.

Scott's words came to them, filled with wonder and delight, distorted by the pummeling, howling speed. *I never knew it could be like this! I never knew it could feel like this!* Janey had to fight to keep her eyes open. Not because there was anything like a real, physical wind blasting her in the face, but because her brain didn't want to process all the information flooding into it. Scott's vision, powered by Sha'dae's Augmentation, swept them north, through the top half of Tennessee and into Kentucky, swung northeast into West Virginia, and dragged them across the tops of hills and trees in a frantic rush. But it wasn't like traveling in an airplane, too far above the ground to see any real detail. Neither was it like a movie special-effects zoom, where the background dissolved into a blur. Instead, every blade of grass, every stop sign, every stray dog, every leaf on every tree stood out sharply in Janey's mind, clear as the proverbial crystal, so well-defined that Janey felt as if she could reach out and touch any or all of it.

The mental tsunami slowed when Janey caught sight of a low concrete building set into the side of a mountain, slowed but didn't stop, and she experienced a touch of vertigo when she and Scott and Sha'dae plunged into the building. They didn't follow corridors or stairwells, though, but instead plowed straight through walls and floors until they came to a shocking stop inside what could only be called a cell. Janey got her first glimpse of Anastasia, sitting on the cot with her back to the corner and her knees drawn up to her chest.

The girl was pitifully thin. Not as emaciated as Julian Roth, but still sick in a different way. She twitched and shifted constantly, not big movements, more like tremors, and her eyes darted everywhere, nervous as a rabbit. They lit on Scott, and then to Janey's surprise, flitted to Sha'dae and Janey in turn. Janey's thoughts raced. *Can she see us? Scott, can she see us?*

"I can see you and hear you," Anastasia whispered. "Please help me, Scott. Please."

The quarry lay in front of Janey, a lake of darkness amid the forest of Atlanta's electric glow. A tall chain-link fence encircled the property, and security lights stood around the pit's perimeter, but Janey had already disabled all of those, and Ashley Strandjev had made short work of the security system. Now Janey stood at the quarry's edge. Nathan and Tim flanked her, both of them outfitted with night-vision goggles. Ashley crouched amid a clump of bushes halfway around the edge, a .50-caliber sniper rifle with a night-vision scope in her hands.

Janey brought her own night vision up to full power. A flicker of movement all the way across the quarry caught her eye. "He's here. Let's go silent. Sha'dae?"

The cool, smooth, comforting silver stream of Sha'dae's thoughts came sliding across the surface of Janey's mind, as clear from the lodge in Tennessee as if she'd been standing next to her.

Got you covered. Everyone hear everyone else okay?

Tim and Nathan's voices joined the stream, acknowledging the telepathic connection.

Janey watched the figure, tiny at this distance, slide down the quarry's far wall and make its way across the rocky ground toward the center. *Everyone see him?*

Nathan pointed. *There. Right in the middle. Just like you told him.*

Janey's fingers brushed the hilt of her katana, protruding from its scabbard over her shoulder. *I'm going to do this pretty quickly once he stops, so everyone get ready.*

Nathan put a hand on Janey's shoulder. *Ready. Yeah.*

She turned to look at Tim, and realized that he'd been reaching for her hand; as she watched, and before she could react, he shifted to take hold of her upper arm instead.

Far below, Simon Grove come to a stop.

All right. Here we go.

A burst of heat slammed out from the spot where the three of them had stood, and in the next instant the group materialized on the quarry floor twenty feet behind Simon Grove. Two much smaller bursts later, and they had Simon surrounded, Janey standing directly in front of him, her katana gripped in both hands.

Simon's eyebrows twitched. "Y'know, anybody else would say something about how good you are at making dramatic entrances. Or maybe they wouldn't, since anybody else wouldn't be able to see you, out here in the dark. But I can see you. Did you know we've got that in common, Janey? The whole see-in-the-dark bit?"

Janey didn't give him her full growl, but she hoped her words came out as clipped and impatient as she felt. "Simon, we've got shit to do. Say what you came here to say."

Simon's head pivoted on his neck, turning to his left, and as Janey watched, her stomach rolling, it just kept turning and turning, like an owl's. "Nathan. Looking good. Been hitting the weights, I see. What do you have to lift to get a good burn? Compact cars?" His neck twisted even further, and yet his voice never changed. "And Tim. Face to face again. Man to man. *Mano a mano*, yeah?" Simon's lips spread in a wide, predatory grin as he lifted a hand and waved to Tim—and his fingers elongated, swaying crazily.

Janey barked, "Cut that shit out or I'll lop it off at the wrist."

Simon's head snapped all the way back around, but the grin stayed in place. "Oh, come on, Janey, you know I'd just grow another one. I'm good like that." His fingers returned to normal. "Okay, fine, fine, let's get down to business. You know about Stamford's little pressure cooker he's got going, thanks to Anastasia, right? Yeah, well, Stamford keeps a really freaking tight clamp on that little girl, and part of it is that he never lets her know exactly where she is, so she can't tell you exactly how to find her."

Tim spoke quietly. "She's a fucking remote viewer. How can she not know her own location?"

Simon's eyebrows quirked up and down. "What an astute question! Ten points to Hufflepuff! Look, it's kind of like being far-sighted. Yeah, she sees things at a distance—about ten or fifteen *miles* distant, at the very closest. So, y'know, unless you want to spend hours and hours combing through better than two hundred square miles of trees and mountains, maybe you should just listen to me."

Janey wished Simon could see the sneer wrinkling her lip. "If her location is all you've got, this meeting is over."

Simon cocked his head a few degrees to one side. "Oh—because you can already find your way to her. She doesn't have to give directions. Got someone to point your way, do you? Or has Scott's range improved that much?" Before Janey could speak, he went on, "No, no, don't tell me. It doesn't matter. You know why it doesn't matter? Because I know every inch of the place. The layout. The patrols. Hell, I know the whole guard staff by name. I can get you inside, and I can tell you just where to hit so it'll hurt the most. And I know you don't have that kind of intel, or you wouldn't be here talking to me."

Janey's grip on the katana hadn't changed at all the whole time Simon had been talking. It still didn't. She stood like a statue. "All right, then. Tell us, and get the hell out of here."

"Oh, for real? You think I'm just going to bow out? Nope. I'm coming with you. And you have to bring me along, because, here in my head? That's where all the good stuff lives."

Janey reached out silently to the group. *Sha'dae—can you tell if he's lying? And if he is, can you just reach in and take the information, assuming he actually has it?*

I don't know. It's not like it was with Aphrodite—when we forced our way into her mind? She'd already opened that door, trying to get to you. Without that, it's not like I can just go fishing until I pull something out. I'm Communications. You tell me things, I tell you things. I relay messages. I'm not... not like that Brenda Jorden person. I'm not an Interrogator.

Simon turned, moving his whole body this time, glancing from face to silent face. "Hmmm...standing there not talking, but looking like you're thinking...whoa. Whoa! Are you serious? You've got a fucking telepath stashed somewhere? Hot damn! That'll make this operation even easier! Provided I'm there to coordinate, of course."

Tim said, "Nathan, why don't you hold this bastard down while Janey hacks bits of him off? Let's see how many it takes before they don't grow back so well."

Nathan glanced at Janey. "I'm game. Just say the word."

Simon's eyes widened a fraction of an inch. "Oooh, the big bad boss lady. Everybody takes orders from you." As Janey watched, his shit-eating grin faded, and his eyes became hard white pinpoints. "Look. Two things. Number one, it would be a lot tougher than you're making it sound to overpower me, and honestly, it's not worth the trouble. Because number two, Derek Stamford is a fucking monster. You hear me? He's the goddamn Grim Reaper, and I want him dead just as much as you do. So let me help you."

Janey still didn't move. "I'm sure you'll understand why we have a problem trusting you."

Simon threw his hands in the air. "God. I know. I *know*, all right? Cards on the table here, people. I used to be a monster myself." Tim snorted, but Simon only threw him an annoyed glance. "Sure, bring the cynicism. 'Cause I deserve it, okay? I killed people. I killed young, innocent people, in the most horrible way I could think of, and I did it because I liked it. I already admitted as much, Janey. Back on the hill, before your new man came bursting out of the woods."

Janey's mouth tightened behind the face plate as she considered his words. She'd had first-hand experience with the way Simon Grove enjoyed wrapping his finger-tendrils around a victim and pulling their blood out through their pores.

"Now, I could tell you guys that I'm different. That I've changed. That what Caroline did for me...it cleansed me. Fixed me. But whether you believe that or not, it doesn't change what I've done. Whether I'm a monster anymore is immaterial." The snark and smugness had faded gradually out of Simon's voice, leaving it cold and hard, each word a chip of ice. "I deserve to die. Don't think I don't know it."

Silence descended on the quarry. The silver stream rippled with Sha'-dae's voice. *Janey? I don't know this guy. I've only heard the stories. But he feels sincere to me. I think I believe him.*

Nathan chimed in, timid. *If he's telling the truth, it sure would be to our advantage, having all that insider info.*

Finally, Janey turned her head and looked at Tim. *What do you think? If we decided to believe him, could you stand to be around him?*

Out loud, Tim said, "We're going to need a minute to discuss."

The mischievous, near-malicious grin reappeared. "Well, now, if you guys all disappear, what's to keep me from changing my mind and scampering off?" Janey took one hand off the katana's hilt and made a gesture. In response, a green laser-sight dot appeared on the ground at Simon's feet and tracked up his body to his forehead. The grin grew wider. "Not bad. All right. Go, confer. I'll just stand here and look pretty."

A rapid-fire chain of heat bursts deposited the three of them up on the quarry's edge again, far enough back to be out of Simon's line of sight. As the others removed the night-vision goggles, Janey took her helmet off and clicked on a small flashlight. She held it up so that they could all see each other's faces.

"This is fucking crazy," Tim said without preamble. "I'll tell you what he's right about. He is a monster. And he does deserve to die."

Janey took a slow, deep breath. "I'm trying to see the big picture here. If he's willing to help with this? Maybe he helps us take down Aphrodite, too."

Nathan said, "You're thinking maybe we could pit one homicidal freak against another? Maybe stay out of it if we can?"

Janey shrugged. "Maybe. Honestly, guys, I don't know what presents a bigger threat. Stamford or Aphrodite. But we know where Stamford is, and maybe we know a good way to get to him. And please, understand, I cannot freaking believe I'm saying these words out loud, but maybe we need to give Simon Grove a chance."

Tim turned away from Janey and Nathan and shoved his hands in his pockets. "So, what, we just take him along with us? Let him sleep in Ashley's cabin, next door to my parents? Janey, he can't be a part of...of whatever kind of club we've started. You've got to see that."

A wave of cold had moved into Janey's stomach. "You're right."

Tim's head turned, one eyebrow cocked up. "You agree with me?"

Janey rubbed the stubble on the side of her head. "No need to act so surprised. I usually agree with you."

Nathan said, "Then, uh...what're you saying?"

Janey put her helmet back on. "I'm saying we take him with us. And we go. Tonight."

I n Kennesaw, twenty-four miles northwest of Janey's apartment building, stood a four-story, square white building. The building occupied the southeast corner of an office park dedicated to medical practices. A sign next to the main entrance read, "OLSEN MEDICAL GROUP." The glass doors of the main entrance only opened with a key card.

Inside the building, in a near-featureless examination room, wearing only a hospital gown, Julian Roth stood and stared at his reflection. A large, horizontal mirror occupied a good chunk of one of the walls, and Julian figured it was probably a two-way deal, so that as long as the lights were off in the room on the other side, he couldn't see through it. He didn't care very much. Let the doctors look all they want, he figured. As long as they kept up the treatment.

Because, for the first time in recent memory, he wasn't starving.

He was still hungry—an empty stomach would do that—but the super-rich nutrient injections Dr. Olsen gave him every hour on the hour had worked a miracle. For the first time in months, Julian wasn't in pain. His hands didn't shake. He didn't have to struggle to focus his eyes.

It was all in the timing. That was what Dr. Olsen said. Julian couldn't maintain a solid form for more than a few seconds, and the strain of even doing that was considerable, so it was all about delivering the maximum nutrient payload in as short a time as possible. Julian looked down at the I.V. port in his forearm. That had been a near thing. Olsen had brought in his best nurse to install it, and she had only just gotten it done before Julian had gone intangible again. But now...now, all they had to do was bring in one of the big-ass syringes full of what Julian thought of as "go-juice," ask him to get solid, and plug that entire payload straight into his system. Took maybe three seconds. He could totally stay solid for three seconds. Shit, he could do *anything* for three seconds.

Julian looked forward to getting enough of his strength back to go and help Janey Sinclair do...well, whatever it was she was trying to do. He didn't care too much about that, either. She'd saved his life. All he wanted to do was help.

The door behind him opened, and Dr. Olsen walked in. Julian had pegged him at forty-eight or forty-nine years old. Still dark-headed, fit, and pretty good-looking for a white guy. Olsen didn't wear a wedding ring, and it made Julian wonder if he had women throwing themselves at him all the time. Probably. He was a doctor, after all, and doctors made *so* much money. More money than Julian had ever had. More than he'd ever have, most likely.

Dr. Olsen held a device in his hands that Julian hadn't seen before. It was kind of like an iPad, but thicker. "What's that? You guys upgrade your charts an' shit?"

Olsen waved the device in the air. "This, Julian, is a tracking device. It taps into a satellite feed, and monitors anomalous thermal readings. The people here have been using it to monitor Janey Sinclair's teleportation."

Julian frowned. "Okay. Why? I mean, why do *you* have it? Are you working with her?"

Olsen smiled, and the irises of his dark eyes shattered and turned ruby-red, becoming a storm of embers swirling against a topaz-yellow background. "You could say that."

───────

In his room in the Special Wing, Parker Schutz lay on his bed, thinking about the feeling that had come over him earlier in the evening. It had taken him a long time to figure out what it was. He felt like…something was coming. Something big.

Parker was very glad his Other Self was almost ready.

12

Janey flickered back down to the floor of the quarry, where Simon waited silently. She said, "All right. We're going."

Simon stretched. "Where?"

Janey got close enough for him to see a hint of her eyes behind the mask's black mesh. "I'm taking you to a safe place. You'll recognize a lot of the faces. And most of the people there want you dead."

He made a sound like *pfff*. "What else is new?"

"I'm telling you this because, if you try anything, if you make any kind of move, if you even hurt someone's feelings, I will kill you. Do you understand?"

Simon folded his arms. "Janey, I can only tell you I'm sorry so many times. I can only promise you I'll cooperate so often, before the words stop meaning anything. If we're going to go somewhere, then let's go somewhere. I'll behave."

Janey put a hand on his shoulder. "Brace yourself. I'm told this is disorienting."

He grinned—not the bizarre, deep-sea predator grin she'd seen before. Just an ordinary grin, like someone about to get on their favorite rollercoaster. "So I finally get to ride the magic carpet, huh?" The grin got even wider. "No double-entendre meant."

Janey growled and, in a burst of heat, took them back to the quarry's rim, where Ashley had joined Tim and Nathan and Sha'dae. Janey flickered the entire group two hundred feet straight up. She had just enough time to hear Simon let out a delighted whoop before they all vanished in a massive fireball.

The darkness surrounding the ski lodge had grown even more impenetrable. Janey wasn't sure what time it was—sometime around midnight, she thought—and had the sensation she'd sometimes felt after a long day of travel, remembering the events of a morning and thinking, *That feels like a week ago.* She knew she and her friends and colleagues had only arrived at the lodge a few hours before, but it seemed like at least a couple of days.

The small group moved out of the darkness into the dim half-sphere illuminated by the lodge's porch light. "I have an idea," Janey said. "If it works, and I don't know if it will, we'll need your help."

Simon eyeballed the lodge. "This is quite a place. My mom used to bring me to places like this when I was a kid. Usually in Vale. We're not in Vale, are we?"

"No. This place where Stamford's got Anastasia. You say you know it well?"

"I did say that, yes. Are we going inside? Or are we going to stand out here in the cold?"

"Listen. This is important. Can you picture the place in your mind? All of it, every hallway?"

Simon frowned, but the frown quickly turned quizzical. "This is going to be some sort of telepathy thing, isn't it? Yeah, I was part of the security detail, as I believe I told you already. I know the place backward and forward."

Janey took hold of his upper arm. "Good. Come on." She pulled him up the steps, and as Tim, Nathan, and Ashley followed them, she said, "Remember. *Behave.*"

As Janey took off her helmet, Simon said, "Yes, *Mom.*"

Everyone who hadn't come with her—with the exception of Vessler and Scott, who lingered upstairs, as Scott had no desire whatsoever to see Simon Grove again—still sat or stood in the living room, and every head turned as Janey and Simon walked in. Simon glanced around and said, "Wow, look at all these people I haven't met yet!" and when Janey saw the reactions from Heather, Sha'dae, and Mrs. Kapoor, it struck her that she'd forgotten how objectively gorgeous Simon was.

Well, when he's not turning himself into a monster.

Janey cleared her throat. "Everyone, this is Simon Grove. Until not long ago, Simon was in the employ of Derek Stamford. But he's had a change of heart, so to speak, and he's agreed to help us."

Zach Feygen had been standing in the kitchen. He walked straight over to Simon and stared him in the eye. "I've read up on you. You're a killer." To Janey: "Why should we trust him?"

Janey said, "Because our already-tight timetable has gotten even tighter." Sha'dae had come over to stand beside Nathan. "Sha'dae, if you're up for one more experiment, I want to try something." She swept her eyes around at Nathan, Agent Grassley, Ashley Strandjev, and Tim. "You guys all come with us. If anything goes wrong, do what you have to do to take him down." She paused. "If I don't take him out myself first."

Simon sighed. "Y'all sure know how to make a guy feel welcome."

Cary said, "So what're the rest of us supposed to do? Just sit around out here?"

As Janey led the way into the master bedroom again, she said, "Yes," and left it at that. Once everyone was inside—standing uncomfortably close, as the bedroom wasn't *that* large—Janey shut the door. "Okay, now, not all of you know this, so let me explain. You know I can go from one patch of darkness to another, in my line of sight. Right? Well, there's another aspect to it. If I know a place really well, like back-of-my-hand well, I can always teleport to that place, if it's dark. I can get to my apartment from anywhere. I used to be able to flicker back to my Basement, before I blew it up."

Simon's eyebrows lifted. "You blow stuff up now?"

Ignoring him, Janey went on. "We need to get to Stamford's place. Now, I could follow directions, look for it, take Sha'dae there, and then use her as a beacon to get everyone else there. Like we did with this place. But, Sha'dae, if you could take a look in Simon's mind and see Stamford's place, and then let me see it too, I think I could take us all there in just a couple of jumps."

Sha'dae's eyes had gone wide at the words "take a look in Simon's mind." She said, "Janey, I've never tried to do that before. I don't—I'm not sure how to—" She faced Simon hesitantly. "Like I said, I can't just dig stuff out of people."

He said, "I would hope not. Gross."

"What I mean is, you'll have to offer up what you want me to see. It's easiest with words. But I can do images. Just…you'll have to help."

Simon spread his hands. "I'm an open book. Let's do it."

Tim put a hand on Janey's elbow. She let him steer her to the back of the room, where he spoke quietly. "Are you sure this is a good idea? I mean, is it worth it? Is saving a little time worth getting inside that guy's skull?"

Janey wrinkled up one side of her face. "Remember when I said I was making everything up as I went along? Yeah, that hasn't changed." She dropped her voice even further. "I'm counting on you to be my eyes, though. If he so much as twitches in some way you don't like, you grab him and do that whole life-draining thing. Okay?"

Tim nodded, his eyes grim. "Count on it."

Janey went back to Sha'dae and Simon. "Okay. Same drill as before? Sitting on the bed?"

Simon cast a doubtful look her way. "I'll stand, thanks."

Sha'dae said, "Standing ought to be okay. I know a little more what to expect, after the other thing." She extended her hands. "Here."

Janey took Sha'dae's right hand, and after a second's pause, Simon took her left. Sha'dae closed her eyes. "All right. Just think about the place we'll be going. Everything about it—the way it looks, the way it smells, the sounds, everything. Vibrations in the walls or the floor. People's voices."

"I got it, I got it," Simon said, and Sha'dae opened the connection, and Janey forgot where she was.

Janey stood in a lobby. Plain gray floors, plain beige walls. Off to one side, what appeared to be a security office. Janey caught glimpses of a bank of monitors, each one displaying a black-and-white image.

Well. Simon's voice held a note of wonder. His words came through with a heavier Southern accent than he used in actual speech. *Don't this just beat all? Here, let me show y'all around.*

Janey began moving, as if on a ride at an amusement park, sliding toward a bank of elevators set into the wall opposite the entrance. She moved *through* the doors, into an elevator—and the floor beneath her trembled as the car began to descend.

Sha'dae's voice floated in. *I don't think we have to do this in real time.*

Abruptly the descent became a plummet, and Janey felt her stomach rise as they fell deep into the earth.

When the doors opened, Janey found herself in a concrete-and-cinder-block hallway lit so brightly it made her squint. A woman in a white lab coat walked past her, heels clicking on the bare floor, and the scent of her perfume tickled Janey's nose. Two men in black fatigues, both of them wearing bulletproof vests, walked by in the opposite direction. They each held an AR-15. Janey thought she recognized the bump stock modification that allowed them to be fired on full auto.

Where are we? Janey scarcely recognized the words as her own.

Her point of view accelerated as if shot from a bow, down to the far end of the corridor, where it swung sharply to the left and entered a carpeted space with multiple TVs, several couches, a few tables set up with straight-backed chairs around them, and two ping-pong tables. Voices echoed around her, phantom conversations held by men and women. Janey understood that this was Simon's memory, understood it on a primal, bedrock-deep level.

On a couch in a corner sat Simon, alone, sipping a beer. Watching the phantoms.

Employee lounge.

Another acceleration, down other bare, starkly-illuminated hallways, and Janey arrived in a small cafeteria. Dim gray ghosts carried trays of food. Faint flirtations wafted through the air, laughter like distant wind chimes. Here and there a raised voice, the occasional burst of anger.

Simon, as clear as if Janey were looking at the real flesh-and-blood person, sat alone at a table near the back, eating in silence.

Cafeteria.

Janey... Sha'dae's words came to her in a whisper, routed around Simon's perception. *Janey, I'm getting more than just descriptions here...*

Janey rushed out of the cafeteria, bolted down more hallways, and rapidly a cognitive map formed in her mind, as Simon's memories of the complex became her memories. No windows. Built directly into a mountain, utilizing the existing structures of an abandoned coal mine. The sights and sounds, the smells, all of it became familiar. Second nature.

Simon. Janey had a more specific request. *We need someplace that's going to be dark.*

Janey's uncontrolled ride through the former mine slowed and stopped, and her field of vision pivoted to the right. Down another corridor, past a big communal bathroom, to a door. Janey slipped through the door as if it were made of fog.

Here. Simon's thoughts came to her quiet and small. *It'll be dark now that I'm gone.*

Janey found herself in a single-occupancy dorm room. A twin bed against one wall, a built-in writing desk, a tiny closet. Almost identical to the setup she'd seen in Anastasia's room. *Simon, this—this is where you lived?* There were no decorations. Anywhere. No art on the walls. No knickknacks on the desk. Aside from the still-rumpled bedsheets, which no one had bothered to change, the room might have been unoccupied.

Oh God. Like my apartment.

Yet she felt Simon there, and as she watched, the phantom Simon came in. Sat down on the bed. Put his face in his hands.

His shoulders shook as he sobbed.

Janey almost cried out when Simon appeared next to her, watching the other version of himself crying on the bed. *Take a good look, if you want.*

Sha'dae touched Janey's mind. *Janey. What I'm getting from him. It's guilt. Nothing but guilt. He could've had friends here, but he isolated himself. Everything he said, everything he told you. It's true. Simon knows he's a monster, and it's killing him.*

Janey didn't know what to say. How could she sympathize with this man? This, this freak of nature who'd tried so hard to kill her? Who'd almost succeeded in killing Tim? This fucked up, vampiric travesty who'd preyed on how many innocents? Janey didn't even know.

I just need to get what we came for.

Janey closed her eyes—or the mental versions of her eyes—and let the essence of Simon's room flow into her. In other places, it would have taken hours, but Simon had lived here for weeks, and Janey took every memory he had, amplified it all through Sha'dae, and boiled it down to a fine distillation. When she finished, all the sensations of the room felt like *her* sensations. She had come back to this place every night. She had eaten here. Slept here.

Wept here.

Okay. That's enough. I've got it.

Sha'dae let go of Janey's hand, and she was back in the lodge's master bedroom. She took a deep breath and turned in a small circle, reorienting herself, and saw Ashley Strandjev slipping a 9mm handgun back into a jacket pocket.

"Well?" Tim said, and Janey found using her ears to communicate strange and jarring. "How'd it go?"

"I know the place as well as Simon does now. We're going to hit these people hard and fast and be out before they even realize we're there. But first—Sha'dae, I hate to ask you for more, but can you link the whole group? We've got a floorplan to memorize."

Sha'dae smiled and shrugged. "Have alien brain, will travel."

O kay. So. We all clear?" Janey spread her fingers on the table. "Out of Simon's room, down the hall to the stairs, down one level, a right and a left. Me, Nathan, and Tim—recon, muscle, and medical if we need it. I'm hoping we won't need it."

Simon coughed. "You're forgetting about me."

Janey said, "I'm not. You've already done what we needed you to do. I'll drop you off before we go. Someplace a long way from here."

Simon tilted his head to one side and let out a short, barking laugh. "Janey! I'm a heavy hitter! What if your plan doesn't work out? What if they've changed something since I left? You're going to need all the help you can get!"

Sha'dae's thoughts touched Janey's. *I think we can trust him. I really do.*

Janey didn't answer. She'd come to the same conclusion herself, more or less, but wasn't happy about it. Janey scanned the living room: Tim's family. Zach and Heather. Grassley. Strandjev, still sulking that she hadn't been invited along, despite Janey's explanation that Sha'dae could only coordinate telepathic communication between Augments.

And Adam. Adam, who'd sat, stony silent, while Janey planned their... what? Should she call this an "operation?" He didn't look scared. Not like Cary, who hadn't stopped trembling for longer than a minute since

Nathan had pulled his trick with the fireplace poker. No, Adam just looked...numb.

To Simon, Janey said, "Yes. All right. Fine." To everyone else around the table—Tim and Sha'dae and Nathan—she said, "We leave in five minutes."

"I still think I should go with you," Sha'dae said, her full lips pursed irritably.

Janey gave her a tiny smile. "And I still think you can do your job every bit as well from here, and not take the chance of getting killed."

Sha'dae waved a dismissive hand. "Give me one of those fancy suits like yours and I'll be fine." As Janey walked over to Adam, she realized that wasn't a bad idea, and made a mental note to ask Agent Grassley about it.

Adam sat in a leather wing-back chair in a corner next to the fireplace, staring into emptiness. Janey knelt down beside him and folded her arms on the armrest. Looked up at him through her lashes. "How you holding up?"

Adam's head swiveled toward her, but his eyes didn't focus any better. "That, that suspicion I had before? About how none of this is real? Yeah, it's powerful right now. Right up here in the forefront." He rapped his forehead lightly with his knuckles. "I just sat here while you planned an assault on a place full of heavily-armed mercenaries and who knows what else." Adam's eyes focused, but Janey wished they hadn't when she saw the fear in them.

Softly, he said, "I married an artist. Y'know?"

She laid a hand on his wrist. Squeezed with what she hoped was a comforting amount of pressure. "I'm still an artist."

He nodded, his eyes out of focus again. "It's just...a lot."

Janey opened her mouth to say, *Yeah, Tim and I have talked about that unreality feeling. We call it "waiting for a commercial." Like our lives have become so bizarre that it's got to be some kind of fiction.* The thought was right there, fully formed, just waiting for her to put it into words, until she realized how little good it would do to reference Tim.

Janey stood. "I have to go."

Adam rose to his feet and hugged her. "You do, don't you? Well, then... knock 'em dead? I guess?"

"Thanks. We'll be back soon."

He hugged her again before she went back to Tim and Nathan and Simon. "All right. Let's do it."

Janey and the three young men stepped outside into the bitter night air. A stiff, soggy wind had kicked up, blowing tiny particles of ice and snow down off the top of the mountain, and Janey said, "Everyone get a good grip on me somewhere."

Nathan and Tim each took hold of one of Janey's arms, while Simon just stood there, looking bemused. He said, "Anywhere?"

Janey growled, "Take my hand, dumbass," and when he did, she sent them flickering high into the sky and from there to the northeast. She could see Simon's tiny room in her mind, smell the disinfectant the cleaning crew used, hear the faint hum of electricity in the walls. Within seconds, all four of them stepped out of nothingness and into the dark of Simon's room.

Janey reached out. *Sha'dae? Everyone still connected? We all good?*

As good as I can make it. Sha'dae's thoughts flowed into Janey's head as swiftly and with the same crystal clarity as if she'd been standing in the room with them.

Simon Grove's mind entered the mix. It made Janey's skin crawl. *We've got about eight minutes before they change the guard. The way to Anastasia's room will be clear then, for maybe three or four minutes, depending on who's coming on shift.*

Janey tapped the back of her left wrist, though she wore no watch. *So we wait.*

Simon sat down cross-legged on the floor. Nathan, conscious as always of how much he weighed, tried not to move at all for fear of making some part of the floor squeal—though Janey figured it was more likely to crack than creak. Tim moved closer to Janey, and to her surprise, his words entered her mind on what she could tell was a private channel. Janey knew from experience that the other listeners would be able to tell they were talking, but wouldn't be able to make out the words. Like hearing a faint conversation in another room.

How you holding up?

Tim wasn't looking at her, but he stood close enough that she caught a whiff of his familiar after-shave through the black-mesh-covered ventilation slits in her face plate. Before she had fully decided whether or not to answer him, the words slipped free. *Just being honest? I don't know. Couple of nights ago, I saw a car wreck, and I got the driver to the hospital. But after that, when I was back in street clothes, I ran into this girl. This young teenage girl, outside the hospital, there to visit her dad.*

Was the dad the driver you saved?

No. Her dad was a guy I had beaten the bloody shit out of the previous week.

Tim's back stiffened. *Oh.*

"Oh" is right. He was selling drugs to kids, Tim, and I've made it clear how I deal with that. I've made it really, really clear. He was standing right in front of an Eyes of the Widow symbol, selling crack to a ten-year-old.

Okay. Then why do you sound miserable about it?

If you'd seen that girl's face, you'd know why. Her dad was the only one bringing any money in. Now she and her mother and her little brother might get put out on the street. Because of me.

Wait. Isn't it because of him? Because of his actions?

Janey did a few light wrist stretches. *Selling drugs on the street is against the law, at least in Georgia. Selling drugs to kids is despicable. But the punishment for doing it is not to have both your knees broken. The guy had a regular job! He trimmed trees! And now I've made it so that he might not ever work again.*

Tim rested a hand on her shoulder. Light, tentative. *You're out there, doing what you think is right. You're protecting the city. Aren't you?*

Janey slowly reached up and laid her hand on his. *That's just it. I made a big splashy deal out of treating people oh-so-harshly if they broke the law, but for what? So I can ruin a man's livelihood? So I can disrupt a family and boot kids out of their home? For fuck's sake, if the mother can't work, then how are those kids supposed to survive? Haven't I just sentenced them to lives of, of, I don't know, of drugs and prostitution, by trying to do what I "think is right?"*

So...okay. So what are you going to do?

Janey made no outward noise, but in her head she let go of a rueful chuckle. She thought Tim would hear it. *I had a thought, actually. Except I'm pretty sure it's stupid.*

Let's hear it.

What if I got some bullet ant venom? And rigged up a couple of batons, so if I jabbed someone with one of them, it would inject the venom, and they'd feel like they'd been stung by a bullet ant?

Tim's forehead wrinkled for a second. *Bullet ant—that's the most painful insect sting in the world, isn't it?*

Supposed to be, yeah.

And you're thinking that would be a deterrent, but wouldn't cause any lasting damage. Classical conditioning without permanent trauma.

That's the idea, yeah.

So what happens if you sting someone, and the pain is so intense they have a heart attack and die?

Janey bowed her head. *See, I told you it was stupid.*

Might just need a little more refinement, that's all.

Tim, I...

Yes?

I miss...this.

A tiny, pained smile flitted around his lips. *Same here.*

Simon's voice came rushing in, obliterating the private thought channel. *It's show time, boys and girl! Let's go commit a bunch of felonies!*

Janey led the way out of Simon's room and down to the end of the corridor, just as planned. Along the way, she noticed that there were no visible light switches anywhere, and that the harsh lighting—every bit as glaring as it had been in Simon's memories—was recessed into the ceiling and covered by what appeared to be thick, perfectly clear sheets of glass. Her first instinct was to use one of her batons, or maybe the katana strapped across her back, and destroy every light source they found, but she didn't want to take the time.

Time was the essence of the plan. One thing Simon didn't know was whether or not the facility had backup generators, and Janey didn't want to tip their hand by cutting off the outside power if it wasn't going to do them any good.

No one on the stairwell. They padded down as quietly as they could. Janey used the same angled dentist's mirror in which she'd first seen Julian Roth, a lifetime ago in a south Atlanta house, to get a look up and down the new hallway.

No one. We're clear. Let's go.

One corner, then another, and just as Simon had envisioned, there was the door. Janey peered through the tiny window set high into it and saw Anastasia, stretched out on her bed, staring at the ceiling. Janey tried the knob. It turned readily enough, and a second later she was inside the room, kneeling next to Anastasia.

"Don't be scared," Janey whispered. "We're here to help you." She shot a look over her shoulder. *Nathan, hit the lights, and we'll all get the hell out of here.*

Nathan obligingly flipped the switch next to the door.

Nothing happened.

Over an unseen intercom, a mechanical voice made an announcement: *"All cells in Special Wing now unlocked."*

Still lying on her bed, Anastasia put her hands over her face and started crying.

———

The latticework now complete, the microscopic machines invisibly spanning the Earth's surface began the synthesis of billions of microbes.

When the time was right—when they received the command—they would spew the microbes into the planet's atmosphere via countless tiny, mechanical geysers.

In their strictly limited, artificial capacity for awareness, the infinitesimal machines knew the command was coming soon.

II

THE STORM

13

Parker Schutz was watching when all the locks made a metallic, ringing sound, like a gunshot, and the doors to the cells swung open. He didn't move. He didn't need to, not yet. Not unless they disconnected Trina's anesthetic drip. If Trina woke up, he'd probably have to do something, but until then, he figured he'd just lie still and see and hear what happened.

He'd been watching, too, when the three strangers came into Anastasia's room. The tall, lean woman in the body armor, and the blue-haired kid with the muscles, and the dark-skinned beanpole with the curly hair, and the white guy who looked like he belonged in a perfume ad. They thought they were going to…what? Take Anastasia out of there? Out of the Facility? No one got out of the Facility unless Mr. Stamford said so.

Well. Except Parker's Other Self. But that was still a secret. It would stay a secret until Parker sent his mind along one of those strands of tissue, and left his small, weak body behind, and moved into his new one. He wouldn't do that until he needed to. But he was ready.

Parker figured Kyle might do something about the three strangers right off the bat. If he could keep it together. If he didn't fall on the floor and start screaming. Or maybe, maybe David, if he was having a good day. Poor David didn't have many good days.

Parker barely had to move his head to look out through his now-open door. He heard a scream that cut off maybe a second after it started, and saw an explosion of blood paint the wall outside his room.

So. Kyle was the one to go and take care of this, then. Not Trina. Not yet, anyway.

Parker concentrated on the images he was receiving from the inconspicuous little eyeball hidden in the ventilation shaft in Anastasia's room.

T im's thoughts came rushed and anxious. *Okay, so, Plan B, right? You've got the blackout grenades?*

As soon as Janey touched Anastasia, Sha'dae looped the girl in on their silent communication. Janey tried to make her unvoiced words pleasant and soothing. *Anastasia. We've come to help you. We're going to get you out of here. Just take my hand.*

Anastasia didn't get up. Tears welled in her eyes. *It's too late. Everything's wrong. They're going to kill us all.*

Janey pulled a black-fog grenade off her belt. She'd brought two of them, just in case. *No, listen, I'm going to set this off, and it's going to get very dark, and then we'll all be gone in a jiffy.* Janey didn't think she'd ever used the word "jiffy" before in her life. *See? All I have to—*

From somewhere else in the Facility, some other floor—Janey got the impression it came from below them—a faint scream pierced the air. Anastasia's tears became sobs, and abruptly Janey felt as if every square inch of her skin were being pricked by millions of needles, and as the air in the room shifted and compressed and pain jabbed through Janey's ears, a man stood there who hadn't been there a second before.

Tall and gaunt and sallow-skinned, Janey thought he might have been Hispanic, and then he opened his mouth and revealed the repeating rows of teeth like black razor blades, and he lifted his hands and Janey saw the fingers extend and writhe and her throat seized up. Because the undersides of his finger-tendrils were a sick gray-green and covered in short, sharp thorns.

From behind her, Simon Grove said, "Fucking hell."

Not even two seconds had passed since the man's arrival, and he extended his arms, the forearms lengthening with a stomach-wrenching sound like branches breaking, and he wrapped one thorn-covered hand around Simon's throat and the other one around Anastasia's ankle. Anastasia screamed, and Simon made a gasping, choking sound, and in the space of a heartbeat the tall man—

—Janey's brain hitched and struggled to comprehend what she was seeing—

—the tall man sucked most of Simon's blood out of his body. The thorn-covered hand released Simon, now drawn and withered like a husk, and the razor-blade smile got broader. He said, "Not allowed, not allowed, it's against the rules, you can't you can't you can't," and he and Anastasia both *vanished*—

—and from where the tall man had just been standing, an explosion of blood detonated, spraying everyone and everything in the room and blinding Janey as it coated the black mesh over her eyes.

Janey slammed thoughts at Nathan. *Shut the door! Keep it shut, brace it!*

Sha'dae's thoughts crashed into Janey's mind. *What's going on what the hell was that Janey get out of there you've got to get out of there now!*

Janey hadn't let go of the blackout grenade. Simon lay on the floor, gasping, his emaciated flesh shrunk to his bones, and Tim hovered over him, the signature waves of healing power emanating from his hands but not yet applied to Simon's body. Nathan clawed blood out of his eyes as Janey pulled her helmet off. Out loud, a testament to how badly he was shaken, Tim said, "What do I do? Do I heal him?"

Janey motioned to Tim and Nathan, beckoning them as she knelt next to Simon. "I'm grabbing him. You two grab me. The plan's gone to shit and we're leaving."

Nathan said, "Fucking-A," and Janey popped the black-fog grenade, and something blew the door of the room out of its frame. The door slammed against Nathan, deflected off of him, and buried itself halfway into the far wall, its hurtling edge missing Janey by no more than three inches. The black fog billowing from the grenade swirled, whirled, raced around the room's edge, and disappeared out the door.

Standing in the doorway, bracing himself with a metal walking cane, was an old white man with an oxygen mask strapped to his face. Shreds of a soiled hospital gown hung from him, more empty space than cloth, revealing the wrinkled, sagging, melted-flesh horror of his body.

His eyes were gone.

Instead of eyes and the bridge of his nose, a hole existed in the man's face, and Janey couldn't see the back of it. His head seemed to contain a bottomless pit, and out of that pit roared the wind that had hammered every molecule of the black fog away, beaten it into submission and chased it from the room. Janey took a breath to say something to the man, she didn't know what, but *something*, and her lungs seized, a white-hot pain blossoming inside them. The horrible, punishing thing that roared from the chasm in the old man's face wasn't wind. It was pure force. And it was pushing every wisp of oxygen out of the room.

Janey coughed, tried for another breath, couldn't find one, and as black spots began to bloom around the edges of her vision, she saw Tim hit the floor beside Simon.

Janey sank to one knee. Nathan was still on his feet, though he'd begun to wobble, and Janey realized Sha'dae hadn't stopped shouting thoughts into her head, and Janey didn't know how much longer she could remain conscious, but she put everything she had into the silver thought-stream. *Sha'dae, please be quiet for just a second, I need Nathan to hear me say this.*

The black spots grew thicker. Faster. Janey pulled the other grenade off her belt, and the roaring wind-force took it from her fingers and smashed it through a ventilation cover set in the base of the wall. She heard it clanging and clattering as it disappeared.

Nathan, you've got to put the old man down.

Nathan took a shuddering step toward him. *Put him down? You want me to kill him?*

The black spots moved out from the edges. Some swam to the center. Janey knew she was about to suffocate. *I don't care what you do, just make him stop!*

Nathan's muscles strained, flexing into steel-hard, wiry bunches as he staggered forward. Janey couldn't tell if the old man knew what was going on. She couldn't tell if he even knew where he was. The expression on his face, such as she could read it, was blank, and as he turned focus the howling wind from inside his head directly at Nathan, Janey saw a string of drool escape from the corner of his mouth.

Nathan hooked a toe around the old man's cane and pulled it out from under him. The old man pitched forward, the raging force cutting off as quickly as if a switch had been thrown, and Nathan brought his knee up into the man's chin. Janey watched through still-dim eyes as the man's head snapped back and he collapsed in a shapeless heap on the floor.

Nathan shoved him out of the doorway, stepped over Simon to pull the door out of the wall, and set the door back in place in its frame. He sank down with his back to it.

Tim.

Simon's thoughts jarred Janey, appearing in her brain. They wavered, fading in and out, like a radio moving out of range of its signal.

You've got the, the, the mojo for this kind of thing...right? I think...I could really use your...help here, buddy.

Janey crawled over to Simon, on the other side of him from Tim. As she caught her breath, Tim directed a private thought to her.

Do I heal him? Really? Heal Simon Grove?

Janey tilted her head back, sucking in breath after deep, sweet breath. *I think you're going to have to. We don't know who else or what else is in this place, and unless we can find somewhere dark, we're going to have to fight back out to the surface.*

You don't think Simon's room would be dark now?

Janey replayed the cognitive map of the complex in her head. *We can see. It's between us and the exit now, in any case. But if Blood Guy comes back, or Face-Hole Man wakes up, we're going to need all hands on deck.*

Simon's silent words prodded at their thoughts. *Tim. C'mon. I don't need much. Just...get me to where...I can move a little...*

Tim grunted, and with an expression on his face that made Janey think he'd smelled something bad, he laid both hands on Simon Grove, one on his neck, the other on his belly.

Simon twitched and surged up to a sitting position, violently enough that Tim pitched backward and slid a few inches on his butt. Simon still looked terrible. His eyes had sunk far back into his skull, his lips barely covered his teeth, and the skin stretched so tightly over his knuckles that his hands looked like bone. "That's it, that's enough," Simon murmured, cutting his eyes at Tim. "Can't let you shoot your wad when you don't have to." Simon got shakily to his feet and motioned at Nathan. "If you'd be so kind as to move the door, I can do the rest myself. Assuming Grampa hasn't crawled away."

Nathan shrugged, got up, and moved the door enough to peer out through the gap between it and the doorframe. Janey went back into the telepathic channel. *Wait a minute. Simon, what're you about to do?*

He didn't bother looking around at her. *Oh, come on, Janey. You know damn well what I'm about to do. You and Tim both.* Simon pulled the door the rest of the way out of the frame, knelt over the old man's limp body, extended his fingers into the long, bone-white, whip-writhing tendrils, and wrapped them around the man's face and neck.

The old man didn't make a sound as Simon drained him of blood.

Janey watched Simon's body complete the process of regenerating him. When he'd finished, the old man's bloodless corpse barely looked human anymore. More like a mummified skeleton. Janey swallowed a threat of vomit. *Where's all the blood? You used to bleed when you did that.*

Simon's eyes had become hard white pinpoints set in jet-black fields, and he turned them on her with an unreadable expression. *I've refined my craft.*

Janey was already running the layout of the place in front of her closed eyes, vaguely aware at the same time of a private telepathic discussion going full-bore between Nathan and Sha'dae. She sent her thoughts to the whole group. *All right, we're going to have to figure out how to get Anastasia some other way. The mission's blown. Nathan, rip the lights out of the ceiling.*

Nathan peered up at the glaring lights behind the layer of glass. He crouched, sprang upward with one hammer-like fist extended, and yelped as the impact knocked his landing off-balance. Nathan hit the floor hard enough to crack the tiles, but the glass remained unbroken, the lights still shining. He rubbed his knuckles. *Okay, that's tougher than I was expecting. I just need to get good and braced, though, I'm sure I can break it—*

Nathan's silent words cut off as the walls shook. A roar so deep and thunderous it sounded more like a collapsing building than a sound made by a flesh-and-blood throat reverberated around them, and the floor trembled with crashing, explosive footsteps. Janey said, "No time for that. Run."

Sha'dae hadn't gotten any less panicked. *What was that sound? Was that a roar? Janey, what's down there with you?*

Don't know, don't want to find out. C'mon, guys, hustle! Retrace to Simon's room. If it's dark, we'll leave from the there. If not, up the elevator shaft and out the door. Nathan, you okay taking point?

Sha'dae spoke to Janey privately again: *Careful. When he gets stressed, Nathan gets awfully honest.*

On the heels of that, Nathan's words filled Janey's mind with what she could only think of as a hysterical booming. *Okay? I'm totally okay! Totally okay because if I'm running toward something it'll distract me from how bad I want to run* from *something because oh my freaking GOD what did I just see in the last two minutes?*

Janey could trace the route in her memories, just as plainly as if she'd walked these hallways herself. The black, peeling tread-strips on the concrete stairs, the latch on the door to Level 2 that tended to stick, the lobby-like area that would've benefited from a potted ficus tree or two. Even if the armed complex staff got in their way, with Nathan and Simon and Janey's own not-inconsiderable combat skills, she didn't think anything could stop them from leaving. Nathan, who had moved into the lead, was roughly a dozen yards from the door to Simon's old room when the pounding footsteps came to them again, crashing louder and louder and louder, and the door and most of the wall into which it was set exploded outward in a storm of dust and metal and concrete debris, the same glaring light as the rest of the place pouring out of Simon's room behind it.

Janey thought the source of the footsteps and the masonry carnage might have at one point been human. She wasn't sure whether it had been male or female. It wasn't much taller than she was, but it was covered head to foot in large, diamond-shaped scales—Sha'dae shrieked *It's a pangolin it looks like a pangolin*—and before Janey or anyone else could react, the creature bared enormous, hook-like claws and flung itself forward.

The scaled beast slammed straight into Nathan, rode him to the floor, and began ripping into him with those huge, bony hooks. Or it tried to. Though Nathan shouted in surprise and pain, Janey saw no blood, the claws unable to penetrate his stone-like skin, and as the creature drew back to smash another bony hand into him, Janey's breathless sprint had closed the distance. Her rainbow-sheen katana—the blade which had lost no sharpness after hacking through brick—tore into the creature's forearm, and Janey thought her hands might break from the impact as the blade crashed to a halt against Augmented bone.

"You made Kyle take Anastasia!" The pangolin creature's words tumbled out like boulders in an avalanche. It seemed angry, furious even, but not overly concerned about the wound. "You killed David!"

Janey wrenched the blade free and sprang backward as the creature howled.

Nathan! Can you move?

Nathan scuttled backward on his butt, pushing with his heels and the heels of his hands, and his words blasted into Janey's head, *What the hell WHAT THE HELL IS THAT THING* but Janey couldn't pay him any attention, or at least chose not to, focused as she was on the wound her sword had left. The creature's diamond-shaped scales, smaller on the arm than on the legs and torso, had a four-inch-long gash carved into them, and dark purple blood, almost black, poured from the wound.

Get back, Nathan. Help Tim and Simon do whatever they're doing. I've got this.

Tim's words flowed in, saturated with mixed incredulity and outrage. *The* fuck *do you mean, you got this? You'll get yourself killed!*

Some fraction of the pain seemed to register at that point, as the creature thrashed about, its wounded arm flailing, spraying purple blood in every direction. Janey risked a half-second glance over her shoulder—and both saw and felt the ice crystals forming on the walls and ceiling at the far end of the corridor. *I'm afraid you guys are about to have your hands full. Just let me deal with this guy. More speed than strength.*

Nathan had gotten to his feet, and out of the corner of her eye Janey saw him turn toward the source of the rapidly approaching cold. He said, "What the hell is—" but Janey lost the rest of the question because the pangolin creature roared and charged.

Janey whipped her torso down and out of the way as a hook-clawed arm sliced just above her, and before the creature could turn she slashed it across the back of its left thigh. Triangular scale tips sprayed against the wall, and the creature screamed again and fell to one knee.

From somewhere down the corridor she heard Simon bellow, "That shit won't work on me, bitch! I'll just grow a new one!"

Janey's blade flashed out and dug deep into the pangolin creature's ribs, and as she wrenched the sword free, she let its natural momentum bring it back around in a tight loop. The blade entered the shoulder scales, drove all the way to bone, and Janey flung herself across its back, ripping the sword up and across the back of its neck.

The creature let out a final, eardrum-piercing shriek and collapsed on its face.

Janey panted, her lungs aching, and just as she noticed that her breath had begun coming out in long white plumes, a living fog bank rolled down the corridor and engulfed her. Something like a hand—*That can't be a hand, it's made of icicles*—clamped down on her wrist, and a narrow, elegant, Asian face drifted out of the icy fog. With a breath so cold it felt like needles on the skin of her face, a delicate female voice said, "We have to kill you all."

The icicle-hand tightened, and Janey's left arm from the elbow down froze solid.

A world of perceptions paraded through Janey's mind as reality slowed to a crawl. She heard Sha'dae, screaming in her brain, a scream mirrored by the tortured sound ripping its way out of Janey's own throat, and she waited for her arm to shatter like glass, shatter into a million ruby-red chunks, and as she envisioned a life with only one arm, a dim, distant part of her watched in wonder as long, bone-white tendrils pierced the cloud of ice fog and wrapped around the Asian woman's throat. Simon Grove's face swept into view just over the woman's shoulder, and the woman tried to turn her head, but Simon was too fast, and his grossly-distended, needle-tooth-filled jaws opened wide. "Say cheese," Simon said, and bit the right third of the Asian woman's face off.

More screams. So many screams, Janey's world was made of screams as she staggered backward, her dead, ruined arm clutched in her right fist. She knew Sha'dae was saying something to her, trying to understand what had just happened, and Janey knew her friend was in shock because Sha'dae could see through Janey's eyes, see exactly what had just happened.

The ice-fog dissipated, wisps and curls of it fleeing around corners and into air vents, and Janey caught a glimpse of the horribly maimed woman's face flashing down the corridor—and then Tim was there, cradling her in his arms, and she realized she'd collapsed against a wall, her deceased arm now lying across her thighs like an alien thing. She knew the pain would come soon…

Except Tim was doing something, something with her gauntlet, pulling and tugging. The gauntlet slid free, exposing her gray-black appendage, and Tim wrapped her dead hand with both of his and for the third time she felt his healing warmth come flooding into her. Both of the other times he'd done this, Aphrodite Lupo had been the one inflicting the wounds. Once he'd repaired her shattered ankle. The second time he'd healed multiple gaping puncture wounds in her chest, wounds that would have killed her if he'd been only seconds later.

Janey didn't know if she'd grown accustomed to the sensation. It bothered her that that might even be a possibility. But sitting there in the strange corridor, her back to Tim's chest, his power saving her limb, saving her life, Janey realized she had never felt safer. At any time, or in any place.

Swift on the heels of that, as she tilted her head and looked up into Tim's deep, warm, ink-black eyes, she also realized she'd made a terrible, terrible mistake.

"Tim." No more than a whisper. "Tim, I think you can stop. Don't—don't hurt yourself." She wiggled her fingers in his, and glancing down, saw the gray-black of her skin had returned to her normal lion's-coat golden brown.

"Oh, sure," Simon said from a few feet away. "Make googly eyes at the Girlfriend Healer. I'm the one that bit that freak's face off for you. *You're welcome*, by the way."

Nathan came and sank to his knees in front of her. "God, I'm sorry. Janey, I'm so sorry, I was fucking useless just then. Worse. Worse than useless."

Privately, silently, Janey spoke to Tim. *Thank you.* She stopped just short of following that with *We need to talk* when she realized how out of breath he was. "Are you okay? It took that much out of you to do my arm?"

Tim's eyes flicked toward Nathan. He managed a smile. "Had to give Nate a hand before I got to you. Frigid Girl came on kind of strong to him."

Nathan's shoulders slumped. "Like I said. Worse than useless."

Out of nowhere, shrieking pain like grenades explosions filled Janey's skull.

She twisted to one side, away from Tim, and vomited all over the floor. The shattered ankle, the shredded lungs, the promised pain of the dead, frozen arm, none of them compared with the agony that shot through every nerve in her head. Janey's vision turned white, then red, as blood vessels burst in her eyes, and the fraction of her that didn't want to die immediately to make this pain stop saw Tim and Nathan and Simon all clutching their heads, exactly as she was doing. Tim collapsed on the floor, writhing, and Nathan smashed his forehead against the nearest wall and screamed, *"Make it stop make it stop make it stop,"* and Simon's body pulsed and changed, pulsed and changed, every heartbeat deforming his limbs, gray-green thorns erupting and sliding across his skin.

Sha'dae! Sha'dae, can you help us, can you make this stop, please, Sha'dae, can you hear me?

The agony grew worse. And instead of Sha'dae's cool, soothing river of communication, an unfamiliar voice ripped and scraped its way into Janey's brain.

{BEVERLY IS RIGHT. WE HAVE TO KILL YOU. SO...DIE. ALL OF YOU. DIE.}

Janey struggled to her feet, screaming and pounding the heel of her hand against the side of her head, and hauled Tim up. "Can you heal this?" she shouted into his ear, her eyes squeezed shut as fire ants burrowed into her brain. All of her blood vessels had been replaced with red-hot barbed wire. "Can you counteract this?"

Tears ran from Tim's eyes, Janey saw, when she finally managed to pry hers back open. Tim said, "Not enough to matter! Where's it coming from? How do we get away from it?"

Janey shook her head. "I don't know! I don't know! But we've got to get Simon and Nathan up! We've got to get out of here!"

Janey thought Simon's screams would haunt her every bit as much as the image of her father's katana taking off his head. His body still pulsating and distorting, he made it to his feet along with Janey and Tim. It took all three of them to pull Nathan away from the hole he'd bashed in the wall and point him past the pangolin creature, toward the exit.

{I KNOW THAT'S YOU IN THERE, PARKER. BACK ON YOUR FEET.}

Janey gasped, reeling, the barbed-wire words lacerating her brain, and her screams shifted from pain to shock. The pangolin creature's back writhed, a broad seam ruptured along its spine, and in an explosion of thick purple blood, the creature rose, renewed and whole, unmarred scales glistening, from the now-discarded husk Janey had damaged so badly. It scraped purple blood out of its eyes and roared, and Janey led Tim, Nathan, and Simon as they ran, staggering, away from the creature and down the hallway, deeper into the complex.

Back in the house on East Brow Road in Chattanooga—where Aphrodite had set the door back into the frame and propped it tenuously in place with a couple of umbrellas—Julian Roth tried to take comfort in the supply of nutrient syringes Aphrodite had let him bring from the Olsen Medical lab. He had enough to last for four more days, stored carefully in the fridge in the kitchen. Watching Aphrodite, Julian figured that if he hadn't come up with some kind of solution in four days, he might as well start writing his own obituary.

Aphrodite paced back and forth in the living room, past the torn, shredded furniture, her footsteps crunching over the shattered floor tiles. Whispers filled the room, sliding and echoing around her. She mumbled under her breath. Julian didn't know how many people she'd eaten since he left the house before, but it must have been a significant number, because Aphrodite was *huge* now. Not Incredible Hulk huge, not quite, but...big. Too big to pass for human anymore. Her red-on-yellow eyes swam and darted, and when she ground her teeth, little bits of enamel flew out of her mouth and made tiny tapping sounds on the floor around her feet.

Aphrodite whirled toward Julian. He jumped involuntarily. "Julian! Get ready to move. We're going to that stupid ski lodge place."

Julian did his best to dampen the black-static-cloud effect of his body. He knew it tended to agitate her. "Wh-wh-what are we going to do there?"

Aphrodite's muscles bunched. Tendons in her neck stood out. "We're going to *kill them all*. What else would we do?" She took a step toward him, and the tiles cracked at each footstep. "Do you not remember what they did to me? Did you not *see?*"

Julian didn't think Aphrodite was aware of how he'd saved Janey Sinclair's life. He hoped and prayed she never would be. "Listen...Aphrodite..."

Another thunderous footstep. "What? What? *What?* Speaking? Is that what you're doing? Got something to say, or just want to buzz some more? Buzz like a bee. Like a swarm of bees. All you're good for. Buzz buzz."

Julian stood his ground. Barely. "Aphrodite, you still want to recruit lieutenants. Right? Isn't that what you want? That's why you went after Janey Sinclair in the first place, isn't it?"

Aphrodite snarled. She'd gotten close enough that Julian felt her hot breath in his face. It smelled like raw pork. He swallowed hard and tried not to think about why. "Didn't *want* to! She didn't! Janey Sinclair. Gray Widow. Wouldn't cooperate."

"But…but you still need lieutenants. More than just me. Right? Especially now that Trent is gone?"

Her eyes narrowed to slits, the volcanic glow shining through her eyelids. "So?"

"So maybe you don't kill them. Maybe that's not the best way to recruit new people. Maybe you can convince them to do what you want."

She hunched over, lowering her face to his, and *sniffed* of him, rapid inhales as her nose grazed his cheeks, his eyes, his lips. "How? Tell me. Tell me how."

Julian took a careful step backward, and laid out his plan.

14

Janey crouched with Tim, Nathan, and Simon behind one of the serving counters in the cafeteria. She thought they'd put enough distance between themselves and the pangolin creature that it might not be *right* on their asses yet.

Sha'dae. Sha'dae, can you help us?

The pain had at least doubled since it had first crashed through her head, and every running step had made it even worse. Nathan's face had taken on a greenish tint, underneath the sweat pouring off him, and Tim had vomited twice. Simon grove sat apart from the rest of them, his body shifting and pulsing, his skull changing shape every few seconds.

Faint, so faint Janey at first thought she had imagined it, Sha'dae's voice reached her. It was like trying to hear shouted words across a battlefield. *Janey! Janey, can you hear me? Am I getting through?*

Sha'dae! Thank God! I'm not sure what's going on—I think there's another telepath here, but all she does is broadcast pain. We're...not holding up...very well.

Every other time Sha'dae had touched her telepathically, the contact had felt like the most soothing stream of cool, deep water. Now Janey felt something like tiny droplets of water, like the beginning of a rain shower blown away by a stiff wind. Strain and maybe tears made Sha'dae's words quaver. *Come on. Come on! Allah, give me strength!* The rain shower came back. Grew stronger. Sha'dae's words came to them, to all of them, Janey could tell because Nathan raised his head and Simon turned to look Janey in the eye.

Guys. Everyone. Can you hear me?

The deep, clear, silvery stream flowed over them, and the pain fell away. Simon's skull stopped shifting, settling back into his human appearance, and Nathan made the kind of tiny, light sound that an infant might make when handed back to its mother.

Across the cafeteria, double doors slammed open. Janey rose up just enough to peek over the counter's edge, and came as close to losing control of her bladder as she ever had.

The icy fog rolled into the huge room, engulfing tables and chairs, the human figure inside it cloaked and blurred. As it moved off to one side, the pangolin creature came in next. Its footsteps shook the floor. It, too, moved to one side, and just as Janey realized it and the ice girl were making way for someone else, a short, slender Hispanic woman strode into the cafeteria. She wore an orange jumpsuit that made her look like a prison inmate, and almost all of what should have been long, straight black hair had fallen out of her scalp. Janey couldn't tell how old she was. Maybe twenty. Maybe fifty.

ALLOW ME TO INTRODUCE MYSELF.

The balding woman's eyes glowed white as the words exploded into Janey's brain, so bright Janey couldn't look at them, and Sha'dae's painkilling telepathic influence shredded like tissue paper. Nathan screamed, and Janey doubled over, both hands clutching her head.

MY NAME IS TRINA. YOU'VE ALREADY MET BEVERLY AND PARKER. KYLE HAD TO LEAVE, AND DAVID...WELL, YOU KILLED DAVID, DIDN'T YOU?

Now that she was in the same room, Janey didn't know how much more she could take of Trina's telepathic assault. Blood dripped from her nose and spattered on the floor.

Got to do something. Something. Anything!

Janey lifted her head again, and even through the life-ending pain, she saw that Beverly and Parker—the ice girl and the pangolin creature—were suffering as well. Beverly's fog-shrouded figure had its hands clamped to the sides of its head, and Parker trembled, grinding his teeth. They just weren't doing anything about it.

Trina walked, slowly, casually, through the cafeteria, approaching the serving counter, and every inch of the distance she closed made the pain worse. Sha'dae's voice drifted to her from an unfathomable distance. *I'm sorry, Janey, guys, I'm so sorry.*

Trina had crossed roughly half the distance between the door and the counter. Close enough now that Janey could see all the pock-marks in her face—Trina had, at some point, had terrible acne.

YOU DESERVE PAIN.

This close, Trina's words felt like individual hammer blows. Janey's nosebleed grew worse.

MR. STAMFORD WOULDN'T HAVE GOTTEN ME UP IF YOU DIDN'T. AND I'M GOING TO GIVE YOU THAT PAIN NOW. I'M GOING TO FILL YOU WITH IT. UNTIL YOU D—

That pock-marked face abruptly creased, and she looked over her shoulder, and Janey heard Trina gasp, just before the pangolin creature she had called Parker picked her up off the floor.

Trina screamed, and the pain made Janey long for death, but then she heard Parker's rockslide voice boom out, filling the cafeteria.

"Told them," Parker said. "Told them last time. Told them, wouldn't stand it again. Wouldn't let you do it again. Told them not to wake you up."

Trina shouted, "Parker, don't, Mr. Stamford said I had to, Parker, it's not my fault," and the pangolin creature tore Trina in half.

The ice girl screamed as Parker opened his jaws and began eating Trina, one huge, crunching bite after another, skin and flesh and bones and clothes, all of it, until there was nothing left but the blood coating his claws and running down his chin.

Parker licked the claws clean.

With Trina's brain-shredding interference gone, Janey initiated telepathic contact through Sha'dae with the rest of the group, awash with relief when the deep, silver stream flowed into her mind.

Guys. Can you all run?

Tim and Nathan both nodded.

Simon eyeballed Parker and Beverly. *I'll run like the fucking wind.*

Janey made a small gesture toward the door into the kitchen. *Out the way we came in. Go. Now!*

Launching themselves out of their hiding spot, they sprinted as hard and fast as they could out of the cafeteria. Nathan put every ounce of muscle he had into the dash. The concrete cracked underneath every thunderous footfall. Janey's enhanced strength let her keep up with Nathan, but Tim lagged behind, so much so that Simon once again changed his body, becoming the panther-like creature that had run Janey and Adam down on the road. Simon extended his shoulder blades into grip-like rods and growled at Tim, "Climb on. I'll carry you."

Sha'dae's connection was still in full effect, and Janey felt a burst of conflicting emotions from Tim at this, emotions mixed with snippets of words and phrases. *Killer*, and *tried to kill me*, and *hate you*, and *monster*. But Janey had always known Tim to be pragmatic, and it took him less than a second to leap onto Simon's metamorphosed back. All four of them tore their way up a stairwell, dashed down another corridor, and made it to an elevator.

Nathan punched the "UP" button. His voice distorted and reverberating from the panther-like larynx, Simon said, "Are you fucking kidding me? We're going to wait for an elevator?" Without waiting for a response, Simon all but dumped Tim onto the floor, wedged massive claws into the elevator doors, and pried them open.

The shaft had been outfitted with protected LED lights, just like the rest of the complex. Tim said, "Damn. Stamford is one paranoid bastard."

Janey threw a worried glance down the hallway behind them. There were no signs of pursuit. Not yet. From above, the elevator descended, and Janey growled in frustration. "I don't even know how far down we are. But it's take this elevator, or try to scale the shaft, or find a stairway and climb a million steps, and I know it's ludicrous to stand here arguing logistics. But I say we take the elevator."

Simon shed mass, shrinking from enormous feline monstrosity back to human. "Fine. But I reserve the right to pop the ceiling hatch and see how fast I can climb if we hear those freaks coming up after us."

The elevator arrived. It seemed to Janey that it took about five hours for the doors to close, and at least six months to get back up to the lobby, but they rode in silence. All of them listening. Janey heard nothing. No signs of pursuit, no distant screams. Nothing. The elevator made it to the lobby, and they poured out of it, sweet, welcoming darkness beckoning from beyond the glass doors of the entrance.

On her way toward the doors, Janey glanced over at the security office, and skidded to a stop. Tim said, "Janey! What the hell are you doing? Let's go!"

But the door to the office stood open, and through the door Janey could see the same bank of monitors that she'd spotted during the mental tour Simon had given them. One of those monitors covered the cafeteria, and when Janey moved into the office's doorway and looked more closely, every bit of blood in her body turned to ice.

There in the cafeteria, standing beside the bloodstain that was all that remained of Trina, was Beverly the ice girl, Parker the pangolin creature...

...and Aphrodite Lupo. The pulsing, static-filled cloud of blackness that was Julian Roth hovered behind her. There was no audio, or if there was, Janey didn't know how to turn the volume up. But she saw Aphrodite walk right up to Parker. Saw Parker bow his head to her. Saw Aphrodite reach up and touch his face...and saw him kneel before her.

Janey! Sha'dae sounded truly frantic. *Janey, what are you doing?*

Janey ran out into the darkness, pulled Tim and Nathan and Simon into a huddle, and teleported the four of them straight back to the ski lodge. She knew the resulting explosion would cause massive damage to the converted mine, if not destroy it outright. She also knew, from experience, that it wouldn't do any good.

As soon as they stepped out of the shadows outside the lodge, the front door banged open and Sha'dae all but threw herself down the stairs in her scramble to reach them. She did throw herself into Nathan's arms, and right there in front of everyone, Sha'dae kissed Nathan full on the lips. Nathan picked her up as easily as if she'd been a stuffed toy, and the kiss lasted long enough for Janey to grow uncomfortable. She said, "Come inside when you're ready," and thought Sha'dae probably heard her. Janey led Tim and Simon up the steps, where Adam waited for her on the porch, his face white as bone.

"Sha'dae told me what was going on," Adam said, his voice uneven. He slid his arms around her and pulled her close, and Janey returned the hug, unsure whether it was supposed to comfort her or him. Adam trembled under her touch. "I'm so glad you're back. So glad you're back."

Janey had just pulled away from the embrace—careful not to look at or even toward Tim—when the door slammed open again. Cary Kapoor stood there, the white visible all the way around his irises. "Hey! *Hey! Something's* wrong! Come, come on, c'mere!"

Janey hurried inside, and gasped. Zach and Heather Feygen lay slumped on the floor, motionless. Tim ran to his father, who half-sat, half-lay on a loveseat, unmoving. Rhonda Kapoor sat beside her husband, fully conscious and near-hysterical, fresh tears rolling down her cheeks. Tim shook Mr. Kapoor, lightly tapped his face, but it had no effect. "Dad! Dad, wake up! Dad! Dad, can you hear me? Dad!"

Janey looked around the room, and caught Ashley Strandjev's eye. "What is this? When did it start?"

"Just now!" Ashley said, and gestured toward the bedroom. "Agent Grassley said she wasn't feeling well and went to lie down, and I was about to go check on her when Mr. Kapoor passed out, and then Zach and Heather did too, and—"

All the color drained out of Ashley's face. Her eyes rolled back into her head, her knees buckled, and she collapsed to the floor.

Adam yanked at his hair. "What is this? What's happening to them?"

Janey rounded on him. "Adam! Look at me! Are you okay?" She pulled off a gauntlet and pressed it to his forehead. "No fever. Do you feel light-headed, anything?"

"No! Janey, what's going on? What do we do?"

Janey left him and went to Ashley, feeling for a pulse. The young woman had one, easily detected and steady. Her skin was cool and dry. "Was anybody vomiting? Diarrhea? *Anything?*"

Tim still hadn't left his father's side. Mrs. Kapoor said, "No! Raj just said he felt strange, and then he passed out!"

Janey ran into the bedroom, where Agent Grassley lay on the bed. She sat down next to her and shook the older woman gently. "Agent Grassley! Nicole! Can you hear me?" Getting no response, she checked again for a pulse and a fever. Nothing strange—no fever, steady pulse.

Zach and Heather, Mr. Kapoor, Agent Grassley, and now Ashley. Janey rushed back out into the living room and locked eyes with Tim. "We've got beds enough. Move them. I'm going to see about getting everyone to a hospital."

"Um...Janey?"

Janey spun toward Nathan's voice, and saw first that he looked as if he'd just been hit in the head with a shovel, and second that he'd turned the TV on. Nathan and Sha'dae stood, arms around each other's waists, staring at the image on the screen, and Nathan punched the VOLUME button on the remote control.

Above a banner that read, "BREAKING NEWS," a female reporter stood outside a hospital's emergency intake, which was clogged with ambulances like a gas station during an oil shortage. The reporter said, "Details are scarce at this point, but the CDC has ruled out influenza. We go now to Dr. Darrell Gilchrist, one of the CDC's leading epidemiologists."

The picture cut to a rotund man in his sixties. The same reporter asked him questions from off-screen. "Have you ever seen anything like this before, Doctor?"

Gilchrist said, "No. Never. If I hadn't seen the evidence myself, I would've insisted it was some kind of hoax. But the calls keep coming in, and we've verified with hospitals and clinics across the country. People are falling into comas. Hundreds of thousands of people, all around the world, if reports are to be believed. People with no commonality. People who've never met. Hundreds of thousands. Maybe millions." Gilchrist's eyes slid from the off-screen reporter to look straight into the camera. "Do not leave your homes. Do not interact with other people. We need to quarantine this if we can."

The image switched back to the reporter. "As Dr. Gilchrist said, if these reports are accurate, we are now in the grip of a pandemic of truly unprecedented proportions."

"What do we do?" Adam asked again. "What are we supposed to do?"

Nathan looked up at Janey. "Well, boss? Got any ideas?"

Janey stared at the TV screen. All her words had left her.

High above Indiana, heading west at well over a hundred miles per hour in his custom-fitted helicopter, Derek Stamford flipped between CNN, Fox News, and the BBC on his tablet. Every news source he'd been able to find was covering the pandemic and *only* the pandemic. He couldn't fault them. The world had never seen anything like this before. In the last hour, how many people had lapsed into sudden, inexplicable comas? A billion? Two billion?

The pilot's voice carried back to him from the cockpit. They didn't have to use headset radios, thanks to the sound-proofed cabin. "Mr. Stamford?" The pilot, a man named Judson, with prematurely gray hair and a chin-cleft that made him look like Kirk Douglas, was having noticeable trouble keeping his voice steady. "I just heard from Minnesota. They're not going to be able to make the usual arrangements. Half the, uh, half the staff has...succumbed? I guess you'd say? The thing that's happening everywhere. It's there, too. Sir."

The low rumble in the atmosphere Stamford had been feeling for days had elevated to a grinding whine earlier that afternoon. Not a shred of doubt remained: this pandemic was of extraterrestrial origin. And now that whatever kind of system had set it in place had finally activated, Stamford knew he could pinpoint it. Isolate it. Understand it, the same way he'd understood the alien communications array under the barn in Texas.

And once he understood it, he'd be able to control it.

"Tell the remaining staff to do the best they can."

"Yes, sir."

Hundreds of millions of victims of the mystery ailment already, according to the BBC, and who knew how many more in the hours to come. Stamford stared out the window, down at the irregular grids and patterns of lights spread out across the landscape.

Maybe one by one. Maybe in clusters. But soon, Stamford knew, all those lights would start going out. It made his fury at Kyle Gutierrez—the fury that had consumed him when he'd learned that Gutierrez had disobeyed orders and made off with Anastasia—seem trivial.

The Plowman's array of deconstructed, reconfigured Earth technology had grown too large for the confines of his previous workspace. Now he huddled, surrounded by his equipment, down in the oil-change bay of an abandoned E-Z Lube near Tracy City, Tennessee. The location, one of the higher geographical points on the Eastern

Seaboard, allowed him much better broadcast and reception capabilities than the last spot.

The Plowman sent out a tentative pulse. He had picked up on the micro-probes thirty-six hours ago, but hadn't been able to tell what function they were serving. Their widespread nature had led him to speculate that his people were conducting a global topographical survey, most likely in anticipation of choosing the best landing sites. But in the last twelve hours, the micro-probes' signal had boosted, and he'd finally decided it was time to contact Janey Sinclair. The pulse he'd just sent out was designed to register teleportation bursts.

The indicator column near his left elbow chimed softly, the glimmering lights on its surface shifting from green to orange. The Plowman grunted and had just turned to leave through the large, round tunnel he had burrowed through the wall at the far end of the bay when a voice spoke from above him. The voice sounded like a dozen cellos playing at once, and could not have been produced by a human voice box.

"Evaluator. Surrender yourself for neutralization."

The Plowman twisted and looked above him, and saw the Assassin standing there at the edge of the bay, glaring down at him. He had just enough time to trigger a message before the Assassin moved.

15

Janey awakened to feelings of intense guilt. She and the rest of the unaffected people in the house had made the ones who'd fallen ill as comfortable as they knew how, before exhaustion, hunger, and dehydration had finally caught up with her. The last thing she remembered was Sha'dae and Ashley both calling to check on their parents—all of whom were unaffected—before Janey had pulled off the Vylar suit, fallen into one of the upstairs beds, and collapsed into a sleep too deep to allow dreams.

She had just sat up and swung her legs over the edge of the bed when Adam opened the door. He held a tray of food—a can of sparkling water and what looked like a ham sandwich. "Hey. Didn't know if you were awake or not, but it's gonna be dark soon. I figured you'd want to be up and about."

Janey nodded. She stood, suddenly self-conscious in a sports bra and her usual boy shorts, and slipped past Adam into the hallway. "Be right back." He set the tray down on one of the twin beds and waited.

Janey used the bathroom, splashed water on her face, and found a travel-size bottle of mouthwash for which she was immensely grateful. She returned to the bedroom, where Adam now sat on the edge of the bed next to the tray, and pulled on a terrycloth robe that had been hanging in the closet. Janey ate the sandwich in four ravenous bites, sitting on the floor, and leaned back against another bed while she sipped from the sparkling water can.

"Where's everyone else?"

"Downstairs. Pretty much waiting for you."

The guilt flared. "Would you go tell them I'll be right down?"

Adam looked as if he wanted to say something else, but finally he nodded and left. Janey took a tentative sniff of the Vylar suit. Stale sweat had mingled with dried blood, and Janey realized with a lurch in her stomach that the suit smelled like the dumpster behind a butcher shop. She held it under one of the showers until most of the funk had washed away, but with no time to let it dry, she decided to put up with the extra chafing and buckled everything but the helmet and gauntlets back in place. Her boots made a sound like *squinch-squanch* with each step as she went downstairs.

The rest of the lodge's residents had divided into two groups in the living room. Tim, Nathan, Sha'dae, and Simon clustered on one side, standing near a window and chatting quietly, while Mrs. Kapoor, Cary, and Adam sat in a little group of leather-upholstered chairs near the unlit fireplace. Everyone turned to look at Janey as she descended the stairs.

"Sorry, guys," Janey said, pulling on her gauntlets. "Did anyone else get any rest?"

A general murmur rose from both crowds. It sounded unsatisfied.

Rhonda Kapoor stood and came to Janey. "Listen...I used to be a nurse."

Janey said, "No shit? Sorry, sorry. What I meant by that was, 'Oh thank God.'"

"That might be premature. It's like this: if someone's in a coma, they can't eat or drink on their own. And of course we'll have to take care of urination and defecation, but that's not the hard part. If they're..." Janey saw Mrs. Kapoor's eyes glisten. After a pause: "If they're not going to come out of this in the next twelve hours, we've got to start thinking about feeding tubes."

Janey's brow wrinkled up. "I will freely admit that I don't know anything about feeding tubes."

"I can get you a list of supplies. The hardware, if you will, and what we need to feed them. But, Janey, we've been watching the TV all day. It makes me really nervous that the rest of us are stuck here, with no transportation, I mean, but…it might be for the best. This, whatever this is, this outbreak, it's hit the entire planet. When you go out there, looking for what we need? I don't know what you're going to find. Please. We need these supplies. But we need you to be careful, too."

From a place of deep honesty, Janey said, "Pardon my French, Mrs. Kapoor, but I'm really fucking impressed with how calm you're staying."

Mrs. Kapoor waved that away. "I cried myself dry while you were asleep. And please, for fuck's sake, call me Rhonda."

From across the room, Tim, said, *"Mom!"*

As Janey hugged her, Mrs. Kapoor said, "I'll observe decorum when the world's not coming to an end, Tim." She let Janey go and looked out the nearest window. "Sun's going down. Good luck."

Janey nodded, and buckled on her helmet.

J aney stepped out of the shadows half a block from the Gavring Medical emergency entrance at 9:48 p.m. She said a silent thanks that the rest of the night stretched before her. After the experience in Stamford's complex, Janey had no desire to get caught out in the open in bright sunlight.

I could be a halfway decent vampire.

She shook the irrelevant thought out of her head. She had already delivered all of the necessary goods Mrs. Kapoor—Rhonda—had asked for, after finding a medical supply warehouse on the west edge of College Park. Now she had a different mission. Janey pulled off her helmet and, reaching through the shadows, set it on her work bench in the storage unit. She shrugged into a long gray raincoat and dropped her armored gloves into its side pockets, buttoned the coat so that the only part of her suit people would see were the non-descript combat boots, and walked swiftly toward the hospital.

Just as she'd seen on the news, ambulances clustered thick, like flies on a corpse. A few police officers tried to maintain order amid the flood of EMT crews, gurneys, and a throng of Atlanta's citizens, many of them carrying limp bodies, all of them trying to get inside.

Janey glanced around, listening before she plunged into the din. Atlanta had become a city of howling screams and blaring alarms and breaking glass. A car sped past her, not stopping at the hospital, and Janey got a split-second glimpse of the driver, a boy no older than twelve. His red-rimmed, frantic eyes pierced her in the single heartbeat she could see them.

How does a city cope with this? How does a country? A world?

No one could answer that. Much like the Augmentations she and her friends were dealing with, these were uncharted waters. Deeper and wider than any ocean.

Janey shouldered her way through the crowd, slipped past a cop when his back was turned, and waded into the tableau of chaos that the emergency waiting area had become. Nurses at the intake desk shouted back and forth with the terrified families of patients. Gurneys lined the hallways, an unmoving body on each one, and more victims of whatever kind of plague had been unleashed on the world sat or lay, comatose, in the waiting area's chairs.

Movement caught Janey's eye. One of the intake nurses had just slumped forward, bracing herself on the desktop. The nurse lifted her head, struggling to get upright again, but her eyes rolled back in their sockets and she collapsed. Screams of horror rippled out from the intake desk. A third of the crowd stampeded toward the door, in a bigger rush to get out than they'd been in to get inside.

Janey spotted Dr. Carla Gates when a set of double doors on an electric motor buzzed and powered open. Janey crossed the space in less than two seconds, pivoting around an orderly rushing toward the nurses' desk, and slid through the doors before they could close again. Dr. Gates stood at a rolling computer kiosk, staring at the screen, her face slack and her fingers twitching. A nurse hurried down the hall, and might have mumbled something along the lines of, "You're not supposed to be back here," but Janey wasn't sure. She made it to Dr. Gates' side unimpeded.

"Doctor. I need to talk to you."

It took a moment for the doctor's eyes to focus. "Listen, everything needs to go through the nurses at the desk where you first come in, all right? I know the situation's bad, but there's nothing I can—"

Janey stepped closer. Dropped her voice to the growl she had practiced for so long. "You know me, Doctor. I was here not long ago with the man in white."

All the blood dropped out of Dr. Gates' face. She grabbed Janey's arm and steered her into a supply closet—*the* supply closet Janey had used more than once to allow her to flicker in and out of the hospital. Gates closed the door and peered up into Janey's eyes. "No mask. Why does that terrify me?"

"Because you're a smart woman. Doctor, a number of people very important to me have been affected by this—whatever this is."

Gates shook her head. "You and everyone else. We got swamped almost immediately. There are no more beds. None. We're past capacity." She took a deep breath. "What do I call you?"

Janey had made the decision to approach Dr. Gates without the mask for two reasons. The first was that she needed Gates's help immediately, and showing this much trust was the best way she could think of to get it. The second was that, if as many people had fallen into comas as the news was reporting, it was only going to be a matter of hours before the entire world went all the way to shit, and maintaining the persona of a masked vigilante just seemed...

Silly. It seemed silly. Janey wondered what she'd been doing with her life for the last year.

"My name is Janey. Seeing what I saw on the way to talk to you, I already figured there might not be much point in bringing them here. I think every medical facility in the country has the same problems."

Gates scowled. "Everyone in the *world*. This is...it's apocalyptic. And I don't use that word lightly. So far, nobody can figure out what any of the victims have in common. They don't all fit into one genetic group. They've been drinking from different water systems. They don't live near each other. They haven't all been to the same goddamn Chipotle. There's just *nothing*. No commonality, no point of origin! It's supposed to be like a fire, see, where you can spot a pattern? At least a rough point of origin? A house doesn't just burst into flames everywhere at once. Except that's what seems to have happened. The whole world just ignited, sometime in the last six hours." The scowl changed, Gates' eyes widening. "Wait a minute. Do you know something about this? About what it is, where it came from?"

Janey rubbed the back of her neck. "Nothing more than speculation. Nothing useful."

"Bullshit! *Any* information is useful! Now spill!"

Janey sighed. "It might—possibly—be extraterrestrial." The Plowman's words echoed in her ears, the same way they'd been echoing for hours now. *It is too late for your world. You will be annexed.* "I'm afraid it's something done to cripple the human species. Probably so we can be invaded."

Janey remembered History class in high school—before she'd gotten shot and left her life as a student behind for good—when she'd learned about the real reason European settlers had been able to move in and take over North America with relative ease: the Native population had already been nearly wiped out by smallpox.

Carla Gates puffed out a quick breath. "Are you—you're serious. This is real. You're telling me Earth has been attacked by aliens? And they're using, what, a virus? Like *War of the Worlds* in reverse. Tell me you're kidding. You're not kidding? You're not kidding." She slumped back against a shelf full of bottles of disinfectant and threw her hands in the air. "Fine. You know what? *Fine.* That makes as much sense as anything else." She folded her arms. "So what do we do? Do you know?"

"I'm working on it. But I wanted to tell you this. Thought it might help you figure out how to treat people better."

Gates scowled. "There's thinking outside the box, and then there's this shit. Yeah. Okay. As I said before, any information helps."

"And if you do figure out something that works, maybe let the rest of the medical community know?"

Gates nodded. "I don't guess you know how long this is going to go on?"

"All I know is that it's a principle of war: wounding a soldier is worse on the enemy than killing one. Because it takes, on average, two people to care for one wounded. So if you kill someone, that takes that single person out of play. If you wound someone, that's three people tied up."

"And the...shit. The goddamn *aliens* have just wounded us. As a species. Really badly. Okay. I'll see what I can come up with. I..."

Janey frowned. She noticed the doctor's left eyelid start twitching. "Doc? Are you all right?"

Gates didn't answer. Instead her eyes rolled back in their sockets, and Janey barely caught her before she collapsed, unconscious, to the floor.

J aney retrieved her helmet, stowed the raincoat in the storage unit, and flickered up to the roof of the hospital. More alarms blared, from homes, businesses, and cars alike, and Janey realized that, in the face of the threat posed by the Plowman's people, she had essentially abandoned the city she had sworn to protect.

Don't be ridiculous. And quit wasting time! Get back to the lodge!

But she stood there, staring out at the chaos rapidly engulfing Atlanta, and realized she couldn't. *No,* a tiny part of her whispered. *You don't want to go back yet. You don't want to face what's waiting for you.*

Janey left the hospital roof and flickered through the city, at the head of a wave of heat that started in Midtown and spiraled outward.

On the roof a house in a residential neighborhood, she heard a desperate kind of crying coming from inside, so she moved to the shadows outside a pair of sliding glass doors that led into the kitchen. Through the doors, she saw a white girl of maybe six, trying to drag a large, unconscious white man across the kitchen floor. Janey tapped on the door, and the girl looked up and saw her and screamed. She dropped the man's hand and ran out of sight around a corner, still screaming.

From her storage unit, Janey pulled a "slim jim," a long, flat, very thin length of metal, which she used to pop open the sliding door's lock. She stepped into the kitchen, pulled off one of her gloves, and knelt to take the man's pulse. Just like Mr. Kapoor, and Agent Grassley, and the Feygens. Steady. No fever. No signs of trauma. Just no consciousness.

Janey looked up to see the little girl peering at her from around the corner. "Hi." Janey waved to her. "I'm not going to hurt you. I'd like to help your…is this your father?"

The girl didn't say anything, but she inched her face further around the corner, so that Janey could see both her eyes.

"Okay, I'm going to stand up and just look around a little. Is that all right? I need to see where I should put your dad so he'll be comfortable."

The girl still didn't say anything, but she didn't move, either. Janey stepped into the living room and, to her relief, spotted several framed photos featuring the man on the floor, the girl staring at Janey, and a woman with short brown hair. The last thing Janey wanted to do was carry the man into the bedroom and tuck him in, only to discover that he was actually a burglar or a kidnapper.

Janey almost tripped over the woman with the short brown hair. She lay sprawled beside the couch, and when Janey bent over to check for a pulse from her, the scent of Jack Daniel's struck her hard in the face. Janey glanced around and saw an empty bottle nearby, and when she sat the woman upright, the woman groaned and slapped weakly at her and said, "Don'…don' touch me…don' touch me none."

Blackout drunk mom and plague-victim dad.

Janey turned to go back to the kitchen, and saw that the little girl had come closer, peering up at her. "That mask is scary," the girl said.

Janey crouched down. "Well, it's supposed to be. It's supposed to scare the bad guys."

"I'm not a bad guy."

"No—no. Of course you're not."

The girl put her hands on her hips. "It's not nice to scare people."

Janey tried to think of something to say. Her mind gave her a heaping helping of nothing. Finally, she managed, "What should my mask look like?"

"Not scary. Different colors. You've got too many eyes. Are you going to help my dad? He was making coffee for mom, but then he fell down."

"You bet I am. Hang on."

Janey went to the man in the kitchen and carefully hoisted him over one shoulder. To the girl she said, "Where were you going to put him?"

"Back in their room." The girl pointed.

Janey carried him into a master bedroom with a king-size waterbed and aggressively plaid sheets. She laid him down carefully, adjusting his arms and legs the best she could, and picked up the phone that rested on a nightstand. She punched in 9-1-1. The line rang, and rang, and rang some more, before the ear-splitting three-tone "technical difficulty" sound played. *"We're sorry,"* the pre-recorded voice told her, *"all lines are busy. Please try your call again later."*

The girl had followed Janey into the bedroom. Janey crouched down again. "Listen. There's something really bad happening outside now. So you need to stay in here. Lock all the doors, and don't go outside, and keep calling 9-1-1. It'll probably be busy, but keep trying. When somebody picks up, they'll come and help. And I'll come back myself later to see if you're okay."

"You're really strong," the girl said. "You picked up my dad like I pick up my cousin's puppy."

"Yeah. I guess I am."

"Your mask should be blue," the girl said. "I like blue. And purple. Make it blue and purple, and not so scary. Then maybe people won't scream so loud when they see you."

"You just…" Janey wanted to hug the girl, hold her tight and tell her everything was going to be okay. But she didn't want to lie, either. "You just keep calling 9-1-1, okay? And stay in the house."

Janey made sure all the locks were in place before she flickered away into the darkness outside.

The rest of the city, she quickly saw, was falling apart.

A young gay Latino couple had run their car off the road when the driver succumbed to the plague. The driver's husband was frantic, trying to get the cops on the phone, and when Janey flickered out of the shadows nearby, he dropped the phone and screamed. It didn't take long for him to pull himself together, to Janey's relief, and he thanked her over and over in both English and Spanish when she dug in her heels and pushed the car back up onto the pavement. Janey helped the man move the driver over into the passenger seat, and made sure the car would start and run, before teleporting away—but only seconds later, six blocks down the street, she spotted a group of teenagers looting an electronics store.

The teenagers scattered as soon as she showed up, but Janey had no way of patching the window, and she discovered a man, most likely the store's owner, comatose in a back room. She tried 9-1-1 on the store phone. All lines busy.

A police cruiser rolled past the store, and Janey sprinted out and flickered after it, hoping to tell the officer about the store owner. But as soon as the cop caught sight of Janey, his eyes bugged out and he stomped on the accelerator, laying rubber as he rocketed away from her. She went back to the looted store, hoisted the owner onto her shoulder the same way she had the little girl's father, and flickered with him to the hospital.

The crowd had gotten worse. They screamed and parted when they saw her, but few of them actually fled. They just ran, chaotic, like spooked cattle in a corral. Janey made her way inside and propped the man in a corner of the waiting room, near a dozen other comatose bodies. Telling herself that was at least a little better than leaving him in the store, she went back outside and pushed through the screaming crowd.

Janey stood in place on the nearest street corner and turned in a slow circle. Everywhere, children had just lost their parents, maybe for good. Huge chunks were suddenly gone out of law enforcement, and medicine, and even though the plague victims were still alive, if there weren't enough people to treat the ones who'd fallen ill, they'd soon die. Janey wondered what would happen at the phone companies. At the offices of Internet search engines. At banks.

There wouldn't be enough people to deliver gas to all the gas stations, or food to all the grocery stores.

Soon America's amazing military, bigger and more powerful than those of the next five or six countries combined, would be reduced to a ragged shell of itself, if it hadn't been already.

Screams echoed up and down the street.

More alarms sounded out.

In the distance, smoke rose from an unseen fire.

It's too big. It's just too big.

Tears in her eyes, Janey flickered several hundred feet into the night sky and returned to the ski lodge.

The only people still up when she walked into the lodge's living room were Adam, Tim, and Tim's brother Cary. Someone had finally started a fire in the fireplace. Janey was too exhausted to decide whether that was a good thing or a bad thing. Would the plume of smoke from the chimney draw attention? Did that even make sense? She couldn't tell.

Tim and Cary seemed to be engaged in some sort of tense discussion, but Adam stood and came to her. She returned the hug he gave her. Her eyes slid closed in his embrace, because she didn't want to meet Tim's eyes accidentally.

"What're they talking about?" she asked, just quietly enough for Adam to hear.

"General attitudes," Adam answered.

Janey let go of him and took a step back, frowning. "Attitudes about what? No, never mind. Has there been any change? In anyone?"

"No. Well, I mean, Nate and Sha'dae are crashed out asleep, and so are Mr. Vessler and his boy. We got Mr. Kapoor in one of the beds, and last time I looked, Mrs. Kapoor was sitting in a chair next to him. She might be asleep now, too. Zach and Heather and Ashley are all in one of the kids' rooms, each in their own bunk. I don't know where Simon went." He paused. "How're things looking? Out in the world?"

"Horrible. But I might as well tell all you guys at the same time. No use in repeating myself if I don't have to."

Adam put a hand on her arm. "I'd like to talk to you. In private."

"In a few minutes?"

Adam hesitated. He shrugged. "Sure."

Janey went over and sat down near Tim and Cary. Adam followed her.

"It's just pointless, is what I'm trying to say." Cary talked with his hands, his freckled features animated. "This is, I mean, come on, this is some race of aliens that have faster-than-light travel, and they're beaming their consciousnesses into freaking robot bodies across light-years, and they're experimenting on humans like we're a bunch of guinea pigs in a lab somewhere, and what? We should *fight* them? It's ridiculous!"

"Okay, then what're we supposed to do?" Tim's voice had risen half an octave, which Janey recognized as an indicator that his patience had almost reached its end. "Surrender? Just like that, just give up?"

"I'm *saying*, we find out what they want, and we *give* it to them. You saw what happened to Dad! And it's all over the planet now! If they did that, what chance do we have? We're outnumbered, outbrained, *severely* outgunned. If we try to attack them? What's to stop them from just killing the rest of us? Just like that? Whereas, if we do what they want, maybe Dad'll wake back up!"

Janey leaned forward and rested her elbows on her knees. "Cary, I know you don't know me very well, and you don't know most of the rest of us here at all. But I might be able to shed some light on this. Maybe make you see things from our perspective."

Cary sat back on the leather couch and folded his arms. "Okay. Enlighten me."

"The reason we shouldn't give up is that humans are, for lack of a better term, wild cards. The Plowman—Tim, did you tell him about the Plowman?"

Tim nodded. Cary said, "Yeah, and that's one of the reasons I think fighting would be pointless."

Janey said, "Well, I saw an Augmented human take the Plowman

155

down. A fellow named Julian Roth. He can do what I do, sort of—he tele-ports. And the Plowman is a walking tank, I mean, the guy's like some kind of mashup of Terry Crews, Clint Eastwood, and Yao Ming…and Julian Roth took him down. Would have killed him, if I hadn't been there."

Cary's forehead bunched up. "Killed him how?"

"Roth teleported big sections of the Plowman's body to…well, I don't know where to. But they were gone. The Plowman was down and out, and if he'd been flesh and blood, he would've been *so* dead. And he repre-sents, basically, the extra-terrestrial state of the art."

Cary frowned and stared at his toes.

Janey went on. "Then you've got Aphrodite Lupo. Another Augment. Someone who's, the best I can figure out—and let me tell you, I've spent a lot of time thinking about this—she's like an evil version of Plastic Man. Changes her body, looks like other people sometimes, and damn if any of us can figure out how to kill her. I burned her, cut her, teleported her *into* the ground. She shrugged it all off. Even after Nathan literally punched her heart out of her chest, her actual beating heart, she's still not dead. It just inconvenienced her for a while."

Janey glanced over at Adam, and saw that he'd turned a faint shade of pale green, but she didn't want him to throw her off her momentum, so she kept going. "Now, here's something the Plowman told me himself. To my face, about the experiments that did this to us."

Cary dragged his eyes off his toes to look up at her. "*Augmented* you, you mean?"

"Yeah. He told me the experiment was a failure. You know why? Because humans are too unpredictable. Right down to the genetic level. He said the experiment was supposed to, to get metaphorical for a minute, it was supposed to mix blue and yellow and make sure it came out the right shade of green. And instead it came out purple with yellow polka dots. These super-intelligent, super-advanced, super-dangerous aliens you're talking about? *They think we're too unpredictable to use.* Let that sink in. We're an entire species of wild cards."

Cary took a moment, but began shaking his head. "Okay, but, like, with respect—so what? Doesn't that just make us a bad batch? Won't they just burn the lab and start over with some other bunch of schmucks on some other planet?"

"They might want to. They might intend to. This thing that zapped your dad is probably part of that agenda. But here's what'll make the difference. There's an Augment out there named Derek Stamford. As far as we've been able to tell, Stamford's Augmentation is all about information. He can learn anything. Understand anything. And he got access to the Plowman's lair...before I, uh, made it inaccessible..."

"More like burned it down," Tim said in a tone that Janey found not at all helpful.

"Anyway. Derek Stamford got access to the aliens' technology. Which means he learned it. Understood it."

Cary sat back up. Janey saw a glint in his eyes spring to life. "So you're saying this Stamford guy can...what? Reverse-engineer some alien tech? Pull some kind of Jeff Goldblum *Independence Day* shit?"

Tim leaned forward, his eyes riveted to Janey's.

Janey let the corner of her mouth quirk upward. "Maybe. Stamford's going to take some convincing, at the very least, but we have the tools. It's possible. If Stamford can figure out what this plague-thing is? Maybe we can figure out some kind of antidote. Maybe we turn it around on them. The point is, we can't just give up. Not when there's still a chance." Janey reached out and put her hand on Cary's wrist. "Will you help us?"

While Janey saw the wheels turning in Cary's mind, Tim said, "Excuse me, but when did you decide to ask Derek Stamford for help?"

"On the way back from Atlanta, like ten minutes ago. I never said 'ask,' though. Plus, we have to find him first."

"All right," Cary said, at first to no one in particular. Then, to Janey: "All right. You're right. If there's a chance...yeah. We've got to try to resist this. I'm in."

Janey's phone buzzed. She pulled it out and, seeing that it just had a string of zeroes displayed, not even an "Unknown Caller" message, she hit DECLINE.

Tim grinned and bumped fists with Cary. "I knew you'd come around."

Cary said, "Yeah, Janey convinced me, I just—just didn't see it...before..."

Janey's throat clenched in horror as Cary's eyes rolled up in their sockets. He slid onto the floor, limp and motionless, as Tim screamed his name.

16

Janey sat on the floor in front of one of the leather couches, her knees pulled up to her chest and her arms wrapped around her shins. She rocked back and forth, her eyes wide but seeing nothing, the icy pit in her stomach growing larger by the second. After five or so minutes, she forced herself to focus on Adam, who sat across from her, watching her, his face creased with worry.

Simon lay stretched out on his back on the kitchen table. He'd found a tennis ball somewhere, and threw it in the air and caught it. Threw it and caught it. He hadn't spoken in a while.

Tim came back down the stairs from one of the bedrooms. "He's as comfortable as I can make him. You guys made any progress?" When neither of them answered him, he slumped onto a couch. "I just don't get why it's hitting some people and not others." Tim ran his fingers through his hair. "You said there were still tons of people on the street, right?"

Janey gestured vaguely at the TV, which had stopped receiving anything but static at some point in the last half-hour. "It's like you see on the news. *Saw* on the news. Yes. Plenty of unaffected. Which goes along with what Dr. Gates told me, before it hit her. There's no point of origin. Nothing linking people who fall prey to it. And why'd it wait so long to hit Cary, when everybody else went under?" She focused on Adam. "Why are *you* immune?"

Adam shrugged, staring at the floor. "Maybe I'm not. Maybe it's just waiting, like it did with Cary."

Tim said, "But if you are immune, we need to understand why." He paused. "We also need to find out how Aphrodite and Julian found us at Stamford's place. Does that mean they can track us here?"

Janey nodded. "I've been sitting here wondering the same thing. I mean, they haven't shown up yet, so maybe they won't? I know, that's not much comfort." She stared through the floor at nothing. "The only thing I can think is that Julian was at the R&D place that Grassley keeps so hush-hush, and while he was there, he saw someone tracking us? Maybe? I'd call them and ask, if I had their number." A burst of realization hit her. "Oh, shit, I completely forgot somebody tried to call me." She dug her phone out and tapped the message. Her eyes got wider and wider as she listened to it, and she immediately put it on speaker and played it again. Simon got up and came over to listen.

"Janey Sinclair." The voice was unfamiliar, machine-modulated, like that of a digital personal assistant. *"This is the being you know as the Plow-man. Since you are hearing this, there is a very good chance that I have been deactivated, resulting in my death. I have located the Augment known as Kyle Gutierrez, who has taken the Augment known as Anastasia Coletti captive. As of the sending of this message, Gutierrez is at the following location."* The voice rattled off a set of coordinates. *"Find young Miss Coletti. With help, she should be able to pinpoint my cognitive signature. If I am alive, find me."*

Janey played the message four more times. On the third play, Nathan and Sha'dae came downstairs, followed moments later by Garrison Vessler and Scott Charles, and they all listened every bit as intently as Janey had.

Scott raised a timid hand. "So...what does this mean? Are you guys going to go get her?" He looked from one face to the next. "Please?"

Tim chewed his lower lip. "Okay, say we're able to go and get Anastasia this time—say this Gutierrez guy doesn't teleport them somewhere else, *again*. What does the Plowman mean, find him? How are we supposed to find a mechanical guy with an alien consciousness floating around inside him?"

Scott said, "We might be able to do it. Anastasia and me. If we worked together. And maybe if Sha'dae helped us."

Adam said, "That's a lot of ifs."

Vessler put a hand on Scott's shoulder. "Son, we're already planning to get Anastasia out of harm's way. You don't need to keep convincing us."

Scott didn't quite bat Vessler's hand away. "That's not what I'm doing! I really think we could find the Plowman if we worked together!"

Janey sighed. "Let's not forget the whole point of getting Anastasia away from Stamford, regardless of the Plowman. She *can* find us, wherever we are. So as long as she's out there, none of us are safe."

Vessler said, "This is also assuming that message isn't leading us into a trap. How far away are they?"

Nathan had been poking at his phone. "Okay, *finally*. Jeez, my network's slow as shit." He glanced at Sha'dae. "Sorry. Language, I know." She patted his knee. "Anyway, if those coordinates are right, they're in Charlotte."

Scott's face fell. "That's too far away for me to see. Sorry, guys." Vessler put a hand on Scott's shoulder.

Tim said, "So who goes? The usual suspects? Nathan and me? Simon?"

Simon cleared his throat. "Let me put something out there. Gutierrez is a teleport. A fucked-up teleport, yes, but the fact remains. And we know what a game-changer that is thanks to Janey."

Vessler said, "What kind of point are you trying to make?"

"A healer fixed my brain. Got me thinking right. Well, got me thinking less wrong, anyway. If we could get Gutierrez off the Stamford teat? That could give us a serious advantage. Which means Beanpole here would take the MVP slot."

Tim scowled. "Yeah. I guess. I could give it a shot, I mean. If we can get him to hold still."

Janey stood up. "If we're going to go do this, let's go do this. And, listen, everyone. Advantages aside, we're not killers. Okay? Yeah, Trent Davis wound up dead, and Aphrodite sort of was, for a while, but that's not what we do. We get Anastasia, and we deal with Gutierrez. Simon's right. If we can turn a foe to a friend, let's do it."

General murmurs of agreement circulated around the room.

Janey paced around the living room. "We've just got to take him by surprise. We can't risk letting him get away again. If the Plowman's in as much trouble as it sounds like, he probably won't be able to clue us in on the location a second time." She stopped and fixed her gaze on Simon. "That means no letting him get his hands on you. Or anyone else."

Simon's expression darkened. The bones of his face rippled, and Adam looked away, half-gagging. Simon said, "Oh, don't worry. Whether we help him or not, he won't pull that shit again."

Janey turned to Scott and Vessler. "While we're gone, would you see if you can get into Grassley's phone, and look through anything else she had with her, and try to figure out where her R&D people are? They might have some gear we can use. Or they might be associated with a hospital. Or both."

Vessler nodded. "We're on it."

Adam said, "Janey? Can I talk to you? In private?" He hooked a thumb toward the front door, and to her own mortification, Janey realized that for a few moments she had forgotten Adam was in the room.

She followed Adam out onto the front porch and closed the door. "What's up?"

Adam shoved his hands in his pockets. "What's up? Seriously? You're about to go off and leave, again, and you're taking a guy who, by your own admission, has tried to kill you a bunch of times."

Janey's jaw clenched and unclenched. "He also *saved* my life very recently. He's an asshole, yes, but he's given us no reason not to trust him." Janey marveled to herself that those words were true. *Simon Grove.* On her side.

"But, but—but you're just gonna go *do* this. Without asking me. You're gonna go fight some super-powered weirdo, and maybe kill him. Or maybe he'll kill *you*. And, obviously, you never even thought to consult with me about it first."

That rocked Janey back on her heels. "Adam, it's...there's no choice. I've got no choice. We need to get Anastasia. That's been the goal this whole time. Well, *a* goal, anyway."

"But—look, I can't believe I have to ask you to do this. Janey, I'm your *husband*. We're a team. Or at least we're supposed to be. Major decisions, we're supposed to make together. Right? And this isn't taking out a loan to buy a new car, or deciding to go back to school. This could make me a widower. And you weren't even going to ask me."

Janey took a long moment, staring into his clear green eyes. Words battled back and forth in her mind, struggling to get out, a verbal logjam for which she was ultimately grateful, because she felt pretty sure she would've said something she'd regret if she'd spoken her mind without careful consideration.

He kept on. "Don't you want us to be a team? Don't you want things to be like they were?"

Janey groaned.

Yes. Yes, of course I want things to be like they were.

But…did she? Truly? And was it even a fair question, since things were *not* the way they were before? Could they ever be again? Shouldn't she just resign herself to the new status of her life, since there was no way to change it?

Or was that a quitting mentality?

Janey felt as if someone had attached a fifty-pound weight plate to her heart with a zip tie. It hurt to beat. And she knew the weight would eventually squeeze it in two.

"Adam…I don't have answers for you. Not now. Not yet. You're right, a married couple is supposed to consult with each other before making big decisions. But what I said before is still true. I don't have any choice. We're going to go try our best to save this girl. And I'm going to try my best to come back in one piece. And…I'm sorry, but that's going to have to do for now."

"Janey—"

"I don't mean to sound harsh. I really don't. But I've got to go."

Janey left Adam there on the porch in the cold.

Before they left, Nathan managed to get a news report to stream on his phone.

According to that one voice, abandoned cars littered the sides of every freeway, widespread rioting and looting had broken out in every city across the country, and hospitals were even more overrun than when Janey had last seen the chaos at Gavring in Atlanta. The percentage of law enforcement and the military affected by the plague was reported as close to ninety—as opposed to the government in Washington, D.C., which seemed to be humming along as if nothing had happened. Only seventeen members of Congress had fallen ill, and both the President and Vice-President were unaffected.

When the newscast abruptly cut off, Janey asked Nathan to pull up the coordinates the Plowman had given them on Google Earth. After a couple of minutes, images began to load, but excruciatingly slowly.

Janey stood, shifting her weight from one foot to the other, spilling over with nervous energy. A thought occurred to her.

"Simon. Something I've been meaning to ask you."

He grinned. "So polite! It's like we're old friends now. What did you want to ask, Fearless Leader?"

"When you change. Physically, I mean. Sometimes, with the bigger changes, your skin takes on a grayish-green color, and sprouts little hooked thorns all over it."

Simon's face adopted a thoughtful cast. "With the bigger changes, she says. That includes when she's shot me full of holes and is about to cut my head off." He seemed to enjoy Sha'dae's shocked expression. "Yeah, I don't really know what that is. It feels sort of...basic. No, that's not the right word. *Primal.* Like, if you strip away all the other layers, that just sort of feels *right*. The bare wood under all the paint and shellac. Why do you ask?"

"I tried to kill Aphrodite Lupo once. Well, I tried more than once, but there was one time when I caught her right in the center of the biggest fireball I could manage. It didn't kill her, didn't even seem to hurt her, really, but for a minute she looked the same way. Gray-green skin. Covered in thorns."

Simon's face wrinkled into a slow frown. "*Did* she."

Janey pushed on. "And the guy we're going after. Gutierrez. He had the long fingers like you, but did you notice the undersides of his hands? Same color. Same thorns."

Simon swallowed. "Sorry, no, I didn't notice that. I guess I was too busy getting my blood sucked out."

"So that's three Augments, who can do three very different things, but all manifest the same characteristics."

When Simon didn't answer, Sha'dae said, "Sounds to me like we've all got some kind of commonality. Some kind of shared foundation."

Tim spoke for the first time since they'd gotten on the road. "Maybe not all of us. You heard what the Plowman said. We're supposed to be military archetypes. Janey's Recon, I'm Medical, so on and so forth. But then you get people like you, Simon, and Aphrodite, and I'm guessing everybody else from Stamford's Special Wing. They're the ones the Plowman's brother activated after he'd been hurt. They're the ones that dumped all the archetypes together and stirred. The Plowman talked about mixing yellow and blue and getting polka dots. Sounds to me like you blend everything together and get gray-green and thorn-covered."

Simon cocked one eyebrow up. "Oh yeah? Well, bear this in mind, Beanpole. You and Muscles and Brain Girl here all got Augmented after *I* did. So what's that tell you?"

Tim's eyes widened. He got very quiet.

Nathan said, "Okay, got the location. It's just a house. A house in a neighborhood." Nathan squinted at the screen, and expanded the view with two fingers. "Kind of a nice neighborhood, from what I can tell."

The front door opened. Adam walked in. He didn't look at anyone as he climbed the stairs and disappeared down the hallway. Janey said, "All right, then. Time to move."

The din of alarms and sirens Janey had heard the night before was all but gone now. A single ambulance wailed in the distance as they materialized inside the gated community where Kyle Gutierrez and Anastasia Coletti were—or at least where they had been recently, according to the Plowman's message. The gates of Winter Breeze, as it was called, stood wide open.

Janey led the way through the neighborhood. It didn't look deserted, quite, since there were plenty of cars parked in driveways and on the curb, but it seemed...dead. Nothing moved. Janey spotted a couple of dogs rooting through trash cans, but aside from them, the place might as well have been an abandoned movie set.

None of them had anything in the way of formal tactical training—Nathan had mournfully commented, "That's what we had Agent Grassley and Ashley for"—so the best Janey could recommend was that they split up and approach the house from multiple angles. She sent Nathan to the front door while she went around to the back, and asked Simon to climb as quietly as he could up to the second floor and try to peek in a window or two. Tim hung back, ready to rush forward if needed.

The house was the kind of place Janey thought of as a McMansion, situated on a plot of land barely large enough to contain it, and she was pretty sure that if she were on the second floor, she could lean out a window and touch the wall of the next house over. Like the other residences in Winter Breeze, it was half-siding, half-mountain stone, with a spacious two-car garage facing the street. As she slipped between two other houses on her approach to the target's back door, she saw that each home did have a reasonably large backyard, most of them with chain-link fences. Enough that the real estate agents could market them to dog owners.

Janey sent a thought to the whole crew. *How we doing, guys?*

So I just walk up and ring the bell? Won't that spook him?

Janey chuckled inwardly—Nathan's actual speaking voice had dropped by an octave, but his thoughts still sounded like the skinny kid she'd first met.

Simon's thoughts rose to the forefront. *I can see the girl. I'm on the roof of the house next door, and I can see her in an upstairs bedroom. She's wrapped up with duct tape, wrists and ankles, lying on a bed. Looks unhurt, near as I can tell. Think she's been crying.*

Janey's mind whirled. Back in Stamford's West Virginia complex, Gutierrez had appeared to need blood, and a good bit of it, before he could teleport. If they could get Anastasia away from him, and prevent him from exsanguinating anyone else, they ought to be able to cart her off problem-free. But what if she'd misread Gutierrez's Augmentation? What if each dose of blood allowed him to teleport a certain number of times?

Janey realized her thoughts had leaked into the group awareness when Simon broke in. *It may be even worse than that. Gutierrez has a couple of similarities to me, I know, and the thing is, once I've gotten to know someone's blood, it's pretty damn easy for me to track that person.*

Sha'dae connected those dots from back in the lodge. *So even if we get Anastasia away, if Gutierrez can track her, and if he's got more juice left in him, he could just grab her and disappear again, and we'd never find either of them.*

Tim's thoughts flowed in. *One question that deserves an answer, though. Why is Gutierrez here? Why'd he bring Anastasia here, instead of taking her to Stamford?*

Janey nodded to herself. *Maybe he's already resisting.* She sidled around the corner of the house closest to their target, and sucked in a sharp, quiet breath. Gutierrez was sitting in the middle of the backyard, on a small, decorative concrete bench, staring at a rose bush. He looked completely normal—no elongated fingers, no predatory, needle-toothed jaw. He just looked...*sad*.

Janey regulated her breathing with some effort. *Okay, I'm going to grab Anastasia and take her back to the lodge. It'll be a few minutes, but then I want to come back and...I guess try to talk to Gutierrez. You guys just stay here and watch him, okay? Don't spook him.*

Tim's thoughts indicated an acknowledgement without using any actual words.

Janey flickered up to the roof of the house next door, appearing out of the shadows right next to Simon. He pointed through the window. Janey vanished and reappeared in the bedroom. She felt guilty about it, but she was grateful that Gutierrez had taped the girl's mouth shut, because Anastasia tried her best to scream her lungs out when she saw Janey. Janey didn't want to create any fireballs that would draw Gutierrez's attention, so she picked the girl up, flickered out the window and down to the street, and moved in a long series of short jumps that took them out of the neighborhood and several miles down the road. By then, Anastasia seemed to have realized who Janey was, and stopped screaming. Janey said, "Don't worry, okay? I'm taking you somewhere safe."

Anastasia hid her face against Janey's collarbone. Janey flickered the two of them several hundred feet in the air and, leaving behind a massive fireball, teleported them straight to the lodge. Vessler and Scott were there at the door, with Sha'dae right behind them, waiting to take Anastasia inside. Janey peeled the tape off her mouth, and Anastasia gasped out, "Thank you. Thank you. Don't hurt Kyle, okay? He's—he's confused."

Vessler said, "You heading back now?"

Janey nodded. To Anastasia, she said, "I'll do my best." Janey moved off the porch, out of the radius of the light above the door, and vanished.

The journey back was much easier, since she knew the way, more or less, and was able to navigate by familiar landmarks. She materialized behind Tim, who waited across the street, right where she'd left him.

Everyone. I'm back. Anastasia asked me not to hurt Gutierrez. She says he's confused, so what we were thinking, about him trying to resist Stamford, might be accurate.

Tim squeezed her upper arm reassuringly. Janey made a few alterations to her wardrobe and flickered across the street.

Behind the house where Anastasia had been held, a gate broke the chain-link fence's perimeter, not far from the bench where Gutierrez sat. Janey crept over to it, making no sound, but once she'd reached it she straightened up and cleared her throat. "Excuse me? Sir?" She had lost the helmet and the gauntlets, and her raincoat again covered the Vylar suit. As far as anyone who didn't know her could tell, she was just a normal, tall, athletic woman.

Gutierrez looked over his shoulder at her. Janey saw his eyes glistening. Tear-tracks on his face. "Who are you?"

"My name is Janey. Are you all right?" She made an expansive gesture around her. "With all of *this*, y'know, a lot of people need help."

Gutierrez turned on the bench to face her. His shoulders slumped. "I don't know what's going on. I don't know what I should do. I know what I was supposed to do, but now it doesn't seem right."

"Would it be okay if I came in? Just to your yard, I mean. Could I talk to you?"

Gutierrez shrugged without looking at Janey. "Sure. I guess."

Janey carefully lifted the horseshoe-shaped latch and swung the gate open. It squealed, metal on metal, as she slipped inside. Gutierrez didn't move as she padded across the recently-trimmed grass. She stopped fifteen feet away. "Can I ask your name?"

"Kyle." He didn't hesitate. "I'm Kyle. And you're Janey, you said?"

She smiled. "That's right. Kyle, I'd really like to help you, if I can. Do you believe me?"

Gutierrez raised his head and cocked it to one side, studying her face. "You look nice. You seem nice. I like your eyes." He squinted, the squint became a grimace, and he thumped the heel of one hand against his temple. "I wasn't going to hurt her. I only tied her up because I didn't know what to do with her. I don't know what to do, I don't know what to do!"

"I can tell you what to do," Aphrodite Lupo said, as she and Julian Roth materialized right behind him.

17

The air behind Aphrodite Lupo buzzed and blurred as Julian Roth disappeared. Over the space of three seconds, the black static shimmered in and out of existence, and disgorged Parker and Beverly, the two other Abominations Aphrodite had recruited in the mine complex. Beverly's face, where Simon had bitten her, had re-formed into something halfway between ice and scar tissue.

"Don't move," Aphrodite said. "The best part's coming up."

The black static cloud reappeared, solidified—and Sha'dae stumbled out of it.

Before Janey could react, Parker wrapped her up in a chokehold. Janey knew the positioning of his arms well. It was a move she'd used herself countless times. Only the tiniest flex of Parker's inhumanly strong muscles would snap Sha'dae's neck.

"Wait—Aphrodite. Don't hurt her. Let her go."

Tim, Nathan, and Simon came racing into the backyard. None of them could see Sha'dae at first, hidden as she was by Parker's bulk and by the haze in the air left by both Julian Roth and Beverly. Janey waved them around Aphrodite's group, pushing thoughts at them: *They've got Sha'dae, don't engage, don't engage!* But Sha'dae's cool flow of information, Janey realized, had disappeared, and Janey's thoughts went nowhere.

"I'm sorry." The pressure of Parker's arm had changed Sha'dae's voice, straining it. "I couldn't—couldn't warn you. She's...in my head...cut me off..."

Janey got in front of Nathan as soon as he saw Sha'dae in Parker's clutches. She knew she couldn't stop him physically, not without tele-porting him somewhere, but she put her gauntleted hands on his chest all the same. "Don't make any moves!" Janey spoke quietly, but packed each word with purpose. "Don't do anything! Not yet!"

Kyle Gutierrez had stood up off the concrete bench, and pivoted between the two clusters of people, eyes saucer-round in the moonlight. His hands fidgeted like those of a little boy who didn't want to see his parents fighting.

Nathan didn't say a word, but the muscles along his jaw stood out in sharp relief. Tim and Simon flanked him, and Janey heard Simon whisper, "They haven't seen what I can do. Just give the signal. I'll rip off some heads."

Janey turned and looked past Kyle Gutierrez to Aphrodite. Only the young woman's head was recognizable. Her body bore no trace of femi-ninity now. Staring, Janey didn't really think it looked masculine, either, not exactly. Aphrodite's limbs and trunk had more of the quality of the Belgian Blue bulls that people on the Internet claimed were pumped full of steroids. Aphrodite's eyes had turned from normal, human blue to their Augmented version, each socket a storm of red sparks swirling against a candlelight-yellow background.

Janey thought she could probably get Sha'dae out of Parker's grip. It was full dark, the nearest light source was a weak light bulb over the house's back door, and with a pair of short flickers, she could carry Sha'dae high into the sky, and from there back to the safety of the ski lodge.

But that would leave Tim, Nathan, and Simon to deal with Aphrodite and her cadre of beasts. And it wouldn't do a thing to address the problem that Janey thought she'd solved on the ranch in Texas: Aphrodite Lupo would still be alive, and would still come after them.

Evil Plastic Man. How did you kill someone like that? Janey had no idea.

"Aphrodite." Janey took a step forward, and saw Kyle Gutierrez flinch. "Can we talk? We've never really tried to talk before. Just engaged in a bit of banter before trying to kill each other."

Aphrodite's left lower eyelid twitched a few times. "I wasn't trying to kill you. I was trying to do for you, what I've done for these fine people." She raised grotesquely muscular arms to gesture at everyone standing on her side of the bench.

"Not to me," Sha'dae ground out.

Aphrodite gave Sha'dae a sidelong frown. "No need to nitpick."

"Okay," Janey said. "All right, you weren't trying to kill me. At least, not at first. And when you were trying to recruit me, you kept saying you needed me to fight with you in the coming war."

Tim leaned forward a couple of inches and murmured near Janey's ear. "*Where are you going with this?*"

Janey ignored him. "Do you still feel that way? Are you still preparing for the war?"

The bones in Aphrodite's face rippled and hitched in almost exactly the same way Janey had seen Simon's do. "Of *course*. We need soldiers. We're *all* soldiers. You were supposed to be a soldier."

Janey took another step closer. She kept her hands open and visible. "Okay, well—let me ask this: who are the two sides in this war?"

Aphrodite frowned. She opened her mouth, and a horrible, forked, green-gray tongue flicked across her front teeth. "It's...it's us. Versus them. Us versus them. That's the way all wars are."

"And...who is us?"

This time every bone in Aphrodite's skull rippled and shifted. The yellow in her eyes flared. Drowned out the red. "Us. Us! Everybody!" Her lips curved, working, working at a word, and three long seconds later it emerged. "*Humans.*"

Janey couldn't help herself. She grinned. "Right. Right! Aphrodite, you are exactly right! All of us are under attack. All of us humans." She gestured all around them. "Everyone getting sick? That's the enemy's first strike. They've hit us hard. Now. Do you know who *they* are? The 'them' in 'us vs. them'?"

Aphrodite grimaced as if in pain. She pushed a finger into her left ear. "It's the, the, the people who...who put me in Command. Who put the voice in my head. Who made the world break apart and go back together and break apart." She dropped her hand and locked eyes with Janey, and her voice pitched low. Conspiratorial. "They're here *now*?"

"They're coming. Yes. And here's the thing, Aphrodite. Here's the important part. We don't have to fight each other. We can work together, and fight them. We can fight for our own world. For Earth. *Together.*"

The momentary confusion leached away from Aphrodite's face, replaced by an icy, cruel smile. "You only say that because you know you can't beat me."

"We beat you once," Nathan said from over Janey's shoulder, and Janey hissed at him and made a *back off* gesture that she hoped was inconspicuous.

"But—but, but I only had two soldiers then. Now I have three. Four, once I convince Kyle what he needs to do."

Gutierrez's jaw dropped open, and he crouched down beside the bench and covered his head with his arms.

Janey said, "That's true. But you could have eight, including the four of us and Sha'dae. Or even twelve, if you count a few more of our friends."

Aphrodite's gaze lowered until she stared at the ground. Janey took the opportunity to shoot Julian Roth a look that she hoped conveyed equal parts confusion and annoyance. Roth winced, and silently mouthed the word, "*Sorry,*" and then what might have been, "*She made me do it.*"

Into the silence, Janey said, "But it's really important to know one thing. Aphrodite... the presence that got installed in your mind. It's from the Plowman's people. Does it...do *you* have details about them?"

Aphrodite shook her head. "Negative. Negative. Data corrupted or missing." She speared Janey with suspicious eyes. "Would you really fight with me? Fight *for* me?"

"If we can all focus on the real enemy, and stop trying to hurt each other? Sure, I'd fight for you." She added a hair more emphasis: "But you need to let Sha'dae go. Right now."

Aphrodite chewed on her lips as she appeared to consider that. "Nnnn... no. Not yet. If we let her go, you could do your flickering thing and all of a sudden we're standing here talking to ourselves. But...but you think that Plowman person...thing... You think the Plowman can give you more information about...about the enemy. You've got a way to find him? You think it'll work?"

Operating purely on gut-level instinct, Janey said, "That's correct."

Aphrodite stretched hugely. Her musculature had grown so thick, for a moment she didn't appear human at all, but more like some kind of evolved gorilla. "Then here's what we're going to do. Parker is going to slide a teeny-tiny little probe up Sha'dae's nose. So tiny she won't even feel it. But if she tries to do something I don't like, that probe is going to poke *so* many holes in her brain."

A wet, pink strand of tissue slid out of the tip of one of Parker's fingers. The strand lengthened, wriggled and waved through the air, and disappeared up Sha'dae's left nostril. Nathan made a sound of anguish Janey had never heard before. She was a little glad she couldn't see him.

Parker relaxed his grip on Sha'dae, and Janey sprang around the bench to her, followed by Nathan half a second later. Janey said, "Are you okay, what'd they do to you, are you hurt?"

Nathan took her in his arms, and moved to kiss her, but recoiled at the up-close sight of the slimy, living tether joining Sha'dae to Parker. Sha'dae gave him a single, sad nod. "Not the time, baby." To Janey: "I'm fine. Just— she's getting stronger. She crashed into my head and I couldn't...I couldn't do anything about it."

Aphrodite said, "That's right. I'm stronger. Muscles, mind, everything."

Janey stepped over, right in front of Aphrodite, and discovered she had grown two or three inches taller than Janey's six feet. "All right, what do you want to do? Why haven't you turned Sha'dae loose?"

"Why do you think? We're *all* going to find the Plowman. *Together.*"

18

"You need to let Sha'dae communicate with us." Janey took a number of deep breaths, willing her body not to tremble.

Aphrodite said, "What's stopping her? She can still talk."

Sha'dae turned, wincing as the slimy pink strand of tissue stretched and moved with her. "It's a matter of getting where we need to go. I need to…for lack of a better term, I need to tune in on someone who's already there."

Aphrodite cut her red-spark-storm eyes toward Julian Roth. "Is that accurate?"

"It sounds plausible." He paused. "I always wondered how she got to places out of her line of sight."

Aphrodite shrugged, muscles rippling beneath skin stretched tight. "Do anything I don't like and she dies." Her eyes slid closed…

…and the cool silver stream flooded into Janey's mind. *Sha'dae. It's going to be all right. We're going to get you out of this.*

Sha'dae's thoughts quavered. Nathan's rushed in: *Sweetie I'm so sorry I shouldn't have let this happen I'm going to kill every one of these bastards rip their spines out and jump fucking rope with them.*

Sha'dae shook her head, all but imperceptibly, but because of the mental connection, everyone in the group understood immediately. *I can't* keep Aphrodite out for long. *Janey, we're going to take all of these people back to the ski lodge? Don't we need to keep them as far away from it as possible?*

Janey sighed. Tim's words rose to the top. *Doesn't look to me like we have any choice. Not when this, what'd she call him, Parker? Not when he's got you in this situation.*

Janey moved close enough to take one of Sha'dae's hands in hers. *We need to let Vessler and Scott know what's going on, and that we're coming.*

Simon's words bulled in, tense and menacing. *Janey. Seriously. We can take these guys. You were there for what I did to your car. Let me cut loose and I'll have them scattered around the yard in drippy little chunks.*

Aloud, Janey said, "Let them know we're coming." Sha'dae nodded and made a show of concentrating, and silently Janey spoke to Simon. *When you change it's not instantaneous, and in the four or five seconds it'd take, Parker could turn Sha'dae's brain into Swiss cheese. I don't like our options here any more than you do. But I don't see us having any others.*

Tim projected a new spark of hope. *Even if he did damage her brain, I could heal her.*

Simon's thoughts surged. *Right. Right! Caroline healed me, and my entire head was off. What's a few puncture wounds in the old gray matter?*

Janey's fists clenched. *The effort it took your friend to bring you back killed her, Simon. I'm not going to risk losing Tim or Sha'dae, or maybe both of them, when we've got an alternative where we all live.*

"All right," Sha'dae said. "Mr. Vessler is about as happy as you'd expect him to be. But they're ready." To Janey: *Scott's ready to serve as your beacon.*

Janey turned to Aphrodite. "I can't teleport a group this big, I don't think, but I can manage four at a time." She scanned the small crowd. "I'll take Kyle, Beverly, and Simon—"*And I'll expect you to keep them in line, Simon, when I'm not there*—"come back for you, Julian, and Nathan, and the last trip will be Parker, Sha'dae, and Tim. Tim, you stay with Sha'dae the whole time."

Parker's rockslide voice rumbled out. "Think he can fix things faster than I can tear them up?"

She made her scowl as authoritative as she could. "It's our goal to make sure it doesn't come to that. Right?"

Parker's beady, dark-brown eyes narrowed at her. He said nothing else.

"All right," Janey said. "If we're going to do this, let's do it. Everyone ready?" When no one spoke, Janey beckoned Kyle and Beverly closer. Simon stepped up behind her and put a hand on her shoulder. Janey peered at Beverly's ice-scarred features, blurred by the freezing mist, and tried to ignore the gooseflesh that rose along her limbs as the air temperature plummeted. "Can you...get less foggy? More, uh, corporeal?"

For the first time, the hard, malicious light faded in Beverly's eyes. "I fucking wish."

"Well, I need to touch you. May I have a wrist?"

Beverly peered over at Kyle, who had already held his arm out, and over Janey's shoulder at Simon. Wordlessly she offered her hand, and when Janey closed her fingers over the woman's wrist, it felt like plunging her arm in ice water. Janey closed her eyes, rode the cool silver stream to Scott Charles's mind back at the ski lodge, and in a burst of heat the four of them vanished.

J aney sagged against Tim. She had just arrived with him and Sha'dae and Parker, and moonlight through the branches above them high-lighted the glistening strand that still connected Parker and Sha'dae. Janey couldn't recall the last time she had used the flickering so *fast*. Maybe never. The time spent in transit with each group had totaled thir-teen seconds, and as she caught her breath, the heat wave from the last fireball, high overhead, made its way down to them, a remnant of her final trip to Kyle Gutierrez's house in North Carolina.

Janey stayed beside Tim and Sha'dae, watching as Parker's great huffing breaths emerged into the chill, damp night air as clouds of steam. Kyle Gutierrez had begun to cry. Aphrodite had a hand on his shoulder, keeping him in place.

Aphrodite took in the lodge with a long, measured look. "So this is your headquarters now. Going to blow it up, too?"

The lodge door sprang open. Adam came rushing out, but saw the crowd—especially Parker—and almost fell off the steps. He sought out Janey, and she went to him.

"Janey, what the *what the hell*?"

She leaned in close to his ear. "We had no choice. Are Mr. Vessler and

Scott still in there?" Janey had had visions of Vessler saying *Fuck it* and hitting the road with Scott before they could get back.

"Yeah, they're here, but—"

"How are all the—" Janey caught herself.

How are all the humans?

Adam seemed to know what she was asking, if not how she almost asked it. "Mrs. Kapoor's still looking after them. Everybody's good. I mean, they're stable, Janey, Scott would only tell me bits and pieces, *who are these people?*"

They're the fucked-up Augments that Derek Stamford was keeping locked up in his basement.

Janey knew she couldn't say that out loud. Not when Aphrodite would no doubt hear her. And not that it would placate Adam in any way. "Adam, I always hate it when people say this in movies, but I just flat don't have time to explain." She turned to everyone else. "All right. Let's get inside."

Janey stood in a corner of the living room and watched as the twisted parade came through the front door. Her own ability to teleport, and the years she'd spent thinking about it and what it meant about the nature of the world around her, as horizon-broadening as it was, had done little to prepare her for Beverly the Ice Girl, or the awful sight of Parker, tethered to Sha'dae, walking into the living room. A small part of her mind insisted that she had stumbled into a Halloween party, that she was simply looking at people wearing very convincing costumes.

Adam came and stood on her left side. Tim moved over to her right. Neither man looked at or acknowledged the other, and Janey felt an entirely different kind of anxiety pour in on top of everything else.

Once everyone had come in, Garrison Vessler emerged from the master bedroom. Janey figured he had Scott stashed in there, probably along with Mrs. Kapoor. Vessler's forehead wrinkled ferociously as he took in the assembled Augments. "Jesus Holy Savior on the mountain," he breathed, and his eyes locked on Parker and Sha'dae. "What the hell do you think you're doing to her?"

Aphrodite Lupo didn't move, but her voice filled every corner of the room. "We're being careful. According to Janey, if we get this one..." She gestured at Sha'dae. "...in the same room with a couple of other mental types, they can figure out where the Plowman is. And he's supposed to be able to tell me about the enemy." The spark-storm eyes glowed. "The *real* enemy. But I'm not convinced there *is* a real enemy. Other than you people. So until we know better, my new friend Parker has a little insurance policy sunk into Miss Wilkerson's nasal cavity, less than an inch from her brain. How's that for a sum-up?"

Vessler's head swiveled. He locked onto Janey. She nodded, and lowered her gaze to the floor.

To no one in particular, Vessler said, "All right. But I'm telling you now. If anyone touches these kids. Either of them. Even *touches* them. I'll fucking kill you with my bare hands."

Janey knew Vessler's own Augmentation, a failed attempt at the same kind of icy ability that Beverly had, was nowhere near powerful enough to take out someone like Parker, let alone Aphrodite herself. But Vessler was decades older than anyone else in the room, and had the experience and confidence to make his words rock-solid believable.

Aphrodite said, "If there really is an enemy out there? One worth fighting? You'll get no trouble from any of us."

Janey almost jumped when Adam threaded his fingers through hers and squeezed her hand. She returned the pressure, but didn't look at him.

Vessler disappeared into the master bedroom and, seconds later, came back out with Scott and Anastasia. Scott had one arm around Anastasia's waist, and it struck Janey that she was looking backward through time. She remembered the tiny, frail, sickly child Scott was when she first met him, and saw those qualities mirrored in Anastasia now. Compared with her, Scott looked like a paragon of health, both physical and mental. Anastasia clung to Scott, and kept her eyes on the hardwood floor.

Vessler said, "So what needs to happen?" His voice came out in a growl more natural than Janey had ever managed, no matter how much effort she'd put into it.

Sha'dae cleared her throat. "Scott. You and Anastasia come over here, okay?" She dragged her eyes up to meet Parker's. "Can you…" Sha'dae wiggled her fingers at the thin pink cable of tissue attaching her to him. "Can you give me some slack, here?"

Parker said nothing, didn't even move, but the tissue cable extended further from the tip of his finger. Sha'dae moved out into the center of the living room and beckoned Scott and Anastasia to her. "Give me your hands, kids, okay?"

Anastasia looked to Scott for reassurance. He nodded, and murmured, "It's all right," and she let go of him and moved over to Sha'dae's left side. Scott stepped closer, so that the three of them formed a triangle, and they linked hands.

"You know who we're looking for," Sha'dae said softly. Her eyes glimmered a beautiful violet. "But this is what you guys do, not me. I'm just helping. So reach out. Do your thing. And if you need a boost, that's what I'm here for."

Scott and Anastasia, who still hadn't made a sound, closed their eyes, and a second later Sha'dae did as well, though violet light glowed through her eyelids. Adam tilted his head closer to Janey's and whispered, "What's supposed to happen?" But before Janey could answer, the lights in the room flickered, dimmed, and an image like a violet hologram appeared in the air in the center of the triangle Sha'dae, Scott, and Anastasia made.

It was the Plowman. Bound by his wrists with multiple loops of heavy chain, suspended in the air, great gashes and craters all over his body.

Anastasia screamed, and in response, the Plowman lifted his head. "Help me." Barely audible, but filled with misery. "Help me. Please."

A shadow fell across the Plowman's image. Huge. Distorted. Nowhere close to human. The image vanished. Anastasia let go of Sha'dae's hand and flung herself against Scott, gripping him tight with both arms, and Sha'dae turned to Janey. "We have to hurry," she said, her eyes shimmering with violet motes. "It's going to kill him."

Janey stood on the side of the disused road, next to a sign proclaiming the city limit line of Cartersville, Georgia. The long, low building that lay before them in the gloom reminded her of a decaying tree, fallen in a forest unheard, its death having made no sound. Janey knew from the Google Maps data Nathan had laboriously pulled up on his phone that this place had once been a community sports complex, hosting after-school basketball programs and boxing leagues. Now it stretched out, falling in on itself, the surrounding parking lot all but reclaimed by the grassy meadow it had once overtaken.

The other nine Augments clustered around her. They hadn't been able to find any kind of blueprint, so none of them had any idea what lay inside the building.

Nathan stood next to Sha'dae, her hand in his, on the other side from Parker. The strand of tissue pulsed and throbbed as it disappeared inside her nostril, and she shivered as Parker moved closer to her, his tendons creaking and squealing like the wooden bones of an old house. "I like you," Parker breathed. "You're pretty."

Janey took a step toward Parker, but Nathan spoke before she could do anything else, cranking his head back to stare up into the creature's tiny eyes. "She doesn't belong to you."

Parker chuffed out a hot breath in Nathan's face, but didn't respond otherwise. Sha'dae pressed into Nathan's side. *If it's all the same to you, I'd rather not provoke the thing with the weird claw inside my head, okay?*

Nathan winced. *Sorry.*

Aphrodite got closer to Janey. "Julian's good at looking for things. Exploring places. Right, Julian?" Aphrodite didn't look at Julian Roth, but he nodded. "So he should go first."

"I'm a Scout, Aphrodite. It's what I was meant to do." Janey took advantage of how the black mesh hid her eyes to study Julian. "He and I will go together. This shouldn't take more than a couple of minutes."

Tim touched her upper arm. *Stay in contact, all right? And be careful.*

Don't worry. We'll be right back.

Janey motioned to Julian. "You start at that end, I'll start at this end, we'll meet in the middle. Sound good?"

"Yeah. Okay."

Janey directed a thought at Sha'dae. *Can you make it so everyone can see what each of us is seeing?*

I think so. I haven't established a link with Julian yet, though.

Janey beckoned Julian over. He drifted closer, the air around him buzzing like an agitated hornet's nest, and Janey held one arm out. "Here. Do this. Sha'dae needs to touch you for a second."

Aphrodite interposed her bulk between Julian and Sha'dae. "Wait, wait, what's this? What're you doing?"

Janey glared up at Aphrodite and put her hands on her hips. "Do you want to see what he sees? Sha'dae needs to touch him. Just for a moment."

Aphrodite's eyes dulled. "She didn't have to touch *me*."

"That's because you can do things Julian can't."

Aphrodite growled, but backed away, and Julian Roth held out a timid hand. Sha'dae laid her palm on the back of it, her eyes glinted violet—

—and Sha'dae and Janey, standing closest to Julian, both recoiled as waves of an intense, agonizing, soul-deep *hunger* washed over them. It faded after only a second, but the memory lingered, gnawing at Janey's mind. Silently, she asked Sha'dae to open a channel just for her and Julian.

I need to talk to you.

Julian's entire mental presence gave off feelings of guilt and sheepishness. *I know. I'm sorry. Janey, I'm so sorry, she found me. I did the best I could. She* wanted *to just show up and kill everyone. I convinced her to take Sha'dae, and try to recruit you all again.*

Janey chewed that over. *Then I guess I owe you a big "thanks."*

Nah. I'm just treading water here. Feels like that's what we're all doing—trying not to drown, hoping the sharks don't come up and start taking bites.

Janey let her face betray nothing. She pointed at the end of the building she'd indicated before. "Okay. Let's do it."

Julian nodded and vanished. No burst of heat, nothing, but thirty yards away—half the distance to the building—she saw him materialize for a split second before vanishing again. *That's his range.* Thirty yards at a time, in line of sight, with or without darkness. Good information to have.

Janey walked a short distance from the group, flickered away in a burst of heat that left the grass beneath her brown and dry, and reappeared at the building's closer entrance. The heavy steel door had once had a small window set into it at eye level, but the glass had long since been broken out, and Janey easily flickered from one side of the door to the other. No moonlight reached the inside of the building. She powered her night vision up to full strength.

A hallway stretched out before her, windows on one side and doors spaced far apart on the other. Near as she could tell from the outside, the structure was a basic rectangle with either four or five multi-purpose gymnasiums side by side down its length. Now, from inside, she could see that each gym was separated by restrooms. Her boots making no noise on the dusty tile floor, Janey crept down the hallway toward the first doors on her left.

Janey felt a wave of pity for Julian Roth. If he couldn't break free of Aphrodite, what could she do to help him?

Janey. Julian's thoughts rushed into her mind, quivering. *You need to get down here.*

Just as she received his words, Sha'dae opened the channel so that, in a strange, organic version of the picture-in-picture feature of a television, Janey could see through Julian's eyes. She heard a collective gasp from everyone still outside, even as she sucked in a sharp breath herself. Two bursts of heat took her down the hallway to Julian's side, where they both peered into the building's middle gymnasium.

The Plowman hung from one of the I-beams high overhead, suspended by his wrists from a heavy chain. He looked even worse now than when Sha'dae had shown them the hologram. One of his legs clung to his torso only by thin threads of metal, which smoked and popped with random sparks. Half of his ribcage had been crushed in, and his neck was broken, so that his head hung down onto his chest.

Julian moved closer to her. *What are those...those things?*

Janey had seen a sight like this before. The Plowman's communication center, buried under the ranch in Texas, had looked like this: a field of chest-high, flexible, metallic columns, each one swaying like the tendrils of some giant, bizarre sea anemone, every one of them aglow with swarms of tiny, multi-colored points of light swimming just beneath their surface. The columns filled the center of the gym floor, surrounding the Plowman, all of them oriented on him as they swayed back and forth as if to an invisible current.

But Janey had never seen anything like the thing that stalked through the columns, circling the Plowman, its glowing, lightning-blue gaze never leaving the Plowman's ruined head.

It's a giant spider.

That was Janey's first thought, but she knew it was inaccurate as soon as it formed in her head. The thing was more like a grizzly bear, but with eight legs instead of four. Eight long, thick, muscular legs—an octopedal mammal. And it had a head, but instead of a muzzle full of fangs, the front of its skull was flat, with four gleaming, blue-white, lidless eyes set in a field of... Janey stared, trying to understand it. The eyes, arranged in a diamond pattern, nestled in a plane of hairless flesh that, near as Janey could tell, had similar color-changing properties as cuttlefish skin. Waves and shapes of iridescent colors rippled and shifted across its surface, never settling, never stopping.

The display left Janey slack-jawed. It was *gorgeous*. Horrifying and gut-wrenching and spectacular.

After a few seconds, Janey managed to tear her gaze away from the creature's face, and she noticed the glint and gleam of metal along its limbs, encasing its torso. As it moved, she heard the faint whirring of motors.

Julian's thoughts reached her. *Janey. Am I nuts, or...is that thing wearing battle armor?*

The octoped lifted one forelimb, and Janey's eyes widened at the movement. Every joint on its body seemed to be a ball-and-socket, rather than a hinge, and as the raised limb moved into the faint light cast by the columns, a *hand* opened at the end of it. Not like a human hand. Eight uniform-length digits were set evenly around a circular "palm," and as she watched the hand move, she thought the joints of the fingers must have been constructed like the joints of the legs as well.

A long, pointed, metal claw clad the tip of each finger in an extension of the armor.

Seven fingers folded up into the palm, leaving one extended. That single digit pointed at the Plowman. The columns all flexed toward the Plowman and turned the same blue-white shade as the octoped's eyes, and the Plowman screamed. Tiny pinpoints of light appeared on the surface of the Plowman's skin, blue and yellow and green and white, but as Janey watched, transfixed, one by one they turned the same shade of blue-white as the columns.

The octoped made a sound. It hurt Janey's ears, but the more she listened to it, the more she realized two things. First, it was language—the giant armored arachnoid thing was talking to the Plowman. Second, it was a language the human brain was not designed to comprehend. Janey's vision blurred around the edges, and she had to grab hold of the door-frame to keep from tipping over sideways, even as her stomach tried to rebel and rise toward her throat.

A voice made its way to her: Tim. *What the* hell *is that thing?*

Janey fought her gorge back down and focused all her mental energy on Aphrodite and Parker. *If we don't stop it, it's is going to kill the Plowman. We need all hands on deck. You have GOT TO LET SHA'DAE GO and GET DOWN HERE.*

Sha'dae's thoughts rushed into Janey's mind on a tide of relief, and for a heartbeat, Janey could feel it along with Sha'dae as the glistening strand of tissue withdrew from inside her head, sliding out and away along her cheek.

Julian. Janey saw the young man turn toward her, and when she dragged her eyes away from the bizarre sight in the gym, she noticed he'd begun crying. *Go get everyone else.*

Julian vanished almost before she'd finished the last word. Janey didn't blame him for wanting to get the hell away. The Plowman was a massive, seven-foot mechanical construct inhabited by an extra-terrestrial consciousness, and the octoped that circled him amid the flexing columns had reduced him to tatters.

The air buzzed around her as, one by one, the rest of the group materialized. Tim and Simon, Nathan and Sha'dae with their arms around each other, Aphrodite with Parker and Beverly and Kyle Gutierrez. Disembodied whispers filled the corridor.

Aphrodite stared. Her eyes switched from red-on-yellow to normal blue and back again, switched and returned, switched and returned. *It's real. The enemy. It's...it's real. You weren't lying.* She put one huge, brick-like, hard-as-wood hand on the back of Janey's neck, but it wasn't a threatening gesture. Instead, it was a gesture one old friend would make to another—an expression of confidence. Of *praise.* Aphrodite lowered her head and looked into Janey's eyes. *You were right. You were right, Janey, all this time.* Waves of elation poured off of her.

The whispers abruptly vanished.

This is what we're supposed to fight. This is the war. This is my purpose! Before Janey realized what was happening, Aphrodite Lupo gathered her up in a full bear-hug and gently shook her back and forth, an ear-to-ear grin stretching her face. *Thank you! Janey, thank you, thank you, I can never say thank you enough!* She set Janey back on her feet.

And you know what we have to do here, right? We have to get the Plowman away from that thing, so he can tell us what he knows about the enemy. We need more information. Aphrodite nodded, still beaming, and Janey turned to face the rest of the group, making sure Sha'dae had opened a channel to each person.

Aphrodite put a hand on Janey's arm. *Janey. Also. I'm really sorry about all the times I tried to kill you. That was bad.*

Janey had no idea what to do with that. She patted Aphrodite's hand.

Tim and Simon stood there, side by side, having just watched that exchange between Janey and Aphrodite, and Janey wished she had time to take a photo so she could capture the looks on their faces. *All right. Everyone. I don't know what that thing is any more than you do, other than the obvious. It's got to be an alien. I don't know its capabilities. But we need the Plowman alive, and it's too bright in there for me to just grab him and leave. Julian, you could do it, but I'm afraid your range is too limited to get him to safety fast enough. That leaves you, Kyle.*

Kyle Gutierrez had withdrawn into himself to such an extent that he reminded Janey of Anastasia. Janey went to him and lifted his chin with one finger. "Kyle," she whispered. "Can you help us?"

Kyle's thoughts crowded into Janey's, wild and uncontrolled. *No I can't I can't I don't want to I don't want to! Mr. Stamford made me do it, I had to do it, don't be like him don't make me don't make me!*

Simon Grove's thoughts boiled and frothed. *All right, he's useless. That leaves nine, and four of us are heavyweights. Let's just go in there and rip that eight-legged motherfucker in half.*

Beverly appeared in the thought-stream. *We could do that. Parker, don't you want to cut loose?*

Janey almost yelped when Parker's thoughts reached them. His mental communication bore no resemblance to the rockslide-voice. Instead, he sounded younger than Scott. *That sounds like fun. Yeah. Hurt the big spider.*

Wait. Kyle Gutierrez closed his eyes and took a deep breath. *Wait. I can try it. I can try it.*

Janey faced him. *Are you sure? All you need to do is get to the Plowman and teleport him away from here. Back to the lodge would be best, but anywhere far away would work, and then we can come and find you. Can you do that?*

Kyle nodded. *David always told me I needed to be brave. Had to be brave. That's what I want to do. Be brave.* Kyle's jaw distended. His fingers lengthened, discolored, and sprouted thorns. *Go and get the big man and be brave!*

Kyle Gutierrez closed his eyes and began to bleed. Janey almost cursed, the effect looked so similar to Simon Grove's warped abilities. The blood appeared all over his skin, beading on his face, his hands, soaking through his clothes—and he vanished.

Kyle reappeared right between the Plowman and the huge octoped, and Janey heard him say, "It's all right, I'm getting you out of here," and Kyle wrapped his fingers around the Plowman's arm, and the octoped drove one of its forelimbs all the way through Kyle's back and out his chest.

Beverly screamed.

The octoped turned its head and looked at the doors of the gym, as it picked Kyle's twitching, spasming body up off the floor, gripped it with two more metal-clawed hands, and tore it apart.

Janey said, "Wait, we need a plan!" as Parker burst through the gym doors and charged across the dirty hardwood with a roar that shook the building's walls. Aphrodite sprinted after them, and Janey had just enough time to catch Tim's eye and say, "Well, fuck me," before the armored, extraterrestrial giant bear-spider turned to face them.

Sha'dae said, "What do we do?"

Nathan almost stepped on Sha'dae's words with, "Do we go in, too? Do we try to help?"

Julian Roth buzzed and vanished, and Beverly disappeared into an air duct with an icy hiss. Simon's jaw had already dropped, filling with needle teeth, and his forearms and fingers elongated as Janey watched, their tips becoming harpoon-like points with backswept barbs.

"Tim, you and Sha'dae hang back, and Nathan, you keep an eye on them. Simon, it's too bright in there for me to do my thing. Let's get rid of as many of those columns as we can. Dim it down some."

Simon grinned horribly. "Works for me."

They raced into the gym just as Parker reached the octoped.

As soon as the armored alien had become aware of the Augments attacking it, all of the flexing columns had bent toward the intruders, but the octoped hadn't moved. It still just stood there, waiting, until Parker launched himself at its mesmerizing face, his scaled, clawed hands drawn back and ready to do damage.

The octoped moved forward and brought one closed fist around and straight down onto the top of Parker's skull, which split wide open, splattering blood and bits of bone as if a grenade had gone off inside his head. Parker collapsed. The octoped reached down and gripped him with three arms, which it used to fling him all the way across the gym. Parker struck the cinder block wall with a wet, crunching, meaty sound, and his thick purple blood sprayed out in a grisly fan on the wall. He slid down and crumpled to the floor in a sodden heap.

Janey and Simon made it to the edge of the field of glowing columns just as Aphrodite reached the octoped.

Aphrodite barreled across the floor, and by the time the armored octoped turned to face her, she had converted both of her fists into dense, bony, spike-covered balls, each one like the head of a mace, and when the octoped took a step toward her, she lunged forward and smashed one of those spiked balls into a knee. The octoped's leg bent sideways, but immediately snapped back into shape, and one of its clawed, metal-clad hands clamped down around Aphrodite's throat. It lifted her off the ground, holding her by her neck, and drew back its other hand to strike, but Aphrodite's head deformed, lost its shape, and she dropped through the giant's fist.

"Nice try," Aphrodite shrieked, in the same tone a child would use while plummeting down a drop on a roller-coaster.

Janey concentrated on the task at hand: mowing down the columns. Simon had transformed his fists into enormous, bone-hard claws, his body gaining mass and turning a now-familiar grayish-green. Janey swung her katana. If the lights from the columns were too bright and too numerous for her to flicker away with the Plowman, well…that left her little choice but to put those lights out.

The katana's rainbow-finished blade sliced into the first column with surprisingly little resistance. Janey had hacked through brick with the sword before, and these things were nowhere near that hard. It took two, sometimes three blows, but she could take a column off its base, and as soon as it came free, the swirling lights within it winked out. Janey glanced over to see Simon enjoying the same kind of success, his massive, muscle-knotted, thorn-covered arms driving back and forth like a pair of scythes. Between them, one by one, they hacked the columns loose, and bit by bit the gymnasium grew darker.

Aphrodite's head had returned to its normal shape as soon as she slipped out of the giant's grasp, and it appeared to Janey that Aphrodite had decided to favor speed over raw strength. She kept the spiked, bony wrecking balls on the ends of her wrists, and began hammering the horse-sized spider creature like some kind of bizarre percussion instrument. The octoped twisted, lunged, tried to grab her, but Aphrodite's body changed in subtle ways. Her limbs elongated, her hinged joints became ball-and-socket, just like the creature's, and while the octoped couldn't seem to get a hand on her, she unleashed a fury on it that made Janey shudder to witness. Janey had taken more than one blow from Aphrodite herself, and to witness the octoped's armor denting and tearing—to see, amid the relentless clanging and crumpling, strips and chunks of it torn off the great flailing body—put Janey right back into the painted room where Aphrodite had driven a cluster of knife-like fingers into her chest.

Movement off to one side caught Janey's eye. She paused, turned her head to see Parker—alive and whole—rise from the ruined husk the octoped had destroyed. But the same motion showed her a red glow from the corner of her eye, and she pivoted to look back the way she and Simon had come in.

The columns were reattaching themselves.

Wriggling across the floor like the severed trunks of giant elephants, they found their bases and melded, metal into metal. In each one, the swarming lights re-ignited, and the shadows in the room retreated.

Simon came to her side, panting. "Now would be a really fucking good time to have one of those blackout grenades, wouldn't it?"

Parker roared and pounded his way across the floor toward Aphrodite and the alien. He batted shimmering columns aside and, as Aphrodite ripped a segment of armor off the octoped's underside, Parker smashed into the creature with the force of a speeding car. The octoped crashed to the gym floor, hardwood planks splintering under the impact, and Parker and Aphrodite piled on top of it, two sets of fists ramming into the metal body like piledrivers.

"Janey…"

The voice was weak, but instantly recognizable. Janey whirled and sprinted to the Plowman's side. His ruined neck forced his head to hang down onto his chest, but he could still talk, and he turned one yellow eye toward her. "You came."

"We'll get you out of here, don't worry. Just let me get you down. Simon, I guess you're going to have to drag him out of here."

Simon's eyes, white pinpoints in black fields, left faint trails of light in the air as he nodded his head. "Sure, he only weighs, what, a ton?" He cracked his knuckles. "Might take a few minutes, but we'll get him out."

The Plowman said, "The Assassin will not allow you to do that."

"That's what that thing is called? The Assassin? Well, I don't think it's going to have much to say about it, considering what Aphrodite and Parker are doing to it."

A tortured metallic shriek filled the gym, and the floor shook as Parker slammed into the wooden planks halfway to the door. Aphrodite smashed into the Plowman's side, her body distorting with the impact, and Sha'dae's and Tim's voices both hit Janey's mind with the force of a fire hose: *Get out of there Janey you've got to get away!*

The Assassin pried itself the rest of the way out of the splintered crater in the floor, and with another metallic shriek, its torso began to *lengthen*. New segments of metal rose from an armored band just above its waist, one after another, and new arms sprouted from its thorax. Janey watched with a cold crawl of revulsion as the Assassin became an enormous, metal-clad centipede, a glowing blue-white eye identical to the ones in its face appearing on the back of each new hand.

"Janey," the Plowman whispered. "I know what you're trying to do with the columns, but you won't be able to damage them fast enough. You've got to shut off the power source."

Janey couldn't take her eyes off the growing, shrieking, twisted monstrosity across the floor. "Where is it? How do I do it?"

"Somewhere below us. That's all I know."

The Assassin's impossible body whipsawed across the wooden floor like someone dying of strychnine poisoning. Before it stopped moving, an icy fog flowed across the planks toward it, and the rear third of its many-limbed body turned white and froze in place. Beverly's ghostly face hovered near it, her lips skinned back into a ferocious snarl, and the creeping, freezing ice worked its way forward.

The Assassin rose up like a striking snake, pivoting 180 degrees on one of its segmented joints and lashed out at Beverly, but its multiple slashing limbs cut through nothing but fog. The air buzzed, Julian appeared right behind the Assassin and calmly stepped forward, and when he vanished again, two of the alien's centipede-like arms vanished along with him.

The Assassin roared. A ripple shook its way along the spine, and in less than a second every bit of ice Beverly had coated it with shattered and blew apart, spraying icy shrapnel across the gym.

Aphrodite picked herself up off the floor, her body writhing and distorting, and forty feet away, Parker shook himself and got up.

Aphrodite said, "Okay. Now I'm pissed off."

The Assassin roared again, and along the creature's entire length, battle armor expanded and encased every hand with blade-like claws.

"Run," the Plowman said. "Kill the power source. Go."

"Yeah." Simon took on more mass, the gray-green thorns growing longer everywhere on his skin, and the scythe-like blades that had once been his fists crackled as their length extended. "Do what the big man says. We got this."

Janey turned and sprinted back to the doors of the gym. *Nathan! Where are you?*

Her question answered itself when she skidded out into the hallway. Nathan, Tim, and Sha'dae stood there, alternately staring at her and at the Assassin with expressions of undisguised horror. "I'm right here," Nathan said in a tiny voice. "Protecting Sha'dae. And Tim."

Janey grabbed his wrist. "You're coming with me. I might need more muscle than I've got." Before he could say anything else, she flickered with him down the length of the corridor.

Janey launched into another flickering search pattern, swiftly and steadily covering every square inch of the building. Nathan didn't try to speak aloud. *What are we looking for?*

The Plowman said there was a power source below us. The place has to have a basement. Boiler room, maintenance room, something. She could barely entertain the thought of the alternative: that the Assassin had simply dug a pit and buried the thing they were looking for. If that was what had happened, they'd likely never find it.

There! Nathan pointed at a plain gray door next to one of the bathrooms, labeled AUTHORIZED PERSONNEL ONLY. Janey flickered to it, tried the handle, and found it locked—and Nathan dug his hands into the metal and ripped it out of the frame.

From down the corridor came more roars and shrieks, and the walls shook. Janey thrust her thoughts into the silver stream: *Are you still watching? What's happening?*

Sha'dae came back. *Oh! Sorry! I let the, uh, the thing lapse.* The picture-in-picture image returned, and Janey could barely even tell what she was looking at. The Assassin had grown even larger and moved with greater speed, and Beverly's freezing assault no longer seemed to affect it, as the creature's armor now glowed red along every seam. Janey saw it fasten one of its razor-clawed hands around Parker's throat, and Parker yelped and writhed as the heat of the Assassin's armor burned into his flesh.

Nathan nudged Janey's elbow. *We're going down there, right?*

Janey peered into the darkness beyond the door Nathan had destroyed —impenetrable for normal humans, but clear as crystal for her. *Stay here, okay? If I need you, I'll come back and get you.*

She expected him to argue, but Nathan just nodded gravely. Janey left him in the hallway and took the concrete steps leading downward three at a time.

The basement of the building had been constructed with someone shorter than Janey in mind. She picked her way rapidly through it, skirting piles of moldy cardboard boxes and ducking under pipes that carried nothing now but stale air and stagnant water. Every few seconds she heard a faint, echoing scream, and another impact shook loose sprays of dust and bits of concrete from the ceiling above her. Janey snuck glances through Sha'dae's eyes at the melee overhead, but only a second at a time. She couldn't afford to let herself get distracted.

It didn't take long for her to find her objective. At the far end of the basement, partially encased in what appeared to be bars of granite, a roughly spherical object had been embedded into a wall. It pulsed and glowed with the same blue-white light as the Assassin's eyes.

Guys, I'm about to take a really straightforward approach to this. Here's hoping it's more like snuffing out a candle than setting off a bomb.

Immediately she heard Nathan's thudding footsteps as he careened down into the basement, and Tim fairly shouted at her. *Bomb? What bomb? What're you—*

Janey threw the katana at the glowing red object with every shred of strength she could muster. She'd thought at first to run forward and stab the sword into it, but the cascade of lightning that lit the basement in a hellish glare upon the katana's impact made her glad she'd reconsidered. The blue-white glare that poured out of the—what was it? An engine? A battery? The glare blasting out of the sphere drove away any chance of flickering out of there, and just as Nathan reached her, the Assassin tore a hole through the ceiling and lunged down into the basement after her.

"Oh no you don't, you fucker," Nathan gritted out, and before Janey could stop him, Nathan launched himself onto the Assassin's shoulders, wrapped his arms around the rippling, four-eyed head, and tore it off the centipede-like body.

The Assassin jerked back up through the hole in the ceiling, dislodging Nathan as it went. Nathan crashed to the basement floor amid a heap of dislodged pipes and chunks of broken concrete, the Assassin's head bouncing away into the shadows. The blue-white sphere had stopped throwing lightning into every surface around it, and now just gave out fitful sparks, and Janey heard Sha'dae's thoughts: *Janey! The lights on the columns! They're going out!*

Janey wrenched the katana out of the sphere. *Julian! Grab everybody but the Plowman and get them out of here! Get as far away as you can, as fast as you can!*

Julian's thoughts came through, weak but steady. *That's a can do. What's about to happen?*

Remember what I did to my Basement, back in Atlanta?

Urgency threaded its way through Julian's words. *Yes! Yes I do! Say no more!*

Janey grabbed Nathan's wrist again as he staggered upright, shaking concrete dust out of his hair, and flickered with him fifteen feet straight up, which put them back in the central gymnasium. The Assassin writhed on the floor, clawed hands ripping up chunks of wood, and Janey saw the stump of its neck glow. In seconds it had a new head, but while those seconds passed, the air in the gym grew loud with a familiar buzzing, the air blurring as Julian Roth worked his magic. When the Assassin finally turned its lightning eyes on Janey, the only beings left in the gym were it, Janey, and the Plowman.

All of the columns, in unison, went dark.

Janey flickered to the Plowman and wrapped her arms around him. *Is everyone clear?*

Julian and Sha'dae spoke in unison. *Yes! Do it!*

Janey teleported herself and the Plowman straight to the ski lodge's driveway in one leap, knowing that covering that distance all at once meant the community sports center had just become a flame-filled crater in her wake, with the Assassin right in the middle of it.

19

Janey and the Plowman flickered out of the shadows onto the gravel driveway. Janey slumped to the ground, exhausted, the gravel pressing through the Vylar along her arms and legs. The Plowman collapsed in a crunching heap. Janey turned her head and saw the yellow glow of his eyes burning steadily.

"What do you need?" she asked him.

"Metal. A lot of it."

Janey sat up and looked behind her as Julian Roth's signature vibration sounded out. She didn't know where he was teleporting people in from—it had to be somewhere close—and she could only imagine what traveling cross-country must have been like for him and for his...passengers? Cargo? Covering miles like that, thirty yards at a time. One by one, with Julian shimmering in and out of existence, everyone from the gymnasium appeared. Janey had only teleported with Julian like this once, and she remembered how much rougher, how much more disorienting, his personal method of transport was than her own. Tim, Sha'dae, and Nathan all staggered in different directions and, within seconds of each other, puked their guts out on the cold, leaf-covered mountain ground. Janey couldn't tell if Parker felt any ill-effects or not. Aphrodite, Beverly, and Simon, on the other hand, could easily have just stepped out of a coffee shop after enjoying a bagel and a latte.

Janey got to her feet and went to Tim. She gestured toward a patch of gravel near the Plowman. "Keep everybody away from there for a few minutes, okay?"

Tim nodded, and had taken a breath to speak, but Janey flickered up and away before he could make a sound. It took her a bit less than two minutes to find an unattended car—a several-year-old Toyota sedan—parked on the road outside a cabin half a mile away, and flicker with it back to the lodge. It was the first time she'd ever teleported anything so big. As the car crunched into the gravel next to the Plowman's outstretched hand, Janey sank to her knees, gasping for breath.

Immediately, the entire back half of the Toyota disintegrated and flowed into the Plowman's hands. His neck turned, aligning itself, recon-figuring until his head sat properly, perched between his shoulders as it should be. The flesh-and-tendon-like cables snaked and coiled inside his body, filling in, repairing. The leg that had hung by tatters drew up into the hip socket. The Plowman climbed to his feet, rolled his head around, and faced everyone. The Toyota sat at his back, half-destroyed. Janey thought it looked more like some kind of modern art installation than a vehicle now.

"Once again, I owe you my life," the Plowman said to Janey. His yellow eyes glimmered and pulsed.

"Not just me." Janey waved at the rest of the group, as those whose stomachs had revolted came back to join the others. "We all took part."

And one of us lost his life. Janey wondered if that was fair, or appropri-ate, thinking of Kyle Gutierrez as "one of them."

The mechanical yellow eyes raked across the small crowd. They narrowed when they came to Aphrodite Lupo. "Ms. Lupo. You and Janey Sinclair are…cooperating?"

Aphrodite's head tilted crazily to one side. "Life is stranger than fiction." She left the group to come and stand in front of him. "Until tonight, I didn't know who the enemy was. Not really." A ripple spread through Aphrodite's grotesque musculature. "But now I do. And it's all real. The whole reason for…for *me*…is *real*."

Adam and Mrs. Kapoor came out onto the porch. Janey saw Adam about to descend the steps, and held up a finger. *Wait.* He did, pausing on the top step.

Tim, Sha'dae, and Nathan came to Janey's side. Janey spoke to the

Plowman. "Now that you're here, and, uh, fixed up—do you know what's going on with this plague? It seems to us that it's got to be something to do with your people, but we didn't know for sure."

The Plowman's head had swiveled in Janey's direction as soon as she started talking. "I can tell you about the sickness, yes, but soon after that I must leave. I have attempted to dampen any signals the Assassin might use to track me, but before I repaired myself, something might have been transmitted. It is not my desire to lead the Assassin here."

"Thoughtful of you," Simon said, from right behind Janey's shoulder, where she hadn't realized he'd come to stand.

She didn't jump—barely—but she jabbed him in the arm with her elbow and hissed, "*Quiet.*" Simon quirked up his face and rolled his eyes, but didn't say anything else.

Janey noticed Tim watching that interchange. *Something you want to say?*

Tim kept his eyes on the Plowman. *If I can think of words to express how freaking bizarre it is that we're all acting like chums with Simon fucking Grove, I'll let you know.*

Sha'dae, moving as far away as she could get from Parker, had huddled up beside Nathan and begun to shiver in the early morning cold. Nathan said, "Hey—guys? Could we move this inside? Some of us didn't think to wear our longjohns."

Janey took note of the eastern sky, which had begun to turn a soft gray. She asked the Plowman, "How long do you have? Before you need to leave?"

"Six point five minutes. Do you have anyone here afflicted by the sickness?"

"Several people, inside, yeah."

The Plowman knelt, drew back one huge, brick-like fist, and drove it into the ground. He pulled it out again, slowly, clutching a handful of dirt, and turned his palm to face the sky. "This. This is the mechanism for transmitting the sickness."

Tim said, "Dirt? It's in the ground?"

"Not dirt. But in the ground, yes. Look." The golden glow from the Plowman's eyes ramped up, burning like twin searchlights, and when that radiance fell on his fist, it lit up a *net*. No, Janey decided, not a net. More like a web. A delicate web of filaments, each one narrower than a human hair. The web led down from the Plowman's hand and disappeared into the ground in every direction. From the looks of it, Janey thought it must have been buried about four inches below the surface.

Nathan stared, bug-eyed. "What the merciful *fuck* is that?"

"The latticework," the Plowman said. Janey got the impression he was keeping his voice carefully neutral.

Parker snorted, snarled, and dropped to all fours, digging into the ground on the far side of the driveway.

Beverly breathed out, "How far does it *go?*"

The Plowman turned his hand back over and released the web, which snapped back into place. Janey could see it glowing in the tiny pit the Plowman's hand had made. When he extinguished the lights in his eyes, the web turned invisible.

Parker grated out, "I can't find it! Where is it? Shine that light over here!"

The Plowman shook his head. "Finding it will make no difference. Your planet has been seeded with it. Micro-drones deposited the seeding modules, the modules deployed and expanded, and now the surface of your world has been covered. It is a nanoparticle configuration. Breaking it will do no good. It will self-repair." The Plowman stood. "This is not something humanity can change. Your world has been permanently altered."

Vessler and Scott had come out on the porch to join Adam and Mrs. Kapoor, and while the Plowman talked, Vessler stepped down and walked over to join Janey. He said, "It's called the latticework, you said? What purpose does it serve?"

"If you will take me to one of the ones touched by it, I can tell you."

Aware of how quickly six and a half minutes could slide by, Janey beckoned him to follow her. "Come on, then." She led the Plowman up the stairs, which creaked alarmingly under his weight, past Adam, who stared at the massive synthetic alien with wide, watery eyes, and into the living room. The rest of the crew filed in after them. Glancing over her shoulder, Janey saw Mrs. Kapoor almost knock Tim down with the force of her hug, and heard her ask her son if he was all right. She didn't hear the answer.

Janey opened the door to the master bedroom and waved the Plowman in. He had to duck to get through the doorway. The Plowman moved to the side of the bed where Zach Feygen lay motionless beside his wife, knelt, and placed the palm of his hand on Feygen's forehead. The Plowman's hand was so huge it covered most of Feygen's face. The yellow eyes slid closed. Janey was the only one who'd followed the Plowman into the room, but she saw Nathan and Sha'dae lingering in the doorway, watching silently.

The Plowman opened his eyes and stood. "It is as I suspected. What you might call a conventional approach."

Janey could barely contain herself. "What? What is it? What's it doing to them?"

The Plowman's gaze slid from the Feygens to Janey. "It has put them into a coma. But that part you already knew. The much more important question is *why*. Why these people are affected, but not others."

Janey nodded quickly. "Right, yes, the doctor I spoke to wanted to know the same thing. Because it happened all at once, all over the world, to people who hadn't been to the same places or had the same food or anything. Why them? And what's this all got to do with the latticework?"

At this point, Vessler, Scott, and Tim joined Nathan and Sha'dae in the doorway.

"The latticework is the delivery system. Once in place, it cultivated a specialized virus and released it into the atmosphere. As you said—all over the world. All at once. As for the objective, my people are, I am sure you understand, much more technologically advanced than yours. They have engineered this virus to attack only non-Augmented humans who display a certain pattern in the activity of their neurons and synapses."

Janey frowned. "Meaning what?"

"Meaning the virus targets those who hold certain specific *beliefs*. Beliefs that can be quantified, targeted, and attacked based on brain activity."

Adam stepped through the knot of people in the doorway and came to stand beside Janey. He looked the Plowman square in the face. "Okay, but what? What beliefs get targeted?"

The Plowman's yellow eyes seemed to bore into Adam as he answered. "The virus targets all those who, when presented with an extraterrestrial threat, will resist. Those who will *not* fight back are unaffected."

Silence filled the room like a noxious gas.

T he sun had been up for better than two hours, but Anna Grove couldn't stop thinking she was having a nightmare. Her best friend in the world, Jessica Siede, lay in the spare bedroom of Anna's secluded house. Anna had tried to move her to the SUV, but she wasn't strong enough to get Jessica all the way through the house and up onto the seat. She had tried for a solid hour the night before, and had only what felt like a torn muscle in her shoulder to show for it.

Her friend Jim Fautsch had not followed Anna and Jessica. He was still in Louisiana, and hadn't answered the phone when Anna called him. Neither had the 9-1-1 operator. Anna had finally maneuvered Jessica into the spare room's bed, using the last of her strength and making her damaged shoulder worse, and then driven the SUV into town to try to get help.

Anna had insisted that she and Jessica move away from their new home outside Nashville after Janey Sinclair found them. The last thing Anna wanted was for anyone to be able to just look her up, like any regular person. This time, she had paid in cash to rent a decent-sized house in rural Ohio, and as far as any public records were concerned, the renter was a woman named "A. Smith."

The nearest town's hospital looked exactly like the others Anna had seen on the news before the station stopped broadcasting: overrun with ambulances, people crowding the ER, doctors and nurses moving, frantic, from one new patient to the next. Anna sat, parked, watching the scene, and saw the hospital staff begin turning ambulances away. She could imagine what they were saying. *No room. No room.*

Anna drove slowly back to her house. Aside from the chaos at the hospital, the rest of the town seemed to be deserted. Nearly a ghost town —everyone holing up in their homes, locking their doors, huddling in fear. She couldn't blame them. That's exactly what she intended to do when she got back.

Anna saw two teenage boys throw a trash can through the front window of a shoe store, but as soon as they heard the engine of her SUV, they darted away like frightened rabbits.

What if Jessica doesn't wake up?

Anna didn't know how to take care of someone in a coma. That was the word the newscasters had used. *Coma.* Anna had never been around anyone in a coma before, not even in any of her movie roles. She had already tried to get Jessica to drink something, but the water had mostly just run off her lips and onto the pillow, and what little did find its way into her mouth had made her gag and cough. Rolling her onto her side had let the coughing fade, but Anna knew she couldn't just do nothing. Jessica had three days. Anna knew a human could live without water for three days.

Anna had pulled into her house's carport, turned off the key, and taken the key out of the ignition when her son Simon opened the door from the kitchen and locked eyes with her, and Anna screamed. She tried to jam the key back into the ignition, but fumbled it and dropped the keys onto the floorboard, and when Simon stepped closer and rapped on her window with his knuckles, she screamed again.

Deep breaths. Deep breaths. Simon's dead. You're hallucinating.

Simon was still there when she opened her eyes. Growing rapidly more detached from her sense of reality, Anna opened the door and stepped out of the car.

"Hi, Mom."

She searched his face. He looked like Simon, and sounded like him, but…it wasn't Simon. Something had changed. Something basic. Down in the bedrock.

"Who are you?"

He rolled his eyes. "Denial. Right on cue. C'mon inside, Mom, I want to talk to you."

Simon, or whoever the person was that looked like Simon, turned and disappeared into the kitchen. Anna shot feverish glances around the garage, looking for a weapon, something, anything to protect herself—but she knew what Simon was capable of, and that nothing she could pick up would make any difference if he decided to hurt her. She also knew how fast he could run. Mutely, she shut the SUV's door and followed her son into the house.

Anna found Simon in the living room, flopped on the couch, his arms spread along its back and his feet up on the coffee table. He motioned to her favorite chair—she'd taken the chair to Tennessee, and from there to

Ohio, one of the few possessions she refused to give up—so she sank into it. Her knees trembled.

"You're dead. You're supposed to be dead. Janey Sinclair said she killed you. She said she…cut your head off."

Simon tilted his head up and pointed to the thin white scar that went all the way around his neck. "And she did, too. Not one to lie, that Janey."

"Then…how are you here?" She blinked. "You're not real. This isn't real. The outbreak, the trauma, it's affected my mind." Anna gasped. "Oh God. Oh God, is this what the sickness does? Does it put you into a coma, and you start hallucinating? I'm in a coma right now, aren't I?"

Simon groaned. "Don't make me regret coming here. I don't have much time, and there's an awful lot of things I could've been doing, but I bribed an associate to bring me to see you instead."

"But she cut your head off."

Simon leaned forward, elbows on his knees. "Yeah, and then someone else put it back on and healed me. Mom. Come on. You know what I can do. You know what *you* can do. And I'm sure Janey let you in on her bag of tricks. Right? So if you can accept all of that, what's to stop you from thinking I could get over a little decapitation?"

Anna's mouth had gone almost too dry to form words. "Then…what do you want?"

Simon's eyes narrowed. He took a while to answer. "Y'know, there's a part of me that's really fucking offended that that's how you greet your son. Your previously dead son. 'What do you want?' That's the best you can do? Not 'Thank God you're all right,' or 'It's so good to see you,' or 'How've you been,' even?" He stood and began pacing. Anna sat still, watching him. "But then I think, okay, it's not like you don't have reason to be freaked out. Like you said, I *did* get my head cut off. And, I mean, beheadings aside, you knew what I was up to. Right? Before I left Louisiana, I mean. The girls. You knew about them."

Anna discovered that tears had spilled out of her eyes and tracked down her cheeks. She couldn't think of anything to say.

Simon went on. "Yeah, there were…there were more girls. Quite a few more. I was on my own at first, but then I got some help. A woman I thought was my friend. She, ah, she provided for me, let's say." He stopped pacing and turned to face her. "Now here's the part I don't expect you to believe. But I wanted to come here and say it. All of it."

He hesitated. Anna swallowed hard. "You...wanted to say...what?"

Simon came over and knelt by her chair and took one of her hands in both of his. Her son's skin was warm and dry and supple, like the finest leather, and chills ran up Anna's spine as she realized it didn't feel like human skin at all. It was more like the time when the animal wrangler on set had talked her into touching a massive python that had been sunning itself on a rock all afternoon.

Simon said, "A couple of things. First, I—okay, *we*—we think we know, pretty much, what this outbreak is now, and we're going to try to stop it. Second..." He trailed off, and gently lowered his forehead so that it rested on the arm of her chair. "Second. I wanted to say I'm sorry." Simon's voice grew stronger as his head came back up. "I'm sorry for all the hurt I've caused. All the hurt I've caused you, and the girls I...I took. And their families. I know 'sorry' doesn't fix anything, doesn't come close to giving back what was stolen away. But I wanted you to know that *I* know. It was all me. Every bit of it. I'm to blame, and I know it was wrong, and if I could go back in time and put a bullet between my own eyes before any of it started, I would do that."

Anna wiped her cheeks dry. "If you're real. If you're my son, and you really mean everything you just said. Why now? Why come here now and tell me all this? Why not sooner?"

Simon let go of her hand and stood. "Well, that's the third thing. I don't know for sure, but there's a pretty damn decent chance I'll be dead soon. So I wanted to say goodbye." He waved one hand toward the spare bedroom. "I looked in on Jess. I know she's one of the ones this plague put the whammy on. What we're going to try to do—I'm doing it for her. I'm doing it for a lot of reasons, but...she was good to me. You were both good to me. And I want to do my best to make it right."

Simon turned toward one of the windows and signaled to someone outside, and Anna heard a strange buzzing sound coming from the carport. Before she realized what he was doing, Simon had bent and kissed her on the cheek. She felt the heat from his face, smelled the scent of his skin, a dark, heavy scent that mingled with a trace of something sweet from his breath. None of it was familiar.

"I don't know who you are," Anna said. "But you're not my son."

Simon straightened up and stood there, gazing down at her, heartbeat after agonizing heartbeat. Finally, he shrugged. "Have it your way. I've said my piece. Goodbye, Mom."

Anna watched the young man who looked like Simon as he strode out to the carport. The buzzing abruptly vanished, and when she went to the door and peered out, no one was there.

I n a converted 747 hangar on a repurposed air field in Minnesota, Derek Stamford floated.

That was how it felt to him, in any case. The brilliant, shimmering, flexing columns that lined the hangar floor buoyed his prone body, passing him along, and every time the tip of a column touched his skin, a flood of tiny, multi-colored lights flowed into him. Stamford's eyelids were closed, but shimmering motes of color shone through them as they danced in his eyes. His engorged penis pressed against the front of his slacks as waves of heat rose from his body.

Almost all of Stamford's human staff was gone now. Collapsed, victims of the outbreak that had crippled the world. He only kept Kay with him now. Stamford didn't need to open his eyes to know that the red-haired, copper-skinned beauty stood at one edge of the communications array, watching him, ready to defend him. His angel of fire. Stamford felt dimly, vaguely guilty that Redfell's brainwashing techniques had reduced her mind to such a shambles.

The millions of pinpoints shifted color, shifted again, and Stamford moaned. He was so close. So close to understanding what had happened to roughly half of the Earth's population in the last twenty-four hours. He had gleaned a word from the extraterrestrial data banks. *Latticework*. So close to a breakthrough. Stamford had mastered every known language of the human species, absorbed every bit of knowledge he could scour from every archive on the planet, and as the heat radiated from his body, he thirsted for more. *So close*. He had spent the last month sifting through all of the information taken from the alien's original comm array, working through it, analyzing it.

Translating it.

Stamford knew, down in his bones, that as soon as he cracked the code, achieved the Rosetta Stone moment and fully understood the aliens' language, he would also understand the purpose of the latticework and the nature of the affliction that had cast so many into coma-like stupors.

Stamford moaned again as another rush of colored lights swept toward him across the array, zeroing in on him, a wave approaching a central point instead of rippling away from it. He was that central point, and as the information poured into his skin, the heat blasting off of him flared like a sun. Stamford's clothes disintegrated, dropping away, reduced to a fine black ash. His penis went flaccid as the lights flooded into him, washing away the coarse, sticky urges that had fueled him for so long. Stamford's hair and eyebrows and eyelashes burned away, just as his clothing had, and where before the lights had ebbed away almost as soon as they had entered him, now they stayed, stayed and built, shining brighter and brighter.

And he saw the latticework. Saw it, felt it. Reveled in it. Saw each and every strand as it crisscrossed the planet's surface. Understood what it had done, producing the virus—the virus that had attacked specific thoughts and beliefs.

No, no, no. Nothing as simple as that. Such a thing can be improved upon.

Stamford reached out, feeling his way along the vast, profound network of information that now encapsulated the planet. Reached out, observed, analyzed…and as the lights swarming and pulsing under his skin grew brighter and brighter—like the throwing of a switch, like the snapping off of a stem, like a sudden idea that presented itself to the mind fully-formed in a nanosecond—Derek Stamford *took control.*

The mantle of that control settled around his mind. He chose to think of it, to perceive it, as a crown. Glowing, golden, woven of the same filaments that made up the latticework. It sank into his brain, and Stamford and the latticework became one.

He sent out a command. The information-dense pulse reached every molecule of the latticework in seconds, and Stamford felt the microscopic engines begin their retooling.

Stamford willed the columns to set him back on his feet at the array's edge, facing Kay, and he walked across the hangar floor to her with no trace whatsoever of a limp. As he drew closer, he could see the lights swarming under his skin reflected in her eyes, a million tiny fireflies in the shape of a man.

"Mr. Stamford, sir," Kay said, "you're lit up like Christmas."

"Yes. Yes, I suppose I am."

In a tone filled with wonder, Kay said, "But what's all those little pointy things?"

Stamford glanced down at his body and noted, with some bemusement, the hundreds of small, curved, wickedly sharp thorns protruding from his suddenly gray-green skin.

20

Janey walked out onto the ski lodge's spacious east-facing deck and held one hand up, shielding her squinting eyes. For once, the sun had burned away all the clouds, providing that rarest of occurrences in the Smoky Mountains: a blue sky, horizon to horizon.

Janey readjusted the T-shirt she'd slept in. She had only awakened five minutes earlier. Just enough time to visit the bathroom and shrug into a pair of jeans. After the Plowman had left, disappearing into another of his holes in the ground, exhaustion had caught up with her again and so, making excuses to everyone else, she had found a quiet corner and curled up in a plush chair for a couple of hours. She knew they were all still deep in crisis mode. But she had very nearly begun to hallucinate, and knew she wouldn't be of any use to anyone if she had a psychotic break from lack of sleep.

Adam sat alone on the steps. The deck overlooked a picturesque mountain stream that wound away from the sheer drop behind the lodge, and Adam had a handful of small pebbles that he chucked into the water every so often. Janey thought Adam knew she was there, but he gave no indication. When he didn't turn around after thirty seconds, she padded across the deck and sat down beside him.

He didn't look at her. "I know what you're going to say."

"Do you?"

A risked glance. Then back to the pebbles. "This is about straws and camels' backs, isn't it?"

The afternoon sunlight turned the cloud of golden curls on his head into a thing of glory. Janey found herself studying it, objectively, as if it were a work of art, rather than part of a living being. She said, "I've never been in this position before." After a sigh, "That's pretty much been the story of my life for the last three years."

Plunk. A pebble disappeared into the water. Janey thought she saw it bouncing and tumbling down the stream bed.

"I wanted it to work, Adam. I really did."

His lips quirked. "It all just...feels like...it feels like it's out of our hands. Or at least, out of my hands. I woke up, and I don't recognize anything anymore."

"It's not fair to you. I know that."

"Y'know...when I met you...I know this is a dead horse I'm beating. But you were an artist. You had your martial arts, sure, but the dojo job was just a way to pay bills when you weren't painting." *Plunk.* "I'd come home and you'd be there, in front of another canvas with paint all over you, and every time I saw you like that I fell in love with you all over again. Standing there, absolutely fucking *radiant*, doing what you were most passionate about, brilliant and sloppy with your hair everywhere, and...I thought I knew what our life was going to be like." Janey took a breath, but Adam said, "Don't apologize. I know you were going to. Please don't."

"But I *am* sorry. I didn't want things to go this way."

Adam shook his head. "All the time I was...*under*. That's how I'm thinking about it. Under. Like I was anesthetized. All that time, I could see the world around me. It was distorted, but the more time I'm awake, the more little bits and pieces come back to me. I can sort of fit them together. Make them make sense. And you know what I remember? I remember you and Tim, showing up there. Together."

"Adam..."

"It's like a...what's the term. A line of demarcation. Looking back, I can see it clearly."

"I don't want you to hurt, I—"

"*Well that's not up to you, is it?*"

Adam stood and took the stairs two at a time. He walked quickly out to the stream's edge, and heaved the rest of the pebbles, firing them into the stream's far bank like bullets from a gun. Janey went after him, but couldn't think of anything to say when she reached him.

"There aren't many relationships that would survive something as traumatic as this," Adam said, and now the bitterness leaked through. "Loss of a loved one...survivor's guilt...these big emotional upheavals. They're fucking poison."

Janey shoved her hands in her pockets. "I don't have to tell you that it's not your fault. Our life was good. It would have been good, if...if things had stayed the way they were."

"But they didn't."

"But they didn't." She nudged a larger pebble with the toe of her shoe. It rolled down the bank and into the water. "My life isn't the same now. I tried to go back to the way it used to be. The way *we* used to be. But I couldn't."

He turned to face her, and his eyes looked ancient. "That's not the whole story, though. You know it isn't."

"Adam, we don't know if what the Plowman said is even true..."

"No. No. I know it is. I've always thought of myself as a pacifist, but how many actual fights have I ever been in? None. Not a single one." He snorted. "I bought that goddamn gun because I thought it could protect me. Protect us. Keep us *out* of fights. I've spent all morning thinking about it, and I can't say the Plowman's wrong. If it came down to it, and everything depended on me doing what you do? Balling up my fists, or picking up a weapon, and saying, 'Okay, it's going to be me dying or you dying.' Or, I guess more likely now, if some weird-ass alien showed up and said he'd kill me if I didn't surrender? It's not a great thing to admit to myself, but Janey, I...I'm not like you. I'm not like..." He waved a hand up at the lodge. "Tim."

Janey's breath had quickened as Adam spoke. "I never asked you to be like me. I never expected you to go out and fight the way I did."

"The way you *do*. Present tense."

She groaned. "Fuck, Adam, I never would've started all this Gray Widow bullshit if you hadn't gotten shot!"

Adam's face went cold. Janey tried to speak, tried to take the words back, but only managed to babble at him. He put a hand up, and after a few more seconds of trying and failing to make sense, she fell silent. He said, "Listen. You, you and all your friends. Tim and Nathan and Sha'dae, everybody here. You're all fighters. This place is like some kind of underground, I don't know, resistance-freedom-fighters thing. I don't belong here."

"But...where—"

"Take me to a hospital. Any hospital. I'm healthy, I'm sane for the most part. I can volunteer there. Help take care of people. I don't know anything about medicine, but I'm good at doing what people ask me to do."

Janey rubbed the back of her neck. "You're handling this really well. A lot better than I would, I'm pretty sure. If our positions were reversed."

He shrugged. It appeared to take a lot of effort. "The fact of the matter is—and I mean no offense by this, it's just the truth—I don't know who you are anymore. I went under, and you were one person. But when I woke up, you were someone else. You'd become something completely different." When she started to protest, he said, "And I'm not talking about the teleportation or the seeing in the dark or how you're strong enough now to make me feel like a dainty little schoolgirl. None of that matters. You've changed on the inside. Your personality, your, your *heart*. And...it's not a bad thing. I'm not saying you've changed for the worse."

Softly, Janey said, "I'm just different."

He nodded. "And that makes *us* different. Listen, I, uh...I hope at some point we can talk again. In a friendly way. Y'know, like...be friends."

"I'd like that, too."

"But it's going to take a while. So...and I realize, this is assuming we don't all end up dead or being living footstools for Zirgnax of Planet Flarglarg. But once I'm gone, for a while, we'd probably better not communicate."

Her eyebrows drew together. "I might not be able to honor that. Especially if I find out you're in danger. I'm going to try to protect you."

Adam laughed. Hollow, distant, like the sound a train makes as it leaves the far end of a long tunnel. "And that pretty much proves everything I've been saying. That'll be another thing for after all this mess is done. The legal part. We'll get that taken care of."

Janey blinked away sudden tears. "Never thought I'd be a divorcée."

"I know. When my parents split up, Mom told me that a big part of what she hated about it was that it felt like failure. Like she wasn't good enough to keep a marriage together. Even though she and Dad knew damn well there was no way to make it work— once they signed the papers, she said it really stung."

Janey was going to say, "That makes a lot of sense," but before she could, the lodge's back door opened and closed. She and Adam both looked up to see Tim standing there, and when he saw them looking at him, he held up a hand in a gesture like *Oh sorry never mind it can wait.* He went back inside, and Adam said, "Y'know...I think I'd like to be alone for a while. Now. I might take a walk."

Janey ran down a list of ridiculous, half-formed thoughts that she might turn into words. None of them seemed appropriate. She said, "Don't go too far, okay?"

Adam nodded, and walked slowly away, following the stream. Janey watched him for ten or fifteen seconds before she jogged up the hill and climbed the steps to the deck. Tim had apparently been watching for her, because he opened the door again and stepped out.

"Sorry about that. I didn't mean to interrupt."

Janey glanced back down toward the stream. Adam was out of sight. She said, "What did you want to talk to me about?"

"Nothing in particular. Just seeing how you were feeling."

Janey worked up the courage to look him in the eye. She'd noticed a quality he'd taken on, ever since he'd healed Adam, that came out whenever he looked at her. Not timidity. More like wariness. Like someone observing a beautiful animal that they knew might bite them at any given second. Janey said, "Can you sit down for a minute?"

Tim's forehead wrinkled up. "Uh...sure?" He led the way to a couple of Adirondack chairs set beside a small wrought-iron table, and waited for her to sit before he did. "What's up?"

"I..." Janey's mind went blank. "I don't know how..."

Tim sat forward. "Don't know how what? Are you okay?"

Well, Tim, now that I've figured out my marriage is over, you get to be my second choice! Isn't that great? Doesn't that do fantastic things for your ego? I bet you've never wanted me more!

"Oh God...I don't know how to say this. And I'm pretty sure you're going to hate me."

Tim's right eyebrow hiked up. "Janey, come on. The only way you could make me hate you is if you, jeez, if you set my parents on fire or something. What is it? What's happened?"

"I just…" She stumbled. "*Shit*, why can't I *talk*? Tim, I—"

Janey choked on her words as the ground beneath them trembled. Every window in the ski lodge shattered, and a terrible voice boomed out, echoing off the mountainsides around them.

"*JANEY SINCLAIR. WE DEMAND YOUR PRESENCE.*"

Janey bolted away from Tim, vaulted over the deck railing and sprinted around to the front of the lodge. She skidded to a stop, her brain scrambling to process the sight that greeted her in the driveway.

Bursting up from a broad hole in the ground, the Assassin's armor-clad, multiple-legged body swayed, towering, the lightning-blue eyes in its re-grown head glaring at her. Its body looped once around the limp, inanimate form of the Plowman.

The Assassin's voice came from somewhere inside it, and Janey thought it sounded like an orchestra playing in Hell. Its words shook the ground with every syllable.

"You. Janey Sinclair is your name. This one—" A couple of the Assassin's forty-plus claw-handed arms gestured at the Plowman's body. "—has let us know that you are amenable to cooperative efforts." Janey heard the front door slam, and felt pounding footsteps, and Aphrodite Lupo, Nathan, and Tim came to a stop beside her, all of them staring up at the alien monstrosity. The Assassin went on. "Yes. Thus demonstrated. You and the Augment known as Aphrodite Lupo now cooperate, where once you were committed to mutual destruction."

Janey traded glances with Aphrodite, and wished she hadn't. Aphrodite's eyes had done their swarming-red-flecks-on-yellow trick, and it made Janey nauseated. Janey said, "That's correct."

Janey heard more footsteps behind her, and felt Sha'dae open the telepathic channel.

Janey! What's going on?

Don't know yet. I can't tell if this thing's going to attack or not. Make sure everyone's ready to fight if it does.

On it!

The ground trembled again. "This one has also told us that you are aware of the latticework."

Janey's thoughts raced, trying to come up with a reason to deny or confirm that. Finally, stretching the words out, she said, "Yes...what does that have to do with anything?"

"One of my functions is the tracing and apprehending of designated parties. It is how I found this Evaluator."

Nathan's voice popped up in Janey's head. *Evaluator? Does he mean the Plowman?*

The Assassin went on. "Ninety-five minutes ago, the human Augment known as Derek Stamford co-opted and corrupted the latticework. This is against our wishes. We must find him."

Tim said, "So? Go find him. You just said that's what you specialize in."

A tremor started at the Assassin's head and ran the length of its body. The Plowman, dangling, slipped a few inches before the centipede arms tightened their grips on him again. "Derek Stamford has cloaked his position. It is not within my capabilities to locate him." The flat, color-shifting face swung up from gazing at Janey to focus on something back toward the lodge. "But you have in your company a collective of Augments which has proven effective in tracking individuals. We propose a cooperative action. A truce. You find Derek Stamford for us, and we will not kill you all."

Garrison Vessler moved up between Janey and Nathan. Speaking as softly as he did, his rumbling voice was almost too low for Janey to make out. "Janey. May I talk to it? To them?"

Just as softly: "By all means."

Vessler cleared his throat. "It would be more convenient if we knew what to call you."

The metal creature trembled again. "Your brains are not configured to understand our name. The appellation the Evaluator provided will suffice. We are the Assassin."

Vessler continued. "All right...Assassin...what will you do with Derek Stamford once you find him?"

No hesitation. "We will kill him."

"And if we give you his whereabouts, you will leave us alone?"

The ground shook. It took Janey a second to realize it might have been what happened when the Assassin laughed. "We will not be the agents of your demise. It will grant a prolonging of life that you may find valuable. But it will not change your individual fates, or the fate of your planet."

Janey said, "We're going to need you to drop the...the Evaluator."

The Assassin immediately quirked its body sideways. The arms released, and the Plowman slid out of its coils and crumpled to the ground. His eyes stared, colorless, dead. "Done."

"And if we tell you where Stamford is, you'll go and get rid of him, and we'll never see you again."

"That is correct, Janey Sinclair."

Tim's voice flowed along the silver stream. *Guys, I don't mean to sound bloodthirsty, but I'm not sure I see a downside to this.*

"You can't kill him," a masculine voice called out—a voice with a pronounced Marathi accent.

Tim yelped and spun around, Janey following less than a second later, and as Tim shouted, *"Dad?"* Janey's jaw gasped. Mr. Kapoor stood on the lodge's front porch, Anastasia held tight against him, a long, shiny butcher knife pressed against her throat. "Stamford is our leader. Our commander. Our god. We cannot allow you to hurt him."

21

"**D**ad, what are you *doing?*" Tim took a running step toward the porch before Janey caught his arm. He whirled on her, black eyes flashing. "Let me go! Janey, *let me go!*"

She pulled him close. Janey was much stronger than Tim, and she tried not to leave bruises. "This isn't your father. I mean, it's not your father's real self. This is Stamford."

Tim jerked his arm out of Janey's grasp, but didn't move. The Assassin's voice rumbled through the ground. "Correct. Derek Stamford has, to use your terminology, reverse-engineered the effect."

Garrison Vessler said, "Shit. *Shit.* It's not attacking specific beliefs now. It's *generating* them."

Mr. Kapoor moved to the edge of the porch. Behind him, Mrs. Kapoor stepped outside, followed by Nicole Grassley, Ashley Strandjev, and Zach and Heather Feygen. All of them held knives. Anastasia wept, her pale eyes shining as tears spilled down her face, but she made no sound.

Sha'dae opened the floodgates on the silver stream—Janey suspected out of shock. A cacophony of voices spilled into her mind, and it took several seconds to sort out those of her friends from Aphrodite Lupo and the rest of her crew. Aphrodite's words were couched in the soft roar of a million whispers.

Enemy must die Assassin enemy kill the Assassin dark-skinned man knife enemy hurt little girl enemy must die must die must die

Aphrodite's mental voice rose into a roar, but Janey projected her own above all the other chatter. *Everyone QUIET! These people are not our enemy! Our enemy is Derek Stamford, and he's forcing them to do this! We have to save Anastasia, but we cannot hurt anyone! Do you all understand that? We cannot hurt any of them!*

Julian Roth's buzzing accompanied his voice. *I think I can shimmer in, grab the girl, and get her out of harm's way before Tim's father has a chance to react.*

Mr. Kapoor pressed the knife into Anastasia's throat hard enough to draw a thin red line in her skin. A single ruby droplet ran down the length of the blade. Mr. Kapoor said, "You all pose a threat to Mr. Stamford. That is unacceptable. You're all going to have to kill yourselves."

Janey saw Tim trembling. *Julian. Are* you *sure* you can grab her before that knife punctures something vital?

The buzzing wavered. *I'm fast. But I don't know if I'm that precise. I might...might grab her and him both by mistake.*

Janey clenched her fists. She called out, "Mr. Kapoor, your plan is flawed. You're telling us to kill ourselves, but your leverage is the death of that girl. If we don't comply, you'll kill her, correct? That's only one death, versus all of ours. It leaves us in a better position if we ignore you."

Scott Charles's panicked voice sprang into Janey's head. *What're you doing? You're telling him to kill her!*

I'm trying to buy us some time! No one's killing anyone!

Janey's eyes flicked over to Zach Feygen. He seemed unfocused. Staring at one of the porch's thick wooden support pillars. *Is he fighting it?* Janey's stomach went icy when she saw Feygen slowly reach behind him and pull a gun from the back of his waistband. He didn't aim it, just held it, his arm hanging straight down.

The ice in her stomach became a freezing, clawing dread. Feygen knew how to use that gun. How many people could he kill with it before they could stop him? How many of the other virus victims would lash out with those knives? Janey's mind raced. *Okay, this isn't a great plan, but it ought to help. Julian, when I give you the signal, you get in there and grab everybody but Mr. Kapoor and Anastasia, and take them out into the woods. Nowhere near each other, and far enough away that they can't just come rushing back here immediately. Can you also get rid of those knives? And Detective Feygen's gun?*

I can do that, yeah, I think so. That's not like pulling someone out of somebody else's grip. But what about Mr. Kapoor and Anastasia?

Before Janey could make any decisions about that, she caught a flash of movement out of the corner of her eye, and turned her head just enough to see Adam, half-hidden behind a broad oak tree. Her brain had time to recognize her husband, then to recognize his posture—it was how he looked after he'd just thrown a pitch at a baseball game—before the fist-sized rock he'd just heaved crunched into Janey's skull.

Janey fell to her knees. She could only see out of one eye. She thought the slow-motion effect with which she witnessed her surroundings must have been because of brain damage. That, or adrenaline, but probably not adrenaline, because she felt no pain, only a warm rushing sensation, as if she'd just been dropped into a rushing, just-the-right-temperature Jacuzzi tub.

Janey saw all of the Augments rushing toward the ski lodge. She heard someone calling her name, and couldn't tell whether the voice was the kind that moved through the air or the kind that just appeared in her head like a spoken ghost. She saw Zach Feygen raise the gun, and the flash of the gun's muzzle, and a different kind of flash, something red and spraying, and Feygen's arm, the gun still clutched in its hand, arced out from the porch and thudded to the ground in front of the Assassin.

She heard Tim's voice, and felt the rumbling of the Assassin as it spoke, and saw another flash of movement off to one side, and her eyes focused on Mr. Kapoor. Still standing on the edge of the porch, still holding Anastasia, still gripping the knife that had begun to part her skin. She saw the shadow of the Assassin as its long body hitched, jerked, one of its arms reaching out, and she realized it had thrown something—a part of its body, it seemed to be, some kind of long black blade, triangular in cross-section. Janey's mind marveled that it could pick out that level of detail in what must have been a tenth of a second.

She saw the black metal blade strike Mr. Kapoor in the bridge of his nose. His skull flew apart like a gourd hit by a shotgun blast, and the arm holding the knife fell limp and useless and dead, and Anastasia ran away from him as his body collapsed, and Tim's raw-throated screaming filled the world.

D erek Stamford swayed atop the tower that all of the columns had become. At his command, the latest communications array had slid across the floor, inch by inch, each column combining with the one ahead of it, and in the center of the vast room the columns had grown into something like a tree. What might have been its branches, radiating out from the crown-like space at its top, cradled Derek Stamford as gently as if he were a newly hatched bird. The lights that swam just under the surface of his skin now pulsed and flared and surged in perfect synchronicity with the lights of the tower tree. Stamford's eyes had lost all color, become a hollow kind of white, and as he lay in the tender embrace of the tower tree, he reached out. Out along all the new strands of perception his elevated status had granted him.

Stamford followed the latticework. That phenomenal achievement, the lace-web that encased all of the inhabited areas of the Earth. His sense of touch, followed quickly by sight and hearing, raced the length of every gossamer filament as they passed through earth and sand and gravel and concrete, as they burrowed effortlessly through steel and traced the contours of the bottoms of rivers and lakes. He traced the latticework's path as it clung to the ocean floor, uniting the web as it spanned from Australia to Asia, from South America to Antarctica.

Never had Derek Stamford loved his planet more than in that moment, and he discovered that, with each passing heartbeat, his love intensified. Stamford wept as the latticework let him feel the stirrings and struggles of countless animals, charging over the strands, burrowing beneath them, some frantic to hide, others frantic to hunt and kill and eat. He felt the sea waters shift and part as vast creatures in the oceans' depths cruised overhead, the gracefulness of their bodies in harsh, hungry juxta-position with their need to prey. Across punishing, barren deserts, along knife-like ridges in the highest mountaintops, through the muck and ooze of the hottest bayous, the latticework was everywhere, saw everything, affected everything.

Stamford knew its purpose. Of course its designers had had no concern with the beauty of the Earth when they deployed it. The lattice-work was a vector, a means to deliver the instrument of subjugation, not a method of observing the intricacies of Earth's ecosystem. And yet Stamford could see it no other way.

His eyes are on the sparrow.

Stamford had heard that, growing up in church. A reference to God, of course. A reassurance that the Lord, all-seeing, all-knowing, the omnipotent, omniscient ruler, knew every detail of every creature ever to live and die on His creation.

But didn't Derek Stamford have that knowledge now? The whole of his life after being changed—after receiving his Augmentation—Stamford had always used the vast capacity of his mind to drink knowledge in, to let it flow into him like a thousand million rivers, filling him so that he became an ocean of knowledge. Now he wondered if he had only ever been seeing half of the picture. Surely no one else had the capacity to understand what he was experiencing now. Surely anyone else who gained access to it would find their poor, unprepared mind fried to a crisp.

Because now Stamford knew everything. Everything on the planet, in the planet, even above the planet, because the latticework measured the air currents and atmospheric patterns just as it knew every molecule of sand and rock and dirt.

That meant Stamford knew every*one*. Every small-town Midwestern farmer, every aspiring basketball star shooting hoops on cracked neighborhood courts, every white-collar criminal on Wall Street sucking the green lifeblood out of the American people. Every construction worker in China, every scientist in Poland, every conservationist desperately trying to keep the Brazilian rainforests from dying a horrible, desiccated death.

Stamford's thoughts turned to his old business partner, Garrison Vessler, now tied to that intensely unpleasant young woman, Janey Sinclair. He knew he could find them. All it would take would be a bit of concentration. A narrowing of focus, rather than the wide-open appreciation of the global existence he had indulged up to now.

But first…

Several times in his tour of the latticework, Stamford had noticed a kind of node. A thickening of the web, through which energy flowed in unexpected directions. He had made note of each location, and now, settling back into the loving embrace of the tower tree, Stamford let his mind flow to the nearest one.

His eyes widened. "Well I'll be damned," he murmured, his voice sounding strange to his own ears. Had it changed? Become harder somehow, sharper-edged? That thought drifted away as Stamford focused on the transmission node.

Because that was what it was: a point of transmission both to and from the source—the author of the latticework—a stream of information gathered by the sprawling web and fired upward. Up, through the sky, into the blackness beyond. Stamford found that infinitely more interesting than Janey Sinclair, and pushed his consciousness into the node, ready to follow the stream if he could.

It felt like...like standing in a wind tunnel. The rush of information battered against his mind. Tore at it. But, if he moved carefully...if he maneuvered just so...

The rush took hold of him. Carried him. Thrust him out, out, out along the screaming pathway.

In the top of the tower tree, Stamford gasped.

"Beautiful..."

Janey watched as Parker scooped the last of the dirt into place, finishing the grave. Tim's father lay there, beneath the earth, and the thought of the latticework reconstructing itself above his inert body filled Janey with the kind of rage that made her teeth grind.

"Thanks, Parker," Janey said.

"I did this because Aphrodite said it was for the best." Parker didn't look at her as he spoke. He turned and began lumbering back toward the lodge. "Not because you wanted me to."

Janey watched him go.

There was little movement outside the lodge at the moment. The Assassin had grudgingly agreed to give them time to recover from the sudden, grisly trauma. Janey didn't know where the spider-like alien was now, but as she followed Parker, she saw Simon huddled over the Plowman's body. Janey wondered if she should think of it as a corpse.

"What are you doing?" she asked as she walked up, but when Simon turned to look at her, the question answered itself. He had taken the battery out of the ruined Toyota and was in the process of hooking it up to the Plowman.

Janey stopped, rocking back on her heels for a moment, trying to figure out why that was a bad idea. She couldn't come up with anything. Finally, she said, "Let me know if that works." Simon gave her a thumbs-up.

Janey paused before she opened the front door. Trying to make sense of the hellish chaos that had descended after Adam drilled her in the head with that rock. Julian had—what did he call it? *Shimmered.* He'd shimmered onto the porch and grabbed Heather first, but Feygen had tried to stop him, and when he teleported her away, that's when Feygen's arm had gotten sheared off. Then the Assassin had thrown the blade at Mr. Kapoor, and... Janey's vision swam. All of the Augments had rushed forward then, and if she could trust her own memory, it was Aphrodite who'd snatched Anastasia away and dropped her at the edge of the lodge's property. Some of the non-Augments were dangerous in their own right, especially Zach Feygen and Ashley Strandjev, but they never stood a chance against the likes of Simon or Nathan or Parker.

Janey knew she'd tried to scream, tried to get the words into everyone's heads, *Don't hurt them don't hurt them it's not their fault* and she guessed the message must have gotten through to some degree, because no one besides Tim's father had died.

She focused on her next clear memory: Tim, crying, as he cradled her head in his hands and healed her. Crying because he'd been too late. Tim could repair the most grievous of injuries, but unlike Simon's Caroline, he couldn't bring anyone back from the dead, and he hadn't been able to heal his father.

Janey remembered sitting up, holding Tim as the sobs tore through his body, and listening as Rhonda Kapoor screamed from the front porch where Parker held her pinned and helpless: "You all have to die! You have to! You want to hurt Mr. Stamford! You deserve to die for that!"

Janey took a deep breath and opened the door. The first person she saw was Aphrodite, a bizarre sight under the best of circumstances, with her Hulk-like body topped by the blonde supermodel head. But now Aphrodite sat on the floor with her back to a heavy leather couch, staring into space, and when she turned to look up at Janey, Janey wondered if maybe the human part of her—the teenager named Agnes Lorch—might have come forward a bit in the last hour or so.

Beyond Aphrodite, Parker lurked in a corner. He had found a can of peaches somewhere, and Janey thought he must have torn the top off with his hands. He stood there, silently and slowly eating peach slices, getting syrup all over his fingers and chin.

Nathan and Sha'dae huddled together on a leather loveseat. Nathan absently stroked Sha'dae's head over the hijab. Beyond the living room, the kitchen was a blurry, cloudy mass, as Julian and Beverly seemed to have taken up residence there. They talked quietly. Janey couldn't make out what they were saying.

Vessler, Scott, Anastasia, and Tim were nowhere to be seen.

Since Aphrodite was closest, and not interacting with anyone else, Janey asked, "Where's Tim? Have you seen him?"

"Everyone in the world is against us," Aphrodite said. In that moment, she definitely sounded like a little girl. "Aren't they? Because of the virus. Everyone on the planet hates us now. They all love Derek Stamford, and they hate us."

Surprising herself, Janey crouched a couple of feet in front of her. "It looks that way, yes."

Aphrodite reached up with a massive, sinewy hand and scratched her scalp, the gesture disarming in its normality. "When I, uh...when I recruit someone...like I tried to do to you. I can see inside them. Inside their heads. Inside what makes them who they are." Her eyes, a very normal dark blue, grew a shade darker. "I saw what Stamford did to them. To the people he kept in the Special Wing. I saw it. All of it. Would you...do you want me to show you?"

"No, no thank you, that's quite all right."

Aphrodite chewed her lower lip. "I don't blame you."

Janey put one knee on the floor and leaned forward. "Listen. Can you tell me who I'm talking to right now? Is this Agnes?"

Aphrodite shook her head, and a wave of sadness rolled off of her. "I don't think there is an Agnes anymore. She really took a beating after what you did, with that room."

Janey flashed back to the blank white room she had covered in her "nightmare paintings," the room where she'd trapped Aphrodite, after discovering that she had a particular susceptibility to the disturbing energy the paintings contained.

Aphrodite went on. "For a while, there was just Command. Now we've kind of... mashed together?" She sighed. "I have good days and bad days. Mostly bad days. But now...all I want to do is fight the enemy. That should be simple, shouldn't it? Point me at the bad guys. Let me rip their spines out. That's why I kept trying to collect people like us. To fight beside me. That's why I wanted *you*." She waved a hand toward the second floor, where Janey knew all the non-Augments were restrained. "But they're not the enemy! Like you said. It's not even their fault. We're out here in the middle of the woods, and they're just regular people, but if everybody on the planet hates us now...*everybody*. That includes all the police officers. All the soldiers. All the people who can, y'know..." She seemed to grasp for the right words. "The people who can push the buttons. That's *everyone*. I can't fight everyone, Janey. I feel like... like maybe Stamford's beaten us."

"Not yet, he hasn't."

"You don't think so?"

"I think it's too early to give up."

Aphrodite stared at Janey for a good ten seconds. She pulled up her knees, wrapped her thick arms around her shins, and hid her face, resting her forehead on her forearms. Her voice muffled, she said, "I hope you're right."

Janey climbed the stairs to the second floor. Vessler was keeping an eye on the captives, all of them bound to chairs in the largest of the bedrooms except for Zach Feygen, who lay on a bed, unconscious. The Assassin had carelessly raked its jagged alien body over Feygen's severed arm where it lay on the ground, reducing it to little more than a red smear in the dirt, which had led to Tim's discovery that he couldn't grow limbs back. Smooth new skin now covered Feygen's stump.

Vessler, leaning against the doorframe, moved most of the way out into the hall as Janey came up to him. He said, "How you holding up?"

"Mr. Kapoor's buried," she said softly. She could see Mrs. Kapoor and Cary over Vessler's shoulder. If they were aware that their husband and father, respectively, had just had his head blown off, neither of them gave any indication. They just sat, like the other captives, their faces creased in hostile, silent scowls.

Janey could not see Adam from where she stood, for which she felt grateful.

"How much time do we have before the Assassin forces us to act?"

"Nightfall. He knows that's when I'm most effective. Where's Scott and Anastasia?"

Vessler nodded toward a room at the end of the hall. "She's pretty shaken up. We all are. But she seems to take a lot of comfort from Scott. I think they do a lot of..." He gestured from his forehead to Janey's and back. "Brain-to-brain type of talking."

Janey did her best to summon up a tiny smile. "You're not worried, leaving them alone together?"

Vessler snorted softly. "Scott's interested in girls. Has been for a while. But he's also scared to damn death of them, and if he touches anything more than her hand, I'll eat my fucking shoe."

"Fair enough." She paused. "I hate what happened to Zach. I hate that we can't take him to a hospital. For his mental health, if nothing else."

Vessler's face darkened. "But you know why we can't."

"Yeah, yeah, everyone wants us dead now, he knows where we are, we can't let him talk to anybody."

"He wouldn't want to put us in danger. You know he wouldn't."

Janey tried to let it go. "Listen, have you seen Tim?"

Vessler pointed up. "Third floor. He wandered up there a few minutes ago."

"Thanks."

Janey left Vessler to his watchman duties and climbed more stairs. She found Tim in what had been intended as a game room, sitting in a chair next to a small square table with a checkerboard pattern inscribed on its surface. Shelves held fifteen or twenty different board games and a couple of video game consoles. Tim had found a domino somewhere, and turned it over and over between his fingers.

Janey went to him and knelt beside his chair and took his hand in hers. He didn't look at her. But neither did he pull his hand out of her grasp.

"Tim, I don't...I don't know what to say."

His words came out flat. All of the energy, the earnest, honest truth that made up Tim Kapoor, seemed to have been crushed to dust. "You don't have to say anything."

"No, but...I do want you to know...I'm here for you. Whatever you need."

He sighed. "You can't be in a great place yourself right now. Since your husband tried to kill you, I mean."

Just saw his father die, and he's thinking of my feelings.

As grossly, insanely inappropriate as the urge was, Janey wanted to do nothing more than climb in Tim's lap and kiss him until he couldn't breathe.

Instead, she brought his hand to her lips and kissed the back of it. "I mean it. I'm here for you."

He seemed to come out of his fog, if only a tiny bit, and frowned down at his own knuckles. "Janey. What're you saying?"

The lodge trembled on its foundations. From outside, the Assassin's voice boomed and cracked like thunder. "Janey Sinclair! Darkness will fall soon! We must prepare!"

Janey groaned, and rested her forehead on Tim's knee for a second. "Can we put a pin in this?" Tim didn't respond, just watched her with widening eyes, as she stood and made her way downstairs.

S cott, Sha'dae, and Anastasia sat at one end of the kitchen table while Janey, Tim, and Garrison Vessler hovered nearby. Those seated had already joined hands, but before Sha'dae's eyes glimmered violet to start the process, Scott leaned closer to Anastasia, his pale eyes full of concern. "Are you sure you're okay? You can do this?"

Vessler spoke near Janey's ear. "Honestly, I don't know whether he sees her as a little sister or a future girlfriend."

The corner of Janey's mouth quirked upward. "Are you in a rush to find out which?"

"I'm too old to rush anything these days."

Anastasia held her head higher than Janey had seen her do before. "I'm not made of glass. Okay? This just makes me tired, is all."

Scott didn't look completely convinced, but he nodded at Sha'dae. "All right. Let's get started."

Sha'dae had already agreed to loop Janey in on what the three of them saw in their...what to call this? Probe? A faint violet luminescence began to glow from Sha'dae's eyes, and spread outward, down her arms and over to Scott and Anastasia, until it surrounded all three of them in a gentle, flickering aura. *That's new.* Janey wondered if Sha'dae's Augmentation was getting more powerful, the way Nathan's and Tim's had. She let her eyelids slide shut, but instead of darkness, she saw movement. The image clarified—and she was gliding, high in the sky, land rolling far below her.

Sha'dae's voice sounded out from all around her, silent, carried on pure thought. *Are you sure we're going in the right direction?*

Anastasia answered. Small, harder to hear, but steady. *I spent my entire life with that man. I know more about him than he realizes. It's not a matter of not knowing where he is and looking for him. It's a matter of keeping him locked out of my mind as a reflex.* Janey's point of view dropped, increased in speed, until she skimmed along treetops and roads and houses. *What's draining me now is trying to overcome that reflex.*

Janey saw something on the horizon. A bluish glow, like a fluorescent bulb. As they drew closer, the glow resolved itself into the shape of a young man, running along a road, headed back the way Janey and the others had come. She put her own voice in the thought-stream. *Who is that? Is he another Augment? Is that why he's glowing?*

She felt affirmation in Anastasia's words. *I know him. That's Michael Walker. He worked for Stamford. He was...like Nathan, more or less. A, uh, a footsoldier, I guess?*

Scott surfaced. *Why's he running away? Where's he going?*

Janey didn't want their purpose getting sidetracked. *Let's not worry about him right now. Once we find Stamford, maybe we can come back to him, see if we can figure it out.*

As a unified presence, Janey, Scott, Anastasia, and Sha'dae swept across the landscape, moving ever northward and, near as Janey could tell, west. After another few minutes, they spotted another glow, this one in a car. Seconds after that, a third. Both of the new ones heading away from what Janey guessed was their destination. Janey directed her thoughts at Anastasia. *Do you know them, too?*

The first one was Bill Krinsky. Second was Darlene Bonner. More of Mr. Stamford's people.

"What's going on?" Vessler asked quietly. "What do you see?"

Janey opened her eyes. She still had the perspective of the seeking telepaths, and the superimposition of that over the real world made her momentarily queasy. "Not sure, but if I had to guess, I'd say Stamford's people either escaped *en masse*, or got fired."

Vessler's steely eyes crinkled at their corners. "That's not comforting."

Janey re-entered the shared point of view. Ahead of them, on the horizon, a thin vertical line of shimmering blue-white appeared, like a laser-cut through the atmosphere—the same color as the Assassin's eyes. As they drew closer, the thin line grew broader and broader, until Janey realized she had become aware of it while they were still hundreds of miles away. Approaching it, the line became a column, grew brighter and broader, and Janey wondered if the heat tightening the skin of her face came from reality or her imagination. They arrived at Stamford's location, and saw Anastasia's true perception of Stamford: the man had somehow become a vast, churning pillar of lightning that shot up from the ground, tore through the sky, and vanished into the heavens.

Janey could barely stand to look at the storm-like pillar. *Anastasia—what are we seeing? Is this how you've always seen Stamford?*

Despair tinged the girl's thoughts. *No! Not at all! That's definitely him, but...I don't know what's happening!*

Sha'dae came through. *I'm not the one who specializes in this stuff, but is that another Augment? Down there, next to him?*

Janey forced herself to look closer. A single glow, tiny in comparison with whatever Stamford had transformed into, flickered near the edge of the lightning-glare. It shone red-orange, like a candle flame, and the closer Janey looked, the more she thought it looked like a woman. *Can we get closer?*

The point of view dipped, traveled down to ground level, and the candle flame resolved itself into the figure of a woman. Someone familiar. Janey squinted, thinking hard, and it came to her. *We've seen her before! At the ranch in Texas. She's one of Stamford's crew, too.*

Sha'dae spoke. *Right. Right! I remember her. It looked like there was something wrong with her. Like, mentally.*

The entire shared point of view wobbled. Anastasia's words, faint to begin with, crackled with something like static. *Guys...sorry...I'm reaching my limit, here...*

Janey snapped back into reality, the superimposition abruptly cut off, as Sha'dae ended the connection. Anastasia slumped sideways in her chair, and Scott leaped to catch her. "Dad! She needs to lie down." As Vessler moved to help Anastasia, Scott said, "It's okay, it's okay, I've got you," in a way that settled any question in Janey's mind. The boy had the mother of all crushes going.

Tim said, "So what's the verdict? Do we know where Stamford is?"

"Yeah." She watched Vessler and Scott support Anastasia as she wobbled to a nearby couch. Scott perched on the couch's edge, holding her hand, as she settled down onto it. "But something's going on that we don't understand. He's sent away all his people except one, and he's...well, come on, I'll tell everyone at the same time."

She started toward the living room, but Tim caught her wrist. A gentle pressure, but Janey felt strength in his grip that hadn't been there before. "We need to talk," he murmured. "What you were saying—before the Assassin butted in..."

Janey dragged her eyes up from the floor until they met Tim's, and in that moment, a truth washed over her that she'd been either unwilling or unable to admit before. For the first time since she and Tim had met, since the day she'd walked into the rental office and seen him sitting there behind the desk, a pathway stretched out in front of her. Not one clouded by guilt, or blocked with obstacles, or haunted by the demons of her life. A smooth, straight, even road. Waiting for her to take the first step.

"I know," Janey breathed, and the sudden, maddening flutters in her stomach became a wave of heat that rushed out along her limbs and downward into her groin.

Not the time. Not the time!

She said, "Soon, I promise," and squeezed his hand. It took everything she had to walk away from him and center her mind on what lay ahead.

Tim's presence palpable behind her, Janey opened the front door and walked out onto the porch, where Nathan had been standing watch over the rest of the crowd. Sha'dae joined him, her shoulder touching his, their fingers intertwined.

Not for the first time, a sense of powerful surrealness settled over Janey, looking out at the assembled throng: Aphrodite and her hulking, blurring, freezing minions, gathered in a loose half-circle around the Assassin, who had emerged completely from the ground and folded his body back into the more-or-less arachnoid shape Janey had first seen. The Assassin crouched over the Plowman's still-inert frame, but had not disconnected the car battery from where Simon had hooked it to the Plowman's right hand.

The sun had already set behind the mountaintop to their west, leaving the sky the kind of cold, colorless gray that made gooseflesh rise on the skin and rendered all the trees and branches in stark silhouette.

Simon stepped up beside Janey. She realized he'd been sitting in one of the porch's rocking chairs. He said, "I've got to hand it to you, you've redefined what the words 'motley crew' mean. This is quite the freak show." When Janey didn't respond, Simon's eyes narrowed. "Ooh, you've got something to say, don't you? That fishing trip the kids went on paid off, didn't it?" His mouth stretched into the grin that Janey now found only marginally less unsettling than she used to. "Y'know, there's another name for us. Aside from freak show, I mean."

Janey looked at him sidelong. "What're you talking about?"

"Look around. You've got bruisers. Shapeshifters. Remote-viewers. Teleporters." He reached over and clapped Tim on the shoulder. "And a medic who's worth more than every other doctor on Earth combined. Janey...what you've got here is an *army*."

She shuddered. There was truth to be found in Simon's words, and Janey knew it. The whole point of the extraterrestrial experiment was to create military archetypes, and in a twisted, chaotic, far-off-the-rails way, that's exactly what it had done. "Yeah. Well. Let's hope we don't have to mobilize."

Simon snorted softly. "What else are all these people going to do with their lives? You think Parker's going to open up a patio furniture whole-sale center somewhere? You think Beverly's going to become a substitute teacher? Hell, what's Nathan going to do the first time he has to take a physical? How's he going to explain why he weighs as much as a compact car?"

Nathan had been listening, and as he shifted from one foot to the other, the deck boards underneath him squealed. He said, "It's a fair question."

Simon folded his arms. "For that matter, you think it'll ever be safe to trust me around regular people? Fuck, Janey, shit like we've been doing is what we were *designed* to do. Point us at Stamford. Let us do it."

Janey had no response for him. She could barely let the words sink in, though they gnawed around the edges of her mind. She could pass for human. She'd done so for years. Sha'dae could. Tim could, no doubt, and she hoped Scott and Anastasia would be able to disappear with Garrison Vessler and just live peacefully off the grid when this was all over.

Except when this is "all over" there's a good chance we might all be dead.

But how could Parker or Julian or Beverly or Aphrodite ever hope to rejoin society? …Did they even want to?

Janey shook the thoughts away. She raised her voice and addressed the whole group. "With Anastasia's help, we've found Stamford. He's in Minnesota. But this won't be another raid, because he's dismissed all but one of the Augments he had protecting him, and he's done something new—something we don't understand yet."

Aphrodite's blue eyes shattered into red-on-yellow sparks. "What do you mean, you don't understand it? What has he done?"

"I mean, the way Anastasia perceives him has changed. He's…I don't know. He's started some kind of transformation, maybe? The point is, we don't have enough information to rush in and try to subdue him. Which is why I'm going to go in and scout out the situation, and once we know exactly what's going on, then we'll deal with Stamford."

"Unacceptable," the Assassin rumbled. "That violates the terms of our agreement, Janey Sinclair. You were to locate the human, Derek Stamford. I was to neutralize him."

Janey put up her hands. "Yes, yes, fine. I won't try to stop you. But it's folly to rush in without proper intel."

"If I may," Vessler said. "You'd do well to take a small team with you. As you pointed out, you don't know exactly what's going on with Stamford. Once you get there, you might need some help."

Nathan said, "If she's going, I'm going."

"So am I," Tim stated from Janey's left. "We're not going to lose anyone because I was too far away to heal them."

Janey sighed. To the Assassin, she said, "I'll take you with us. If everything checks out, we won't stop you from 'neutralizing' him."

Simon waved his arms. "Whoa, whoa, whoa, now, hold on a minute! You can't just leave the rest of us behind!"

Janey's said, "Look, if we need backup, I'll let you know, and Julian can bring in the cavalry. Can't you, Julian?"

Julian's black-static-cloud body snapped back to fully corporeal for a second, revealing his true nature as a rail-thin young man in clothes that hung on his frame. "Yeah—yes, I can. I'll do that."

Janey said, "Then it's settled. Nathan, Tim and I will take the Assassin and go in for an observe-and-report. Once we know what we're dealing with, we'll either take him out, or go to whatever kind of Plan B the situation calls for." She looked straight into what she guessed was the Assassin's dominant eye. "Is *that* acceptable?"

The Assassin made a sound halfway between a hum and a purr. It sent chills up Janey's spine and into her scalp. "I have not yet experienced the teleportation of which human Augments are capable. Much data can be gleaned from the process. Yes, that is acceptable."

Janey said, "Fine. Now, we don't know what we're walking into, and I want everyone at peak capacity when we do this. It's going to take Anastasia about another forty-five minutes to get back on top of her game, in case we need her." Janey checked the time on her phone. "So we'll go at 7:30 sharp. Agreed?"

A general rumble of assent made its way through the crowd.

Nathan turned to Sha'dae. "Forty-five minutes, huh?"

Sha'dae dipped her head. She took Nathan's hand and led him back inside the lodge.

Tim put a gentle hand on Janey's upper arm, turning her toward him. "Janey—"

She placed a finger across his lips, then pulled it back: *One second.* "Mr. Vessler, can you keep an eye on everyone until it's time to go? Let me know if I need to get back here in a hurry?"

Vessler frowned. "I suppose so. Where are you going?"

Janey took Tim's hand, flickered the two of them a hundred feet straight up, and in a blast of heat that boomed like an Independence Day firework rocket, teleported them directly into her storage unit in Atlanta. Tim stumbled in the dark, but Janey held him up, held him close to her. "Here. Light." She reached out and pulled the chain that lit up the bare overhead bulb.

"Janey, what is this? Where are we? What are you doing?" He glanced around, taking in the unpainted metal shelves, the rough wooden work bench, the peg board, and the Vylar suit Janey had hung from a hook to dry after its last washing. She saw the recognition in his face. "Oh—so this is your new Basement, huh? Nice. But why are we here? What about getting ready to go to, what'd you say? Minnesota?"

Janey put both hands on Tim's chest. She felt him tense, felt the muscles tighten through his shirt, and he took half a step backward, but when she lifted her gaze to his, he was right there. With her. The bottomless black of his eyes peering straight in the winter-sky blue of hers. Janey slid her hands up, over his collarbones, and glided them around to the back of his neck. Tim hadn't moved, hadn't even blinked, but she heard his breathing get ragged. He brought his hands up, took hold of her wrists. "What about…"

Janey hadn't been this close to Tim in…how long? Weeks. The scent of him filled her nostrils, and she drank it in, the deep, primitive part of her brain flaring as all of the memories slammed to the forefront.

Tim said, "What about Adam?"

She'd known it was coming. Inevitable. Of course Tim would ask about Adam, because that's who Tim was. Janey could see his pulse thumping in his neck, could see how dilated his pupils were, could all but hear his heart pounding in his chest, but he didn't move. Hands on her wrists, ready to push her away. Ready to honor the vows she'd made with another man.

"It's over," Janey breathed. "Adam. He and I are done."

Tim's hands twitched. Their grip loosened, but he didn't let go. "Does he know that?"

"He does. I talked to him…" She couldn't bring to mind how long ago she'd had the conversation. "I already talked to him. There's no time right now, but we're filing for a divorce as soon as we can."

Tears filled Tim's eyes. His hands moved from her wrists, up to her forearms. "Are you sure?"

She kissed him. He wasn't expecting it, and it wasn't the best kiss she could have managed, but she kissed him because she wanted him to know how sure she was. Janey felt Tim's tears spill onto her cheeks, his breath fluttering against her skin, and he returned the kiss, his fingers kneading along her spine, pulling her against him now as if he wanted them to meld into one being. When his lips left hers and nuzzled her earlobe and left a trail of kisses along her neck, Janey said, "I'm sorry, Tim, I'm sorry I put you through this," and before she could stop herself, "I love you, God I love you so much, I don't ever want to be with anybody else," and Tim said something just then but Janey could barely hear him over the rush of blood through her ears, and she worked the buttons of Tim's shirt, more and more of his deep copper skin exposed in the wake of her fingers. Janey wanted to touch every inch of that skin, explore every contour and line and ridge, every part of him. She raised her arms as Tim pulled her shirt over her head, and grabbed the bedroll she sometimes used after an exhausting patrol through the city. The bedroll flopped to the floor, unrolling, and Janey spun Tim around and lay him down on it and climbed on top of him.

He gazed up at her, his nails grazing along her thighs as she unbuckled his belt, and when she stood again, he sat up and undid her jeans. Janey reached behind her and unhooked her bra as Tim slid her jeans down, his fingers catching the waistband of her boy shorts at the same time, and his breath grew ragged again as he wrapped his arms around her, hands cupping her ass, and pressed his cheek against her nakedness. "I've wanted this for so long. So long." He looked up at her. "I thought we'd never—after I—I didn't—"

Janey kicked off her shoes and socks, gently stepped out of her pants, knelt, and slid Tim's pants down. She pushed his shoes off, catching his socks along with the pants, and left him wearing only the unbuttoned shirt. Naked now herself, Janey let her eyes rake over the length of Tim's body, soaking him up. She wanted every part of herself saturated with every part of him, inside and out, skin and flesh and blood, soul and hopes and fears and dreams.

Janey crouched, straddled him again, and moaned as his shaft, still lying flat against his abdomen, pressed in between her folds. Tim breathed out, "Oh God...Janey..." She leaned forward and kissed him, long and deep, tongue swirling against tongue, and the thunder of his heart beat against her through his cock. Janey slid up, just enough to let his lips find her breasts, and as he sucked one hard, dark brown nipple into his mouth, his hand caressing and massaging the other one, Janey reached down and guided him inside her.

Tim groaned, his mouth still worshiping her breast, and as soon as she glided down, taking his entire length inside herself, his back arched and he came in a spasm that nearly bucked her off.

Tim collapsed under her, panting, his arms flopping at his sides. His head thumped against the bedroll.

After a few seconds he opened one eye. "I guess I should've seen that coming. No pun intended. Ha ha."

Janey kissed him and ran the backs of her nails along his cheekbone. "It's been a long time, I know." She straightened up and moved to lift herself off of him—and felt him stir, just as his hands came up and held her hips in place.

He said, "Whoa, now, where you going?"

A grin wanted to dance across her lips, and Janey let it. "Well...don't you need—I don't know—ten or fifteen minutes to recover...?"

He sat up, hands still on her hips, and Janey gasped as he moved her body against his. Slowly, grinding her deliciously, rock-hard again deep inside her. In full control now.

"I recovered from a gunshot through the head in less time than that." He planted another line of steam-hot kisses along her collarbone. "You'd better buckle up."

Forty minutes later, Janey and Tim reappeared in the darkness on the edge of the lodge's driveway. Janey had left her civilian clothes behind, and now wore the Vylar suit again, the helmet tucked under one arm. She took a step toward the lodge, but Tim pulled her back and wrapped his arms around her and kissed her again.

She chuckled. "No more time for that, I'm afraid. We've got work to do." But she kissed him back, savoring the taste of him, still feeling traces of his lips and tongue and hands all over her, his cock deep inside her. She wondered if she was walking funny as she and Tim made their way up to the front door. She was pretty sure they both smelled of sex.

The Assassin emerged from the shadows at the side of the house, one long, multi-jointed leg blocking their way to the front door. His four lightning-blue eyes peered down at them out of the field of swirling, shifting color. "Are you ready to depart, Janey Sinclair?"

The front door opened, and Nathan, Sha'dae, and Simon stepped outside. Janey sent a mental request to Sha'dae, and the silver thought stream flowed into her mind. *You guys ready?*

From the glow of Sha'dae's skin, Janey suspected she and Nathan might have been spending their last minutes alone together the same way Janey and Tim had. *As ready as we're going to get.*

Janey beckoned to Simon, who obligingly descended the stairs. "All right, look, I might be insane to ask you this. But I can't think of anyone else more qualified to make sure things don't go straight to hell here while we're gone. Will you do that? Play lion-tamer, if you have to?"

Simon grinned. For once, there was nothing predatory about it. "I have to admit, it's nice to be trusted. Don't worry, Janey, I'll hold it all down." His eyes flicked from her to Tim to Sha'dae and Nathan, and settled on the Assassin. "You just make sure I don't have to do it for too long, okay? And don't put Dr. Beanpole under too much stress." Something in his eyes changed—grew mirthful—and he sniffed the air. Just loud enough for Janey to hear, he added, "Not any more than you already have, in any case."

Janey gave Simon a glare so exaggerated she was sure it came across as comical before she turned her back on him and pulled her helmet on. *All right, Sha'dae. Let's see if this works. Give me a boost.*

Rather than words, images flowed into Janey's mind: the location where they'd found Derek Stamford. The place used to be an airfield, but had since then been turned into an office complex, all the hangars converted and the runways turned into park land. As long as Janey held that image in her mind—crystal clear, just as real as if she were seeing it with her own eyes—Janey was pretty sure it would function the same as line-of-sight.

Another improvement on an Augmentation. Fleetingly, Janey thought about the kind of damage she and Sha'dae and Scott and Anastasia could do, versus something as normal as regular Earth military. It would be... unfair, she decided. And terrifying.

Janey addressed the recon team as Simon went back inside—more for the Assassin's benefit than anyone else's, since Tim and Nathan had traveled with her many times before. "Okay, we'll be moving pretty high up in the air, and I know it's disorienting, but don't worry. I won't let anyone fall. Once we get there, we'll find a good vantage point and take stock of the situation. Got it?"

"How does this mechanism work, precisely?" the Assassin asked, but by then Tim and Nathan had gotten a good hold on Janey's arms and shoulders, and Janey reached out a gauntleted hand and gripped one of the Assassin's legs, and in a burst of heat sent them straight up into the night sky. In the tiny fraction of a second before she reoriented and sent them hurtling to the northwest, she heard the Assassin screaming, and took more than a little pleasure in it.

When Janey set the group down, several hundred yards from the nearest hangar on the airfield and behind a thick decorative hedge, the Assassin was no longer with them. Tim looked around, his mouth opened to speak, but Janey beat him to it. "He's about thirty miles southeast of here. That's when we dipped low to the ground."

Nathan was in his usual posture after one of these trips, doubled over with his hands on his knees, but he sounded relatively stable. "So we stick with the plan? Get in, grab Stamford, and get out before the Assassin catches up to us?"

Janey knew it wasn't a perfect plan. She figured it probably wasn't even very good, as she'd never considered herself a strategist. But she didn't want to leave the Assassin at the lodge, where he might do a lot of damage to people she cared about, and she had no desire to bring him with them on their "recon" mission, either.

"Right. Now you guys sit tight and let me see what's what." She squeezed Tim's hand, took a step backward, and flickered away in a burst of heat.

Janey couldn't tell if the office complex was abandoned, or if Stamford owned all of it and simply wasn't using much of it, or what. Given the fact that, until a few hours ago, half the population of the planet had been comatose, it probably wasn't any surprise that no one had come to work today. For whatever reason, all the hangars were dark except one.

She would have missed it if she'd only made one pass around the airfield. No exterior lights burned on the hangar in the far northwest corner, but as she crept across the roof, she noticed a faint glimmer coming through one of the skylights, and peered down through it into the massive space below.

At first Janey didn't know what she was seeing. The floor space appeared to have been some kind of bullpen at one point or another, judging by the patterns of holes in the floor, meant to hold up a warren of cubicles. Now all the office furniture had disappeared, and in its place, in the center of the cavernous room—swaying atop a tree-like pillar lit up with millions of tiny, multi-colored lights—was Derek Stamford himself. It took her a few seconds to make a positive identification, thanks to the swarms of tiny lights that now swam underneath his skin. The ambient light cast by the tree pillar was just bright enough to keep her from flickering directly down there, but as far as she could tell, Stamford was alone in the room.

Janey flickered back to Tim and Nathan and Sha'dae, and broke down the situation for them. "Now, I know we saw that other Augment, when we were looking at this place with Anastasia and Scott, so there's no reason to think she's gone now. And she's probably massively dangerous, or he wouldn't have kept her around. So let's approach the building, really freaking carefully, and see if we can maybe get past her."

Nathan said, "And grab Stamford and get out?"

"Yeah. That."

Nathan went on. "And I know we're grabbing him so we can make him undo this whole we-all-worship-Stamford-as-our-god thing, but once he's done that, what happens to him then?"

Janey spread her hands. "I haven't planned that far ahead."

Tim said, "I want Stamford."

Janey said, "Tim—"

He shook his head, and held up a hand. "That rat bastard is the reason my father is dead. The reason Zach Feygen's going to have to wear a prosthetic arm. I want him to be unable to hurt anybody else, ever again, and I want to see to it personally."

No one said anything. Finally, Janey shrugged. "I can't fault you. We ready?" She took their hands and, peering through the hedge at the hangars, flickered them away.

They emerged across from the entrance to the hangar where Janey had seen Stamford and his light-swarm tree-pillar. A set of glass double doors led into a lobby, on the other side of which a large, heavy-looking wooden door kept her from seeing anything else. Another flicker and burst of heat, and the four of them materialized in the lobby. Janey tested the wooden door and found it locked. *Nathan? How quietly do you think you can break the lock on this thing?*

I might be able to do you one better. Nathan stepped over to the door's hinges and, with a pinch of his thumb and forefinger, pulled one of the pins up and out. The other two followed suit, and Nathan worked the door out of the frame, pulled it loose from the deadbolt lock, and set the whole thing aside. The whole process had made no more noise than slowly crushing a couple of soda cans.

Which didn't matter, as a two-foot-wide beam of fire blasted out from beyond the door and engulfed Tim. Janey screamed and tried to push him down, tried to get him rolling so she could put out the flames, but the intensity of the beam increased, heat washing out from the doorway so intense Janey couldn't get anywhere close to him. The light all but blinded her, and she staggered away, looking back just in time to see Tim, charred and brittle, thud to the floor.

Nathan screamed, "Run, Janey!" as the dark-skinned, red-haired woman stepped into the lobby.

Flames danced around her hands, wrapping them in a brilliant, searing aura, the dazzling, blinding light filling every corner of the lobby, and Janey threw herself out of the way as another beam of fire tore through the air where she'd just been standing. "Mr. Stamford said don't disturb him," the woman said, and even through the flames and the carnage and Tim's horrible burning death, it struck Janey that there was nothing behind her voice. No emotion, no inflection. She sounded like an automaton. Like a child on heavy sedatives.

Nathan picked up an office chair from behind a desk and flung it at the woman. Janey had no doubt that with Nathan's strength behind it, the chair could have gone completely through the wall, but another fiery beam turned it to smoke and dust and tiny bits of melted metal in mid-air.

"Get out!" Janey motioned frantically at Nathan. "Get out, I'll deal with her!" She had to dive again as another white-hot gout of fire chewed through the floor beneath her feet.

"Are you fucking crazy?" Nathan bellowed. "Is that suit fireproof?"

"No, but neither are you, and I'm faster!" Janey drew her katana. If she could get close enough, it wouldn't matter how hot the woman got, she could still take her head off.

"None of that's going to be necessary," Tim said from right behind the woman, and clamped his bare arms—still flecked with the charred, melted remains of his clothes— around her head and throat in a choke-hold that Janey had taught him. The woman tried to scream, and the fiery aura that surrounded her blazed so hot that Janey had to turn and stumble away, but in another three seconds the heat faded.

Janey saw Tim lower the woman to the floor. That last burst of heat had burned away most of the soft tissue on the front of his body, but as Janey stared, all of the muscle and tendons and ligaments and skin re-formed, threading themselves back together almost as fast as they'd been blasted away. Tim knelt, naked as the day he was born, the woman's head still in his arms, and Janey waited for the waves of power that came rolling off of him whenever he used his Augmentation to drain someone instead of heal them.

Instead, Tim's face grew slightly more gaunt. He grunted with effort, and Janey ran to him. "What the hell are you doing? Are you *healing* her?"

Tim looked up at her, his jaw set with determination. "Anastasia said Stamford brainwashes people. Drugs them. And you heard her talking. There's something wrong with her." He laid the red-haired woman down gently on the floor. "I figured, if I could fix it, maybe she'd be, y'know. Sympathetic." He shrugged with his eyebrows. "Not sure if it worked. Not sure how long it'll take her to come to, either."

Janey shook her head. The horror of Tim's fiery death hadn't had time to sink in, but its reversal had given her something like emotional whiplash. "You just." She shook a finger at him. "You just, just—you just *wait.*" Janey crouched next to the unconscious woman, took her by one wrist, and flickered away.

When she returned to the hangar office's lobby, Tim had Nathan's shirt tied around his waist. Nathan said, "Where'd you put her?"

Janey hadn't had many options of places to stash the red-haired woman. Reaching back to the storage unit, she'd grabbed a number of zip-ties, a gag, and a blindfold, and left the woman bound securely to the steel walkway right below a huge billboard beside the closest freeway, about an eighth of a mile from the airfield. It would have to do for now.

"She's safe enough," Janey said, and pulled her helmet off and threw her arms around Tim. She kissed him, and then shoved a finger hard into his chest. "You have *got* to quit getting killed! Okay? My heart can't take it!"

Tim grinned and rubbed the place where she'd poked him. A bruise the size of her fingertip turned his skin darker, but immediately faded. "Duly noted."

Janey took a deep breath. "All right. Now. Stamford."

"That's why we're here," Nathan said.

The three of them walked through the door and into a long hallway. Halfway down its length, through a door on the left, a multi-colored glimmer shone out.

They found Stamford, not in the branches of the tree-pillar, the way Janey had seen him through the skylight, but slumped onto the floor at the pillar's base. The lights inside the pillar had dimmed to almost nothing, and all of the lights that had been flowing and moving under Stamford's skin had either left or gone out. He was simply a small, slightly-built, nude man in middle-age, and didn't appear the least bit threatening.

Janey propped him up against the tree-pillar. Stamford's eyes were open, but focused on nothing, and his jaw hung slack. "He's breathing. I don't see any signs of injury." *Sha'dae—can you take a look in his head? See if you can tell what's going on in there?*

Sha'dae's thoughts reached all three of them. *Maybe if I was there. Can you come get me?*

Janey shrugged at Tim and Nathan. "What are teleports for, if not shit like this?" She kissed Tim, walked back out into the dark corridor, and flickered away.

She and Sha'dae returned in under three minutes, and Sha'dae threw her arms around Nathan and kissed him, and through a grin Nathan said, "Good to see you, too."

Sha'dae knelt beside Stamford. She put one hand on his head and closed her eyes...but in the next instant her eyes popped back open, and she sprang up, away from him, an expression of revulsion on her face. "There's—there's nothing there! It's like he's just *empty*. Like somebody scooped out his brain or something."

Janey said, "Literally? His brain is gone?"

Sha'dae shook her head. "No, no, he's not physically hurt, I don't think. Well, I mean, I think there's something wrong with his brain, yeah, but it's still there. I think..." She glanced up at the tree-pillar. "I think whatever this thing is sort of, uh, fried it."

Tim's lips thinned. With a snarl, he said, "No, no, no. You're not getting off that easy, motherfucker." He knelt and clamped both hands around Stamford's skull, his face creasing in concentration.

At that moment, the room's far wall buckled and exploded, and the Assassin crashed through it, body extended into the centipede-like battle form. "You deceived me!" the Assassin roared. "I shall kill all of you!"

Janey flickered across the floor and latched onto one of the Assassin's many claw-tipped arms. "Been wanting to do this for a while," she said, and in a series of small jumps followed by a much longer one, teleported the two of them three miles straight up. Janey left the Assassin there and flickered back down to the surface alone. She watched as his massive, grotesque, twisting body plummeted and slammed into the ground at terminal velocity, and much as Trent Davis had done when she'd pulled the same trick on him, the Assassin more or less exploded. Tiny bits of hair-covered flesh and mangled armor rained down around the point of impact. Janey stood there and watched long enough to be sure that none of those bits were moving before she returned to her friends and Derek Stamford.

Tim sat by himself a few yards away, panting, his face even more gaunt now. Beyond him, Stamford sat up under his own power, glaring murder at Nathan and Sha'dae. Janey went to Tim. "You all right, baby?"

He nodded. "Little more of a workout than I usually get, but yeah."

Janey moved over to Stamford, who transferred his death-stare to her. She took off her helmet and squatted on her haunches in front of him. "So you're back."

"Sinclair." He spat at her. The spittle didn't go very far, and plopped on the floor between his knees. "You don't matter. None of you matter. You're not getting shit out of me."

"Well, then, it's a good thing we don't want any shit. What we *do* want is for you to turn off this mind-control thing, so that people stop thinking you're some kind of god and realize you're just a tiny little dumbass."

His narrowed eyes took on a cruel glint. "Not a chance. Not a *fucking* chance."

Janey stood, eyeing the tree-pillar. "And what were you doing with this thing, anyway? Why'd it fry your brain?"

Stamford said nothing.

Janey sighed. "All right. Sha'dae, now that Mr. Stamford's back among the mentally sound, relatively speaking, but not so inclined to cooperate with us…" Janey pointed at Stamford's head and made a swirling motion with her finger. "What do you say we do a little poking around in there? See what we see?"

Sha'dae took a second or two to think about that. "I…Janey, I don't think I can. Like I've said, I'm Communication. Not Interrogation." She touched her lower lip, her eyes distant. "But…working with Scott and Anastasia like we have? I think I've got an idea about how we can do what you want."

Janey said, "Okay, I'll bite. How?"

Sha'dae eyeballed Stamford as she spoke. "Why don't you go get Aphrodite, and we'll talk about it?"

23

Derek Stamford hadn't moved from his seat, his back to the tree-pillar. He seemed to be trying to push himself through it, shoving at the floor with his heels, twisting his head left and right. Sweat ran from his brow and dripped off the end of his nose. Janey had bound Stamford's hands with more zip-ties, and had draped a towel across his crotch.

"I don't know," Aphrodite said. She took a step back and turned away. "It's not working. It doesn't always work." Aphrodite favored Janey with an expression Janey could only think of as *sheepish*. To Janey's further astonishment, Aphrodite followed that with, "I didn't want to disappoint you. I'm sorry."

Sha'dae stepped close to Janey's ear and murmured, "What kind of alternate reality have we stepped into?"

The light from the pillar had continued to dim, so that now Janey, Sha'dae, Tim, Nathan, and Aphrodite stood there watching their captive in near-darkness. Janey could see Stamford's face just fine. She didn't miss a second of the hate-stare he was driving into her.

"It's his brain." Aphrodite turned her gaze, normal blue-and-white now, to Tim. "Maybe you healed him too much. It's like a bank vault. Even with Sha'dae helping me, I can't make a crack in it."

Stamford let loose a mirthless chuckle. "I translated a fucking alien language and took control of a nano-scale construct covering the entire planet. Do your worst. Fucking amateurs."

I think you might be going about this the wrong way. Nathan's words surprised Janey, emerging from the thought-stream.

How so?

Nathan went on. *When you guys did this, uh, mental overpowering thing to Aphrodite—no offense, I don't mean to talk about you like you're not here—*

Aphrodite's voice, buoyed by the silver stream in Janey's mind, came couched in a faint susurrus of whispers. She sounded bemused. *None taken. What're you trying to say?*

Well, I mean, Tim sort of softened you up first. You would've torn a bunch of heads off if they'd tried it when you were at full strength, right?

Aphrodite smiled. If Janey only looked at her from the neck up, it was a beautiful sight. *Damn straight I would have.* The smile faltered, and thoughts jumbled against each other. *I really didn't—it's not what—that day wasn't my best moment, guys. I'm sorry.*

Janey surprised the hell out of herself by patting Aphrodite on the forearm.

Tim pursed his lips. *I could do the same thing to Stamford, I guess.*

Nathan shook his head. *Nah, you don't want to make him pass out, right? He's not like Aphrodite. He's not like the Juggernaut. Physically, he's just a dude.*

I'm like the Juggernaut? Aphrodite smiled again. *...That's good, isn't it?*

Janey turned to Nathan. *What do you propose?*

Well, you know I used to take martial arts, right? I mean, I was never anywhere near as good as you, Janey. Not even close. And now I'm sort of too heavy. I'd have to start all over, figure out some moves that'd work with me being this big and, y'know, I'm not all that fast, either. Maybe wrestling...that might work...

Sha'dae broke in. *You were trying to make a point, sweetie?*

Right! Sorry, okay, what I'm trying to say is, we still ought to try to soften him up, just not in a way that might kill him, y'know?

That piqued Janey's interest. *Got something in mind?*

Sure. One of my instructors showed me this. Nathan moved over to Stamford and squatted down in front of him. "Okay, Mr. Stamford, here's what's going to happen. My friends are going to take a peek inside your brain, y'know, poke around, see what they come up with. And you're going to cooperate with them, okay? Don't keep throwing up walls or booting them out or anything. Got it?"

Stamford rested the back of his head against the pillar and stared at Nathan from below heavily hooded eyes. "Why don't I get your mom down here and fuck her in front of you?"

Nathan's eyebrows rose. He made a sort of strangled, snorting sound, and Janey realized he was stifling laughter. "Oh, dude, if you only knew what you were saying. Believe me, that'd be a lot rougher on you than it would on me. I mean, I don't know, do you hate yourself?"

"Eat shit, you stupid little cunt."

Nathan said, "Here, let me help you out," and reached out and grabbed Stamford's face.

Janey recognized the technique Nathan employed, though she hadn't seen it in years and didn't think she'd ever actually witnessed it used on someone. Nathan dug the tip of his thumb in on the right side Stamford's nose, stretched his hand out, and hooked his fingers behind the hinge of the jawbone below Stamford's left ear. Stamford's eyes went wide, and Nathan squeezed, and Stamford starting screaming and thrashing.

Ordinarily, the person applying this hold—a hold which, Janey knew, was designed specifically and exclusively to cause immense amounts of pain—would have moved a little with the victim, their hand and arm shifting, maybe their shoulders adjusting to maintain the grip. Nathan didn't move at all. It was as if Stamford's face were caught in some kind of industrial vice. Janey had seen Nathan Pittman bite a revolver in half, she'd seen him kick a Jeep so hard it buckled the frame, and in the last month, he only seemed to have grown stronger. She lightly touched her own jaw, glad she wasn't the one in Stamford's position.

Nathan didn't bother looking over his shoulder. *Okay, I think he's in the mood to be more helpful now. Or at least distracted enough not to try to stop you.*

Sha'dae's words flowed out, laced with a kind of gallows-flavored amusement. *If we ever have kids, I'd better be the one to do the disciplining.* Sha'dae held out her hands. Janey and Aphrodite took them.

Janey gave Tim a wink. *Wish me luck.*

She and Sha'dae and Aphrodite disappeared down the rabbit hole.

No. Rabbit hole wasn't right. It was more like a well.

A well filled, instead of water, with burning, grinding, tearing pain.

WHAT ARE YOU DOING GET OUT OF MY HEAD GET OUT OF ME GET OUT GET OUT

The voice echoed thunderously all around them as they descended, the three women, their minds drawing closer together in a sort of defense mechanism until Janey was sure they were looking out of each other's eyes. Except their eyes weren't real, none of them was real, no bodies, no selves.

Only pain.

Janey plunged through an icy barrier. It felt like bursting through a plate-glass window, the jagged shards ripping and cutting, and the searing agony settled in her lower back. From there it shot down her leg, an unbearable damaging torture that felt as if all the muscles and ligaments and tendons were being sawed through with a dull knife. From somewhere, on some distant level of her mind, Janey understood that this was a pain that Derek Stamford felt every single day of his life, without fail.

GET OUT GET OUT GET OUT GET OUT

The splintering, brittle crash of broken glass and broken ice rewound, settled into the hum of an engine, and dread clamped down on Janey's heart with such force that she forgot how to breathe. Someone was about to die. Someone close to her. Someone she loved.

NO DON'T LOOK DON'T LOOK

Janey turned her head and saw Derek Stamford's wife, sitting there in the passenger seat, a lovely woman in her early forties, wavy dark brown hair framing a heart-shaped face with kind brown eyes and lips bracketed with smile lines. The dread tightened its grip, and the interior of the car became a hellstorm of broken glass and torn metal as the truck hit them head-on, and the body of the truck's driver came bursting in through the shattered windshield and slammed into the dark-haired woman and the top of the driver's skull caught the kind-faced woman right under the chin and tore her head off her body.

NO DON'T LOOK DON'T MAKE ME LOOK DON'T DON'T DON'T

Sha'dae swam into focus in front of Janey. Her skin had turned a lifeless shade of gray. *Janey, we can't do this. We can't get lost in Stamford's suffering. We have to focus. And you have to help me.*

Janey couldn't see Aphrodite anymore. She sent out a questing thought. *Aphrodite? You still with us?*

A grunt answered her—a sound of physical strain. *Sorry—just—keeping the doors—wedged open. Do what you've—gotta do.*

The ungodly crash played on a loop behind Janey's eyes. She didn't think she'd ever be able to stop seeing that horrendous impact. *Right. Okay. Yes. Sha'dae, how do I help?*

We need to find out about the virus, right? What he did to it?

Right. Right. Okay.

Janey's non-corporeal self drew a deep breath. She knew whatever communication she engaged in here would be purely mental, but it seemed right to approach this from the other side of a boundary. "Derek Stamford! We need to talk to you!"

The booming, disembodied voice wailed. It made Janey's bones hurt.

"Derek Stamford! It's Janey Sinclair! Show yourself! Talk to me, so we can leave you alone!"

The images of the wreck dimmed, dimmed, faded altogether, and in the lightless void, a body took shape. Dark blond hair. Pale skin. A silver-headed cane. Derek Stamford limped out of the shadows. He looked like a man who'd been beaten, starved, and left for dead—but he wore a *crown*. Golden, delicate. Janey realized it was made of the same gossamer threads as the latticework. "What do you want?"

Janey glanced down. She still wore the Vylar suit, even here, and a quick touch to her temple confirmed that she had on the helmet as well. She pulled the helmet off. "We need to know about the outbreak. About the virus, and the latticework. What did you do to it? How did you do it?"

Stamford's mental projection sneered. "You only want to know so you can *un*-do it. Fuck you. The world is mine. The entire world. *More* than the world." His eyes narrowed. "You'll soon realize that."

Sha'dae stepped up beside Janey. She said, "I see we're going to have to go in the hard way."

"You can take the lead?"

"With Aphrodite helping us? Bet your ass I can."

A brilliant violet line appeared on Derek Stamford's forehead, and in the next second had extended up into his hair and all the way down to his groin. Stamford had enough time to look shocked before he split open, his two halves swinging on a hinge, his body filled with nothing but more violet light. Janey suppressed a delighted chuckle.

Sha'dae grunted. "This isn't as easy as I'm making it look. Now I get what Aphrodite's doing." Another grunt. "Go on. Get in there. Get what you need."

Janey wasted no time. She stepped forward, *through* the doorway Derek Stamford had become, and found herself floating in a dead-black void, looking down at a small-scale version of the planet Earth. The latticework enveloped the planet, and as Earth turned slowly, gracefully, on its axis, Janey could see every fine, tiny strand of it. Here and there, a stream of energy shot up from the latticework, leaving the planet behind, and Janey raised her head, following the stream's progress. She moved slowly here. As if underwater.

The latest energy burst climbed higher, higher, pierced the edge of the atmosphere, continued into space. Slowly, slowly, yet moving at thousands of miles per second, Janey traced the stream's path, until it met a curved metal object floating near the moon, redirected, and—

Janey couldn't breathe. Her throat locked up tight. She wasn't sure her heart was still beating. There, on the far side of the moon, hidden from human eyes, lurked five immense structures. Spherical giants, they lay in wait.

And they were made of glass.

Janey wanted to move closer, to get a better look. The starships, she realized that's what they must have been, seemed to be composed almost entirely of some kind of transparent substance, all of their inner workings visible to the naked eye, even as billions and trillions of pinpoints of light flowed and swirled and ebbed across their surfaces.

She heard a sound. Coming from the ships. No—from the biggest ship, the one poised in the center, the hub around which the other four orbited. Faint, distant, but the longer she listened, the more certain she became. The sound was Derek Stamford's voice.

Screaming.

"Janey. Janey, we need to know about the virus."

That was Sha'dae. Still with her. There to remind her, to keep her priorities in check. Janey tore her gaze away from the glass ships and plummeted toward Earth.

The latticework glowed as she rushed down to meet it. Glowed and pulsed, glowed and pulsed, and Janey recognized the pulsing as belonging to a heart not her own. *Stamford's tied to it. But how?* She dipped closer.

The latticework touched every human. She wouldn't have thought it possible, but every single human on the planet had been affected, and Janey knew, on an instinctive, lizard-brain level, that each and every member of *Homo sapiens* had a corresponding node on the latticework. The entire structure functioning like a quantum computer. Quadrillions of equations taking place every nanosecond as the latticework monitored its human hosts, reading them, reacting to them, recording them down to the molecular level, down to the DNA...

Janey gasped, as a truth presented itself to her. Written there in the latticework, written on the faces and hearts and minds of every member of her species. The dread she had felt before witnessing the death of Stamford's wife paled next to this.

If it's true...if it's true...

From somewhere around her, Derek Stamford's voice reached her as the tiniest of whispers. *"Don't look too closely. You won't like what you see."*

That was the last push Janey needed. The voice, the familiarity of it, the texture and sound and intonation, all of that acted like a beacon. Not unlike the way Sha'dae let Janey find her way to an unfamiliar place, Janey followed Stamford's whisper. She found his node on the latticework, saw the energy stream rising from it, and rather than ride it up to the glass Titans in the sky, Janey dove down. Down into territory she could tell Stamford had claimed as his own.

Down into the latticework itself.

"No. You can't do this." The whisper grew louder. "You can't! You'll burn your mind out!"

Janey wasn't listening. What she was doing felt like forcing open a long-rusted door. She knew the hinges were there, knew the movement could come, *would* come, if only she worked at it. Chipped and scraped and filed away the rust.

The door opened. Derek Stamford screamed as Janey moved past him...and the crown vanished from his head. Pain flared through Janey's head as the golden crown appeared on her own brow, encircling her mind, sinking countless burning needles into her brain. She reached out, into the latticework—the latticework that was now hers to command—and made a change. She felt it as the seven billion nodes released another cloud of microbes.

Success. She'd done it. But...

If it's true...

The truth she had witnessed. The fact staring at her with baleful eyes.

She knew it *was* true. The weight of what Janey had learned threatened to snap her neck. *Sha'dae. I think we can get out of here now.*

Glad to hear it. Hold on—out's a lot faster than in.

Janey blinked. She stood in the converted aircraft hangar, next to Sha'dae and Aphrodite. Derek Stamford still sat, his hands bound behind his back, his face wrinkled into the sourest hatred. Tim came and put his arms around Janey and kissed her cheek. "Made it back. I never doubted you would. Are you all right?" He squinted into her eyes. "*Janey?* You look like you've just seen the mother of all ghosts. What's wrong? What happened?"

Janey closed her eyes. Squeezed them shut and rubbed them.

Hold it together, hold it together.

"I...I think...I fixed one problem. *We* fixed it, I mean." She gave Aphrodite a genuine smile, which the young woman returned.

Tim said, "*One* problem?"

"Yeah. We have another." She gestured with her chin toward Stamford. "He's got more he needs to tell us. Nathan? You feel like engaging in some more persuasion?"

"That's not going to happen," the red-haired woman said from behind them, flames dancing around her hands. "Because I'm about to kill him." She stood in the doorway, wrists bruised where Janey had zip-tied her, and when no one moved, she said, "I don't know who any of you are, and I don't care. Move away from that bastard so I can burn him into ash."

Aphrodite snarled, muscles flexing, but Janey stepped in between Stamford and the red-haired woman and flung her arms out. "Wait! Wait! Nobody do anything! Please!" Through the sea of tension that had filled the room, Janey said, "I know you want to kill him, and I don't blame you, I know what he's done to the Augments he had working for him."

The red-haired woman's eyes blazed like furnaces. "You don't know *shit*. That motherfucker *lobotomized* me. I don't know how I came back from that, but I goddamn well *am* back, and you'd best move your ass or I'll burn you down too."

Tim stepped up beside Janey, facing the woman. "You're back because I healed you." He waggled brief jazz hands at her. "That's my thing. Look, nobody wants Stamford dead more than I do. But if Janey thinks we need to keep him alive, then we *need to keep him alive.* Please. As the guy you can thank for bringing you back, I'm asking you. Thank me by listening to her."

The woman's eyes slowly dimmed. She glared at Janey. "That's you, I'm guessing? You're Janey?"

"Right. What can I call you?"

The woman's lip curled in disgust. "My name is Kay. And you've got thirty seconds. Talk."

2 4

Janey had just stepped out of the shadows in front of the ski lodge when the first wave of pain struck. She gasped, doubled over, and emptied the contents of her stomach on the gravel, which didn't amount to much, since she had no idea when she'd eaten last. Tim was instantly at her side, arm around her shoulders, words tumbling out. "Janey what's wrong what happened are you hurt?"

She straightened up as much as she could. Around her, Aphrodite, Sha'dae and Nathan—Nathan holding Derek Stamford with one hand, that hand clamping Stamford's elbows together behind his back—and the red-haired woman named Kay gathered, varying degrees of concern on their faces.

The pain started in a corona around Janey's skull and snapped down along her nerves, very much like the sensation of getting shocked. She had accidentally touched an electric fence once as a girl, and remembered the sensation vividly. The pain subsided for a few seconds and then hit her again. Harder this time. She ground her teeth together.

I don't have time for whatever this is.

But she knew what it was. The mono-filament crown she'd taken from Derek Stamford, the control, the key to the latticework. Stamford had told Janey that her mind, her brain itself, couldn't handle it. As the agony ripped and tore all the way down to the tips of her fingers, she began to think he might be correct.

No. No. Fuck no. Not when we're this close. Not when I know what to do.

The front door opened, and Mrs. Kapoor and Cary came rushing down the steps. Tim's mother ran to her son and latched onto him, her face wet with tears, and a brief, silent explosion of grief and pain stabbed out along the silver thought-stream. Cary hovered near his mother and half-brother as Tim burst into sobs, but not even ten seconds passed before he pulled away, wiping at his eyes. "Mom. Mom, listen. We don't have time—we can't do this right now."

Mrs. Kapoor sniffled. "But…your father…"

Suffering washed through Tim's face, but steel lay under it. "I know. I know, Mom, and we'll mourn him. I will. Just not yet. I can't." He turned to Janey. "Are you okay to go in?"

Janey nodded. She didn't want to try to talk. While Tim had been embracing his mother, Janey had done her best to contain the shearing agony in her head, channeling it away, redirecting it, but another wave clawed and tore its way through her body. Janey gestured toward the lodge, and everyone followed after her. Stamford only grunted at the pain in his arms and shoulders.

Inside the lodge, Vessler had freed the rest of the non-Augments. Zach Feygen sat on the couch, hollow-eyed, the stump of his arm hidden under a blanket, and Heather sat beside him, dried tears on her face. Janey spotted Adam slouched at the breakfast bar in the kitchen. He didn't even look at her. Aphrodite joined the rest of her crew, clumped together on and around the stairs. Julian Roth and Beverly blurred and wavered on the first landing.

Nicole Grassley and Ashley Strandjev immediately came to Janey, both of them clear-eyed. Grassley said, "I can't begin to tell you how fucking mortifying this was."

Ashley zeroed in on Stamford. Nathan and Sha'dae stood in the corner to the right of the front door, Stamford still in Nathan's grip. "Is that the guy? The guy who did this to us?" Her shoulder hitched, and a big black semi-automatic pistol appeared in her hand. "Why is he still breathing?"

Janey slammed her eyes shut as another wave of pain rocketed through her. "I'll explain. Everyone, listen. I need you all to listen." She tried to project her voice and fill it with as much urgency and authority as possible. Zach Feygen's eyes focused on her. Julian Roth blurred and reappeared at the bottom of the stairs. Even Adam stood and drifted closer to everyone else.

"Thanks to Sha'dae, I was able to make a kind of mental connection to Stamford. It confirmed a couple of things. Number one, to nobody's surprise, he's the reason everyone who'd been affected by the virus suddenly woke up and turned on us. Number two, that's because he...*merged* with the latticework. Bent it to his will, I guess you could say. But that connection, that mental link, while I was in his mind—I took that away from him."

She heard Tim suck in a sharp breath.

Nicole Grassley said, "What do you mean, you took it away from him?"

The invisible crown around her head blasted another wave of pain through her. Janey breathed deeply until it had mostly passed. "I mean I saw how he did it. And I transferred that connection to myself. I'm still... I'm still figuring it out. It's like I got handed the access code to some God-awful huge super-computer, but not the owner's manual."

Stamford spoke. He sounded flat. Like a man who'd made grudging peace with his own imminent death. "I told you it would overwhelm you. You're either going to die or go insane."

Janey said, "Nathan, would you shut him up?"

"Gladly." Nathan pulled an armchair cover off the nearest recliner and shoved it into Stamford's mouth.

Janey went on. "Okay, so, I've learned a few things, thanks to this—this connection I've got now. The latticework is like a huge transmitter. It's beaming off information pretty much constantly."

Garrison Vessler said, "Beaming it off to where? Their—the aliens' homeworld?" He looked faintly embarrassed to have said those words out loud.

"No. A lot closer than that. There are five alien spacecraft hiding on the other side of the moon. One gigantic ship and four smaller ones."

Gasps and murmurs and exclamations rippled throughout the crowd. Janey waited for them to subside. "And it gets better. Stamford used his own Augmentation—which, I don't really know a good way to describe, it has to do with the manipulation of data, of information—anyway, he used the latticework to transfer his consciousness into the base ship's system. He'd already done it when we found him, and I don't think he meant to come back to his flesh-and-blood body. Tim fixed that, though."

Stamford glared at Tim. It was hard for Janey to consider his expression too menacing, though, with the armrest cover poking out of his mouth.

Scott Charles, in a tiny, awed voice, said, "Janey—you're telling us the aliens...they're here? More than just the Assassin?" He turned a little paler. "Where *is* the Assassin, anyway?"

Nathan, pride in his voice, said, "Janey took care of him. Well, *gravity* took care of him, but Janey made it happen."

Another murmur ran through the room. Janey thought it sounded a tiny bit relieved. She said, "The ships up there have brought what the Plowman called an 'annexation force.' They seeded Earth with the latticework, spread the virus, crippled half our population, and were going to wait until our infrastructure had finished collapsing before moving in to wrap up the job. In a way, we should be thanking Stamford. He screwed that up with a vengeance."

Beverly spoke from inside her frigid, icy cloud of fog. The air temperature dropped with each word. "But you said the latticework was a transmitter. Don't the aliens know what's happened? Won't they just take control of it again? Change the virus? Maybe just kill us all this time?"

Jagged pain crashed through Janey's head. "I think they're trying. Them and Stamford both, but Stamford's fucked everything up. He's embedded in the alien system—trying to take the ships over, just like he took control of the latticework."

Simon Grove hadn't said a word up to that point. He cleared his throat. "And what's he going to do with these ships?"

Janey had seen this in Stamford's mind. Clear as day. Vivid. "He's going to bring them into low Earth orbit. Let everyone on Earth see them. And then zap everyone back into worshipping him."

Sha'dae said, "That doesn't make any sense. So he takes over Earth. That'd be like...like some random nutjob taking over Guam. We're dealing with *aliens* here. They've got faster-than-light travel! They've got technology we can just *barely* even grasp! Does he think they won't just send more aliens to take their ships back? And what're the odds they won't turn Earth into a big glowing lump of rock while they're at it?"

Alarmed murmurs threaded their way through the group.

"Good point," Janey said. "Earth wasn't Stamford's endgame. He wanted to ride those ships away from here. See the universe. Do some exploring. Seed enough planets with the latticework, convert all the inhabitants into worshippers, and what do you have?"

Simon let out a low whistle. "There are worse things than becoming an intergalactic space god, I guess," he said, as Stamford stared hot death at him.

Sha'dae said, "Sorry, Janey, I'm not trying to be negative, I just don't see—I mean, how could—what are we supposed to do?"

"I think I know. I think I've got a plan." Janey took another deep breath. "We're going to go up there. To the spacecraft. We're going to get rid of Stamford Mark 2. And we're going to convince the Plowman's people to leave us alone. Permanently."

The murmurs escalated into random bits of speech loud enough for Janey to pick out. *How are we supposed to do that,* and *Go up there? Like, go into space?* and *What, in like space suits or something?*

Janey said, "Agent Grassley. You said your R&D people had some gear meant for Mars colonization. Does that mean they have pressure suits?"

Grassley nodded slowly. "Yeah. Yes. I believe so. I'm not sure how many, but I can check."

"Do that. After I've told you the rest of it, I mean."

Simon said, "Yes, please. I am *dying* to hear more details."

Before Janey could speak, Sha'dae spoke up again. "Wait, Janey. Stop. Think about this. You're saying you want the aliens to leave us alone for good."

"I'm saying I think that's our only way to survive."

Sha'dae didn't appear to be enjoying the words she was saying. "But—couldn't there be some sort of middle ground? If we do this, if we warn the aliens away from us for good—what I'm trying to say is, let's look the bigger picture. We just recently found out we're not alone in the universe. There's at least one species of extraterrestrial out there, probably two, since we were designed to fight in whatever war they're mixed up in. And that means there's who knows how many *other* alien races out there, too?

There could be hundreds, or thousands, or millions. And we want to cut ourselves off from that? What if one of them could *help* us? And—and even if nobody wants to help...won't this doom us to stay on this planet? Forever?"

Simon stretched. "Sounds like it. We're *way* likely to render ourselves extinct before we figure out reasonable space travel on our own."

Janey frowned. "You're making good points, Sha'dae. I hear you. But I'm not seeing any alternatives." She looked around. "If anyone else has any other ideas, I would be more than happy to listen."

Silence fell. Stretched. No one said anything.

Janey's tone grew even more grim. "Okay, now...this part...this isn't easy to say, so bear with me, please. If we do this. If we go up there to those space ships. I don't know exactly what's up there, and—shit. I'm just going to say it. It's really damn likely we won't come back."

Into the silence that followed those words, Julian Roth said, "You're asking us to go on a suicide mission?"

Janey swallowed hard, and clenched her fists as the latest cascade of agony burned its way down her limbs. "I'm saying, if we don't do anything, the aliens are going to come and kill us all. This way...this way we might be able to make a difference for everyone else."

Tim moved closer to her. Took her hand in his. *Wherever you go, I'm going with you.*

Janey would've enjoyed the butterflies in her stomach if her head hadn't hurt so much.

"And there's something else." She squeezed Tim's hand and let it go. "I need a—I don't mean this in any kind of discriminatory way, I just can't think of a better way to say it—I need a human to go with us. Someone non-Augmented, I mean. And I'll explain why, but first I have to tell you. The odds of any of us coming back are slim to none, but for the human who goes...I can't see you coming back at all."

Zach Feygen said, "Count me in."

Heather rounded on him. Janey thought if Heather had been a cobra, her hood would've been all the way out. "Like *hell!* What the *fuck?*"

Feygen fixed weary eyes on his wife. "I've been nothing but dead weight for days now. I've got one good arm left. Let me do something worthwhile."

Heather's anger grew incandescent. "Of all the bone-stupid, testosterone-splattered, fucking *moronic* things I've ever heard anyone say, that tops the *fucking* list! So you've got one arm now! So fucking what! Are you dead? Are you not my husband anymore?" Tears started in her eyes, and she drew back a fist and punched Feygen hard straight in the chest. He recoiled and made a sound like *whoulf.* "Don't you fucking dare go off and leave me, you bastard!"

Without a trace of that fire, Ashley Strandjev said, "Hey. Janey. I'll go." Grassley started to protest, but Ashley held up a hand. "No disrespect, ma'am, but I'm a Marine. This shit is what we do. Besides, if it puts a thumb in that son of a bitch's eye—" She nodded toward Stamford. "I'll even enjoy it." To Janey, she said, "Ready for mission briefing whenever you are."

"This is all bullshit."

Janey's head snapped up. She focused on Adam. He said, "It's all, it's *ridiculous.* I mean, even if everything you're saying is a hundred percent accurate, if *you* believe it, you just told us you were messing around inside this guy's head. Who's to say you're thinking straight now?"

Tim took a step toward Adam, but Janey put a hand on his arm. She said, "Adam, I'm telling you all the truth."

Adam started pacing. "Okay, let's say you are, it's *still* bullshit! There's a bunch of fucking space ships up there, and you're going to just take a bunch of people who don't know what the hell they're doing any more than you do, and you're going to kick all the aliens' asses! What is this, a fucking fairy tale? Have you lost your goddamn mind?"

Sha'dae came to her over the thought-stream. *Why is he doing this?*

Janey knew Tim and Nathan could hear her. *It's guilt. Guilt and self-hatred. He can't come to terms with trying to kill me, and he's lashing out.*

Tim made a low, gritty sound deep in his throat. *Yeah, well, he's not helping.*

It was true. Adam's fear and disbelief moved through the crowd like a virus itself. Adam picked up on that. It seemed to embolden him. "How are you going to fight these things? I'm assuming there's a shit-ton more alien freaks up there like that Assassin thing. And Sha'dae had it right, this is a super-fucking-advanced society! We're being *invaded by aliens,* people! We ought to be trying to find someplace to hide, not planning, what'd you call it, Julian? A suicide mission! Because that's what it'll be!"

Worry colored Sha'dae's thoughts. *You're losing the crowd, Janey!*

Janey hesitated, gritting her teeth again as she fought back another agonizing wave. Almost every face she saw bore expressions of mixed fear and skepticism. The muscles in her neck taut, Janey strode forward and stepped up onto the coffee table, right in the middle of everyone.

"Listen. Listen! You're not thinking about this the right way. Okay? The Plowman said it himself. Humans are unsuitable for the experiment his people were running. You know why? Because we're too unpredictable. Our DNA goes in too many different directions." She pointed at Adam. "He's trying to tell you what our story is. He's saying it's about getting invaded by aliens. That we all need to run and hide, dig some holes and crawl in and pray no one finds us."

Everyone in the room had fallen silent. Janey turned in a slow circle, making eye contact with every single person, and her voice built in intensity, slowly, word by word.

"I'm telling you that's *not* what our story is. You *know* our story. Humans have told it to each other a thousand times. It's the one where the scientists find something ancient, buried in the ice. It's the one about the explorers who set down on an unfamiliar planet. It's the one in the books where the dwarves *dug too deep.* Do you hear me? *Do you hear me?*"

Aphrodite Lupo hadn't said a word, hadn't even made a sound, this entire time. She had simply sat on the stairs, watching. Now Janey knew Aphrodite understood. Aphrodite got it. Her eyes became glowing storms of infernal embers, and she began to *pant.*

Janey's voice ratcheted up further. She hammered every word, every syllable. "Don't you see? The Plowman's people are the ones who tried to play God! They tampered with forces they didn't understand, and they got *us! We* are the prehistoric microbe dug up from the glacier. *We* are the creatures that wipe out the landing party! *We are the fucking Balrog!*"

Parker began growling. He thumped his fist into his hand, again and again. From off to her side, she heard Nathan whisper, *"Fuck yes."*

Janey continued turning in the slow circle. The pain in her head had vanished. Every eye was riveted to her. "They made a fucking *critical* error when they came to this planet. They have awakened something they were never prepared to deal with! Because *we* are the masters of this world. We are the monsters. We are a *planet of demons!* And we're going to go up there and *rip them to fucking shreds!"*

The lodge's windows rattled with the collective roar.

Adam turned and walked through the kitchen and out into the dark.

Janey didn't care. She was panting, riding a high she'd never felt before, but when Tim put a hand on her wrist and she turned to face him, the unreadable expression on his face stopped her in her tracks. "Tim? What's wrong?"

Sha'dae and Nathan were staring at her, too. So was Kay. So was Stamford.

Tim leaned in close. "Janey. You've got *fangs.*"

"...What?"

"You've got fangs. And...your eyes..."

Janey ran her tongue along her teeth, and almost shrieked when she felt the long, pointed canines. She turned to look in the nearest mirror, and saw that, on top of the fangs, her eyes had gone solid black, with tiny white pinpoints in their center.

Janey slumped down onto the edge of one of the twin beds in an upstairs bedroom. Tim and Nathan and Sha'dae came in after her, and Tim shut the door and locked it before he came over and sat down next to her. Janey ran her tongue over her teeth again. The fangs were gone.

Tim put his arm around her. "Janey? What's going on? What's—what's happening to you?"

A soft knock sounded at the door, and Simon's voice came through from the other side. "Hey, is this strictly a cool-kids club meeting, or can anyone find out what the hell we just saw?"

Janey grimaced. The pain in her head had returned. She called out, "Just wait downstairs, okay?"

His words growing fainter as he retreated, Simon called out, "Sure thing, Mom."

Sha'dae sat down on Janey's other side. "It's a fair question, I'm afraid, sweetie. Is there something going on we need to know about?"

Janey stared at the floor without really seeing it. The truth she had discovered when she was inside Stamford's head, the truth mirrored in every molecule of the latticework, danced in front of her. She said, "Y'know, I've always hated it when characters on a TV show don't tell each other things for no good reason. Like, a couple of people find out something's going to happen to one of them, and that one tells the other one, 'Whatever you do, don't tell my brother!' And then you spend two or three episodes with a bunch of stupid, unnecessary drama and lies and misunderstandings that could all be avoided if people just had a shred or two of basic, decent honesty and laid it all out at the beginning."

Nathan said, "I've seen that show. I've seen a bunch of that show."

Tim put his hand on Janey's knee. "What do you have to tell us?"

"Guys...when I was in Stamford's head? Um. Sha'dae, you don't know this either."

Sha'dae's eyes flashed. "What? What don't I know?"

"I saw something. I guess, more accurately, I found something out. Something I know to be true. Now, I don't know if it has to do with that, or with what Stamford said—he said my brain couldn't handle the connection to the latticework. That it would overload me. That might be it. My body might be...I don't know. Destabilizing? Maybe I'm starting to be sort of like what Simon is. Or, y'know. Aphrodite."

Tim said, "God above, don't say *that*."

Janey shrugged. "It might be true, though."

"You still haven't told us what you saw," Sha'dae said. "You *are* going to tell us, aren't you?"

Janey took a deep breath. And another. And she told them.

When she'd finished, Sha'dae got up and went to Nathan and buried her face in his chest, his shirt quickly soaking through with her tears. Tim sat, visibly stunned. He ran his fingers through his hair. Janey said, "I'm not any happier about it than you are."

"It's...I mean...it is what it is. Right?" Tim peered up at the ceiling. "And the latticework...there's no way we can get rid of it?"

Janey gave her head a tiny shake. "I don't know. Maybe there is. It's a... a nano-scale construct that's wrapped around the entire planet, and it's self-repairing, and if I understood what I saw correctly, it's powered by ambient heat. So...I don't know. I can't think of a way. I mean, if we try to burn it, it'll burrow deeper until the flames are gone. Freezing won't bother it. We could get a backhoe and pull a bunch of it up, but it would repair itself as soon as the scoop was gone. Maybe there's a way. But I don't know what it is."

"Nothing we have access to," Sha'dae said. "Not on Earth. *That's* what we should do, up there in those space ships. Look for something to get rid of that…thing. Some kind of off-switch."

Janey didn't say anything. The latticework, and its effects, were crucial to what she had planned. She knew Sha'dae knew that, too.

Nathan frowned. "Hey, I just thought of something. If those ships are still on the far side of the moon, how are you even going to get up to them? Get us all up to them, I mean? Don't you need to see a place, if you've never been there before, if you're going to teleport to it?"

Janey mashed her fingertips into her temples at another flare of pain. They weren't quite as powerful as they were before her—what, her fang incident? But they were coming more frequently, and she could feel what that meant. "I can get us there. With Sha'dae's help, and probably Aphrodite again, and Stamford. That's why we can't kill him, much as a lot of us would love to. Sha'dae can tap into his mind again. I can—I think—direct the latticework to give him access to the copy of his own consciousness that's up there, screwing shit up for the aliens. And through *that* I can visualize the interior of the base ship." She sighed. "It might not be necessary, though."

Tim said, "Why not?"

Janey stood up. "Because the ships are moving. Stamford 2 is bringing them down. Soon they'll be visible to the naked eye." She popped her neck back and forth. "Which means I need to go talk to Agent Grassley. And then to Sgt. Strandjev. …Better do that away from everybody else."

Janey opened the door and stepped out into the hall. Tim followed her, closed the door again, and—glancing around to make sure no one else was within earshot—said, "What are you going to do about Adam?"

She groaned softly. "He thinks I blame him. For throwing the rock, trying to bash my brains out. I know that wasn't him—that was Stamford. But, I swear, I just…I just don't have the emotional space to deal with him right now. He's not hurting anybody, and…I've got more important things to do." Janey moved closer to Tim. Gently pushed him against the wall, her body pressed to his, only leaning back enough to look him in the eyes. "Tim, I know things are fucked up. And I'm afraid they're going to get a lot more fucked up. A *lot* more. But I want you to know…you remember when we were in the old theater? And you said you loved me, and if you could, you'd ask me to marry you?"

Tim caressed the side of her neck. Traced the line of her jaw with his thumb. "Vividly."

"Well…if it turns out you can? I'll say yes."

Janey kissed him and left him standing there in the hall with a big stupid grin on his face.

25

Two hours later, Janey stood with a large contingent of the bizarre group of individuals whom Nathan had, at some point, dubbed the Widow Society—a name Janey fervently hoped would not stick—in a brilliant white-and-chrome laboratory. A handful of men and women in white lab coats stood on the far side of the room, gawking at them, while a dark-haired white man in his fifties, also in a white lab coat, explained things to them. Agent Grassley stood nearby, observing. She had referred to the dark-haired man as Olsen.

When they'd first arrived, Olsen's eyes had widened at the sight of Julian Roth standing at the back of the group. "Mr. Roth. Nice of you to rejoin us."

"Yeah, sorry about skipping out, Doc. It, uh…it seemed like a good idea at the time."

Now Janey stood in the center of the group, wearing what Olsen had called a "slim-line pressure suit." It felt like a bulked-up version of her Vylar body armor, except ten times more cumbersome and fifty times hotter. Olsen lowered a helmet over Janey's head and, when it connected to the collar plate, touched two switches. A series of lights came on inside the helmet, air hissed around Janey's ears, and after a few seconds, the temperature became much more bearable.

"You've got three hours of oxygen," Olsen said. His voice came to

Janey through speakers in the helmet. "We sure as goddamn *fuck* didn't design these suits for fighting giant spider aliens, so if it gets torn, you're up shit creek. But this is the best we can offer."

Grassley said, "As far as we can tell, the aliens breathe the same kind of atmosphere we do. At least, the one we've encountered breathed our air, without any kind of helper apparatus that we could see. So we might not need the suits at all."

"Bring them back if you can," Olsen said, eyeballing the seal between Janey's helmet and collar. "Each one only costs about eighteen million dollars."

Janey looked over at the rest of the group. Joining her in Grassley's R&D lab were Tim, Sha'dae, and Nathan, along with Aphrodite, Parker, Simon, Julian, Beverly, and Kay. Ashley Strandjev stood next to Grassley. Vessler, Scott, and Anastasia were back at the ski lodge with Adam. Heather had already taken Zach to a hospital, plenty of which had openings to spare, now that everyone afflicted by the outbreak was back on their feet. Mrs. Kapoor and Cary had gone home.

Janey knew Tim hadn't truly dealt with the death of his father yet. She hoped to be there for him when it really hit him. She hoped they all lived that long. Janey touched the two switches, waited for the lights to go out, and pulled her helmet off. "We're grateful, Dr. Olsen. How many of these suits do you have? And can they fit..." She gestured toward Parker, Julian, and Beverly. "Non-standard sizes?" Following Olsen's instructions, she hit another switch under a flap on the chest, powering down another series of vacuum seals, and stepped out of the pressure suit. Released from its confines, the Vylar body armor felt like a track suit in comparison.

"I can wear one of those, no problem," Julian said. "My clothes go with me."

"I can get inside one as long as it won't punk out in the cold." Beverly drifted closer to Janey and peered down at the now-empty suit lying on the floor. "But I'd guess they're insulated, right? I mean, they're space suits."

Olsen nodded. "Correct." He narrowed his eyes at Parker and pursed his lips in thought. "As for your large friend..."

"My name is Parker," Parker grated out.

Olsen took that in stride. "I believe we can accommodate you, Parker. Come with me." To Grassley, he said, "Give me half an hour?"

Grassley seemed to find that acceptable. "Got a break room around here?"

Olsen waved vaguely down a nearby hallway as he and Parker left. "First door on your right." Janey heard him say to Parker, "If you don't mind me saying so, young man, you and your friends are the fucking coolest people ever to set foot in this place."

Parker laughed. It was the first time Janey had heard him make that sound. "No shit?"

Janey moved among the rest of the Augments. "Everyone still good to go? Ready to kick some ass?"

Aphrodite began panting again. "Kill them all," she breathed, making Janey wonder if she was about to have one of her less-articulate "bad days." "Kill them tear them apart rip them into pieces kill them and eat them all."

Simon clapped Aphrodite on the shoulder. "That's the spirit!" He turned his head so Aphrodite couldn't see his face and widened his eyes at Janey, a subtle gesture that clearly meant *Oh my God what a psycho.*

To Simon, Janey said, "Keep everybody in line while Parker's getting fitted, would you?"

Simon frowned. "Where're you going?"

"Nowhere, I just need to talk to Tim for a few minutes."

Sha'dae flowed in on the silver thought-stream. *Everything okay?*

Yes. Hundred percent. I just need a word. Janey turned to Grassley. "Tim and I are going to go discuss something in private. Give a shout if you need us."

Grassley waved one hand: *fine.* Janey motioned with her jaw at Tim, and he followed her past the slack-jawed, wordless researchers and into what appeared to be a darkened office. Using her night vision, she saw a nameplate on the desk: DR. BERNARD OLSEN. Janey hoped he wouldn't mind, and that he wouldn't be back immediately, what with taking care of Parker. She closed the door and quietly locked it.

"What's up? Are you okay?"

Janey flipped the light switch and half-sat against the edge of the desk. "I'm a wreck, is what I am. I wouldn't let anybody else know it, but my brain's going in a thousand different directions at once, and this damn latticework crown thing is about to split my head open, and I just want to crawl off under a rock somewhere. I don't know if I can do this, Tim. I need you to coax me down off this ledge."

He came and leaned against the desk next to her and slid an arm around her waist. "Talk to me."

"I know I gave everybody that speech…"

"It was a kick-ass speech. Seriously. I wish I'd recorded it."

"I think Nathan *did* record it. And I know everyone's fired up. But…"

"Yes?"

Janey buried her face in her hands. "But it's *ridiculous.* We're about to teleport into space and fight *aliens?* It's not real! My mind refuses to believe it's real!"

Tim kept his tone mild. "Even after the Plowman? Even after Simon, and Aphrodite, and the Assassin, and…and the stuff you and I can do? The stuff the rest of us can do? You know it's all real."

"Yes, yes, I know *that's* real. But we're talking about fighting aliens. Actual, honest-to-God *aliens*, Tim. This isn't the real world anymore! Everything's gone off the rails. Off the rails, over a cliff, into some kind of bottomless pit. And…" Hot tears threatened to start in her eyes, and she willed them back. "It's true, what I told everyone. I don't know if we're coming back from this. We might all die. *I might die.* And that doesn't seem real either, because if we do die, we'll die *fighting fucking aliens.*"

Tim steered her around so that she faced him, and pulled her up against him, her legs between his as he still leaned on the desk. He took her hands and kissed them, kissed the scars on her knuckles, the calloused palms. "You're not going to die. We're not going to die. I believe what you told us. These asshole aliens are not prepared. Like you said—we're the fucking Balrog."

She came close to a chuckle, but didn't quite make it. "Plus my plan sucks. I mean, we poked around in Stamford's head enough to know what needs to happen once we get to the system core. Where Stamford's got his digital clone stashed. But before that? My whole plan is 'beat up all the aliens.' What kind of weapons do these things have? What if we get there, and they just hit a button and paralyze us all? What if they've got, like, disintegrator guns? We might show up and die in the first five seconds."

Tim thought about it. "I don't know about the paralysis thing. I guess that's something we'll have to gamble on. But I don't see a space-faring species using hand-cannons and such inside a space ship. Aliens or not, they've got to breathe, don't they? They won't want to go blowing holes in the hull."

"And...even if we make it back..."

"Yes?"

"I used to think what I do is so black-and-white. Go out into the city, find people doing bad things, and hurt them until they stop."

"Well, it's working, isn't it?"

"I don't know. I don't know if it is or not. I kind of think it's not. I've been thinking about that girl—the one I told you about before, whose father I put in the hospital? She *hates* me. And I think she might be right to."

"But her father *was* selling drugs to kids. You prevented that from ruining children's lives."

"At what cost, though? Am I not just perpetuating a circle of violence? Isn't there a better way? There *has* to be a better way."

Tim seemed to pick up on the note of finality in her words. "Janey... what are you getting at?"

She lifted one of his hands. Kissed the back of it. "I think...if we do this, and survive...I think there might not be a Gray Widow anymore."

"Seriously? I find that hard to believe, if you'll pardon me saying so. You're not going to use your abilities at all?"

"No, no, I didn't say that. I just think...maybe I'd be...maybe I should do more with things like search-and-rescue efforts. Or recovering kidnap victims. Helping out after natural disasters. Things where I'm not, y'know, breaking people's kneecaps when I don't have to."

"There's still a need to protect innocent people."

She gave him a rueful chuckle. "Maybe I'll become a cop."

Janey's hands trembled in Tim's gentle grasp. She saw him notice that. "I just, like I said, I'm nervous as all fuck, and my head's killing me, and I know getting everyone up there is going to take a lot out of me, and I'm nervous about that, too, because I'm pretty sure I'll need to be firing on all cylinders right from the first second, and I don't know what to do about it. Sorry. Sorry."

"Janey. Please. Don't apologize."

Tim put his hands on her waist and turned her so that her back was to him. Janey leaned into him and let her eyes drift shut as he slid his arms around her. "This is nice," she said, "but I don't think it's the time for snuggling."

"Do you trust me?" he murmured at her ear.

"Why?"

"If you trust me, I think I can help you."

Still with her eyes closed, Janey felt Tim's fingers undo one of the Vylar suit's buckles. She knew he was familiar with their locations, as he'd had to strip the first-generation suit off her before, when she'd been close to death after an encounter with Aphrodite. Another buckle came loose. "Tim...honey. We don't have time to—"

Janey's words turned into a gasp as Tim's hand slipped inside the armor and cupped her left breast. He covered the side of her neck in kisses, and when he gently rolled her suddenly-hard nipple under the tip of his finger, a low moan got away from her. Janey reached back and pushed her hand into his hair. "What're you—I—"

More buckles opened, and Tim brought a hand to his mouth and wet two of his fingers, but it wasn't necessary, as he discovered when he slipped his hand down underneath the band of her boy shorts. Janey was already soaking wet, and she gripped his wrist, but not in an effort to stop him. "Should I—I can bend over, we—"

"Sshhh. No, no. Just relax."

Tim spent some time on the precious bit of flesh between her lips, long enough for Janey's breaths to grow shorter and closer together, the fire building inside her, but then he moved his hand further down and slid two fingers up inside her. Tim's hands were long, slender, elegant, the hands of a pianist, and as his fingers slipped farther in, they found exactly the right spot—the sweet spot—the magic spot. Janey wasn't sure whether she'd cried out, but she knew her back arched, and she twisted her head around and kissed his mouth, and while his fingers touched her deep inside, touched her center—

Janey gasped.

She knew what was happening. She'd felt it before, more than once. The heat, the waves of power.

Tim was healing her.

But God in Heaven, it had never felt like *this*. With his breath hot on her skin, Tim unleashed wave after wave of energy into her, channeled it through his hand and into the deepest, most sacred recesses within her, and Janey clamped her lower lip between her teeth and squirmed and held on for dear life as the power built, built, crashes of energy quivering through her, spots and streaks of light flashing across her vision, and Tim whispered, "Janey..." and she came like a thousand lightning strikes at once.

The controlled explosion continued, rolling through her, the blood rushing in her ears loud as thunder, and when it finally reached its end, Janey slid out of Tim's grasp and collapsed, panting, to the floor. She rolled over onto her back and stretched her legs out. Toes quivering. The ceiling swam in and out of focus.

Tim knelt beside her. She watched as he slowly licked his fingers clean and dried them on the tail of his shirt. When she could talk, she said, "Dr. Olsen's going to think his office smells suspicious."

"How do you feel now?"

Janey stretched. Slowly, luxuriously. Her head didn't hurt at *all*. "I didn't know it was possible to feel this relaxed."

"So that helped?"

She took his hand. Nibbled on the tips of his fingers. "How often can you do that?"

"How often would you *like* me to do that?"

Janey grinned. "Those alien motherfuckers don't stand a *chance*."

26

As a group, they walked out of the laboratory and into the parking lot, Parker shuffling along in the rear, wearing a pressure suit that no one would have called "slim-line." Nathan kissed Sha'dae, deeply and long, right there in front of everyone, and she didn't admonish him when he finally pulled away. They had all decided that, since Sha'dae's telepathic range had expanded to right at two thousand miles, there was no point in risking her life. It was a point made easier to swallow thanks to Dr. Olsen having run out of pressure suits.

Janey craned her neck and stared up into the sky. The five points of light were up there, tiny but visible. Swords of Damocles, hanging over the entire planet. "All right. I'm going to handle the big jumps. Julian, you get us inside, and once the time comes, you're on ship-to-ship duty as needed. So stay out of combat unless you're threatened directly, because if you get your ass killed, none of this is going to work. Got it?"

Julian said, "Yeah, I've got it. And in the meantime, everybody does as much damage as possible, right?"

Janey scanned the group. Each of them stared back at her through the transparent faceplates of their helmets. "Right. We get up there and…we wipe them out. We need to get to the system core, but to do that, what do we do?"

In a ragged attempt at unison, everyone said, "We wipe them out."

"We what?"

Louder, more in synch: *"We wipe them out!"*

Ashley Strandjev hadn't sealed her helmet yet. Janey saw Agent Grassley step over to her, and read the simple question on Grassley's lips: *Are you sure about this?*

Ashley gave the older woman a thumbs-up, her face stony.

"All right," Janey said. "I've got visual." She nodded at Sha'dae, whose eyes glimmered violet. "Plus I've got the link between Sha'dae, the flesh-and-blood Stamford, and the digital clone on the base ship." She held her arms straight out. "Everybody get a good grip." Tim held Janey's left hand. Parker, Aphrodite, Nathan, Simon, Kay, and Ashley all crowded around her, gripping her arms, her shoulders, her thighs.

We good, Sha'dae?

Sha'dae nodded in answer to Janey's silently spoken question. *Rock solid.*

Janey took a deep breath, cleared her mind as best she could, and took the entire group two hundred feet straight up. They only blinked into existence for a minuscule fraction of a second before Janey took them the rest of the way, leaving behind a thunderous crack and a fireball a hundred feet across.

Janey knew what she'd seen in Stamford's mind. The interior of the ship was composed of metal every bit as transparent as the hull, and the lack of visual barriers lent itself to bizarre optical illusions. Objects that were very close appeared far away, and vice versa. Solid planes seemed to disappear. She knew becoming disoriented would be all too easy, in much the same way someone suddenly plunged into deep water might not know which way led back to the surface.

And there was light everywhere. No opaque surfaces meant very, very few shadows, and while the illumination was far from harsh—the whole place existed in a kind of twilight, filled with glimmers from machines and devices swimming with the now-familiar swarms of tiny pinpoints of multi-colored lights—Janey couldn't find a single place dark enough for her to flicker into it.

She'd been prepared for all of that, or had tried to be.

What Janey was not prepared for, as Julian took the group from right outside the hull to the ship's interior, was the stomach-churning, perception-warping reality of it. The rational part of Janey's mind realized that the aliens' vision must not function at *all* like humans', and that human eyesight was, at its most basic level, incompatible with the alien architecture. Her mind couldn't even make sense of what she was seeing—

—other than the several hundred gigantic alien octopeds that came rushing at them as soon as they appeared. None of the creatures appeared to be wearing the kind of combat armor the Assassin had. Janey found little comfort in that.

Julian had taken them to some kind of very large space within the ship: a hangar deck, or a staging ground, or some kind of training floor. Janey couldn't tell, and didn't have time to try to analyze it.

Overhead, a series of broad yellow strips in the ceiling began to flash.

The octopeds swarmed at them, moving in silence—but their color-shifting faces flashed and rippled in repeating patterns, and Janey realized they didn't *need* to speak to communicate. At some color-based, wordless signal, every single alien drew weapons from sheathes along their backs.

Tim had been right, Janey thought, as icicles formed in her stomach. The aliens didn't seem to want to take a chance on blowing holes in their hull with firearms, so they all had swords, instead. At least two per octoped. Many of them had four—long, black, gleaming blades, each of which looked heavy and sharp enough to take down a good-sized tree with one swing.

Nathan's voice crackled through the suit helmet. Either he had forgotten they had a telepathic communications channel, or something on the ship was interfering with it. "Janey! Holy *fuck!* What do we do what do we do?"

"Kay!" Janey barked. "Burn them! Burn them all!"

Janey was expecting Kay to say something. Crack a joke, rattle off a one-liner, something like, "Time for a barbecue!" Kay didn't say a thing. She simply stepped out away from the group, raised her arms, and became a being of fire.

Back in the hangar, Janey had only seen Kay's ability manifest around her hands. Now, facing hundreds of huge, sword-wielding, homicidal aliens, Kay didn't bother with things like restraint or moderation. Her pressure suit vaporized, along with the clothes she'd worn underneath it, and she blasted out twin fans of flame from her outstretched hands so hot that Janey and the rest of the group had to back off and shield their faces. Through the insulated pressure suits,

Janey felt a heat that seemed to be somewhere between "cycled up jet engine" and "surface of the sun."

The aliens screamed as they died.

Not human screams. Not even animal screams. They sounded more like the steam forced out of the bodies of lobsters boiled alive, an involuntary, mechanical, shrieking atrocity that made Janey want to puke in her helmet. After long seconds, during which the roaring of Kay's flames grew louder and louder, Janey risked a look at the carnage the red-haired woman was causing.

The aliens' bodies reacted to the burning, fiery death in a uniform way. One after another, they flipped over onto their backs, their blackened, scorched limbs bending and drawing toward their torsos so that each octoped became an eight-pointed star. Janey started counting. Beneath the sheets of blue-white flame lay dozens of corpses. Dozens upon dozens.

A tiny spark of hope appeared in her heart. Could it be this easy? Was it just a question of using the right tool for the job—Kay being that tool? Janey had heard of submarine crews dying, to a man, because of a gas leak on board. What if this was that kind of situation, in which the ship's crew simply had no defense against a certain kind of hazard, and everyone died?

Janey didn't see the octoped until it was too late. All of Kay's flames had sprayed out parallel to the staging ground floor, blasting apart the aliens. Neither she nor anyone else in the group had thought to look up, and an alien with a sword in each of its forward-most hands dropped from the ceiling right behind Kay and split her in half. The flames cut off abruptly as the pieces of her body thudded to the transparent floor, her blood sheeting out across the deck, a plane of bright red liquid.

Nathan grabbed one of the creature's hind legs and tore it off.

While the alien screamed, Aphrodite Lupo launched herself onto it, her hands transformed into massive, hooked, bony blades, and ripped it apart. Sapphire-blue blood sprayed across the floor and, like Kay's, turned it into a wet but recognizable solid surface.

Across the deck, emerging from doorways at floor level as well as crawlspaces along the walls and ceiling, more octopeds appeared. The sound of their blades pulling free of their sheathes scratched through Janey's helmet speakers.

Oh no. Sha'dae had been watching through Nathan's eyes. *Oh no, no, Tim! Tim, can you help Kay? Can you heal her?*

Janey didn't wait for Tim to respond. *No. She's gone.* She willed the view of the new wave of octopeds along the thought-stream to Sha'dae. *The quick and easy way isn't going to work, people.*

Parker picked up one of the swords the alien had used to kill Kay. It wasn't designed to fit his hand, but he clutched it tight.

Then the octopeds were on them, and chaos descended.

Parker charged out in front, smashing into the front line, and whatever the aliens had been expecting from the surprise Earth visitors, Parker did not seem to be it. The sword he'd picked up was easily as long as he was tall, but he swung it as if it weighed no more than a pool cue, and the octopeds he first encountered flew apart as easily as had the one that had killed Kay.

Janey wondered if these aliens were not of as tough a breed as the Assassin.

For that matter, were they soldiers at all? They had deployed the latticework and used the virus to conquer the planet. Maybe they had no business on a battlefield. Maybe this was like a crew of researchers suddenly forced to defend themselves against hostile aliens.

Janey decided she could live with that scenario just fine.

The octopeds beyond the ones Parker had taken down grew cagier. They sprang back and formed a circle around him, dashing in when his back was turned, denying him easy targets. Few of them appeared to be expecting Aphrodite and Nathan to join the fray, however, and though a couple of them did land devastating sword-strikes along Parker's back and legs—enough to drive him to his knees—the entire wave withdrew when Aphrodite threw herself onto the nearest one, her head bursting out of her helmet and distorting into something crocodilian, and bit one of its legs off.

Simon dashed past Aphrodite. He had detached the pressure suit's gloves, and his hands become the same kinds of bony scythes he'd used to cut down the communication columns in the sports complex. Fountains of sapphire blood sprayed as he dug into the aliens.

An octoped landed near Janey, and immediately ate a stream of bullets from the AK-47 Ashley Strandjev had brought with her. Ashley calmly reloaded as the creature staggered and died, blue blood spreading across the deck. "Kinetic energy's a bitch, alien or not," Ashley said—

—and a thought leapt into Janey's mind. She sent out a broad message: *Guys! Guys, can you all hear me?*

Janey watched as an octoped swung a sword straight into the back of Nathan's head, and stifled surprised and delighted laughter as the blade broke. She could hear the anger in Nathan's thoughts as he responded. *We're all kind of busy, Janey!*

I know! I know! Don't stop! But, if you could—could you get as much of their blood everywhere as possible?

Simon interjected. *You're asking us to be messy?*

Yes! Get it everywhere! Floor, walls, ceiling! The more the better!

Parker grunted, grabbed an alien, and swung it toward Nathan. Nathan caught the other end, and they tore it in half, both halves geysering sapphire blood in every direction.

"Just out of curiosity," Ashley said over the helmet radio, "what's with the finger-painting?"

"I need shadows. There weren't any, not with everything transparent. But check that out." She pointed at a huge splotch of blood on a nearby wall—and the pool of shadow created just beyond it. "Beverly. Can you stick by Ashley and Tim? Help make sure they stay in one piece?"

An octoped came crawling out of a tunnel-like opening in the wall behind Ashley, and halfway out, a frigid fog enveloped it. The creature screamed and froze in place, stuck in the opening, and the fog flowed over the rest of it, freezing it solid. Beverly's face drifted out of the fog. "Sure thing. Go. Have fun."

Janey sprinted along the edge of the Parker/Aphrodite/Nathan/Simon destruction zone, dove into a shadow, and emerged from another one on the far side of the fray. The rainbow-blade katana proved more than enough to slice through the back legs of the nearest alien—trauma which sprayed more thick blood along the floor and wall—and Janey flipped backward and flickered away before the whirling octoped could touch her.

Janey. She recognized Julian. *They're, uh...they're bringing over spiders. More spiders. From the other ships.*

How many? Can you tell?

Janey flickered through the staging area's floor, scrambled to another shadow, came up through the floor and sliced an octoped's torso along its center line, and flickered away again before the downrush of blood even touched her.

This—this is the kind of thing the aliens weren't expecting. A battle that gets easier to fight the more blood gets spilled.

Janey flickered, slashed, flickered, slashed. She couldn't tell if the fight actually was going well, or if she was still riding the massive endorphin high of the attention Tim had paid her before they left.

Julian went on. *Hard to say. They're in, I guess they're shuttle craft? I don't know, twenty or thirty in each one?*

Janey's enthusiasm wilted a degree or two. She had no idea how long everyone could keep this up.

Janey spotted Aphrodite across the floor...or at least, it must have been Aphrodite. Her body had gained mass, the way Simon's had when he'd chased down Janey's car. Now she topped out at nine feet, her skin had gone gray-green and sprouted thorns, and instead of two arms she sported two pairs of thick, muscular tentacles encrusted with razor-sharp, hooked, bony blades. Nathan, Parker, and Simon were definitely holding their own—Parker had split open his sword-damaged skin and emerged, whole again and furious—but Aphrodite was an engine of destruction in the truest sense. The octopeds' blades touched her, but didn't cut her. Didn't hurt her. She didn't even seem to notice them. Jaws wide and roaring, she slashed and crushed and twisted the eight-legged aliens like a grizzly bear killing squirrels.

"Janey Sinclair!"

The voice hissed and popped over her helmet radio. She recognized it, though this version had a different timbre. "Stamford 2."

"Janey! This was a mistake! It was all a mistake! You've got to get me out of here!" Terror saturated the digital clone's voice. "I thought I could take over! I didn't, I didn't understand, I uploaded into the system but it's cold and sharp and it keeps pulling me apart and putting me back together Janey it's killing me please help me please help me!"

A flash of movement caught Janey's eye. She thought her brain must be slowly acclimating to this environment, or maybe it was the creation of opaque surfaces and shadows, but the awful queasiness and disorientation had backed off. To one side of the staging area, more octopeds had arrived, sprinting up a walkway. Jane figured they had to be some of the ones from the other ships.

Good. Get them all here.

Janey spoke to the clone. "If you help us, I'll see what I can do to get you out."

Pop. Hiss. *"Anything anything help me it's killing me!"*

The new octopeds didn't just have swords. They had firearms, or something that looked like firearms, and one of them appeared high on the wall above Tim and Beverly and Ashley. Janey rolled into a shadow and emerged forty feet from Tim, just as the alien dropped to the floor and leveled the weapon, and Janey shouted, out loud and into the thought-stream both, as the creature fired the weapon directly into Beverly's frigid mist.

Beverly screamed under a massive blast of white-hot plasma, a scream that cut off in a choke as she died, her charred body exploding into black dust as it hit the floor. Ashley emptied the AK into the octoped, but it seemed to be wearing some sort of transparent armor, and the bullets only staggered it.

Janey sprinted toward the octoped, searching for a shadow, anything to let her get there in time, and the creature regained its footing and leveled the gun at Ashley, and in a blurred, static-filled burst of darkness that mingled with a hoarse, anguished cry, the front half of the alien's body vanished.

Julian Roth materialized next to the ashes that marked what was left of Beverly, and the missing chunk of the octoped followed him out of the darkness a second later, falling to the deck with a thick, wet splat. Julian's eyes dragged up from the ashes to the other octopeds, armed and armored, pouring into the staging area, and Janey said, "Julian, you have to stay alive! This won't work without you! Don't put yourself at risk!"

But he either didn't hear her or didn't care, and for the next handful of heartbeats—Janey wasn't sure how long it lasted—the air above the deck blurred. This time the octopeds didn't scream. They didn't have time. Julian moved through them like a wraith, like the angel of death itself, and took away the centers of their torsos. Eight-legged bodies fell in two pieces in his wake.

The aliens realized what was happening almost immediately, and they began firing their horrible white-hot weapons at the blurring cloud of dark static, but all they managed to hit was each other. One bolt struck Aphrodite, but it only made her angry, and she took the weapon away from the creature and beat its head in with it.

The digital Stamford clone screamed and wailed into the helmet radio.

"Stamford!" Janey barked. "Tell me where you are! Let me come to you!" To Sha'dae, she sent, *Now. Help me.*

The clone cried, "I don't know, I don't know, I'm everywhere, I'm in everything," but with those words came a mental impression, its clarity boosted by Sha'dae's Augmentation and her link to the flesh-and-blood Stamford on the planet below—the location of the system core.

Janey returned her attention to the carnage on the staging area floor. One more platoon of octopeds from one of the other ships had just arrived, but this time Aphrodite was waiting right outside the doorway, and she pulled them out one by one, grabbing them with one set of tentacles and shredding them with the other. Janey couldn't tell what color Aphrodite's skin actually was now, because she was so thoroughly coated in sapphire blood.

When those octopeds were gone, silence fell. Janey sent a wide message. *Guys. It's working. Everybody—follow me.*

She headed for a pair of transparent doors—made slightly more palatable to her brain thanks to a spray of sapphire blood across them—and the doors slid open as soon as she approached. Nothing moved around them. No octopeds, nothing. They took an unobstructed path deeper and deeper into the vessel. Aphrodite had shed some of her mass, shrinking back down to a paltry six and a half feet, and lost her quadruple tentacles in favor of arms again. Julian Roth trailed at the back of the crowd, expression unreadable. Janey hadn't realized how close he'd gotten to Beverly.

Tim caught up with Janey, and his words flowed into her mind on a private part of the thought-stream.

How you holding up?

Janey had been debating whether to mention this part of her plan to Tim before reaching the system core. She kicked herself for having brought up her earlier argument against dramas that relied on characters being dishonest with each other. *I can't believe we might actually pull this off.*

Not without paying a price. Kay didn't deserve that. Neither did Beverly.

True. Tim...you told me—before we came here. You told me you loved me.

And I meant it.

I love you, too. I want you to know that. Really, truly know that. I don't want there to be any doubt in your mind.

Janey—why're you saying this?

I...because...because we're not out of the woods yet.

Before Tim could respond, another door slid open, and Janey led the surviving Augments into a long, low room. On the far wall, a transparent tube a foot in diameter ran in a maze-like pattern from floor to ceiling all along the wall's length, its interior so tightly packed with swarming, swirling pinpoints of light that it resembled a neon sign.

Nathan had come up to Janey's side. He said, "*That's* the system core? The ship runs on a big lava lamp?"

"What are you doing?" Derek Stamford's duplicated voice echoed around the chamber. It seemed to emanate from the core tube. "Help me! Help me! Get me out of here!"

Janey said, "You need to do something for us first."

The voice grew more frantic. "What? What? I'll do anything! Anything, just help me!"

"We want to speak to the Plowman's people." Janey gestured around her. "The people who built this ship."

"You want to *talk?* Are you crazy?"

"Send a message, Stamford. Hail them. Whatever you call it. Get their attention. We'll take it from there."

The lights swirled again, and shifted from ruby red to emerald green. Seconds passed. Janey said, "Well?"

The Stamford clone groaned. "Oh...oh God...oh, God, they're angry... they're going to talk through me *aaaahh—*" The anguished cry distorted, digitized, cut off.

The lights in the tube pulsed and shifted into a vivid shade of green, and Stamford's voice boomed out, this time with absolutely no inflection or emotion. "Identify yourself."

Janey cleared her throat. "I speak for this group. My name is Janey Sinclair."

"Janey Sinclair. You have committed crimes against the—" The digital Stamford broke in. "*Aaargh*, you can't, you can't translate their real name! I'm, I'm, *aaaahh*, I'm calling them 'the Nest!'" The emotion dropped out

again. "You have committed crimes against the Nest. You will be appre-
hended and executed."

Simon said, "So much for due process."

Janey tried her best to speak as clearly as she could. "No. I am going to
tell you what will happen. But first a demonstration is in order. Do you
have recording devices on this ship? Can you review what has taken place
here in the last hour?"

A pause. The green lights pulsed. "Yes."

Janey beckoned to Aphrodite, who stepped up beside her. "This is
Aphrodite Lupo. She was one of your experiment subjects, as were all but
one of the humans here. You saw the damage she did to your people."

The voice took on a frigid edge. "Irrelevant."

"No. Extremely relevant. Because she is about to demonstrate the kind
of damage one such person can do to an entire ship." Janey nodded at
Julian, and to Aphrodite said, "You *can* survive in a vacuum for a second
or two, right?"

Aphrodite showed Janey a grin filled with dagger-like teeth. "Just get
me over there."

Julian appeared next to Aphrodite. "Don't worry, boss. As soon as the
job's done, I'll pull you out of there." The two of them vanished.

Janey sent a message straight to Sha'dae. *Can you hook us all up so we see
through Aphrodite's eyes?*

Janey's vision split in half. She could tell Sha'dae was worried, since
the experience was rougher than usual. Janey saw Aphrodite and Julian
materialize on one of the four other ships. Julian took her deeper into it,
following the vision Janey had wrested from Stamford's brain, the flash of
understanding and knowledge he'd received just before the transfer of his
consciousness had completed.

Out loud, Janey said, "Aphrodite is approaching your vessel's drive
core. She's going to damage it badly enough to render it inoperable. We're
going to turn your ship into a hunk of space junk."

The green lights pulsed, but the voice said nothing else.

Janey watched as Aphrodite approached a door that failed to slide
open. As if to prove a point, rather than letting Julian teleport her through
the transparent door, she increased her mass again, sprouted the blade-
covered tentacles, and ripped completely through the door as well as the
wall beside it.

"Your actions have no point," the cold voice said. "Our drive cores are designed for ships of war. What use would they be if they could not withstand damage?"

Aphrodite reached the drive core. It was just as Janey had seen it in what passed for Stamford 2's memories: a spherical red object roughly the size of a washing machine, much like the one Janey had destroyed under the sports complex, sheltered in the center of two larger transparent spheres. Aphrodite struck the outer sphere, to no effect. Her blow more or less bounced off of it.

The voice said, "As stated. Pointless."

Aphrodite struck it again. And again. Her tentacles began to shift, flowing from blades into pick-like appendages, enormous weights concentrated into single, needle-sharp points. Her mass increased, increased again, and as she rained blows down on the sphere, Aphrodite *roared*. Janey had never heard a sound like it. She hoped never to again. Blow after blow, with ever more muscle behind it, the roar growing louder and louder, until the sphere *cracked*.

The cold voice said, "Impossible."

The crack grew larger, and the next blow shattered the sphere. Aphrodite ripped its broken debris away and, still roaring, attacked the second sphere. Now she seemed to have developed a technique, or grown the proper amount of muscle to supply the needed strength, because it cracked almost immediately.

"The forces that sphere was designed to withstand..." The cold voice trailed off.

The second sphere shattered. Aphrodite broke it loose piece by piece and tossed it out of her way, drew back an enormous, pick-like fist, brought it down on the drive core—

—and the double image in Janey's vision flared white and vanished. A second later something massive smashed into the base ship and slammed everyone into the floor.

"Holy God," the digital Stamford said. "That ship just detonated."

Janey heaved herself up. "What? It's—it's *gone*?"

Sha'dae screamed over the thought-stream. *What just happened? What just happened to Aphrodite and Julian? Janey, I can't reach them! What happened?*

The cold voice filled the room. "You have proven yourselves far too dangerous to be allowed to live. You and your verminous, flawed artificial intelligence. Goodbye, Janey Sinclair."

Janey scrambled to her feet and rushed back toward the tube, shouting at the top of her lungs. "Hey! We're not done talking! And you *really* want to hear what I have to say!"

The cold voice adopted a note of weariness. "Speak, then."

"You saw Aphrodite. You recognize her as an aberration. An unintended consequence of your experiments."

The voice said nothing.

"And she may be dead now, but she single-handedly ripped through shielding you believed to be impregnable. And destroyed an entire ship. Herself."

A faint whirring sound preceded the voice—detached, mechanical. "What point are you trying to make?"

Janey took a deep breath. "I have yet to reach the limits of my teleportation ability. The ability you planned to serve as a short-range reconnaissance method. I've already covered thousands of miles in one leap. And if I can visualize a place perfectly...I can reach it. Do you acknowledge that?"

The voice only whirred.

"Now, you may be thinking, so what if Janey Sinclair can teleport great distances? She's no Aphrodite Lupo. She couldn't just show up out of nowhere and wreck another of our ships. But I learned something, when I was inside Derek Stamford's mind. Something shown to me by the connection the latticework made to the structure of human DNA."

More whirring. Faster. "What are you saying?"

"I'm saying I *can* show up out of nowhere. And when I do...it won't be as Janey Sinclair anymore."

She hit the switch on the pressure suit's chest plate, disconnected her helmet, and shrugged out of the suit, letting it fall to the floor. Janey stood there, wearing only a sports bra and underwear, and reached inside her own mind. Tapped into the roiling, churning energy in the shape of a crown. Reached into that miniature churning sun—and redirected part of its power.

Janey felt the change in her fingers first. A heat that started in her bones and surged outward, rushing up through her arms and into her torso, down her legs, into her head.

The woman who had been Janey Sinclair for the last twenty-eight years became something else.

She felt her skin turn a slick gray-green even before she glanced down and saw it. She felt the short, sharp, wickedly hooked thorns rise all over her. She felt her body come alive in a way it never had before, her flesh and bones and organs bending to her will, her physical makeup much closer now to a mass of sculptor's clay than a rigidly ordered set of components. Janey grinned, and her jaw dropped and distended, and all her teeth lengthened and became daggers, stilettos, and her eyes turned bright white and left glowing trails in the air as she shook her head back and forth.

Janey realized she was roaring. She'd been roaring. She wasn't sure for how long.

The lights in the tube churned and shifted to a deep violet. Janey took a step toward the lights, the floor shaking under the sudden weight of her massive, clawed foot, and she wrapped the long, sinuous tendrils that had been her fingers around the transparent metal. "You see," she said, not recognizing the scraping, guttural tone of her own voice, "when you tampered with human DNA...you turned a key in a lock. You released something that should have been kept caged. And now that one of the Augments you created has embedded himself in your systems...? He gained access to your records. Your archives. Your navigation charts."

The digital Stamford said, "Janey..."

She ignored it, and kept speaking. "Now—and I want you to under-stand this—now we can *all* become this. These engines of destruction are within *all* of us. And *we know where you live.*"

The voice's whirring ground to a sudden stop. "A paltry threat. How many Augmented humans exist? Twenty? Thirty? No, Janey Sinclair. Your species as a whole remains weak. Pitiful. *Vulnerable.*"

Janey turned her gray-green, thorn-covered, white-eyed head and fixed those eyes on Ashley Strandjev. "Ready?"

Ashley stepped up beside her. She had already shed her pressure suit. "Do it."

Janey wrapped the long, barb-ended tendrils of her right hand around Ashley's head and neck and shoulders, and channeled more of the minia-ture sun inside her brain directly into the Marine sergeant.

The whirring voice said, "*No.*"

Ashley screamed and staggered away from Janey. She fell to her knees, retched up a bit of thin clear liquid...

...and began laughing. Ashley's skin went gray-green faster than Janey's had, and each thorn that rose from her body bore a serrated, knife-like edge along the inner curve. Ashley's eyes turned a glowing blood-red, and as the muscles surged along her arms and legs and back and chest, scattering the tattered remains of the underwear she'd worn beneath the pressure suit, a pair of massive *wings* sprouted from her shoulder blades. The laughter continued, deepening, until it became a booming basso rumble that made Janey's bones shake.

"Holy fucking shit," the massive, winged, reptilian creature growled out from crocodilian jaws. She turned her blood-red dragon's eyes on the swarming lights inside the tube. "You alien sons of bitches don't even *realize* how bad you fucked up."

"Janey!" The digital Stamford clone's voice rose to become a wail. "I think they *do* realize! They're sending all three ships straight down!"

Janey found it hard to concentrate. "Straight down? What?"

Nathan caught her arm. She'd forgotten he was there. He barked, "They're going to crash all three ships into Earth!"

The digital version of Stamford was near jabbering. "The impact— Janey, it's going to be extinction-level!"

Static filled Janey's mind. Thoughts fit together only reluctantly. "What...I don't..." It felt as if her brain had been suddenly split, divided, the different sections refusing to communicate with each other.

But, as she watched, like a detached observer, light flared in the gaps. Reorganizing. Re-forming.

And deep within herself, Janey saw another truth. It rose before her like the sun at dawn.

Simon grabbed Janey's jaw and hauled her head around, so that she had no choice but to look at him. "We've got to destroy all four ships. And now that Julian's gone, you're the only one who can get us there."

Janey understood Simon's words. She knew the plan they'd worked out—the plan she had spared Tim from knowing about in its entirety. Once she and Ashley had changed, become Abominations themselves, Julian was to leave Janey on the base ship and teleport Ashley, Parker, and Simon to the remaining three, and then evacuate Tim and Nathan while the other four copied Aphrodite's destruction of the drive cores. Janey had hoped that destruction would simply render the ships inert.

But now that plan was no longer necessary, suicide mission or not. Janey held her hands out, and her long, waving fingers shot forth, gripping everyone else in the room, wrapping around arms and legs and, in Ashley's case, her elongated, scaled neck.

Tim shouted, "Janey! The hell're you doing?"

The truth shall set you free, Janey said to herself, embracing the new reality that her transformation had granted her.

Janey knew that truth now, deep in her bones, in her soul. She was no longer human.

And no longer limited to the dark.

The base ship detonated in a cataclysmic explosion, the fireball perfectly spherical in the vacuum of space, as Janey teleported herself and the remaining five members of her crew to Earth's surface. She ignored the screams of fear and confusion and flickered away, first a few hundred feet into the sky, then to the hull of the nearest undamaged ship, then to the chamber housing its drive core.

The cold, hard voice—the voice of the Nest—cried out, "Janey Sinclair, hold, do not—" just as Janey teleported five hundred miles away, out into the welcoming blackness of space.

The static in her head grew louder. The light flaring between the newly re-formed sections of her brain faltered. Dimmed. For a few moments she forgot her name. In those moments, she didn't think it mattered very much anymore.

A burst of incalculable heat took her to one of the two ships left.

Eighteen seconds had passed since the demise of the largest spacecraft, and as the walls around her trembled with the shockwave of the second ship's destruction, she teleported again out into the cold, black emptiness.

The sight of the beautiful blue planet below her filled Janey with awe. As static crackled through her mind, her thoughts skittering away from her in a dozen directions, she wondered whose planet it was. The fiery, pulverized remains of the alien spacecraft drifted along the edge of Earth's atmosphere like jewels on black velvet, but there was still one left. One intact ship, still dropping toward the surface.

The static grew louder. More intense. Words drifted in her mind, words she thought she might have heard somewhere before. *Your brain isn't equipped to deal with this. It'll burn out.*

The transparent membranes across Janey's slitted-pupil eyes protected her from the vacuum, just as others closed off her nostrils, her ears. Her skin had become armor, her blood cells clinging to more than enough oxygen. It was peaceful, out in the emptiness. No conflict. No destruction anymore. And she didn't mind the cold. Janey could simply float there, away from everything, away from everyone. The last spacecraft moved slowly, so slowly, its forward surface glowing orange as it entered the atmosphere, and...

Tim.

Tim would die.

And all of her friends with him.

Janey flickered and vanished. It took her four seconds to find her way from the hull to the drive core, but before she could teleport away again, destroying the core in another mountain of flame, the cold, hard voice said, "Not fast enough this time, Janey Sinclair."

The cool, silver stream of Sha'dae's telepathy had just flowed back into Janey's mind when the aliens detonated the ship's drive core.

The last thing Janey felt was being crushed by the fist of God.

EPILOGUE

Derek Stamford had the top down. He cruised through Miami Beach, a smile on his face and the wind in his hair. It had been easier than the proverbial child's play to lock out Sha'dae Wilkerson's annoying telepathic habits, once Aphrodite Lupo and Janey Sinclair had disappeared, and he hadn't left a footprint traceable by non-Augmented humans in years. Especially now that he'd spent enough time around Scott Charles, and knew what to look for from him and Anastasia. No one would find him. Not until he was ready to be found. Or do the finding himself.

As far as he could tell, and as much as he didn't want to admit it, Janey Sinclair's argument to the extraterrestrials seemed to have worked. At least in the short run. The latticework was still in place, and after re-establishing a connection to it, he'd tapped into it now and then, just for a nanosecond at a time. Just long enough to see if there had been any activity.

There hadn't.

That meant his chances to venture off-world and explore the universe were more or less dead for now, but he'd already made his peace with that. While the latticework still existed, it presented a prime target for manipulation. For that matter, the virus the latticework had created—the virus that had infected every living human—may still be active. Ready for instructions from the right person. Someone who could see humanity's true potential. And if the virus wasn't still active, well, the latticework could no doubt engineer and release another one.

Stamford imagined an entire species of creatures like Aphrodite Lupo, but with Janey Sinclair's teleportation ability and capacity for rational thought. He could make it happen. His penis engorged almost painfully. Such plans he had…

Stamford's car came to a halt in the middle of the street as if it had rammed into a telephone pole. His airbag deployed, and Stamford sat there, stunned, trying to understand what had just happened. His jaw dropped open when a column of silvery, serpentine, mechanical constructs rose in front of the car, combined, and resolved into the Plowman.

"There you are," the Plowman said.

Stamford tried to put the car in reverse, but the engine had died, and the vehicle didn't respond. Briefly, he considered running. Instead he remained in his seat, while the Plowman glared down at him with blazing yellow eyes. Pedestrians screamed around them. Teenagers on sidewalks filmed them with their phones.

Stamford said, "Look, we can talk about this."

The Plowman sank his fingers into the car's hood and pulled it free. He cast the hood aside, reached into the engine compartment, ripped out the entire engine block, and threw it through the windshield at not quite the velocity of a bullet leaving the muzzle of a handgun.

The engine block tore into Stamford. It collapsed his ribcage, shredded and burst his internal organs, and obliterated his skull, spraying bits of his brain all over the back of the car and the street beyond it. Amid the horrified screams, the Plowman lifted one arm, exposing a nozzle that protruded from his wrist, and sprayed a jet of fluid all over the wreckage of the car and Stamford's scattered, ruined corpse. He snapped his enormous fingers, which sent a spark flickering through the air, and watched as the fluid caught fire.

The Plowman stood and surveyed his work for a few more seconds. Wordlessly, while approaching sirens wailed around him, he dropped into the hole in the street from which he'd come and disappeared.

J aney stared into a white light. She knew she was dead. No one could have survived the drive core exploding in their face. Was this the light that everyone talked about? Should she be trying to move toward it?

Her mouth felt as if it had been carefully and tightly packed with sand. She might have tried to spit the sand out if she'd been able to move, but being dead seemed to mean that she couldn't move at all. She couldn't close her eyes to get away from the harsh white light. Or maybe her eyes *were* closed, and the light was so bright that it didn't matter. Or maybe she didn't have eyelids anymore. Maybe they'd been burned away.

Janey wondered if being dead meant hallucinating. Did that make any sense? Why would the dead hallucinate? And why would it grow louder? She lay still, because she couldn't move, and stared into the agonizing white light, because she couldn't close her eyes.

"Janey!"

There it was again. The hallucination. Auditory…that was the word. Hearing things that weren't there. She couldn't be hearing Tim's voice. Because she was dead.

"Janey!"

She wished she could at least turn her head. A terrible thought struck her. What if this was hell? This pain, and this light, and this torment, making her think she could hear Tim's voice? She didn't think she deserved to be in hell. But then a lot of things had happened to her that she didn't think she'd deserved.

"Janey, oh my God, Janey, I'm here, I'm here!"

Something blocked out the light, and she thought she might have felt someone's hands touching her, but she passed out before she could get any more irritated at the tormenting dreams.

The voice drifted through the mist in her head. "Whoa, whoa. Janey. Come on, now. Wake up. Here—"

Something wet touched her lips. *Water.* Real water? She couldn't help herself. She swallowed, and water had never tasted so incredible, too incredible, it couldn't be real, couldn't be.

"Janey, come on. Open your eyes. Janey, look at me."

She did. God help her, she opened her eyes, even though she was dead, she had to be dead.

She *wanted* to be dead.

But she opened her eyes, and there was Tim's beautiful face, and he was holding her, cradling her head in his lap. Janey squinted—the light still bright, glaring, all around her, even if it wasn't shining directly in her eyes now—and saw that she lay, completely naked, in the middle of a twenty-foot-wide crater. No more gray-green, no more thorns, no more long wiggly fingers. Just her. She seemed to be on some rocky beach somewhere.

Janey turned her face away. "You shouldn't be here."

"Janey. You're okay. Do you hear me? You're okay."

She closed her eyes. Sure this time that her eyelids were working. "I should be dead."

"Yeah, well. You're not. Aphrodite made it, too. She's the reason we were out looking for you—she turned up first. Honestly, she's more lucid now than she was before she got blown up. I think it did her some good." He paused. "Still no sign of Julian, though."

Janey made a pained sound, deep in her throat. "You should leave me here. Go. Get away."

Tim pulled his shirt off and draped it over her. It covered just barely enough to afford some modesty. "Why would I do that?"

Finally, grudgingly, Janey looked up at him. Straight into his stunning black eyes. "You saw what I became. That's what I am, Tim."

He stroked her hair. "According to you, that's what we *all* are."

"But I...my mind...Tim, my mind was going. I wasn't...it wasn't me. I was becoming something—something else..."

"Janey, you did it. You destroyed those ships. You and Aphrodite. You literally saved the goddamn world."

"But...I don't know if I can *control* myself. What if I—what if I turn? What if I become that *thing* again?" She clutched his wrist. "You don't know what it was like. The feelings. The *power*. What if I wind up some kind of, of *monster?*"

"I'm willing to bet you won't. Also, I don't care. I'm not leaving you. It's a God-given fucking miracle you're alive, Janey, and I'm not ever leaving you again. Not ever."

He paused.

"Besides...it's not like you could hurt me."

Janey curled against him and held him tight, and couldn't tell whether she was laughing or crying.

END

ACKNOWLEDGEMENTS

As with every novel I've done, this has not been a solo effort. I owe enormous debts of gratitude to the valiant few who've helped me, advised me, and put up with me as I've brought this story to a close.

Thanks to Stephen Zimmer, Holly Marie Phillippe, and Linda Sullivan, for being there at the beginning.

Thanks to John Hartness and Tuppence Van der Vaarst for making this new, even more highly-polished incarnation possible.

Thanks to the best beta readers anywhere: Clint McInnes, Zach & Sarah Caylor, and Tracy Jolley.

And a special thanks to Bethany Kesler, not only for a super-helpful beta read, but also for providing some much-needed and valuable insight.

You guys rock.

ABOUT THE AUTHOR

Dan Jolley began writing professionally at age 19. Starting out in comic books, Dan has worked for major publishers such as DC (*Firestorm*), Marvel (*Dr. Strange*), Dark Horse (*Aliens*), and Image (*G.I. Joe*). He soon branched out into licensed-property novels (*Star Trek*), film novelizations (*Iron Man*), and original novels, including the Middle Grade urban fantasy series *Five Elements* and the urban sci-fi *Gray Widow Trilogy*.

Dan began writing for video games in 2007, and has contributed storylines, characters, and dialogue to titles such as *Transformers: War for Cybertron*, *Prototype 2*, and *Dying Light*, among others.

His latest work includes the best-selling Audible Original Middle Grade urban fantasy audiobook *House of Teeth*, and a Middle Grade post-apocalyptic sci-fi novel series for German publisher Fischer Verlag called *Bad Tide Rising* (published in Germany as *Waterland*).

Dan lives with his wife Tracy and some largely inert felines in northwest Georgia. Readers can learn more about him on his website, www.danjolley.com.

ALSO BY DAN JOLLEY

ADULT FICTION
The Gray Widow Trilogy:
Gray Widow's Walk
Gray Widow's Web
Gray Widow's War

YOUNG ADULT BOOKS
The Alex Unlimited Trilogy:
The Vosarak Code
Split-Second Sight
True Chemistry

MIDDLE-GRADE BOOKS
The Five Elements Trilogy:
The Emerald Tablet
The Shadow City
The Crimson Serpent

House of Teeth (Audible Original audiobook)

FRIENDS OF FALSTAFF